Little Bits of Karma

LAURA SIMMONS

outskirtspress
DENVER, COLORADO

Outskirts Press, Inc.
http://www.outskirtspress.com

ISBN: 978-1-4787-5716-0

PRINTED IN THE UNITED STATES OF AMERICA

Prologue

This is a story of reincarnation and forgiveness. The main character, Holly O'Rourke, learns of her past lives by visiting a psychic medium and later experiences some of those lives through past-life regression hypnosis. The people in her current life she has known in previous lives and sometimes she discovers their names from that particular era. Here is a listing of characters and their identities in previous incarnations:

Holly O'Rourke–Sanjay/Krista/Emily/Minori/Dayani/Renata/Mary/Ursula/Joseph/Friedrich

Charlie Thomas–Erik/David/Kam

Roger Chasen–Gustaf/Fumito/Clive

James Macklin–Natom/Marcus/Thaddeus

Patricia Swain–Moriko

Alyssa Thomas–Lisa/Paul

Amber Conner–Laneesa

Alex Manning–Caleb

Jack Briggs–Stefano

Neil Peters–Hantoro

Matt Weedon–Margan

CHAPTER 1

The Two of Cups

Holly O'Rourke wished she could be lying on a beach soaking up the sun and forgetting her troubles. She took a break from the mind-numbing task she was working on to look out of her office window at the cheery, bright, and sunny day. Her office was on the tenth floor of a commercial building in downtown Washington, D.C., and she could see for miles. She had a great office. It was filled with light from two tall windows, and although it wasn't a large office, it had an inviting feel with everything she needed to get her work done. She worked as an executive assistant for a Department of Defense contractor, Military Technology Analysis Corporation (MTAC), directly supporting one of the company senior vice presidents. It was mid-September and summer would soon be fading. She loved the summer and hated to see it end. Sunny days and warm temperatures lifted her spirits when she was feeling down, and she was not in the best mood this morning due to an argument late last night with her significant other, James Macklin . . .

. . . "What's happened to us? These last 2 years, you spend less and less time with me. I understand your needing to spend time with the guys now and then, except that I only get to be with you twice a month,

and that's if I'm lucky! We've become two ships passing in the night, or rather the morning," Holly said angrily to her longtime lover.

"You just don't understand the kind of pressure I'm under. I need a break from working at that place. I need an outlet. We keep having this same fight over and over. What more do you want from me?" James snapped back at her.

"I want your time and attention without having to beg for it. You used to give it freely. When you come home after hanging out with the guys, it takes you about 2 days to come back to your normal, loving self. I feel like you take me for granted. Are you tired of being in this relationship?" she asked him, her eyes glaring and her hands on her hips.

"Holly, I love you . . . however, when you keep harping on me like this, I want to pull away. I'll work on spending less time with the guys if that's what you want," he replied with a sigh.

"You'll WORK on it? I didn't know being with me was work. All you care about is having a place to sleep at night and a warm body for sex once in a while. I don't want to talk to you anymore; I'm sleeping on the couch tonight!" she yelled at James and stormed off into the living room carrying her pillow.

James came after her and said, "If you don't want to sleep next to me, I'll take the couch tonight . . . you can have the bed."

"Just go away," she replied and turned her body away from him as she lay down on the sofa . . .

They had been living together for 11 years and the last 2 years were challenging for them. James would frequently disappear on his days off. He would justify his absences saying he went to the shooting range to let off steam due to stress at work, and then he would visit one of the guys and hang out. He used the excuse of not wanting to drive home while intoxicated, as he usually drank a lot when he was with his buddies so he would crash for the night with a friend. During this time he never called to check in with Holly. When these disappearing episodes would happen, James became distant, moody, and emotionally unavailable after he returned home. A wall was building between them, and she wanted to tear it down and get back to the way things used to be.

When James and Holly first met, she felt like she knew him from somewhere. They met at a speed dating event. She was immediately attracted to and comfortable with him, and they could talk and laugh about anything. James was a handsome man. He stood 6 foot 3 with blond hair, blue eyes, and had a nice body. He lifted weights and liked to go running. James was now a man of 53, and he was still in good shape and not losing his hair, although it was more white than blond these days.

The first 9 years of their relationship were great; she thought she had found the love of her life. However, things were changing now. She hated his disappearances and resented him not spending more time with her on his days off. He worked long hours as a chef at the American Steak Bistro and Pub, a five-star restaurant in Arlington, and his shifts would change every few weeks. The restaurant overworked their kitchen staff, yet they paid better than most of the other area restaurants and James put up with it. The restaurant served breakfast on Saturdays and Sundays, and lunch and dinner only Monday through Friday. The weekends were the busiest time, and the kitchen didn't close until 10:00 p.m. There was a large bar area attached to the main dining room for the late-night revelers.

She reflected on her life and the lousy choices she made in selecting mates as she watched the people walking on the street below. She had been married twice. Her first husband, Roger Chasen, was a wife beater. Her second husband, Alex Manning, had a drug problem and was bisexual. Alex was one who often disappeared too. At least James told her where he was going; Alex would take off for days to do drugs with his friends. She didn't have any children by those men, and was thankful for that. The only way she would ever consider motherhood was if she could be a stay-at-home mom for a few years. Just the thought of trying to work full-time and take care of a baby made her feel exhausted, although she thought that if she accidentally became pregnant by one of her former flames, she would have loved the baby dearly and been a good mother. Holly's thoughts were interrupted by a knock on her door. She turned around to see that it was her good friend, Patricia Swain, stopping by for some chitchat.

"Wishing you were somewhere else?" Patricia asked, looking at her over reading glasses that slid down her nose, her big blue eyes indicating mischief.

"Every day!" Holly replied emphatically. "What are you doing up this way?"

"I just finished talking with Neil Peters, and he told me an interesting tidbit about Charlie Thomas," she said.

"Spill . . . I need something to spice up my day," Holly replied.

"Did you know that Charlie was divorced?" Patricia asked.

"No, I don't work with his group much anymore," she replied.

"Apparently he's been divorced for 3 years. His wife was a pistol; she embarrassed him by punching a contractor in the nose who was doing some work on their house, and then began pummeling the poor guy. She was convicted of assault and spent 90 days in jail . . . along with a hefty fine. Prior to that, she totaled two of Charlie's vehicles at different times, trying to chase down people who cut her off in traffic. Those were a few things that Neil mentioned; there must have been others too. I guess he had enough of her tantrums and kicked her out," Patricia said with a laugh.

"I remember when he first started working here. He got married a few weeks later, and Matt Weedon asked me to get a card and gift for Charlie and his new wife on behalf of the group. I collected money and bought them a gift card for Macys. I think it's sad that they are no longer together; marriage is hard work. Actually, any long-term romantic relationship is hard work," Holly said, thinking about her current situation with James.

"I think I married the last good man on the planet," Patricia said with a sigh of relief.

"I would have to agree . . . Andy is a gem," Holly replied thinking . . *I never wanted to marry James. I was afraid marriage would ruin our relationship, and yet it's sliding downhill anyway.*

"Speaking of Matt Weedon, have you heard anything from him lately?" Patricia asked sarcastically.

"You know I haven't, and I don't want to," Holly replied with a laugh. Matt Weedon was her former boss; she worked for him for 5 long years and wanted to dance on a cloud the day he announced his resignation.

"I've got to run . . . too much work and not enough time to do it. I'll catch you later," Patricia said as she turned to leave.

"Have a nice day," Holly said cheerfully.

Patricia Swain was Holly's best friend at work. She was 57 years old, tall and slim and looked the part of the quintessential businesswoman. She was wearing her perfectly tailored navy blue suit, designer pumps, expensive white silk blouse, with salt-and-pepper hair cut into a stylish pixie. Patricia could carry off the short haircut without looking matronly, and her exuberant personality made her seem years younger. Holly and Patricia bonded when working on a project several years ago. They had been located on the same floor and would seek each other out for gossip and lunch; they worked in different areas now. They still saw each other several times a week. Holly often talked to Patricia when she had problems with James. Patricia had issues with her boss. She didn't like him, and he was difficult to work for. Patricia was happily married though, to the same man for 32 years. Holly wished she could say the same.

Holly put her unhappy thoughts aside and went back to crunching numbers for another hour. Lunchtime was approaching, and she started to get hungry. She decided to walk to the nearby deli, two blocks away. As she left the building and walked down the sidewalk, she reveled in the feel of the warm sun on her face. September was warm and the weather today was perfect and inviting. She thought about continuing her backyard tan this upcoming weekend. She was a redhead who loved the sun and carefully nurtured a light tan. Lying in the sun was therapeutic for her. It made her feel relaxed.

Holly stood 5 foot 7 with long and thick auburn hair that fell well below her shoulders. Her large, hazel green eyes were framed with naturally curling eyelashes. She didn't need to wear much makeup. She had a slim and slightly athletic build from regular workouts, and she looked good today. She was dressed in a dark purple suit with a knee-length skirt and black, low-heeled pumps that showcased her toned calves. She noticed more than one man checking her out as she walked down the street. Holly was a strikingly pretty woman who didn't realize how beautiful she appeared to others. She was 45 and did her best to stay in shape; she was afraid of growing old and fat.

As she entered the deli, she recognized the tall man standing at the end of the line. He turned around to see who was behind him and greeted her warmly.

"Holly! How are you today?" Charlie Thomas said with a flicker of excitement in his eyes . . . *My fantasy girl just walked into the room . . . I wonder if she still has that live-in boyfriend.*

Holly was surprised to see him. It was a funny coincidence after talking about him with Patricia earlier. "Hi, Charlie. I haven't seen you in months. Where have you been hiding?" she asked pleasantly.

"I've had to travel lately, although I don't like to travel for business much anymore," he replied. "It's such a nice day; I won't be surprised if my staff doesn't return from lunch."

Holly noticed how handsome Charlie looked today. She never looked at him in this way before. He was tall, standing 6 foot 4. She looked into his brown eyes as he talked, noticing his long eyelashes. She saw that his dark brown hair had streaks of gray which gave him a distinguished look. She thought to herself . . . *What a good-looking man; I wouldn't kick him out of bed.Why didn't I notice him before? It's like I'm seeing him for the first time.*

"I hear you. I certainly don't want to return to work either. Hey, do you want to run away? We could hop a plane to the Bahamas or something," she said to him teasingly while placing her hand on his arm . . .*Why did I reach out and touch his arm like that? . . . I'm flirting with him . . . having visions of the two of us holding hands, walking along the beach.*

"I'd follow you anywhere," he replied with a charming smile, thinking . . . *Leave your boyfriend and run away with me.*

She was startled by the way he was looking at her and how it made her feel . . . happy inside, and her heart was beating a little faster. Holly started to reply, "Well, it sounds like a plan. You can buy the plane tickets and—"

"Charlie! I have some news to tell you!" Their moment was interrupted when Charlie's boss, Mitch Devlin, suddenly bolted through the door and struck up a conversation with him.

Holly didn't like Mitch. She thought he was obnoxious and pretentious. He gave a cursory hello to her and proceeded to talk to Charlie about one of their client's issues. Holly let Mitch cut in front of her so he could talk to Charlie more easily. Mitch was a nice-looking man with a buzz haircut and brown eyes. He had prominent facial features and a Native American look to him. He liked expensive cars and had the money to afford them. He was demanding of his workers and not particularly compassionate.

Charlie and Mitch became involved in conversation, and she stood behind them in line thinking romantic thoughts about Charlie. He was 8 years older than she, the same as James; she knew that from handling personnel records when he was working in her group several years ago. He had a master's degree in operations research, a bachelor's degree in mechanical engineering, and served as a pilot in the air force. She loved that he was tall and he didn't slouch. He had broad shoulders, a flat stomach, and obviously worked out. There was a small bald spot on the back of his head; however, it didn't detract from his looks. She was enjoying her thoughts of running away with him.

In her previous relationships with Roger and Alex, when things started to go wrong, she would get crushes on other men. Granted, neither one of them treated her well. In the 11 years she lived with James, she never had thoughts like this until now. It was happening again. She hoped it would be a passing thing. Charlie was looking too good to her today. An uneasy heaviness was forming around her heart. She decided that she would make things right with James, and that her thoughts about Charlie were a warning signal. She still loved James, and missed him when he wasn't around.

Charlie and Mitch ordered their sandwiches to go and turned to leave the deli when they were ready. Charlie looked at Holly and said to her, "Have a nice day."

"You too, Charlie," Holly replied and turned to watch him and Mitch walk out of the deli, still in awe of Charlie and the strange new feelings she was having for him.

Holly got her lunch order to go and walked back to the office. She started thinking about her situation with James again. He was her third and longest significant relationship. She wasn't getting any younger and didn't want to start over with someone new. It took so long to build a relationship, and she had time and effort invested in him.

She arrived back at her office, ate her lunch, and devoted the rest of the day to various administrative tasks that were piling up. The day went by quickly and soon it was quitting time. Holly changed into her flat shoes to walk to the subway station, or the "Metro," as everyone called it. As she left the office and walked out of the building, she had a thought to stop by the bookstore three blocks away. The bookstore was a small, privately owned business called "The Book Store," an unassuming name and easy to remember. Despite the simple name, it was a great place for books and the selection and variety were good.

Holly was drawn to the New Age and Philosophy sections. She loved to read books about reincarnation, spiritual healing methods, how-to books on developing psychic ability, communicating with angels, books written by psychics describing the afterlife, and anything with spiritual or metaphysical content.

She glanced over the available selections in the New Age section and was drawn to a book written by a hypnotherapist who performed past-life regressions for his clients. It was titled, *Welcome to Yesterday,* by William Livingston. A light turned on in her head and she thought she would look into seeing if there were any people in the Washington area who did this kind of work. She bought the book and left the store. She was excited at the prospect of being hypnotized into a past life. She believed in reincarnation and read much about it over the years.

On her ride home that afternoon, she overheard bits and pieces of a conversation that two ladies sitting behind her were having about calling a psychic hotline. Their voices went from soft to loud, depending on the sensitivity of the subject.

". . . and the psychic I talked to was amazing," Lady #1 said.

"What did she tell you?" Lady #2 asked.

"She told me that I shared 15 lives with my husband, and 10 lives with my mother," Lady #1 said. "She said in seven of the lives I shared with my husband that I was a man and he was a woman!"

Lady #2 let out a laugh which sounded more like a cackle. Both women were laughing now. The train came to a stop and both ladies got up and exited. Holly was sorry to see them go. She enjoyed eavesdropping on their conversation and wanted to hear more. She consulted phone psychics at various times throughout her life, but since she had been with James, she never felt the need to consult a psychic. Her life was filled with love and happiness, and there was no anxiety about the future . . . until recently. She was beginning to think there was a message here. First, she was drawn to the bookstore and bought a book about reincarnation, and then she heard these ladies talking about psychics and past lives. She decided to investigate seeing or calling a psychic, and look into consulting with a past-life regression therapist.

Holly arrived home to a quiet and empty house, as usual. She and James lived in Alexandria, Virginia, near the Huntington Metro Station which made commuting to downtown Washington tolerable. Their house was a small, single-family home on a large, flat lot. There was a wooden privacy fence around the property, and she nurtured a sunflower garden in the backyard, along the back part of the fence. She loved sunflowers and grew Kong Hybrids, which can grow up to 14 feet tall. She enjoyed looking out her kitchen window over the summer and watching these giant beauties rise. She measured them yesterday and most were close to that now. There was a concrete patio just outside the dining room, and it was perfect for having guests over for cookouts and lying in the sun.

The ranch-style house was made of brick with a finished basement. It was a two-bedroom, one-bathroom house. She liked to joke that she lived in a box, as the house was plain-looking on the outside. From the street it looked like a simple, one-story house with two large windows on each side of the entry door. She planted boxwood shrubs underneath each window when she first bought the place, and they were now thick and full. The inside was pretty, with honey-colored hardwood floors throughout and off-white painted walls. The furniture was plush and comfortable in shades of dark olive green, orange-red, and beige. A brightly colored area rug in coordinating earth tones was the centerpiece of the living room and helped bring it to life. The sheer curtains on the two main windows were an orange-red color which helped the living room pop, and blended nicely with the area rug. She was a good housekeeper and took pride in her home.

As she walked through the door, the cat woke up from its slumber, stretched, and jumped off the sofa and came over to her. She and James recently adopted this cat from the local animal shelter and called her

Fate. They didn't choose to name her "Fate," that was her name at the shelter, and it seemed appropriate to keep it. She was a 5-year-old Tortie with beautiful, light green eyes. She had thick, silky, luxurious fur. She meowed at Holly because she was hungry and she knew that Holly fed her when she got home from work.

"I'll feed you in a moment, sweetheart. Let Mommy get settled first," she said to the cat.

Fate followed Holly as she went into the bedroom to change into more comfortable clothes; she sat waiting patiently for her to finish up what she was doing. Holly turned on her computer in the spare bedroom which they set up as an office, and then went to the basement to prepare Fate's meal as the cat followed her, bounding down the stairs.

After she fed the cat, she made her own dinner. She opened a can of tomato soup and cooked a grilled cheese sandwich. She gulped her soup and ate her sandwich quickly. She was anxious to get on the computer and search the Internet for local psychics and hypnotherapists.

When she finished eating, Holly went into the home office and began to search the Internet. She searched for past-life regression therapists and found several in the area. She noticed that none of them had their fees listed. This was a concern for her as she didn't want to spend a small fortune on this venture and not seeing any prices led her to believe that it was expensive. She was able to find one hypnotherapist who listed her fees. For a 2-hour session, this therapist was charging $350. The maximum Holly would spend for something like this would be $150. After all, there was no guarantee that she would be able to be hypnotized, definitely something to consider when spending that kind of money.

She thought that her next option was to visit a psychic medium. She hoped this would be more affordable. She continued her Internet search and found one located in the Dupont Circle area of downtown D.C. Dupont Circle was easily accessible by the Metro and was an interesting part of the city with restaurants, shops, small museums, and galleries. The psychic's name was Martina Preston, and her business was called "Martina's Psychic Services." She was a medium who claimed she could talk to the deceased, angels, spirit guides, see past lives, and tell the future. She charged $150 for a 45-minute session. Holly thought this was expensive, yet she wanted to find out about her past lives and decided to go for it. She noticed that Martina had evening hours until 9:00 p.m.; she looked at the clock on the wall and saw that it was now 8:15 p.m. She called and was able to connect right away.

"Hello, this is Martina," the psychic answered.

"Hi, my name is Holly, and I would like to make an appointment for this Saturday. I would like to have a past-life reading," Holly said.

"Certainly . . . I have an opening this Saturday at 11:30 a.m. Will that work for you?" Martina asked.

"Yes, I will be there. My name is Holly O'Rourke," Holly replied happily.

"Great, I look forward to seeing you then. If for some reason you are unable to make it, please call to let me know," Martina said.

"I will. Thank you. See you Saturday," Holly replied and hung up the phone.

Holly was so excited that she had a hard time falling asleep that night. Tomorrow was Friday, and she wouldn't have to wait long for her reading. She finally dozed off and was slightly awakened by James getting home from work and crawling into bed next to her. She acknowledged him in her state of half-sleep, and he kissed her on the cheek. She caught a whiff of fragrance that smelled like sweet vanilla. She thought for a half-second that he must have taken a shower before coming to bed, and then she rolled over and went back to sleep.

James was sleeping soundly when she woke up for work the next morning. She went through her usual morning routine, thinking about her upcoming psychic reading. As she was taking her shower, she vaguely recalled James smelling like vanilla and realized that neither of the soap bars in the shower smelled like vanilla. *Maybe he was making or sampling desserts last night,* she thought to herself.

She was ready to walk out the door when James appeared in the living room looking handsomely disheveled in his gray lounge pants, muscular shirtless chest, and tousled hair. She admired how sexy he looked. Their sex life wasn't what it used to be; the arguments and fights these past 2 years, combined with him not being around, had taken their toll. She had a momentary impulse to call in sick to work and stay home in bed with him, and then realized she had to finish a report which was due Monday.

"Good morning beautiful," James said to her.

"Good morning," Holly replied casually, remembering the fight they had yesterday.

"I have Sunday and Monday off and I thought we should do something fun. Anything you want," he said.

"We haven't done anything fun together in a long time. I don't want you to do something with me if it's going to feel like WORK," she replied tersely.

"I know I haven't been the best partner. I'm sorry, and I want to make it up to you," he said and walked over to her and pulled her close to him, nuzzling his head into her hair. She noticed again the faint smell of vanilla.

"You smell like vanilla," she said.

"Oh, that's from the new room spray we started using in the kitchen. Not only does it smell fantastic, it gets rid of stale food odors too," he replied . . . *I sound like a friggin' commercial . . . I wish I had taken a shower before coming to bed last night.*

"I like it, bring some home. I've got to get going. I'll see you late tonight," she said and kissed him lightly on the lips.

"Have a good day," he replied and watched her get into her car and pull out of the driveway.

As Holly drove to the Metro station, she felt somewhat relieved by James apologizing and wanting to spend more time with her and hoped he really meant it this time. She was curious as to what the upcoming psychic visit would uncover concerning their relationship.

When she stepped off the train that morning, she noticed Charlie in the distance. He was too far ahead for her to catch up with him, so she admired him from afar. He was so tall and yet he carried himself well, and didn't have a lumbering or goofy walk. She watched him get on the escalator, smiling to herself and having mental pictures of the two of them engaged in a steamy kiss. *Why am I thinking stuff like this? It must be because I'm sex-deprived . . .* she thought to herself. Watching Charlie made her feel like a teenage girl hoping to catch a glimpse of her dreamy crush on her way to class.

Holly settled into her work routine and drank three cups of coffee, hoping the caffeine would help her focus on her work. There must have been 100 e-mails in her inbox this morning. She had many tasks to get done today, including travel reservations for several program managers, each of them going different places. One of the managers she supported, Jack Briggs, left her 20 documents that needed to be scanned. She didn't want to do any of it. She took five documents from the stack of 20 and walked to the copy room. It was a large room with three copiers, two black-and-white and one color. There was a fax machine and wall cabinets containing various office supplies. While she was standing at the copier, Neil Peters entered to fax a document and he struck up a conversation with her.

"Hi, Holly. Got any plans for the weekend?"

"Not really. James has to work most of the weekend. I'm going to see a psychic tomorrow, just for fun," she replied thinking . . . *It isn't just for fun . . . I don't want to ruin my credibility by admitting the truth.*

"That sounds cool. I've been to a few psychics in my time. Some of them were good, some not so much," he replied. Neil Peters was an interesting guy to talk to. He was a retired naval officer who had been around the world in his career. He was a short man, standing 5 foot 6 and probably 40 pounds overweight. He was in his early 60s with hair that was still brown, showing no hint of gray, and he wore plastic-framed glasses. He told colorful stories of the places he visited and was well-liked by everyone. He continued, "What kind of reading are you going for?"

"I'm going for a past-life reading," she replied feeling self-conscious.

"Whoa, I bet that will be a hoot! I've never had one of those. Let me know if the psychic is any good. I might want to get a reading myself. I've had a strange recurring dream for a long time where I'm participating in some weird, native ceremony that involves fire and naked, writhing bodies," he replied with a laugh.

Holly started laughing. "Sure. I'll let you know," she said with a smile, relieved that he didn't think she was crazy.

"Have a good weekend," Neil said as he left the room.

"You too," Holly replied and continued to scan documents.

Patricia stopped by Holly's office later that afternoon to see if she wanted to join her for drinks after work. She knocked on her door to get her attention.

"You're working too hard," Patricia said to her.

"No, it just looks that way," Holly replied. "What's up?"

"I stopped by to see if you want to join us for happy hour at Jake's Joint."

Jake's was a fun, beer-themed restaurant four doors down from The Book Store. It had an outdoor, rooftop bar area that was open late spring through early fall, weather permitting. It wasn't fancy, just a concrete rooftop bar set up with outdoor furniture and a fantastic view of historic landmarks like the Capitol Building, the Washington Monument, and others. Patricia wasn't one to frequent happy hour, and neither was Holly.

"That's surprising, you don't normally do happy hours," Holly replied.

"Normally I don't. Andy's in the area on business, and it was his idea," Patricia said.

"Sure, I'd love to. It beats sitting alone at the house tonight," Holly said, overjoyed that she had an opportunity for some fun this evening.

"I'll come by and get you, and we'll walk over together," Patricia said.

"Great, see you then!" Holly replied.

Quitting time came 3 hours later, and Patricia and Holly walked down the street to Jake's. The sun was still high in the sky, and it was quite warm. Andy Swain was waiting outside the restaurant for his wife. Holly liked Andy; she thought he was the perfect husband. He adored Patricia, and she never said one bad thing about him. Andy and Patricia were the same age. They were college sweethearts. Andy stood 6 feet tall, with blue eyes and gray hair that was receding in the front. He had a warm and friendly personality.

"There are my two favorite ladies," Andy said, and then he kissed Patricia and shook hands with Holly. "Let's go get some drinks. I'll buy the first round." The three of them took the elevator to the rooftop. Holly loved the city view from there. As they stepped off the elevator, Holly heard someone call her name.

"Holly . . ." Charlie Thomas called out to her.

She looked in his direction, waved, and said, "Hi, Charlie." She was suddenly delighted to see him. He was sitting at a table with two of his colleagues, Henry and Nathan, who Holly didn't know well. They were sharing a pitcher of beer.

"Come on over, bring your friends," Charlie said and motioned to a vacant table next to his.

"He seems friendly; the more the merrier," Andy replied and the three of them went to join Charlie and his companions.

As Holly approached the table she felt her heart pounding . . . *Why am I having this reaction?* Charlie got up and moved the adjoining table close to his and rearranged the chairs so they would be comfortable. Patricia immediately noticed the sparkle in Charlie's eyes as he held out a chair for Holly. Charlie wanted Holly to sit across from him so he could look at her.

"Good to see you, Charlie," Patricia greeted him with a smile. "This is my husband, Andy." The two men shook hands, and Charlie introduced them to Henry and Nathan, who seemed kind of quiet and were just happy to sit and drink their beers. A waitress asked to take their order, and Andy got the first round as promised. Patricia and Andy ordered scotch on the rocks and Holly ordered hard apple cider.

"If I'm going to drink, I should order something to eat when the waitress comes back. I want to make it home in one piece," Holly said.

"Would you like to share a basket of potato skins?" Charlie asked.

"Yeah! That sounds great," Holly replied.

When the waitress came back with their drinks, Charlie ordered food and Nathan and Henry finished their beers and said they had to leave and get home to their wives and kids. It was now just the four of them sitting around and talking about work. The alcohol helped Holly to feel more relaxed around Charlie and the conversation flowed easily among the four of them. Two hours later, Andy and Patricia had to leave as they had company coming to visit.

"Drive safely," Holly said to them as they left.

"You too," Patricia replied. "See you on Monday."

Patricia and Andy left the bar and Holly and Charlie were alone together, sitting across from each other. Charlie consumed five beers over the course of happy hour and he was feeling good and buzzed. Holly felt on top of the world. She was more relaxed and happy than she had been in a long time. Charlie was looking at Holly like he could devour her as they continued to talk, and she loved every minute of it. *Charlie, I could drown in your eyes . . .* she thought, unaware that she was glowing.

At that moment, music began to play in the background. The bartender turned on the radio and speaker system. It was tuned to an oldies station playing hits from the 1970s. The dreamy, ethereal song,

"I Only Have Eyes for You" sung by Art Garfunkel filled the air.

"So . . . are you still living with James?" Charlie asked her.

"Yes," Holly replied.

"Too bad," he said with a sigh, looking into her eyes.

Holly held Charlie's gaze for a few seconds, and then asked him with a teasing look on her face, "Why is it too bad that I'm still living with James?" *Here I go, flirting with him again.*

His dark eyes appeared serious and he replied, "It's too bad because if he wasn't in your life, then I would have a chance with you."

"Charlie, that is so sweet," Holly replied a little breathlessly and continued, "If I were single, you would" . . . *I would do way more than just go out with you . . . and you would like it* . . . she thought.

"Good to know," he replied with a big smile and looked at her lovingly. "I hope I'm not making you feel uncomfortable. I like being here with you, and you are fun to talk to. I think you are beautiful . . . I'm saying this because I've had a few too many beers."

"It's okay, Charlie. I've had a few too many myself" . . . *I'm quite drunk, and crazy, happy, silly, and trying not to say or do anything stupid . . . I'm doing my best to refrain from throwing myself at you.* "I don't want to pass out on the Metro. My head is spinning a little," she said and started giggling. She drank at least four hard ciders since eating the potato skins, which were gone in the first hour.

"I take the Metro too. What station do you get off at?" he asked thinking . . . *I'm going to help her get home tonight.*

"Huntington," she replied.

"I take it to Springfield," he said. "I can ride the Metro with you to Huntington and make sure you get to your car okay."

"That's out of your way. You'll have to backtrack to Springfield," she replied.

"I don't mind. I'd feel better knowing that you made it home safely. That is, if it's okay with you," he said . . . *I could stay here talking with you all night.*

"Yes, it's okay. I guess we should go before you have to carry me out of here," she said jokingly.

"I would happily do that," he replied smiling.

Holly and Charlie got up to leave. The radio was now playing the joyful, romantic song, "Laughter in the Rain," by Neil Sedaka. The bar was getting crowded and their vacated table was taken before they stepped on the elevator.

They walked down the city sidewalk toward the Metro station. The sun was setting, and it was beginning to get dark. Holly looked up at the sky and saw a glimpse of the moon. There would be a full moon later tonight. The early twilight air was pleasant and warm. Charlie was walking close beside her, and she felt like she was on a first date. She enjoyed being with him and didn't want their evening to end. The city was busy tonight, lit up with cars and buildings, and a street band was playing their instruments hoping for money from the passersby. One of the band members began to sing another old song from the 1970s. He began to belt out the words to "Me and Mrs. Jones" by Billy Paul. The song was about an extramarital affair, and it was one of Holly's favorites. She loved the smooth, jazzy tune and prominent saxophone.

"That's one of my favorite songs," Holly said . . . *I would jump Charlie's bones if I was unattached, and that song fits in perfectly with the way I feel right now.*

"I like it too. That guy sounds exactly like the original singer," Charlie replied and continued, "I like a lot of '70s soul music. I even like old disco tunes."

"So do I!" she replied enthusiastically.

"You weren't old enough to be into the disco scene," Charlie playfully said to her.

"I have an older sister who listened to the Bee Gees, Donna Summer, Gloria Gaynor, The Village People, and a bunch of others. I grew up listening to that kind of music," Holly replied.

"Would you like to stop and get a pastry and coffee? I'm concerned about you driving home. I think you need more food to absorb the alcohol," he said.

"I'd love to. There's a Starbucks across the street," she replied.

"Let's cross here . . . There's no crosswalk further down," he said and reached out to take her hand as they hurried across the street. Holly felt like she was walking on air. He held onto her hand for a few moments after they reached the other side of the street, and then gradually let go.

They walked into Starbucks, and there wasn't a line. As they were standing at the counter, Charlie placed his hand on the small of her back and said, "This is on me. What would you like?"

I love how I feel when you touch me . . . "I'll have a skinny vanilla latte and that big piece of chocolate layer cake that's looking at me," she replied happily and asked, "Are you going to get anything?"

"Yes, I'll have an espresso and that pastry over there that looks like tiramisu," he replied, his hand still on the small of her back. Holly resisted the urge to lean into him.

Charlie paid for their items, and they took a seat to wait for their order. "A skinny vanilla latte and a big piece of chocolate cake . . . Are you the type who orders desserts with Diet Coke?" he said lightheartedly to Holly.

"Yes, and proud of it," she replied with a wide smile . . . *It's so easy to be with him.*

A few minutes later their order was ready. Charlie walked up to the counter and got their coffees and brought them back to the table.

"Thank you, Charlie . . . Now I can dive into this chocolate cake," she said.

"If you want to try my tiramisu, you better do so now, because it won't be around for long," he replied.

Holly stuck her fork into his dessert and tasted it. "This is fantastic. I think I should concentrate on my cake or I'll end up eating most of yours." . . . *This feels intimate, like we've been a couple for years.*

"I'll buy you another one," Charlie offered.

"No, I'll have to work out extra tomorrow to make up for splurging tonight," she said . . . *I feel like I'm with my lover . . . This feels wonderful.*

"Me too. I plan to go running and hit the gym tomorrow," Charlie said.

James does those things too . . . "You're in great shape. I think it's important to exercise regularly," she said to him.

She thinks I look hot . . . She's gorgeous, and I know she takes care of herself . . . "Isn't this a great dinner? Beer, potato skins, cake, and coffee," he said, highly amused.

"The BEST!" she replied. They finished their cake and coffee and resumed their walk to the Metro.

"I feel more alert. That was a good idea to stop for food, even though technically it wasn't food," Holly said smiling up at him.

"Dessert and coffee make life worth living," Charlie said with exuberance.

They walked two more blocks and the Metro station was on the other side of the street. When they saw the crosswalk signal, they instinctively reached for each other's hand and hurried across. This time they didn't let go until they reached the escalator for the ride down to the turnstiles. As luck would have it, the train they needed was right there waiting for them. The seats were small and cramped, and this was one time she didn't mind.

As they sat down in the small seats, Charlie said, "Normally I detest these cramped seats. However, tonight, I'm thankful for them."

Holly laughed and said, "I think you're flirting with me."

"Yes, I am, and I know you aren't currently available. If that changes, I hope you'll let me know," he replied and touched her hand.

"Oh, I will," she said sincerely . . . *You bet I will.*

"So, what other types of music do you like?" Charlie asked, wanting to keep the conversation interesting and light.

"I like country and classical along with instrumental and orchestral music. What I don't like are sad songs. I think music should be uplifting. I work hard to stay happy and upbeat. What about you?"

"I'm not a big fan of country music, although I find myself listening to it on occasion. I'm with you on the classical, instrumental, and orchestral music. I could go to a National Symphony concert and enjoy it immensely," he replied with enthusiasm.

"Me too. I don't know many people who have the same musical taste as I do. It's nice to know I have a kindred spirit working at MTAC," she said.

"What about movies and TV? What do you like to watch?" he asked, wanting to know if they had similar tastes in that area too.

"I like comedy, suspense, adventure, mystery, and horror stories if the focus is on the supernatural and not a crazed slasher. I'm not a fan of heavy emotional drama and tearjerkers. Romantic movies are okay if they are not clichéd. I like happy endings. I'm a big fan of the History Channel, HGTV, and the Discovery Channel," she replied.

"We have a lot in common. I like everything that you just said, with the addition of war stories and anything military, typical guy stuff. I know you like chocolate cake and potato skins, what other comfort foods do you like?" he asked.

"I love macaroni and cheese, scalloped potatoes, and any type of bread with gobs of real butter. I don't eat that stuff often, and when I do, I savor it, like tonight," she said fondly . . . *I wish I had met you before I met James.*

I could fall hard and fast for this one . . . "Same here. If you ever want someone to eat dessert with, don't hesitate to give me a call," he smiled.

"So, if I should get a raging sweet tooth at 2:00 in the afternoon while I'm sitting at my desk, I can call you and we can sneak out for a piece of cake?" she said laughingly.

"Sure, if I'm not in a meeting," he replied smiling.

The train reached Huntington, and they stepped off and began the short walk to the parking garage and her car, a white 2010 Lincoln MKX. It was parked on the top level of the parking garage. It was dark and the full moon was hovering over them. The night sky was clear and filled with stars.

"Do you live far from here?" he asked.

"No, probably 2 miles at most," she replied and looked up at him.

"Good. I think you can make it 2 miles," he said looking in her eyes, not wanting to leave. They stood gazing at each other for a few seconds, and then she broke the silence by saying, "Thank you so much for making sure I got to my car okay, and for the good eats. You're a great guy, Charlie. You went out of your way tonight."

Charlie leaned down and kissed her on the lips. She smiled up at him and said, "Thanks again. Please drive home safely. I don't want anything to happen to you." Her heart was pounding in her chest, and she wanted to kiss him again . . . and again.

"Don't worry, I'm fine to drive home. I'll see you at work next week," he replied and squeezed her hand, continuing to hold her gaze and wanting to kiss her again. He then opened her car door and she stepped inside.

"Thanks, Charlie. Have a good weekend," she said to him.

"You too, drive safely," he replied.

She waved to Charlie before she drove away. He watched until she left the parking garage, and then he walked back to the Metro to get the next train to Springfield. As he made his way back to the station, he hoped he didn't scare her off. The alcohol really got to him. He liked Holly, and he knew he couldn't have her . . . yet. He secretly hoped she would break up with James soon. *I think that things aren't too happy at home . . . Women in happy relationships don't usually carry on like she did with me, holding hands and flirting . . . I'll have to contain myself at work . . . I'll be a gentleman and hope things aren't awkward between us next week.*

I can't believe Charlie kissed me! Oh . . . my . . . God! I won't be able to stop thinking about him . . . she thought over and over as she drove home. She watched her speed closely. She hadn't driven under the influence in years and didn't want to get pulled over tonight. *I feel young again . . . I had so much fun this evening . . . and Charlie kissed me!*

She pulled into the driveway, got out of her car, and unlocked the door to the house. As soon as she walked through the door Fate began voicing her displeasure. She was hungry. She fed the cat, and then went into the bedroom to change her clothes. She lay down on the bed for a few moments while still fully dressed, thinking about Charlie. Her head started to spin and she passed out.

James returned home in the early hours of the morning. He put his key into the front door and discovered it was unlocked. Holly never left a door unlocked. He was panicked now. He entered the house and went into the bedroom and saw Holly asleep on the bed fully dressed. She still had her shoes on. He thought it was strange and woke her up to find out if something was wrong.

"Holly, wake up. You're sleeping in your clothes," James said as he gently shook her awake.

Holly woke up. Her head was throbbing, and her mouth was dry. She sat up on the bed and said, "Hi, James. I went to happy hour with some coworkers and drank too much. My head feels like it's going to explode."

"You left the front door unlocked. Anybody could have just walked in here. How did you get home? Did you drive?" he asked her angrily. His voice was loud, and he was thinking of several guys who would like to mess him up.

"I'm sorry I left the door unlocked. Fate was hungry so I fed her first and must have forgotten to lock the door behind me. I was going to take off my clothes, and when I lay down on the bed I must have passed out. I got home just fine, as you can see. The Lincoln and I are in one piece," she replied abruptly.

"Don't let it happen again," he scolded her.

"What do you mean by that?" she said, and felt her anger rising.

"Leaving the door unlocked," he replied with exasperation. "I don't mind if you want to go out with your coworkers, just please, be more careful."

"Okay. I'm sorry," she said, feeling guilty that just a few hours ago she kissed a handsome man under the moonlight, or rather she let him kiss her, and she liked it.

"I've had a rough day and I want to get to bed," James said, somewhat irritated.

"Me too," Holly replied. They both changed into sleepwear, got into bed, and were asleep within minutes.

Later that morning Holly woke up first and went into the kitchen to make the coffee. She looked at the clock on the wall. It was 8:15. She had her psychic reading later this morning and James had to be at work at 3:00. She felt better, although her head was still aching. She took two aspirin with her first cup of coffee and sat down at the dining-room table. She got back up and opened the curtains so she could look out onto the patio.

She thought about last night and Charlie. The song "Me and Mrs. Jones" was running through her head like a freight train. She was having mental pictures of the two of them in the coffee shop and thinking of how they held hands walking to the Metro. *I guess I sort of cheated on James last night, holding hands with another man, even though it wasn't for very long.* One part of her brain was thinking. . . *Don't be so hard on yourself. James has taken you for granted for a long time. He repeatedly hurt your feelings by choosing to spend time with his guy friends over you, and you never do fun things together anymore . . . no wonder you're attracted to someone else . . . Charlie is HOT!* The other part of her brain countered with . . .

Stop making excuses . . . you have years invested in James and you know you still love him . . . Work it out, don't ruin it by having an affair. Her troubling thoughts were interrupted by James coming into the kitchen.

"Good morning," he said as he poured his coffee into a bright yellow mug.

"Good morning," she replied, feeling the unspoken coldness between them.

"So, what are your plans today?" he asked.

"I have an appointment at 11:30 downtown to see a psychic," she replied.

James laughed out loud, and it broke the tension. She started to laugh too.

"Why the hell do you want to see a psychic?" he asked, still laughing.

"I overheard some ladies on the Metro talking about past lives and I thought it would be a fun thing to explore," she replied.

"Past lives? I know you believe in that stuff . . . I don't. I believe you get one chance at life, and then you turn into worm food," he said with smug satisfaction. "Let me know what she says."

"I will. It should be interesting," Holly replied. She was used to James not taking any of this seriously. He sincerely believed you turn into worm food and that is the end of the road.

"I'm sorry I jumped on your case last night," he said.

"That's okay. I understand. It wasn't smart, forgetting to lock the door," she replied.

"How did you get home? You must have driven drunk," he said, looking serious now.

"I told you last night that I got home fine. By the time I got to my car I wasn't drunk anymore, just buzzed. I drove fine," she replied, slightly agitated.

"How about I make a sausage, ham, and cheese omelet for us?" he asked, hoping an offer of food would calm the residual irritation between them.

"Sure. I'm extremely hungry right now," she replied.

James cooked a delicious omelet for them. She loved that he could cook. There were advantages to living with a chef. James liked to invent new meals for the restaurant, and he often asked Holly to try them first, although it seemed like it had been months since he created a new entrée. Holly scarfed down the omelet like a starving prisoner. James watched in amazement. He wasn't used to seeing her eat like that.

"You just inhaled an omelet stuffed with meat, and it wasn't a small one either. I'm still working on mine," he said with a look of surprise on his face.

"The last thing I ate was a piece of chocolate cake last night and some potato skins several hours before that. No real dinner," she answered.

"I'm surprised you aren't sick this morning. Please be more careful in the future and never forget to lock the door behind you, especially late at night," James said to her, trying his best to not sound scolding.

"Yes, Daddy," she replied with a laugh and glanced up at the kitchen clock. "I need to get ready for my appointment."

She took a shower and later as she was putting on her makeup, James took one. By the time he was finished showering, she was ready to go. He was blow-drying his hair in the bathroom when she went to kiss him good-bye.

"I'll see you when I get back," Holly said and kissed him.

"What do you want to do tomorrow?" James asked her.

"Oh, I don't know. Let me think about it," she replied.

"Whatever you want is fine with me."

"See you later," she said.

This Saturday morning was sunny and warm and Holly was feeling anxious. She hoped this woman would be able to tell her about her past lives. She arrived 10 minutes early to the appointment. Martina was located within walking distance from the Metro. She lived in a small row house with a sign in the front yard indicating her services by appointment only. Holly rang the doorbell, and Martina opened the door.

"Hello. Are you Holly O'Rourke?" Martina Preston asked her.

"Yes. Are you Martina?" she asked excitedly.

"Yes, I am. It's great to meet you. Come on in," Martina said with a smile and extended her hand. Martina's demeanor was friendly and inviting and Holly instantly felt at ease.

Martina was a little lady, standing no more than 5 foot 1. She was in her mid-30s with a round, pretty face with crystal blue eyes, medium brown, curly hair that fell past her shoulders, and a voluptuous figure. She was wearing a red checkered sundress and matching solid red Espadrille shoes. She led Holly into a small room with gleaming hardwood floors and two white leather chairs and a round wooden table. There were two windows in this room. Martina pulled down the shades to block the sun. There was a large wooden cabinet next to one of the windows. The room was practically empty.

"Have a seat, Holly, and we'll talk for a few minutes," Martina said. The two women sat in the white chairs across from each other.

"So, you are here today for a past-life reading, correct?" Martina asked.

"Yes," Holly replied.

"First, I want to tell you what will likely happen during this session. I go into a trancelike state, and my voice might change. I sometimes take on the behavior of whatever spirit guide is there to speak through me. Usually it is my spirit guide working together with your spirit guide to access your past lives. Each of us has spirit guides to help us in our earthly incarnations. Your primary spirit guide is assigned to you before reincarnating into your current body. As you go through life, the circle of your guides expands, depending on the work you need to accomplish. When you reincarnate, you go through a veil of amnesia, and as you learn and grow in this life, you wonder, what the heck am I here for?

"We come from heaven, a place of total love and happiness. Your enemies in this life are dear friends on the other side. By incarnating into physical bodies, you learn a deeper appreciation for good things and even the bad. The potential growth from experiencing the bad is tremendous. There is no 'bad' in heaven, and if you never reincarnate you won't know the difference between good and bad. There are many wonderful worlds to advance to in heaven after your schooling on Earth and your incarnations are completed.

"We plan our lives before we are born, and our spirit guides are here to help us achieve what we came here to learn and do. They do this by giving us intuitive nudges in the right direction, although we don't listen to them most of the time. They do their best to keep us on track and guide us for our own good.

"Today, we will be accessing an area of the spiritual realm called the Akashic Records. This realm contains detailed records of your past lives and the past lives for every soul who has reincarnated. Your thoughts, dreams, and actions are recorded for eternity. Do you have any questions before we start?" Martina asked.

"No, I understand. We can begin whenever you are ready," Holly replied thinking . . . *Even our thoughts are recorded for eternity? That's embarrassing . . . Thank goodness not just anyone can access them.*

"Okay. I will ask the guides to show the past lives that might resonate with you at this point in time," Martina replied and became quiet.

It took several seconds for Martina to enter a trancelike state. She began to speak and the voice was not her own. A deep male voice was speaking with a distinct Middle-Eastern accent.

"Hello, Holly. My name is Kavi . . . I am your guide.

"You lived a life in Atlantis and fell deeply in love with your college teacher. He was married and would not leave his wife. You became pregnant with his child . . ." The voice paused for a few seconds.

"You lived a life in India in 1500 BC. You were a man in that life, and we were brothers. Your name was Sanjay. We were devout Hindus and ran a spiritual center together where we helped people better their lives . . ." Again he paused for a few seconds before continuing.

"I see a life as a Roman gladiator during the year of 47 BC. You were a prisoner of war and forced into fighting for the Romans' entertainment . . ." More silence.

"You were a baby left on the doorstep of a monastery in Ireland in the year of 816 and raised by monks. You died young, as the monastery was raided and burned to the ground by Vikings. The Vikings gangraped you before cutting off your head . . ." Still more silence.

"I see a life in Germany in the 1340s. You were a young boy and your mother was mean and cruel to you. You left home on the day you turned 16 . . ." The voice again paused.

"I see you and the man who was your abusive German mother. You are both on a Spanish sailing ship in the late 1480s. You are engaged in a fistfight and you kill him." More silence ensued.

"You lived another life in Germany in the 1560s. During this time they killed women suspected of witchcraft, similar to the Salem Witch Trials in America. The townspeople believe that you are a witch and burn down your home. You escape your burning house and lose everything you own. A man traveling through the countryside comes to your rescue and helps you get back on your feet. This is the same man who was your married lover in Atlantis . . ." The voice paused for a moment.

"You lived in Japan in the early 1600s, where you were a prostitute and killed your pimp. This is the same man who was your abusive German mother and enemy on the Spanish sailing ship. You killed him in self-defense . . ." The voice hesitated for a brief moment before continuing.

"You lived in Sweden in the 1740s during a time of war. You tended to wounded soldiers, like a nurse. You fell in love with a married soldier from an allied country and carried on an affair with him for over a year. This affair cost him his position, and he was stripped of rank and sent back home. This broke both of your hearts . . ." Again, the voice was silent.

"In another life in England in the 1850s, during the Victorian Era, I see that you and this same man were again secret lovers and married to other people. You were best friends with his wife, and your husband was often away from home due to work. You had a falling out with his wife that ended your friendship, and the two of you began having a secret affair. One day your husband came home from work and caught the two of you in bed together. He shot and killed your lover. You turned to alcohol to ease your depression and died 1 year later . . ." Moments later, the voice continued.

"You lived a frontier life in the American West during the late 1890s with the man who was your Atlantis lover. He treated you and the children poorly. He preferred getting drunk with his friends. You were extremely unhappy as you did most of the work on the farm to ensure the family's survival.

"Holly, we reincarnate to experience life from different perspectives so that we can grow both as a human and a spirit. You have lived many more lives than what I have just shared with you. Earth is a classroom, and you choose what you wish to learn before reincarnating. It can take many lifetimes to learn your desired lessons. There is no time in the spiritual realm and you choose when and how to clear the negative karma that you have created. I want to add that you are not required to clear bad karma, nor are you required to reincarnate. As an eternal being of light and love, your soul desires to clear it and make things right for the greater good, and you make the choice to do so, in agreement with the other souls involved . . . That is all for now, my dear . . ."

Martina came out of her trance. Holly sat there flabbergasted at what she had just heard. She didn't know what to think or say. If Martina was a hoax, she was a damn good one.

"Kavi has left. Do you have any questions, Holly?" Martina asked.

"I don't know. I'm in a state of astonishment at what just happened," she replied.

"Did any of those past lives resonate with you?" Martina asked.

"Interestingly, in this lifetime I've never been unfaithful to any man that I was seeing. The Hindu life that he mentioned does resonate with me because I have several CDs of Hindu mantras that I chant on occasion to help me with occasional bouts of depression. I'm stunned, amazed, and fascinated by everything that was revealed. It's one thing to read books about reincarnation and other people's experiences. Having a reading like this just increases my curiosity. I want details. Are these men in my current life?" she asked thinking . . . *Hearing my spirit guide's voice was pretty freaky*.

Martina paused for a few moments and said, "Yes, you are currently in a relationship with one of them, and you have crossed paths with the other two. One of them is a work acquaintance, and the other was your first husband. I see that this first husband was physically and mentally abusive. You have shared many lifetimes with him."

"I looked into having a past-life regression session with a hypnotherapist and it was too expensive. Do you have any recommendations on how I can further explore this?" Holly asked.

"You could read a book on how to do your own past-life regressions and practice the techniques, or you could purchase a CD that includes a guided meditation similar to what a hypnotherapist does, and keep practicing until something happens. I think repeatedly listening to a past-life regression CD would help you eventually regress to other lifetimes and help to find the details. I see a lot of them listed on Amazon," Martina replied.

"That's a great idea . . . I think I'll pursue that," Holly said excitedly.

"If you happen to experience some past lives, interesting things will happen during these regressions. You will know the people you interact with, you will know who they are in your present life even though they look completely different, unless you haven't met them yet in the here and now. Your soul knows who they are. We have 20 minutes left. Is there anything else you would like to know?" Martina asked.

"Yes. I've had some problems with my significant other, James, these past 2 years and want to know where our relationship is headed," Holly replied.

Martina was silent for a moment, and then she said, "I feel there is something he is hiding from you. He is deeply troubled. He is trying to work through his issues. Would you like a quick, three-card tarot reading on this?"

"Yes, definitely," Holly replied.

Martina got her deck of tarot cards from the large wooden cabinet and asked Holly to think about her question and shuffle the deck. Holly shuffled the cards thinking about her situation with James. When she was done, Martina told her to place the cards in a pile on the table. Martina drew three cards from the top of the deck. The first card was the past, the second card was her present, and the third card was the future.

The first card she drew was the Two of Cups. It showed a picture of a man and a woman standing face-to-face sharing their cups (which look more like large chalices) with each other. The overall feeling of this card was joy and happiness.

The second card she drew was the Three of Swords. It showed a heart with three knives pierced through it. A large cloud was above the heart, and it looked like rain was pouring down onto it. Holly tensed up when she looked at this card. She was familiar with tarot cards as she had several decks of her own, and this wasn't a good omen.

The third card she drew was the Tower. It showed a building on fire at night. The top of the building has been blown off and there were figures jumping out the windows. Lightning is striking the building. Holly remembers when she used to do her own readings, and she often took this card out of the deck. This card alarmed her because of its catastrophic appearance.

Martina began to interpret the meaning of these cards. "I'm sure I don't have to tell you this, however, I tell each of my clients that there is nothing mystical or magical about tarot cards. They are simply a tool to help access your intuition and the subconscious mind. If your thoughts are scattered and you are unfocused, the reading will not be clear. I feel that in your case, this three-card reading gets to the heart of the matter. The card meanings are not set in stone. If you look at a card and something about it echoes a particular feeling or thought within you, pay attention to it," she said and continued . . .

"The Two of Cups in the first position signifies the past. Cups relate to emotions. This card typically indicates attraction and the beginning of a love relationship. In addition, it can indicate a business partnership or a truce, or a meeting of the minds. I feel that this card signifies the beginning of your relationship with James, although I also feel it could indicate someone you recently befriended." *Holly thought of Charlie when she said this.*

"The Three of Swords in the second position relates to the present. Swords relate to action, force, and power. This card indicates heartbreak and betrayal. You just have to glance at this card and the meaning is blatantly portrayed. I think you know this already. It doesn't mean that you will break up with James. However, I feel that you should take this as a warning that some type of upset is possible for you soon."

"The Tower in the third position relates to the future. I'm getting a feeling of fear and apprehension from you. Please don't let this card scare you. It portends sudden change, upheaval, the possible dissolution of a relationship, and letting things go. However, it is not necessarily a negative card. In my experience, it often indicates a sudden revelation which sets you on a new and better path, or circumstances beyond your control that force a much-needed change."

Holly manages to suppress the tears and emotions building inside her. She is an emotional mess from her new and unexpected feelings for Charlie, and her conflicts with James, and now this reading. Martina watches her and explains that she doesn't sugarcoat readings, yet she thinks it is important to point out the positive aspects too.

"Holly, my advice for you is to find out what is troubling James and work with him to get through it. Don't dwell on the negative aspects of these cards. The future is constantly changing. It changes with every thought and action we undertake in our daily lives. Live your life day to day and focus on the things in life that make you happy and that you are thankful for. If you continue to dwell on the negative parts of this reading, you will attract the negativity it portends," Martina advised her, and then she asked, "Why don't I draw a fourth card to shed additional light on the situation?"

"Please do," Holly replied.

Martina drew a fourth card from the top of the deck. It was the Ace of Cups. This card showed a hand coming out from the sky holding a chalice which was overflowing with water. A white dove was hovering over the chalice. It was one of the most positive cards in the deck. Holly let out a sigh of relief when she saw it.

"The Ace of Cups in this upright position portends good things. Whatever problems arise from the previous cards' messages, you will overcome them and your life will be filled with love and happiness. I feel that a strong, happy, joyous love will come into your life. The relationship will be lovingly balanced. See, things aren't completely bad," Martina told her with a smile.

"Maybe things will turn around with James," Holly said hopefully, yet she felt a strong feeling of discontent and a heaviness in her chest area as she spoke those words.

"It is too early to know, and like I said before, the future is constantly changing," Martina replied. "There is one more thing I want to tell you. You have strong psychic ability which I believe could be further developed, should you wish to explore it. You have the potential to be a psychic medium. Just something to consider."

"Wow! I don't know what to say to that. I've been intuitive my entire life, yet I haven't followed my inner guidance, and I've made plenty of mistakes. But the older I get, the more I try to listen to it. Thank you, Martina. I appreciate the readings, and I will try to focus on the positive. All this information is overwhelming," Holly replied.

"Thank you. I hope that both readings were helpful. Feel free to make another appointment anytime you need to. It has been a pleasure getting to know you," she said.

"You too," Holly said happily.

Holly paid Martina for her services and left the building. The sun was hot, and there was no breeze for relief. It was lunchtime and there were many people out for a stroll, walking their dogs, jogging, eating and drinking at the outdoor cafes, and taking in the beautiful day and everything that the city had to offer. Holly walked to the nearest Metro station thinking about the tarot card reading she just experienced. She barely noticed the other people around her or the beauty of the day. She was in her own little world, feeling a jumble of mixed emotions. She was excited about the future, but worrying what might happen with James and feeling like she needed a drink of water or anything cold and wet. She was still dehydrated from her bender last night. She didn't drink alcohol often. She reflected on last night and Charlie, replaying the entire evening over in her head. She forced herself to stop thinking about him and instead began to recall what Martina told her about her past lives.

On the train ride back to Alexandria, she decided she would get on the computer and order a past-life regression CD when she arrived home. Her past lives weren't anything like she imagined they would be. She killed the same guy twice, had secret love affairs, was a man more than once, and lived in Atlantis. The Atlantis aspect was fascinating to her. She believed that Atlantis existed, even though it could never be proven. She wanted to know who was the man she had secret affairs with . . . *Could it be Charlie?* . . . and she was sure that Roger was the abusive mother and the one that she killed twice. James liked to drink and hang out with his guy friends. Was he the lousy frontier husband?

Chapter 2

Exploring the Past

Holly arrived home and hoped to have lunch with James before he left for work. However, when she pulled into the driveway, she noticed that his truck was gone. She walked into the house and saw that he left a note on the dining-room table.

> Holly, they called and asked me to come to work early. I'll see you late tonight.
>
> Love, James

She was disappointed because she wanted to tell him about her psychic reading and wanted to gauge his reaction to what Martina said about him hiding something. *Did he really get called into work early or is he avoiding me?* It would have to wait until tomorrow. She wanted to know what he was hiding, and she felt nervous about approaching the subject. She went into the office, logged onto the computer, and ordered a past-life regression CD from Amazon. She had the rest of the day to herself. She decided to lie out in the sun while it was beating down on the backyard and shop for groceries this evening.

She changed into her bikini and took a portable radio with her to listen to while sunning herself. She wanted to pretend that summer was going to go on indefinitely. She spread a beach towel over the chaise lounge, doused herself with sunscreen and turned on the radio. She couldn't believe what was playing . . . "I Only Have Eyes for You" was just beginning, and Holly was immediately mentally transported back to happy hour with Charlie. She let herself go and once again relived the course of events in her mind. When the song ended she thought . . . *What are the chances of hearing that same old song 2 days in a row? It just keeps Charlie stuck in my head.* She let out a heavy sigh and turned the radio dial to a classic rock station instead, thinking to herself . . . *I've known Charlie as an acquaintance for the past 6 years, never paid much attention to him or even talked to him at length until I ran into him at the deli . . . and then ended up getting drunk with him last night . . . Why on earth am I feeling like this? It can't be purely because I've been neglected by James . . . although that might be part of it . . . I feel there is something else too . . . Why has he suddenly come on the scene?*

James didn't go into work early. He had to make a delivery to a posh area of Arlington. One of his clients was having a party tonight and needed "the works." The works consisted of cocaine, marijuana, ecstasy, and heroin. James wanted the extra money. He lost $4,000 in a poker game a few weeks ago and his ass was on the line to repay it. James was a big, brawny guy and could hold his own one-on-one in a fight . . . unless it was with Bryce Decker. James had a permit to carry a concealed weapon. However, when you are up against two or more armed thugs who are out to get you, the only thing that might save you is a prayer. That's why he got so upset at Holly last night for leaving the front door unlocked. He had been slow to pay back the money. He was building a secret stash for himself, and Bryce was breathing down his neck. James never did any illegal drugs; he just sold them for money.

He was into physical fitness and keeping his body in shape. The basement of their house was set up with a Total Gym fitness system and an elliptical machine for cardio workouts when the weather didn't allow for running.

As he waited in his new and shiny, gray Ford F150 4X4 truck for his client to appear, parked in a ritzy subdivision, the regrets started again. He was tired and getting too old for this. He left this life behind when he first got together with Holly. He lived on the straight and narrow for 9 years. He knew she was a kind, classy lady, and he wanted her to be proud of him; he wanted to be a better man. He never told her about the gambling and drug dealing. He had never been arrested. He was clean on paper. He was an excellent chef, he loved to cook, and took pride in his work, yet he was drawn to the seedy side of life and living on the edge. He loved poker and blackjack. He was a member of an underground gambling club where the stakes were high. He loved the adrenaline rush it provided. He started gambling again 2 years ago. It started with a simple poker game in the bar with some old friends before work, and he gradually wound up here again. Dealing drugs was a quick-and-easy way to make the money he wanted, and James kept in touch with his underworld connections through the years.

This secret life drove a wedge between him and Holly. He used the excuse of wanting to hang out with the guys to cover his gambling and drug dealing. In his mind he wasn't really lying to her, he just didn't tell her the whole story. He knew their relationship was hanging by a thread. Things change when you hide a secret life from your significant other. He was thankful that Holly was trusting and patient, as the drug dealing and gambling were only part of it. He would eventually figure a way to get out of this situation like he did when they first started dating. Once this debt was paid up he would consider going to rehab for his gambling compulsion, although he would have to keep that a secret from her too. He was fighting many internal demons.

James didn't have to wait long. A clean-cut young man dressed in jeans and a Hawaiian shirt waved to him as he walked toward the truck. This must be his client, or his cover, sent to pick up the works. The drugs were hidden inside a beautifully wrapped large box to look like an expensive gift. James got out of his truck to greet the young man.

"Hey. Are you Mac?" the young guy asked him.

"Yes, nice to meet you," James said as he extended his hand.

"Got the present?" he asked.

"Sure do," James replied as he retrieved the present from his truck and handed it to him.

"Looks beautiful. Here you go," the young guy said as he handed James a manila envelope filled with cash. "Thanks, man."

"Thank you," James replied and watched the young guy walk down the street with the present in hand.

James got back into his truck to go to work. He decided this would be his last drug deal; he was going to get back on the straight and narrow. He was looking forward to spending tomorrow with Holly and forgoing an upcoming poker game. When he pulled into the restaurant parking lot, he noticed Bryce was waiting for him in his black, Hummer H3. Bryce saw James pulling in and got out of his H3 to meet him. Bryce was an enforcer for the underground gambling club. He made sure debts were paid . . . or else, and he was an intimidating figure. Bryce was tall and built like Hercules, and his head was completely shaved. He had a large nose, blue eyes, and a wide, mischievous smile which showcased perfect white teeth. He practiced martial arts and owned several studios in the Washington area. You didn't want to make him angry. Bryce was dressed casually in khaki pants and a form-fitting black polo shirt which showed off his muscular physique.

"James, good to see you," he said as he walked up to James's truck.

"Bryce, how are you?" James asked.

"I'll be doing fine once I get payment from you," he replied.

"Here you go," James said as he handed Bryce the envelope with

$4,000 in it. James made a profit on the drug deal by jacking up the price and hid the rest of his money in the glove compartment.

"Awesome . . . Thanks," Bryce replied coolly, and discreetly counted the cash. "See you tomorrow night?"

"No, I've got to spend some time with my lady. She hasn't been too happy with me lately," James replied with a nervous laugh.

"She's a fine-looking woman, don't let that one get away," Bryce replied.

"Oh, I won't," James said . . . *I've got some major work ahead to patch things up with her.*

"Catch you later," Bryce said, and then turned to walk back to his H3.

James felt like a weight was lifted from his shoulders once again, and he walked into the kitchen for his shift.

"Hi, James!" Amber Conner said excitedly as she saw him enter the kitchen.

"Hey, Amber." James didn't want to deal with her today. He was turning over a new leaf and cleaning up his act.

"What's wrong?" she asked.

"Nothing. I just have a lot on my mind, and I've got to get to work," he snapped back.

"Okay," Amber replied feeling slighted. She picked up the order for her table and left the kitchen. She was hurt by his abrupt greeting. She had important news to tell him.

When Sunday morning arrived, James woke up ready to make love with Holly. She happily obliged and enjoyed finally having him to herself. It had been over 3 weeks since they were intimate with each other.

"I've really missed being with you," she said to him.

"I've missed you too," he replied. "What do you want to do today?"

"I want to relax and just be with you. Why don't we have breakfast, read the paper, do the crossword puzzle, and then take a long walk?" she suggested, hoping to get to the root of what was bothering him.

"Sounds like a good plan," he replied and kissed her.

They went into the kitchen to make breakfast. James made her favorite, chocolate chip pancakes. They usually ate healthier as they both had to fight a raging sweet tooth. Holly made sure the conversation stayed light. She wasn't going to start probing him until they started their walk. James was content to have an easy morning with Holly. He realized how much he missed times like this. He didn't ask her about the psychic reading she received yesterday. He was going to, and then got a sudden case of guilt. He hoped the psychic didn't uncover his secrets.

Later that day they went out for a walk around the neighborhood. The sky was overcast, but it was warm. Holly finally got up the nerve to ask him what he was hiding.

"James, I want to talk to you about the visit I had with Martina, the psychic."

"What did she have to say?" he asked, suddenly feeling alarmed and trying to act calm.

"Well, she went into a trancelike state and channeled my spirit guide, whose name is Kavi. Her voice changed into a deep male voice with a Mid-Eastern accent, so it was actually Kavi speaking through her. He told me about my past lives, and then Martina read my tarot cards. She said she got the feeling that you were hiding something from me, and you were deeply troubled."

HOLY CRAP . . . I've been caught . . . Holly will kick me to the curb . . . James thought to himself and felt his heart pounding in his chest, and then he laughed. Stopping in his tracks he turned to face Holly, look her in the eyes, and lied, "Honey, I'm not hiding anything from you. She was right that I am troubled. I am troubled because I want a career change and don't know which way to turn. I'm having a midlife crisis of sorts and trying to work through it. She must have picked up on my inner discontent," he said. James was an expert at lying. He had lots of practice. Lying saved his life on many occasions. He continued, "This lady must be something else if she can imitate deep male voices with ethnic accents. Maybe she should be working in a carnival." *This lady picked up on some things . . . however, she must have faked the male voice. I just don't believe in that crap . . .* he thought.

Holly felt a wave of relief flood over her. She believed James and ignored his comment about Martina speaking in a male voice. "James, why didn't you talk to me about this? I know you're tired of working at American Steak. What kind of career change are you looking for?"

"I'm 53 years old and working as a head chef. There is nowhere to go. I'm not trained for anything else, and I'm tired of cooking for the masses and the restaurant business. I'm looking for direction and don't know where to turn," he said, knowing that these words were partially true. He wanted to get into another line of work and leave the restaurant business behind, and he was having a midlife crisis on top of it. He hoped this would be enough to stop her questions.

"You have bachelor's in hotel and restaurant management, and years of experience as a chef. Have you thought of going back to school and getting an MBA? Maybe you should talk with a career counselor at one of the colleges in the area," she suggested.

How can I change the subject? I've got to say something to change the subject. I'm not going to any damn college at my age . . . I'll ask her about her past lives . . . "Holly, I'm not a kid anymore. I'm not going to consult with any career counselor, and I sure as hell don't want to go back to school! Sweetheart, I'll figure it out in time. I'm curious, though, what did Kavi say about your past lives?" he asked, hoping to change the subject.

"Oh, that was interesting. Apparently I was involved in two secret love affairs in two different lives which ended up getting my lover killed in one life and sent away in the other. I lived in Atlantis, I was a man in Germany, and my mother was abusive. I was a Japanese prostitute in the 1600s, I was left on a monastery doorstep as a baby and raised by monks and died young because Viking invaders raided the place, and I was a Roman gladiator, a Spanish sailor, and a Hindu holy man. Kavi was my brother in the Hindu past life," she replied.

James laughed at her explanation and was pleasantly amused, relieved that he was no longer the focus of the conversation. "Do you really believe that?" he asked, mildly charmed by her seeming naivety.

"I have no frame of reference so I have to say yes, I do," she replied. "I ordered a past-life regression CD to try to find out more about these past lives."

"That's interesting. I hope you find what you're looking for. Maybe you'll get to meet Kavi," he teased and began laughing again.

Holly and James continued their walk around the neighborhood and the conversation turned to everyday subjects. She was satisfied with his answers. Things seemed to be back to normal, at least for now, and they enjoyed the remainder of the day together.

Monday arrived too soon, and as she took her shower that morning, she reflected on the nice Sunday she had with James and how she felt closer to him. There was still an uneasy feeling nagging at her, though, and she hoped it would soon pass. He was sitting on the sofa, drinking his coffee and reading the paper when she was finally ready to leave for work.

"So, what are your plans for today?" she asked him.

"I haven't thought that far yet. It's just so nice to have the day off," he replied. "I do plan on making dinner for you tonight. What would you like to eat?"

"I would love for you to make baked macaroni and cheese. I love how you use four different cheeses and sprinkle the parmesan on top," she said happily. "It's a diet buster for sure, although I think we can splurge on it now and then."

"Sure, I'll make that. It's easy, and a favorite at the restaurant," he said.

"Great. I will see you tonight," she said and kissed him good-bye.

"You look beautiful today, I love you," James said to her.

"I love you too," she said with a smile, and then walked out the door to get in her car.

As she got into her car and turned on the radio, "Me and Mrs. Jones" was playing and she immediately thought back to Friday night and walking down the city sidewalk with Charlie. In spite of her pleasant Sunday with James, hearing that song put her in a dreamy state of mind and she recalled her enchanted evening with another man. When the song ended, she turned off the radio and shook her head, thinking to herself . . . *Am I going to be continually haunted by these songs? . . . Something is definitely there with Charlie. James and I reconnected and you would think that my feelings for Charlie would have dissipated like any normal crush . . . and they haven't . . . I guess I'll just have to deal with it.* She was both dreading, and looking forward to going to work and seeing Charlie.

Holly was relieved that she didn't run into Charlie on her walk to the office. She settled in at her desk and logged onto her computer. It was a quiet morning. Mondays generally started out calm. Her quiet time was interrupted when Patricia came up to see her. As usual, she knocked on the door to get Holly's attention.

"Good morning. Did you have a nice weekend?" Patricia asked her friend.

"Good morning. Yes, I had a great weekend," Holly replied.

"What happened after we left on Friday?" she asked with a probing look in her eyes.

Holly's facial expression changed and became slightly serious, and

Patricia knew right away that something was up.

"After you and Andy left, Charlie and I stayed and talked for probably 30–45 minutes, and then we went for coffee and dessert. He rode the Metro home with me," Holly replied.

"He did what?!" Patricia exclaimed and questioned at the same time.

"Yes. He rode the train home with me to make sure I got to my car okay, and then he got back on it to go home to Springfield," Holly said dreamily, and she was glowing.

"I knew it. That man has a thing for you. I saw the way he was looking at you on Friday night. I think you like him too," Patricia replied.

"Well . . . there's more . . . He kissed me," Holly said softly.

"What kind of kiss? Was there tongue?" she asked excitedly.

"No . . . just a nice, soft kiss on the lips . . . one time . . . and then I thanked him for seeing me to my car, and he watched me drive away," Holly replied.

"Did you tell James?" Patricia asked.

"No way! He would have a fit if he knew. Besides, you know things have been rough for us these past 2 years. It's not an excuse for kissing Charlie. It just happened, and now I can't stop thinking about him," Holly said with a sigh.

"So what's your next move?" Patricia asked.

"I don't know. Suffer in silence, I guess. James and I reconnected yesterday and things seem to be getting back to normal. I'm not ready to leave him for another man," Holly said.

"I understand. What if Charlie makes a play for you?"

"I will politely decline his advances, or at least attempt to," Holly replied with a laugh . . . *I'm not the cheating type . . . although Charlie would be the true test of my resolve.*

"I've got to get going, I just wanted to check in with you," Patricia replied. "Don't work too hard and have a great day."

"You too, Patricia. Thanks for checking up on me," Holly said.

Holly meant to tell her friend about the psychic reading and got carried away talking about Charlie. She figured she would tell her some other time. A few hours later Holly got a call from Charlie. She saw that it was him on the caller ID, and her heart started racing. She picked up the phone.

"Hi, Charlie," she said.

"Good morning, Holly. Did you have a nice weekend?" he asked.

"Yes, did you?" she asked.

"Yeah. The reason I called is that I wanted to apologize if I made you feel uncomfortable on Friday night," he said.

"Charlie, it was wonderful being with you on Friday, and I didn't feel uncomfortable, not once," she replied with enthusiasm . . . *In fact, it was the best time I've had in ages.*

"I feel a lot better now," he said with relief. "So, you'll still speak to me when we run into each other?" he asked jokingly.

"Of course, I'm happy I made a new friend," she replied with sincerity.

"I'm taking some leave this week. Tomorrow I'm going to Florida to visit my daughter, Brianna. She's going to have a baby and is scheduled for a C-section on Wednesday. This will be my first grandchild," Charlie said proudly.

"Congratulations! That is fantastic and exciting," Holly said happily. "When are you coming back?"

"I'll be back next Wednesday and show you the photos," he replied.

"Okay, Charlie, have a safe trip," she replied and hung up the phone, her heart still pounding in her chest. It suddenly struck her that many men in their 50s were becoming grandfathers. She didn't think of Charlie like that. He was handsome, in good shape, and certainly not "grandfatherish."

She didn't run into Charlie that day and his phone call had relieved the anxiety and fear she had about seeing him again after Friday night. She was looking forward to crossing his path when he got back. Until then, she would try to put him out of her thoughts and get on with life. Holly realized that it was going to take more than one good day with James to get their relationship firmly back on track, although they were off to a good start. She hoped that eventually she would have no more thoughts of romance with Charlie.

James enjoyed his day off and gradually got around to doing some chores. He mowed the grass, pulled the weeds in Holly's sunflower garden, and welcomed being outdoors. It was great to not have anyone breathing down his neck. He knew he had himself to blame and really wanted to make things right with Holly, now that he could breathe again.

He took the money he made dealing drugs and hid it in the small closet underneath the staircase which led down into the basement. There was a narrow space beneath the first shelf and the floor and this was where he stashed it. He put the cash in sealed cardboard boxes shoved back against the wall underneath that shelf. At first glance it looked like a small empty area. Holly didn't like the dark and cramped closet and most of the things in there belonged to him. The money was adding up and would be there if or when he needed it. He currently had $200,000 in cash from drug dealing and gambling. He could have easily paid the $4,000 to Bryce without batting an eye or selling drugs, except that James was greedy and he wanted to make as much money as he could on what he intended to be his last deal. A part of him was tempted to go to the next poker game and bet everything. If he won, he would have a small fortune indeed.

On Wednesday of that week, Holly received her past-life regression

CD. She took time in the evenings to listen to the CD and tried to allow herself to be hypnotized into reliving her past lives by following the speaker's gentle voice and instructions. Her persistence paid off, and on Saturday night she was able to go back in time. She had a past-life experience which took place in the 1700s, but it wasn't a continuous sequence of events and things seemed to jump around . . .

. . . Holly watches a handsome man dismount from his horse and she knows that he is Charlie. He is a high-ranking soldier who oversees strategic aspects of the war. She hears someone call him Erik. In this life he is 6 feet tall with light brown hair and blue eyes and a handsomely chiseled face. She is instantly attracted to him.

She is working as a nurse (or someone who helps attend to the sick and wounded) in a building close to where Erik is stationed. She hears someone call her by the name of Krista. She knows, somehow, that she is in Sweden.

She seems to cross paths with Erik often, as he comes and goes into the clinic she works in. They exchange glances and smiles and chat about everyday things. Erik goes into the clinic when he doesn't need to, just so he can see and be around her. They develop a huge crush on each other. During this time, it was not appropriate for a higher-ranking official to become romantically involved with any of the staff or support group. However, Erik was determined to ask her out.

Krista finds herself at a birthday party that is held for Erik at a nearby tavern. She is with a group of soldiers and other staff members who were able to attend. Erik is drinking heavily and the group is singing and laughing. Once the singing stops, Erik stumbles over to her and they strike up a conversation.

"You look beautiful tonight," Erik says to her, and he kisses her on the lips in front of everyone. Krista laughs and makes light of this, and says out loud, "You're drunk! You need to go home and sleep it off. Soldiers, please take this man home before he passes out."

"Come on, let's get him out of here," one of the soldiers said to the group.

"Krista, get Krista to come with me," Erik keeps repeating. He is so drunk it takes two men to hold him upright, and they proceed to help Erik into a carriage.

"Are you okay to watch over him tonight?" a soldier asks her.

"Yes, I'll make sure he survives the night," Krista replies, and she gets into the carriage with Erik and two other men.

One of the soldiers riding in the carriage with them looks familiar to Krista. He begins to talk to her, and then she realizes who he is. She knows him in her soul, and not in a good way.

"Are you sure you want to watch over him? He might take advantage of you. I don't think it's safe," Gustaf says. Krista recognizes this man as Roger Chasen.

"Yes, I'll be fine. Look at his condition. The only thing he can do is pass out. It wouldn't take much strength to fend off his advances," she replies with a laugh.

"Okay, be sure to scream if he tries anything with you," he warns her sternly. Gustaf is a nice-looking man, same height as Erik, with blond hair and light brown, caramel-colored eyes. However, something in his facial expression looks mean. He has a slightly crooked nose, and it detracts from his otherwise handsome face. Krista feels a strong dislike for him.

They arrive back at the fort and help Erik to his quarters. He has a small room inside a larger building. The higher-ranking soldiers have their own space.

Erik falls down on his bed and passes out. Krista notices a mirror on the wall and looks into it. She sees that she looks Swedish. She has pale blond, almost platinum-colored hair, large, wide-set blue eyes, and soft and feminine facial features. She thinks that she looks plain, pale, and quite young, 17 or 18 at best. It was a strange feeling, looking at a past-life version of yourself.

Krista tends to Erik, taking off his boots, trying to make him more comfortable. She lies down next to him and eventually falls asleep. Morning arrives and Erik wakes up and sees Krista asleep next to him. He kisses her softly on the cheek, lightly touches her face, and she wakes up.

"I love you," Erik says to her.

"I love you too," Krista replies.

In the weeks that follow, Erik and Krista become involved in a secret affair. They often sneak away to an inn outside of the military base to make love. Their passion is intense. They can't get enough of each other and go to this place whenever time permits. This goes on for almost a year, until the day when Gustaf sees them going into the inn together and decides to tell his superiors about this.

Erik is given a warning to end his affair with that woman or he will lose his position and be sent home. He tells Krista that they must be more careful. Gustaf keeps his eyes open for further indiscretions between Erik and Krista, and he spies them together one evening, kissing passionately outside of the inn.

"I think someone is watching us. Please, Erik, don't kiss me in public like that. I don't want them to strip your rank," Krista pleads.

"I can't help it, I am crazy for you!" he replies and kisses her again, consumed by his passion.

Gustaf reports Erik to command the next day, and Erik is reprimanded by his superiors, stripped of his rank, and ordered to leave the station and return home.

Erik walks into the clinic where Krista is working and tells her that they must talk. She looks in his eyes and knows something is terribly wrong. She finishes tending to a wounded soldier, and then walks with Erik outside of the building.

"Krista, we were caught again. I know that Gustaf is the one who reported me. I have never liked him. He wants my post and continually tries to undermine me. This time he succeeded. I just lost my position

and must return home," Erik tells her with a heavy heart.

"Can you stay here and get a job in town?" Krista asks.

Erik breaks down in tears and says, "No. I have a wife and son back in Bavaria, and I must return to them. I'm so sorry I didn't tell you. I have never loved my wife. It was a marriage of convenience. I will return home to divorce my wife and tell her I am coming back for you. I love you. I promise I will come back for you."

"How could you do this to me? Why didn't you tell me you were married and had a child?" Krista says indignantly to him.

"Would it have made a difference? Would it have stopped you from falling in love with me?" he asked.

Krista begins to cry and shakes her head no. She knows she would have fallen in love with him anyway. She feels betrayed, guilty, and full of shame.

"And then what? If you come back and get me, what about your son?" she asks through her tears.

"Krista, I promise I will return for you and take you with me back to Bavaria. I will divorce my wife. I want to spend the rest of my life with you," he said, and took her in his arms. They clung to each other, and he stroked her hair and tried to comfort her. He was crying too; his heart was breaking.

Krista continues to cry while holding onto him. Erik is abandoning her, and she gets a sinking feeling that she will never see him again, he will never return. They finally kiss good-bye and Erik steps into a carriage that will take him to where he can board a ship and return home.

Later that day, Krista walks to the outskirts of the base. There is a thickly wooded area nearby, where she can be alone with her thoughts. She feels cold, the sky is gray and cloudy. A chill is in the air, and it feels like late fall. She kneels on the hard ground behind a large tree and cries her eyes out. She knows in her heart that she will never see Erik again. Something will keep him from returning to her. A few moments later, she hears footsteps and looks up. Standing before her is Gustaf.

"Krista, do not waste tears over him. He is not good for you," Gustaf says to her softly. She looks up at Gustaf's face and sees a trace of compassion in his expression. However, she knows he was the one who told on them.

"It was you. You told on us. He said it was you! Why? It was none of your business," she yells hatefully to him.

"He was not an honorable man. He broke the rules. Rules must be followed," Gustaf says to her with a hard look on his face.

She is standing up now and facing him. She is filled with fury, and she raises her hand and slaps him hard across the face . . .

Holly is suddenly awakened by Fate jumping onto the bed. She looks around the room and is startled to be back in the twenty-first century. She takes off her headphones and places them on the nightstand. Random thoughts and questions run through her mind . . . *Martina was right . . . I did live in 1740s Sweden and lost a man I deeply loved . . . and that man was CHARLIE! Should I tell him about this? No, he will think I'm crazy. No wonder I am so attracted to him in this life . . . Why now? I've known him for years . . . and what was Roger doing in that life? . . . Did he try to date me after Charlie left? Should I try to go back again and pick up where I left off? Do I have unfinished business with Charlie to resolve in this life?*

Holly hears someone unlocking the door and realizes it's James coming home from work. She gets up and walks to the living room to greet him.

"Why are you up?" James asks her.

"I was awake and heard you unlocking the door," she replied.

"Normally you are dead to the world. What woke you up?" he asked.

"I finally had a past-life experience, and Fate jumped on the bed and snapped me out of it," she said.

"So, who were you?" he asked . . . *I'll play along with this reincarnation stuff . . . although I think she's nuts . . . Reincarnation doesn't happen.*

"It was one of the secret affair dreams. I dreamt I was some sort of nurse in 1740s Sweden, and I was having an affair with a married soldier who got stripped of rank because of it and had to leave and go back home to his wife," she replied.

"Who was the soldier?" James asked.

"No one I recognize in this life," she lied to him . . . *I can't tell James the truth . . . He can't know about my attraction to Charlie.*

"Oh . . . I kind of hoped it would be me," James said disappointedly and feeling a little jealous, wishing that he was the secret lover in her strange dream.

"If I can keep doing this, maybe you will show up soon," she replied with a laugh.

James got an uneasy feeling about the dream she just told him, and he thought . . . *Is my guilty conscious getting to me, or am I jealous of a dream? Holly is perfect, and I'm the one who's been a bad boy.*

"Did you have a busy night?" she asked.

"Yes, and I just want to hit the sack," he replied.

"Oh, the vanilla air freshener, you don't smell like that tonight. It was nice. Did you run out of it? I guess I expected you to smell like vanilla every night," she said to him.

"Yeah, everyone likes it. It will be hard to keep it stocked. I don't think I should bring any home," James replied, hiding his annoyance that she was asking about it again. Thankfully she bought this lie, and he would have to make sure he didn't come home smelling like vanilla any more, or she might keep bugging him.

"Let's get to bed," he said to her.

Holly yawned and they both got into bed and crawled under the covers for sleep. Tomorrow was Sunday, and James was off on Sunday and Monday. Holly was too excited to sleep. She had just glimpsed her past, and while it was heartbreaking, it was interesting and she wanted to know more. She thought about her recent psychic reading and thought . . . *Maybe the Three of Swords is the heartbreak I experienced from my past life bleeding over into this one. I hope that is it, although it wouldn't explain the Tower card . . . unless I uncover a more horrible past life.* Holly wanted to have another past-life experience, so she put her headphones back on and started the CD again. She was able to travel back in time to Victorian England . . .

. . . Holly sees herself in a lovely Victorian-era bedroom. The heavy velvet drapes are olive green, and the furniture is ornately carved with cherubs and painted a cream color with gold detailing on the dresser drawers. She is looking into a mirror and sees that in this life she was medium height and slim. She has long, dark brown hair pulled back and partially up. Her eyes are a gray-blue color, her lips are full, and she is wearing a medium blue dress with a high neck, a nipped-in waist, and a bustle in the back. She looks stunning, and she twirls around looking at herself from every angle. She is a beautiful woman.

"Emily, sweetheart, I'm home," a man's voice calls out to her.

She walks out of the bedroom and down a long staircase to greet her husband. She sees him at the end of the staircase smiling up at her. He has been gone for several days. He's wearing a policeman's uniform. He is over 6 feet tall with red hair and blue eyes. Quite a few freckles cover his face. He is attractive in an ordinary way. She recognizes him as Roger. In this life he is named Clive. She is glad that he is smiling. He usually comes home from work in a bad mood. She never knows when he is going to be home, and he is gone for long stretches of time. She feels apprehensive around him. He is often irritable and likes to pick fights with her.

She sees pictures in her mind of the last fight they had. He came home and wanted some brandy right away. She went to pour him a glass and realized they were out of brandy. He became furious and accused her of not paying attention to the things he liked. He grabbed her by the neck and pushed her up against the wall and threatened to divorce her, telling her she was a lousy wife. Similar situations like this happened frequently. He was becoming a monster.

"Hello, my dear, welcome back," she says and greets him with a kiss on the lips and a forced smile. She is not happy to see him.

"It is good to be back," he says and pulls her close in a tight hug.

"How long are you home for this time?" she asks him.

"Oh, a day or two. What have you been doing since I was away?" he asks.

"I have tea with Lisa in the afternoons. Sometimes we go shopping. When I am bored I clean the house or read a book or write a letter to my sister," she replied.

There's a knock on the door and Clive opens it to find Lisa and her husband David.

"Good evening. We were on our way to the pub and wanted to see if you would join us," Lisa said to them.

"Clive, it's good to see you again," David says and extends his hand.

"Good to see you, David," Clive replies and shakes David's hand.

She recognizes David as Charlie. She doesn't recognize Lisa as anyone she knows in her present life. She is strongly attracted to David and wishes she could trade places with Lisa. David is tall like Clive. David has thick, curly, chestnut-brown hair and blue eyes. His dazzling smile lights up his face. Lisa is the same height and size as Emily. Emily has images in her mind of them borrowing each other's clothes. Lisa is a pretty woman with golden blond hair and green eyes. She has a vibrant, friendly personality, and Emily enjoys her company. She would love to join them for drinks tonight.

"Thank you for the invitation, but I think Emily and I will stay in this evening. I just got home and want to be alone with my wife," Clive said to them with a wink.

Emily knew that Clive wanted to make love with her tonight although she could care less. She was disappointed not to go out with their friends.

"I understand," Lisa said. She looked at Emily and said, "We can meet tomorrow afternoon for tea. Is that okay with you, Clive?" Emily and Clive both nodded their heads yes.

"Have a good evening. Cheers," David said as he and Lisa began to walk away. David and Emily exchange admiring glances that neither Lisa nor Clive can see, as they are looking in different directions.

Emily finds herself having tea with Lisa sometime later. It feels like it has been a week or two since Lisa and David stopped by to invite them out for drinks. They are at Lisa's house in her parlor room, sitting at a heavy, wooden table covered with an intricate white lace tablecloth. Emily notices that Lisa seems distressed. Lisa pours tea for them and they each add two cubes of sugar.

"Lisa, is something wrong?" Emily asks.

"David. It seems he does not want to make love much anymore. He would rather read books than make love. We have been married for 3 years and the first 2 were lovely. He constantly wanted me. Now, rarely, and when we do make love, I feel that his mind is somewhere else or thinking about someone else," Lisa said woefully.

"Have you talked to him about this?" Emily asked her.

"Yes, and he denies there is a problem. I am starting to think that the reason he is losing interest in me is because of you," Lisa said in a hateful tone.

"Me! Why?" Emily asked, suddenly feeling alarmed.

"He often talks about how beautiful and kind you are, and what a lucky man Clive is. I have seen the way he looks at you. Actually, it just occurred to me that ever since you and Clive moved here he has gradually lost interest in me. He wants you!" she said angrily, and set her tea cup down hard on the table, its contents spilling onto the pristine white tablecloth. She continued her rant. "It is your fault. He will not admit it, but I know he wants you. I am ending our friendship. The only way my marriage can survive is if you are out of the picture.

Please leave and do not talk to me again!"

Emily is shocked and hurt by her friend's words. She tries to change Lisa's mind and says, "Lisa, you are my best friend. I do not want to lose you. I am not after your husband."

"Just leave. I do not want to see you anymore," Lisa coldly replied and glared at her.

Emily leaves Lisa's house in tears. She walks the one block to her home and on the way she encounters David coming home from work. He sees Emily, but she doesn't look at him. He stands in front of her to block her path, and then confronts her.

"Emily, what's wrong?" he asks, alarmed at the tears on her face.

"Lisa ended our friendship. She thinks that I am the reason you do not want to make love to her anymore," she says through her tears. She is crying harder now.

"Let me walk you home and we'll talk about this," he said.

"Okay," Emily says softly.

They walk to Emily's house, and she opens the door. They head to the parlor and sit down on the soft, burgundy velvet sofa facing each other.

David takes Emily's hands in his, bows his head in shame, and says, "I am sorry that you and Lisa are no longer friends. However, she spoke the truth. I have fallen in love with you, and it is hard to stay interested in her when I am constantly thinking about you. I have been trying to find a way to end it with her. I know you are not happy with Clive. I can see it in your face whenever we are gathered together. I know he does not treat you well."

Emily has stopped crying. She feels both relieved and torn over this declaration of love from David. She feels the same way about him, and she knows that Lisa was correct in her judgment. She continues to hold hands with David.

He is looking in her eyes and she says to him, "Yes, I love you too. I am not happy with Clive. He has a cruel streak, and I look forward to him not being home. In the beginning, I hated when he would have to leave for long periods of time. I was lonely. These past several months I would rather be lonely than be with him."

David leans in to kiss her, and neither of them wants to stop. Emily takes him by the hand and leads him upstairs to the bedroom. They make love that afternoon and decide to keep their love a secret until they can figure out a plan to run away together. They have trysts at Emily's house while Clive is away. Their secret affair goes on for 6 months.

They become careless, however, and one day Clive comes home unexpectedly and walks in on Emily and David making love in his bed. He opens the bedroom door and Emily screams. David rolls off of her and pulls up the sheets. Clive is shocked and angered at his wife's betrayal. He pulls out his gun and points it at David and says loudly, "YOU ARE A DEAD MAN."

"NO!!" Emily screams. "Clive, please, NOOOOOOO!"

He pulls the trigger and shoots David in the heart. He pulls the trigger again and shoots him in the head. David's dead, naked body falls out of the bed onto the floor. Emily is screaming and crying.

"YOU ARE A WHORE AND DESERVE TO DIE," Clive yells at her. He shoots his gun and fires several shots at her, purposely missing her, wanting to scare her.

"CLIVE, PLEASE STOP . . . I'M SO SORRY . . . PLEASE DON'T KILL ME!!" she screams.

Clive stops shooting and says, "I am going to tell the police that he broke into the house to rape you. If you say otherwise, I will kill you. Understand?"

Emily nods her head yes; she is in shock. Clive proceeds to vandalize their home to make it appear that David broke in to rape her. The police show up a short while later, and they believe every word of Clive's story. Clive is a fellow police officer, and they have no reason to doubt him. Emily is sitting in bed the entire time, wrapped up in bed sheets, crying and looking at David's dead and bloody body lying on the floor . . .

Holly wakes up and feels extremely sad. This was her second secret affair past life and it involved Charlie again. She understood the message that cheating is wrong, and it is better to get out of a bad relationship first than to cheat on your partner. Secret love affairs often end badly and hurt more than the two people involved. Roger was in this life too. She wondered if this twisted karma was the reason she married him in this present life. He was physically and mentally abusive to her in the past and the present. She wasn't sure what to make of this, seeing Roger appear again. She decided to turn over and go to sleep. No more trying to revisit the past tonight.

CHAPTER 3

Three of Swords

On Sunday morning James woke up before Holly and went into the kitchen to make breakfast. The smells of coffee and bacon woke her up, and she walked into the kitchen. She was hungry.

"I thought you would wake up when I started cooking," James said to her.

"Good morning," Holly replied and yawned, still feeling sleepy. "I could have slept another hour except that I'm starved."

James noticed she seemed distracted and not her normal, happy self. "Is something wrong?" he asked.

"I had another past-life session, and it wasn't pleasant," she replied.

"Tell me about it," he said as he gently flipped the bacon with metal tongs.

"I was married to Roger in this past life and I was having an affair with one of our friends. Roger was a policeman and came home one day to find me in bed with this other man, and he shot and killed him. He covered his tracks by telling his police friends that the guy broke into the house to rape me. It's hard to get the image of my lover's dead body out of my head. Roger shot him in the heart and the head. He fired shots at me too, deliberately trying to scare me. It's like I just witnessed a shooting death, even though it was sometime back in the 1800s," she replied while pouring cream and sugar into her coffee.

James found himself feeling jealous of her past-life lover and recalling the times he watched men get killed for not paying their gambling debts. He didn't believe in reincarnation and thought that Holly was having self-inflicted bad dreams. He was starting to wonder if there was another man . . . *No, Holly wouldn't do that, she's not the type,* he thought.

"Who was the guy you were having an affair with?" he asked.

"In the past life he was called David. I don't know him in this life," she lied . . . *I don't like lying to James . . . I don't want to upset him. I don't think I can get the image of David/Charlie's dead and bloody body out of my mind anytime soon though.*

"I think you should take a break from visiting the past," he suggested.

"I think I will, although it was exciting to actually see some past lives," she replied.

"You didn't go grocery shopping last night. We're almost out of food," James said to her, mildly annoyed and wanting to change the subject.

"I know. I was on the phone with my sister for an hour, and then I got involved in a stupid TV show and I didn't feel like grocery shopping," she replied.

"We can go today," he said. "We haven't gone grocery shopping together in a long time."

Holly and James went to the grocery store later that day. It was another glorious, sunny, and warm day. They went to a Giant Food store near their house. Holly was looking at the produce when James noticed Amber Conner. She was several feet away looking at the gourmet cheese. *I've got to hide so she doesn't see me,* he thought anxiously. *Where the hell can I go? What do I tell Holly? . . . No, this can't be happening to me . . . I don't want to see her . . . I'll tell Holly I have to use the men's room.* James pushed the cart over to Holly. This way he would be out of Amber's immediate line of sight.

"Hey, babe, I've got to run to the men's room. I'll be back," he said and quickly walked in the direction of the restrooms. Holly nodded and continued to examine the organic pears, looking for the best ones. She heard a woman's voice call out her name.

"Holly," Amber Conner said and waved to her from across the aisle.

"Hey, Amber," Holly replied and waved back. Amber pushed her cart over to the produce aisle so she could talk to the girlfriend of her romantic interest.

"Do you have a rare day off?" Holly asked her.

"Yes, finally. I serve people constantly. If I'm not wiping up after kids, I'm catering to adults," Amber replied. "Is James here with you?"

"Yes, he went to the men's room," Holly said.

He probably saw me and wants to avoid me . . . Well, I'm not going to let that happen . . . I'll keep making conversation with Holly until he gets back . . . Amber thought to herself.

Amber Conner worked as a part-time waitress at American Steak in the evenings and on weekends. She worked full-time at a day care center during the day. It was expensive to live in the D.C. area, and she didn't have a roommate to help her with rent. She was crazy in love with James. She was 33 and not interested in men her own age. She had her eye on James from the first day she started working at the restaurant. She enjoyed flirting with him.

"Holly, I really love your sandals. Where did you get them?" Amber asked, trying to bide time until James reappeared.

"Oh, I got these from DSW. They have the best shoe selection, and shoes are my weakness. I counted my shoes the other day, and I'm embarrassed at how many I've got," Holly said.

"Me too. I had 36 pairs the last time I counted," Amber said.

"I don't feel so bad now. I counted 40," Holly replied with a laugh.

James made his way back to the produce aisle and saw Holly and Amber talking. *Damn it . . . I was hoping to avoid this. I guess I'll have to play along . . . I really wished Holly had gone grocery shopping last night . . .* he murmured to himself. *Oh well, here goes.*

"James, good to see you," Amber said happily, intending to turn on the charm and see if she could make Holly jealous. Holly noticed how Amber's face lit up when she saw James.

"Hi, Amber. Enjoying your day off?" James asked, doing his best to remain calm and collected. He thought Amber looked good today. She was a hot little number, standing 5 foot 2 with a wonderfully curvy figure and long blond hair. She had a strong effect on him. Today she was wearing a short, black sundress that showed her ample cleavage.

"Yeah, I'm taking a short vacation soon and will spend a few days at Ocean City," she said, hoping to spark his interest. She had no plans to take a vacation, although she would make plans with James if he was interested.

"When are you planning to go?" Holly asked.

"Two weeks from now. It's easy getting time off from waitressing since it's just a second job," Amber replied and continued, "Holly, did you know that James is the best chef at the restaurant? I've noticed that people leave less food on their plates on the nights that James is cooking than when the other two chefs are in charge. You are such a lucky woman." Amber was looking at James like she could eat him up.

"She's exaggerating because I came up with the special recipes for the baked mac and cheese menu," James said humbly, hoping to end this conversation as soon as possible. He didn't have to wait long, as Holly was getting annoyed at Amber's fawning over James.

"Well, she's right. I know you are the best chef there. We've got to get going though. We need to get our groceries and get back. It was nice seeing you, Amber," Holly said.

"Nice to see you too. James, I'll see you at work soon," Amber replied, and winked at him while Holly was looking in another direction.

Holly pushed the cart into another aisle to get away from Amber, and James followed without protest. "It looks like someone has a crush on you," Holly said with a smirk.

"Yeah, I think so. I try to stay out of her way," James replied, his heart was pounding and his palms were sweaty.

"You are pretty awesome, and you cook well too," Holly said with a smile and reached up to kiss him. "She's right . . . I am a lucky woman."

"No, I'm the lucky one," he replied . . . *Lucky that Holly doesn't suspect anything.*

The rest of the day passed without incident, and Holly was feeling better about everything between her and James. They were spending more quality time together, and she was convinced that the upsetting tarot card reading was tied to her past lives, which were starting to rise to the surface and were full of heartbreak. Holly was ambivalent about continuing to investigate her past. The lives she discovered with Charlie had rocked her world in an uncomfortable way. She wasn't ready for more dreams about him. He would be back at work on Wednesday. She was secretly looking forward to the middle of the week and aggravated with herself for still thinking about him.

James was off on Monday. It would be his last Monday off for several weeks. He would get the new schedule when he went into work tomorrow. He enjoyed this lazy Monday morning by himself. As he was reading the paper his phone rang and he saw that it was Amber.

"Hello, Amber," he said coolly.

"Hi, James," she cooed. "I'm right outside your house, parked along the street. Is it okay if I come in?"

"Aren't you supposed to be at work?" he asked.

"I called in sick. Day care workers can't be sick around the kids. I told them I had a stomachache. I was hoping we could get together," she said to him in a soft, sexy voice.

She got to James. He wanted to resist her, and he tried and tried, yet he was getting excited just hearing her voice. He never really cheated on Holly once they moved in together . . . until he met Amber. There were a few hookers on occasion, although they provided just blow jobs and he didn't consider that cheating.

"Okay, you can come in. Don't stay long. I don't want to arouse the suspicion of any nosy neighbors that might be home," he said to her sternly. He let Amber into the house and was caught off guard with how sexy she looked. She was wearing another low-cut and short cotton sundress in a floral print that was slightly see-through. Thankfully she didn't smell like vanilla today.

Amber made the first move and reached up to kiss James. He returned her kiss and picked her up and carried her into the bedroom. They were naked underneath the sheets and going at it less than 2 minutes later. He loved having sex with Amber and was torn between two women. He was tired of lying to Holly, yet he didn't want to stay away from Amber. This had been going on for 8 months.

He wasn't proud of himself. He wasn't unhappy in his relationship with Holly, and he didn't want to break up with her. He felt a strong attraction toward Amber, and the more she flirted with him, the more difficult it became to ignore her. They first got together when Holly went out of town on a business trip. James and Amber stayed for drinks at the bar one night with other coworkers and ended the evening at her place having sex. Since Holly was out of town for an entire workweek, he spent his nights at Amber's apartment.

He wasn't frequently with the guys drinking or going to the shooting range when he wasn't with Holly. He spent half of that time with Amber, especially in the last year. Since Holly didn't suspect anything like this, he continued with the double life. He had the best of both worlds, having sex with two hot women who were crazy about him. He wasn't prepared for the doozy Amber had in store for him today, however. When they finished their zesty session she broke the news to him.

"James . . . I'm pregnant. This baby is yours. I haven't been with anyone else since we started seeing each other," Amber said to him and continued, "Don't even suggest that I have an abortion. I'm having this baby whether you like it or not. I'm 6 weeks pregnant. If you don't believe me, I will give you the name and phone number of my doctor, and you can call her to verify this," Amber said defensively.

"When did you stop taking your birth control?" he barked at her with an icy-cold look in his angry blue eyes.

There was a moment of silence, and then tears began to fall down her face, and she said, "I've been off of the pill for 6 months. I love you, James."

James was extremely upset. He was standing up facing Amber who was sitting on the bed, and he began to rant, "You did this on purpose to trap me. I'm 53 years old. When this kid is 20, I'll be 74. YOU HAVE JUST RUINED MY LIFE!" He screamed these last words at her and wanted to punch a hole in the wall. This woman had deceived him. He was angry with her for trapping him, angry with himself for getting involved with her, and the gambling, and the drugs. He didn't feel bad for yelling at her. At this point in time he never wanted to see her again. Amber was crying uncontrollably, and he knew he needed to calm her down until he figured out his plan of action. He didn't trust her, and he was afraid that in her current state of mind, she would go directly to Holly.

"Look, I will support the baby. I'm going to have to tell Holly, and I'd rather wait until you are farther along before I do that," he said . . . *Keep Amber calm until you can find a way out of this.*

"You want to make sure I'm not going to have a miscarriage before you break up with her, is that it?" Amber said resentfully.

James let out a frustrated sigh and nodded his head. "Yes. I never made any promises to you when we got involved. Remember how we said it was just for fun, no commitments?"

Amber remembers and backs down. "Don't you love me even a

little bit?" she implored.

"I care greatly for you, Amber. I don't know if I love you. I know that I still love Holly," he replied casually . . . *Maybe this will turn her off and she won't want any more to do with me.*

"Sure—you love her so much that you cheated with me, right?" she said spitefully.

I deserve that . . . he thought. "Amber, I'm a lousy excuse for a man. I've never been able to be faithful to one woman. What the hell do you want me for? You're a beautiful young woman. What's wrong with finding a man your own age?" he asked, frustrated with this new situation and remembering a dalliance he had shortly before he moved in with Holly. She was a sexy bartender at American Steak named Gina . . .*Yeah, I did cheat on Holly with Gina . . . however, I stopped once I moved in.*

"I fell in love with you at first sight," Amber said softly.

"I don't deserve you or Holly," James replied. "This is a huge surprise, Amber. I need some time to process. Will you please leave now?"

Amber put her sexy little sundress and sandals back on and walked to the front door.

"I'll see you at work," she said coldly to him and walked out the door.

"Yeah, see you there," James replied and shut the door after her. From the living-room window he watched her walk to her car, get in, and drive away. *My life is over . . . I should just end it here and now. Once I tell Holly that will be the end of us. I won't be surprised if she burns my belongings in the front yard* . . . he thought.

He went back into the bedroom and made up the bed. It was a good thing Holly was too busy getting ready to make it this morning. He decided to vacuum. The last thing he wanted was for Holly to find a long blond hair lying around and ask him about it.

James didn't want to be a father. He was enraged at Amber for not taking her birth control pills and getting pregnant. He needed to do something to quell his rage. He decided to go for a run. He put on his running shoes and gym clothes and left the house. The late-morning air was comfortable and the sun was bright. As he ran down the sidewalk, his mind raced trying to figure a way to get out of this predicament . . . *I can't believe that bitch trapped me. I could arrange it so that she disappears. Bryce might be able to help, for a price. I don't know if he's ever had his goons take out a woman before. I won't know unless I ask. Surely he would understand this type of thing. He only has sex with high-class call girls because he doesn't want any woman trapping him. I'll be a baby killer . . . I can't believe I'm even thinking of this . . . killing a pregnant woman. That makes me a monster . . . I don't care! She trapped me. She deceived me . . . I'll talk to Bryce and see what he can do. Maybe there are other options, and she won't have to die.*

James was miserable for the rest of the day. It was going to take a superhuman will to keep everything hidden until he could gather enough courage to tell Holly about the pregnancy or make arrangements for Amber's disappearance. He decided to be the best, most loving man toward Holly until that time. Maybe Amber would have a miscarriage and Holly would never know about this. He realized how much he loved her and hated himself . . . *Why did I get back into the gambling and drug life again? . . . Why couldn't I keep it in my pants?* He knew he was weak.

On her way home from work, Holly was looking forward to spending the evening with James. When she arrived home, it seemed liked something was bothering him. She walked into the house and found him drinking a beer and watching TV. She could smell dinner cooking in the oven.

"Hi, honey," she said cheerfully as she walked in the door.

"Hi. How was your day?" he asked.

"It was good. I got caught up on a bunch of miscellaneous things. What about you?" She sensed that James was preoccupied with something else.

"Uneventful and calm," he said . . . *If that isn't a bold-faced lie, I don't know what is* . . . he thought.

"Is something bothering you, are you okay?" she asked.

"I'm fine. I'm just dreading going back to work tomorrow," he replied thinking . . . *At least that part is true.*

"What's for dinner?" she asked.

"Tonight we are having TV dinners. I put in a flatbread pizza for you, and I'm having a Hungry Man fried chicken dinner. I didn't feel like cooking tonight," he said trying to sound normal.

"That sounds good. Those dinners have been in the freezer for a long time," she replied.

She went into the bedroom and changed into a blue, tank-style dress to lounge around the house in. It was short and showcased her shapely legs. When James saw her walk into the living room he felt like he was seeing her for the first time. He had a knot in his stomach that felt like a piece of lead. He hated what transpired earlier with Amber. He thought Holly was the prettiest, most wonderful woman in the world. Those feelings were intensified by the guilt and regret he was harboring in his heart.

"I don't tell you often enough just how beautiful you are," James said to her with deep sincerity.

Holly smiled at him and playfully said, "Thank you, James. I agree, you don't tell me often enough."

"I think dinner is ready, let's eat," he said.

Holly was in the mood for lovemaking later that night when they got into bed. James was far from aroused. He would have to make up an excuse for not being in the mood.

"What's wrong, are you tired tonight?" Holly asked him.

"My stomach doesn't feel that great. I think the TV dinner was bad. It tasted like cardboard and I think I'm paying the price now," he said hoping she would buy that line, and it wasn't a total lie. His stomach *was* upset, but it wasn't from the chicken dinner which tasted pretty good.

"Okay, there will be other nights," she said and kissed him. "I think I'll see if I can uncover another past life tonight."

"I thought you were going to take a break from that?" he asked.

"I changed my mind. My curiosity has gotten the best of me," she replied, putting on her headphones and turning on the CD player on her nightstand.

James turned out the light and knew he wouldn't be able to sleep. He would be quiet so he didn't disturb her. Holly focused on the narrator's soothing voice instructions, and soon, she was taken to Japan in the 1600s . . .

. . . Holly is in a fancy, gilded room with several young Japanese women and they are drinking tea, laughing, and discussing the physical attributes of the different customers who have visited with them. She realizes that this is a house of prostitution and understands everything that is said in Japanese. She recognizes one of the girls as her friend Patricia. She is known in this Japanese life as Moriko.

She hears a door open and an angry man rushes in to break up their lively chatter. He is heading straight for her. She knows he is the house pimp and recognizes this mean-looking man as Roger. He is taller than a typical Japanese man, and his facial features hint of European lineage. He is not handsome. His nose is straight and quite large, and he exudes brutality. His eyebrows are overly arched. He looks like the devil. He marches over to Holly, takes the tea cup from her hand, and throws it up against the wall, smashing it to pieces.

"Minori, you are not bringing in enough money.You are spending too much time with each customer. Consider this a warning. Either bring in more money, or I will get rid of you," he yells at her. He slaps her hard across the face for added emphasis.

The other girls are huddled together holding on to each other and terrified of him. He continues his tirade. "And that goes the same for the rest of you. Revenue is down. You are not servicing enough customers." His face is now red, and he stomps out of the room.

Moriko says softly to her, "I hate Fumito! Make sure your money is hidden where he will never find it."

"Oh, I have. I can't buy my way out of here soon enough," Minori replies tearfully.

Moriko continues, "I heard the Portuguese sailors will be here soon . . . That is a good opportunity to make a lot of money."

Sometime later she sees the girls in their fancy clothes flirting with the men who arrive at the house. Men from several different races and nationalities frequent this establishment as well as the local men.

A group of Portuguese sailors enters the room. One of them locks eyes with Minori and walks toward her . . . it's James . . . He looks so different in this life. He's not tall, and he has brown hair and eyes. He is rather average looking.

"Good evening, sir. Can I help you?" she asks him.

"You are the prettiest thing I have seen in a long time. Are you available?" he asks.

"Yes, follow me," she replies and leads him down a long hallway to her room. She services James, and then tells him he must leave. She cannot spend too much time with one customer.

"I will come back to see you again. This was fun," he says and kisses her on the cheek. He leaves her a generous tip.

She bows and thanks him. She feels tired and sad and decides to lie down on the bed for a few minutes before returning to the main room.

Minori lies down on her bed and accidentally falls into a deep sleep. She is rudely awakened when Fumito slams open her bedroom door, and then quickly slams it shut again. He yells at her, "WHAT IS THE MATTER WITH YOU, BITCH? You should be in that room making me money. I saw your customer leave an hour ago and you just stay in here lazing around instead of working." His face contorts into a sinister grin and he continues, "I found a large, hidden stash of money, and I know it belongs to you . . . not anymore, though. It's mine now."

Minori recoils in fear and gets up off the bed as he moves toward her.

"No-good whore, I should kill you now and be rid of you." Fumito goes for his knife intending to stab her in the stomach. She manages to evade him and in the process he trips over something on the floor and falls hard to the ground face-first. The knife falls out of his hand. She jumps on his back and grabs a nearby scarf and wraps it around his neck, pulling and twisting it. He begins to choke.

"I HATE you, you nasty, evil, horrible man! That money is mine. You can't have it . . . You are dead now. DEAD! DEAD! DEAD!" She screams these words at him furiously as he chokes and gasps and takes his last breath.

Fumito's body goes limp. She continues to strangle him, afraid he is tricking her. She quickly rolls him over and kicks him hard in the groin to make sure he is really dead, and he is. Her heart has almost stopped beating. Minori can't believe what she has done. She has to discreetly get rid of his body. His enforcers will kill her if they find out. Fortunately, he isn't bleeding. There is no mess, which is a good thing about choking someone to death.

There's a knock on her door. Her friend Moriko says, "Are you okay in there?"

Minori opens the door and lets her in. She sees Fumito's dead body lying facedown on the floor.

"You killed Fumito!" Moriko says excitedly.

"He was going to kill me. Fumito tripped and fell on his face. I had to stop him. Help me get rid of the body or his enforcers will kill both of us," Minori says breathlessly in a state of panic.

"The enforcers are in the main room trying to break up a fight between the sailors and the locals. There is no one in the hallway. We can drag his body to the vacant room at the end of the hall and throw

it off the balcony," Moriko says hurriedly.

"Let's do it," Minori replies.

The girls drag Fumito's body down the hallway and into a vacant room. There is a balcony and a steep drop into the surrounding moat. They go out onto the balcony, continuing to drag the dead body.

"Are you ready?" Moriko asks her friend.

"Yes! I never want to see him again . . . He deserved to die," Minori says, and together they struggle mightily to lift and throw him off of the balcony into the murky water of the moat . . .

Holly comes out of her hypnosis, takes off her headphones, places them on the nightstand, and thinks . . . *Well that was interesting . . . It figures that Roger would be a pimp . . . It suits him. Patricia is going to laugh when I tell her that we were prostitutes in another life, I killed Roger, and she helped me get rid of his body . . . I need to thank her for that . . .* Holly giggles to herself, and then concentrates on falling asleep.

The next morning she wakes up and goes into the kitchen to eat something before taking a shower. She chooses two granola bars and a glass of milk. She hears James get out of bed and get in the shower first. She thinks . . . *That's strange. He doesn't have to be at work until noon . . . maybe the shower will help him feel better. I think I'll take this into the living room and watch a few minutes of the morning news.*

Holly takes her breakfast into the living room and turns on the TV. A news segment is talking about the latest software programs and high-tech items. The man they are interviewing looks familiar. She then sees his name flash on the screen: *"Roger Chasen, President/CEO of Chase TechNet, Inc.,"* She can't believe her eyes. Here is the very man who caused her grief and pain through at least two past lives and the present life, acting professional, congenial, and smart as he talks to the interviewer. She doesn't believe this is a coincidence. Roger has put on weight, his hair is thin and gray, and he is well dressed in a black suit, white shirt, and a multicolored tie. His company is based in San Diego, California, and he has opened an office here in Washington, D.C. She is shocked at this news and knows that she is going to cross paths with him soon.

She continues to watch him on the screen, not hearing anything he says, remembering everything that ever happened between them. She doesn't regret killing him back in Japan, yet at the same time, she is surprised that she doesn't feel an intense hatred for him. She is simply amazed to see him. He's just an average-looking, middle-aged man. James finishes showering, dries off, and walks into the living room and sees Holly glued to the TV.

"What are you watching?" he asked.

Holly jumped and suddenly realized she must have been in a daze. "Roger Chasen is on the news. Look!" she said as she pointed to the screen. "He owns a tech company and opened an office in D.C. I had a past-life session last night, and he was in it. I was a Japanese prostitute, and he was my pimp. I killed him, and Patricia and I got rid of the body."

James began to laugh. "Do you know how crazy that sounds? That must have been one hell of a dream," he said and continued laughing, and then said sarcastically, "He's a real looker. He must have looked good when he was younger to have landed a woman like you" . . . *It feels good to laugh . . . I should enjoy it while I still can . . .* he thought.

Holly finished eating her breakfast and went to take a shower. *ROGER!! I can't believe it . . . That wife-beating son of a bitch is opening an office near me. I wonder if he ever remarried . . . If he did, I hope she knocked some sense into him.* When Holly was ready to leave for work, she walked into the living room to kiss James good-bye. He was watching TV, yet the expression on his face looked to be one of pain, and he looked pale.

"Honey, are you feeling sick?" she asked.

"Yes. My stomach is churning again," he said.

"You should call in sick if you don't improve by noon," she replied.

"We'll see. I hope you have a good day," he said to her.

"Thanks, honey. I'll see you late tonight. I hope you feel better soon," she replied and kissed his cheek.

Holly was still thinking about Roger as she got into her car. It was raining hard this morning, and she thought it was appropriate after seeing Roger on TV. She remembered back to when they first got together, once upon a time in the late 1980s . . .

. . . Holly first met Roger Chasen when she was a junior in high school. He had moved to her neighborhood and lived on a nearby street. She remembers seeing him walking up and down the sidewalk and being instantly attracted to him. He was a tall young man with light brown hair and brown eyes. He seemed friendly, and they gradually got to know each other.

She didn't start dating him until the last part of her senior year in high school. They stayed together after graduation for about 1 year, and then he enlisted in the navy. They wanted to get married and eventually did. The first 6 months of their young marriage was easy and fun. They soon got stationed overseas, in Spain. From there, the marriage fell apart.

He began trying to control her, who her friends were, what she wore, etc. He hated being in the navy and had frequent temper tantrums where he would throw things and act like a child. She got a job on base and made money as a typist. When payday came, she had to cash her check and give it to him. He gave her a small pittance for an allowance, and she was supposed to come to him if she needed any more money. Holly didn't like this, however, she thought that this was the way married life was supposed to be. You combine your money and share it.

Roger was no fun to be with anymore. They would make plans with friends to go to the beach, and he would back out at the last minute saying he didn't feel like going.

"I don't feel like going to the beach today. Tell John and Dana that they can go without us," Roger said to her.

John and Dana were an American couple they befriended who lived in an adjacent apartment building.

"Why don't you want to go? Are you feeling sick?" Holly asked him.

"No, I feel fine. I just don't want to go. We need to clean the apartment. It's a mess," he replied.

"No, it isn't!" Holly exclaimed. "There isn't much to clean. It's a beautiful day, and we'll have such a good time. We can clean it later. This will be the third time we've canceled on them."

At that moment they heard a knock on the door. It was Dana.

"Are you ready to go?" Dana asked them.

"I don't want to go today, maybe next time," Roger said.

"Oh, I'm sorry to hear that," Dana said. "Holly, do you want to go with us?"

"Yes, I'd love to," Holly replied, then remembered she should confer with Roger first. "Is that okay with you, honey?" she asked.

"No, I need you here today. I want you to help me with a project," he replied.

"I'm sorry, Dana. I know John's waiting in the car. Tell him we're sorry," Holly said with deep regret. She was hoping this time that Roger would let her go. She knew if she pressed the issue a big fight would ensue. Fortunately, Dana knew Roger was an asshole and she understood. She felt bad for Holly.

"Hey, it's okay. We'll talk to you later," she said with a knowing look and left to join her husband on their way to the beach. Holly closed the apartment door, and then asked Roger a question.

"What is the real reason you don't want me to go with them?"

"Because I don't want any guys looking at you when I'm not around," Roger hatefully retorted.

This scene played out many times after that. If it wasn't the beach, it was some other place or event. Holly never knew if the plans they made would come to fruition. She was afraid to look forward to anything because her hopes were usually dashed. Life was miserable. She grew jealous listening to her friends at work talk about the trips and places they visited on the weekends. They were in Spain, with easy access to the rest of Europe, and the only thing Roger wanted to do was stay home. They were just 21 years old. They should be having the time of their lives. Instead, they usually ended up cleaning the apartment and doing mundane, boring things. Roger was continuously in a bad mood and would verbally abuse her, often calling her "shit for brains."

Then the physical abuse started. At first it was light. He would occasionally hit her in anger, and then start crying and apologizing, saying he would never do it again. On their first anniversary, they had a heated argument, and he kicked her in the stomach. The force sent her reeling across the room and into a wall, leaving her breathless, frightened, and shocked.

"I don't want to be with you anymore," she said, holding her stomach and crying. "I want to go home."

"Honey, I'm so sorry . . . I will never do that again. Please don't leave me, I love you," Roger begged, and began bawling like a baby.

He cried and begged for her forgiveness. And he did hit her again after that incident. He slapped her now and then. She forgave him out of fear. Any love that she had for him at that point was gone. She stayed with him because she loved Spain and her job on the naval base. She had a lot of friends there, both American and Spanish. She wasn't ready to leave yet.

Roger began pressuring her to have kids. Holly was not going to bring children into their relationship, not with the way he treated her. She imagined herself big and pregnant and him slapping her and being cruel when she was vulnerable.

"I want to get to work on making a baby; no more condoms," Roger said to her.

"I'd rather wait until we save some money. I don't want to work full-time and have to take care of a baby too," she replied.

"We can't afford for you to stay home. You will have the baby and go back to work right away," he demanded.

"Roger, why don't we do this . . . Let's wait until next summer to try to make a baby. Between now and then we can start saving money, and I'll keep my eye out for a part-time job on base. This way, we can be a little more prepared. I think we can afford for me to work part-time," she replied calmly, hoping that this would buy her time until she could make plans to leave.

Her sensible reasoning convinced him to wait a little longer. She knew right then and there she couldn't stay married to him. She finally summoned up the courage to ask him for a divorce 3 months later.

"Roger, I want a divorce. I don't love you anymore," she told him one evening after a nasty, heated argument earlier that day.

"Holly, we've only been married for a little over a year . . . I still love you," he said.

"Can you promise that you will never hit me again—I mean REALLY promise?" she asked him.

"No, I can't promise that. You'll do something stupid again," he replied.

"Then we're done. I'm going to call my parents and ask them to send me the money so I can fly home," she said coldly.

"How can you do this to me?" he said and went to get their photo album of wedding pictures. "I didn't go through all of this just so you can leave me!" he said and showed her happy pictures of their wedding day. "Why are you doing this to me?"

"Because you treat me like shit! I can't do anything right enough for you, and you can't promise that you will never hit me again. I'm not living with that anymore. It's over," she said without shedding a tear. She hated him, and the wedding pictures filled her with disgust.

He wanted both of them to take time off from work and spend quality time alone together and work out their problems. He dragged her to a chaplain on base for counseling. She reluctantly agreed to it, knowing in her heart it wasn't going to help. She had already emotionally checked out of this relationship.

They took a week off from work, and the chaplain counseled them on the things they needed to do to get their marriage back on track. Roger gave it lip service in front of the chaplain, except that he refused to do any of those things when they were alone together. He would blame her for starting these problems in their marriage and putting him through this. She wasn't perfect, but she did her best to put up with him. She should have left him right after he kicked her in the stomach. During their week alone, he would slip into frightening moods and tell her he was going to kill her.

"I'm going to drive you down a dirt road and kill you. If I can't have you, no one will have you. They will never find your body," Roger said to her.

He said this to her at least twice during their week of "quality time" together. She didn't say anything back to him when he threatened her. She didn't think he was a killer. However, she wasn't going to stay and find out. She was afraid of him and wondered how in the world she was going to escape. She had thoughts of spiking his drink with something that would put him to sleep for a few hours and allow her to get out. They were just thoughts because she was afraid if she did that, she might end up killing him instead.

When she went back to work, she confided in her coworkers what was happening, and they told her she had to leave him now.

"Holly, you must leave him today! Antonio and I will drive you to the apartment and you can get your things. You can stay with me until you go back to the States," Mia said to her. Mia was her best friend at work. Antonio was an engineer that worked in the office with them, and he often rode into work with Mia. He was a large and imposing-looking man.

"Yes, Mia is right. You must leave now. We will go there at lunchtime and get your things," Antonio insisted.

"Thank you," Holly said with deep gratitude.

They left work during lunch and drove Holly to her apartment to get her clothes and personal items while Roger was still at work. She was able to gather everything quickly, throwing items in her suitcases as fast as she could.

Roger called her at work the next day and begged her to forgive him, but she told him it was too late. He didn't know where Mia lived, so he wouldn't be able to stalk Holly or try anything crazy. Roger was smart enough to know that he had to let Holly go and not make trouble. He respected and feared his commanding officers. He sent her flowers and candy and love notes and attempted to woo her back before she left. Holly was unfazed by this and excited about going home.

Her parents sent her the money for a one-way ticket home. She returned to Virginia with two suitcases and the clothes on her back. She was 20 pounds thinner, and her mother thought she was anorexic. Holly wanted nothing more from Roger . . .

Holly got off of the Metro train and headed to the office. Her life with Roger felt like a past-life session . . . *It happened so long ago it might as well be*. She had grown into a mature, confident woman who was happy with her life. The years she spent with her second husband, Alex, felt like a past life too. She decided not to think about either of them right now. She was on her way to a job she liked and people who appreciated her.

Meanwhile, a few blocks away, Roger Chasen was getting settled into his new office. Chase TechNet Inc. was winning new business like crazy and recently won a large contract with a branch of the government to provide cybersecurity services. He would still maintain his California address and live in two places until he could get the new office fully staffed and operational.

Roger was a happy man these days. He met a woman named Alyssa Thomas. He liked to call her Lisa, and she inspired him to go on a diet and start getting into shape. She lived in Arlington, Virginia, a short distance from his new office. She was 5 years older than he. Lisa was assertive and bossy, and a classically pretty woman with shoulder-length blond hair, blue eyes, and a curvy figure. She was tall, standing 5 foot 10. He thought she looked like a beauty queen.

Roger wondered if Holly still lived in the area. He thought about her now and then and was truly sorry for the way he treated her. He regretted taking his bad moods out on her, hitting her, and driving her away. He sought counseling for his anger issues shortly after she left him. It took many years and a lot of hard work to become a well-adjusted man. Roger learned some hard lessons from his time with Holly and later from the breakup of his second marriage to Olivia. Olivia Harper was a rough-and-tumble, redneck type of woman who was a stripper. She was pretty, with long dark hair down to her waist and clear blue eyes. She was unusual in that she liked to hunt and fish and do guy things. She had a body most men fantasized about, and he kept going into the strip club to watch her and get her attention. Her stripper name was "The Big O."

. . . Roger married Olivia 5 years after his divorce from Holly. He was living in Seattle at the time. Olivia stopped working at the strip club and settled down into domestic life for a short while. Roger tried not to be controlling and jealous. Olivia had a lot of ex-lovers and guys who used to frequent her club, and they managed to run into at least one of them every time they went out together. Olivia knew Roger had the intelligence and drive to make a lot of money, and he was doing extremely well when they first started dating. He was a computer

geek and bringing home big bucks. She was a gold digger with expensive tastes and used to men groveling at her feet. She liked to flirt and fool around and did this behind Roger's back. He eventually found out about Olivia's cheating and confronted her one day while she was rinsing dishes before putting them into the dishwasher.

"Olivia, we need to talk," Roger said to his wife as she was rinsing off a large frying pan in the sink.

"Sure, sweetie, what's wrong?" she asked.

"I ran into Mark at the auto store, and he said you've been screwing several guys from the gym, including him. Is that true?" he asked her in an accusatory tone. He was now standing a few inches from her.

"No! I would never cheat on you. How could you think a thing like that?" she said defensively.

"Because he gave me a pair of sheer white panties with your name embroidered in sequins on the back. They're just like the other ones you have in multiple colors. Just how many women named Olivia have sequined embroidered panties? You are a lying, cheating bitch. I'm going to divorce your ass!" Roger said and slapped her hard across the face.

Olivia was shocked by this aggression and before Roger could utter another insult she wacked him hard on the head with that frying pan. He fell to the floor unconscious.

When he came to, paramedics were standing over him and Olivia was explaining what happened. "He slapped me hard across the face so I wacked him with the frying pan," she said to them and continued, "This isn't the first time he has hit me. He loves to use me as his punching bag whenever he gets angry." She was lying, trying to get sympathy.

Roger was disoriented but managed to say, "Don't believe anything that whore says. Yes, I hit her, and it wasn't the right thing to do, but this tramp has been cheating on me."

The paramedics packed him up and took him to the hospital to make sure he wasn't seriously hurt. In the meantime, Olivia packed her bags and checked into a fancy hotel. Roger stayed in the hospital overnight. They released him the next day. He had a concussion and was ordered to take it easy. He was lying in bed that evening when he heard the front door open. He knew it was Olivia. He could hear her stiletto heels on the hardwood floor. She came into the bedroom with some news for him.

"What do you want?" he asked her.

"I wanted to give you back the house key," she said and threw it on the bed.

"Why did you cheat on me? I gave you everything I had, and then some. What do they have that I don't?" he asked.

"I got tired of being married. I wasn't meant to be tied down to one man. Life with you is boring." She sneered the words at him.

"I'm filing for divorce tomorrow," he told her.

"Good, I look forward to it. However, you should know that I'm pregnant. I'm not sure if you're the father. We won't know until the baby is born," Olivia said coolly.

"Oh, Jesus, this is just wonderful," he said scathingly.

"Since you are divorcing me, and I don't have a job, you will have to pay me alimony. No one is going to hire a pregnant woman. If this kid is yours, you'll be on the hook for child support too," she said, and began laughing.

"You can go back to stripping and whoring to make money," he barked at her.

"Not around here. They closed down the club last month," she said, and flipped her hair back as she walked out of the room.

As luck would have it, the child was his, a little girl they named Denise. He ended up paying alimony for 10 years until Olivia remarried, and child support until his daughter turned 18. Roger had a good relationship with his daughter and despite her slutty mother she grew up to be a lovely, smart, and good-natured young lady. He was putting her through college; she loved biology and wanted to be a teacher . . .

Roger had a few more relationships through the years, although they weren't serious and long term. He never hit another woman again. He never raised a hand to his daughter either. He met Lisa through an Internet dating site and thought she was the perfect combination of sassy and sexy, although she had a hot temper. Roger could deal with that, having overcome a hot temper of his own. He worked hard over the years to become calm and centered. He knew Lisa was trying, and he was happy to help her in any way he could. They had been dating for 3 months.

Chapter 4

The Fool

Holly woke up thinking about tarot cards and decided that she would start using her own deck and draw a card every morning to get a feel for what the day would bring. *I might be better prepared if heartbreak is coming my way . . . The daily cards I draw might be able to predict when and what it will be . . . Please don't let it be James . . .* she thought. After she ate breakfast, she shuffled the tarot deck and drew the Fool. The Fool's message represents a new beginning and an end to something in your old life. The card depicts a young man carrying a knapsack and walking toward the edge of a cliff, looking out at the world. A small white dog is at his feet and the sun is shining brightly behind him. It portends important decisions ahead, which may be difficult to make, and carries an element of risk.

She thought to herself . . . *It's a sign pointing to change . . . possibly difficult change . . . Something is coming . . . Fools are usually happy people in real life, blindly going on their merry way, seeing what they want to see . . . Am I a fool? If so, how am I a fool? What am I blindly heading toward?* She looked at the card again and thought . . . *If the Fool keeps walking, he will walk off the cliff.* She remembered Martina's sage advice on this . . . *"If you look at a card and something about it resonates a particular feeling or thought within you, pay attention."*

Today was Wednesday, and Charlie was supposed to be back in the office. Holly kept an eye out for him when she stepped off the Metro. She didn't see him. She had the image of his past-life dead body stuck in her mind and wanted to tell him about it. *Should I call him or stop by his office to say welcome back? . . .Will he be happy to see me? . . .Will it be odd and uncomfortable? I loved him deeply in those two past lives. If it wasn't for my relationship with James, I could easily fall head over heels for Charlie . . .* she thought.

After working on various things for the first few hours of the day, she was dying to go see Charlie. She took the elevator to the eighth floor, and she could feel her heartbeat quicken as she entered the lobby area and walked to his office. He was sitting at his desk, looking at the computer when she knocked softly on his door.

"Hi, Charlie. Welcome back," she said.

"Holly, nice to see you," Charlie replied with a welcoming smile.

"Did everything go okay with your daughter?" she asked.

"Yes, everything went great. Brianna and the baby are doing well. She had a boy and named him Douglas Stephen. My ex-wife Kelly is staying with them for a few weeks. We arranged it so I would be there for the first week, and then Kelly would come down and stay for several weeks. How have you been doing?" he asked.

"I'm doing okay. I went to see a psychic last weekend, and she told me some wild stories about my past lives," Holly said, curious to know what he thought of such things.

Charlie laughed and said, "Now *that* is interesting. What kind of past lives did you have, and what prompted you to visit a psychic?"

"Curiosity. I've always been interested in reincarnation and recently bought a book written by a hypnotherapist who helped his patients recall their past lives. I also bought a past-life regression CD to help me learn to do it on my own," she said thinking . . . *He's going to think I'm totally nuts and do his best to avoid me from now on . . . I won't mention*

Martina's voice change to anyone else . . . I should have never told James.

"I think that's fascinating, Holly. I believe in reincarnation and have had numerous dreams about people and places that seem too real to be just ordinary dreams. Have you been able to regress on your own?"

Should I tell him? . . . How much should I tell him? . . . "Not yet. I've been practicing every night so I expect to find out something eventually," she said with a nervous laugh . . . *I'm not ready to tell him yet. Thankfully, he hasn't pressed me about what kind of past lives Martina mentioned.*

"If you do, I would be interested in hearing about it. Did the psychic say you would befriend a tall, dark, and handsome man at the office?" Charlie asked with a mischievous look in his eyes.

"No, because that happened before I went to see her," Holly replied with an equally mischievous look and smile . . . *He really lights my fire. I want him to engulf me in flames.*

Charlie's phone rang, and Holly took that as a sign it was time to leave. "I'll see you later, Charlie," she said sweetly.

"It's Mitch. I'll talk to you later," he replied and picked up the phone.

Holly got back on the elevator and ran into Patricia. "Hey, girl. I haven't talked to you in days. What's the latest?" Patricia asked her.

"Oh, do I have a lot to tell you!" Holly replied excitedly.

"Walk with me to my office and we can talk for a few minutes," Patricia said.

"I'll give you the abbreviated version for now," Holly replied. Patricia worked on the seventh floor. The two of them walked to her office.

"What were you doing on the eighth floor?" Patricia asked as they walked down the hall.

"Talking to Charlie," Holly replied, smiling.

"Are you going to leave James?" Patricia asked with raised eyebrows and a grin. Holly knew that Patricia didn't think highly of James and thought she could do better.

"No," Holly replied. "I went to see a psychic last weekend and had a past-life reading. I was so enthralled that I bought a past-life regression CD and went back in time to find out more," she said.

"Wow . . . Did you have a past life with Charlie?" Patricia asked.

"Yes, we were secret lovers in two different lives," Holly admitted.

"Seriously?"

"Yeah, I swear. I experienced it myself, under hypnosis," Holly replied.

"Were you telling him about it?"

"No, I don't think I'll tell him. I mentioned to him that I saw a psychic and got a past-life reading, and I found out that he believes in reincarnation. He doesn't think I'm crazy, thank God," Holly said with an expression of relief.

"How are things with you and James?" Patricia inquired.

"Much better. I think we are on our way back," Holly said.

"I still think that he isn't good enough for you," Patricia said.

"Thank you for saying that. I know I say bad things about him, and he's been a jerk for a long time, but I think everything will work out," Holly replied confidently.

"Time will tell," Patricia answered.

"Oh, I wanted to tell you that we shared a past life together too. We were prostitutes in Japan back in the 1600s," Holly said laughing.

Patricia had a surprised look on her face, and then burst out laughing. "Are you serious?" she asked, wondering if Holly was joking with her.

"Yes, I'm completely serious. I killed our pimp in self-defense, and you helped me get rid of his body. We threw it over a balcony, into a moat. What's even crazier is that our pimp was my first ex-husband in this life, Roger," Holly said with a smile. "I want to thank you for helping me get rid of his body."

"You're welcome. I'm here anytime you need help getting rid of a dead body!" Patricia exclaimed and laughed out loud.

Just then, they both saw Patricia's boss, Ian Smith, and figured it was time to get back to work.

"Thanks for the advice. I'll talk to you later," Holly said.

"See ya," Patricia replied still laughing at Holly's story and went into her office.

Holly went back to her office on the tenth floor, sat down at her computer, and a few moments later her boss, Stan Bowman, entered the room.

"Welcome back. Did you have a wonderful time?" Holly cheerfully greeted him. She liked working for Stan. He was much easier to work for than Matt Weedon. Stan had been on vacation for 2 weeks in Aruba with this wife, and this was his first day back. He stood 5 foot 10 and was a distinguished-looking black man in his early 60s, with graying hair and round, wire-framed glasses that made him look like a college professor. He had been with MTAC since he graduated from college and rose up through the ranks to a senior vice president position. He was well-liked and respected throughout the company.

"Yeah, we had an amazing time. I'm trying to get through 500+ e-mails and need more than a full day to get caught up. Please don't schedule anything for me until midday tomorrow," he said.

"I promise to keep the hordes away," Holly replied.

"Your old friend Matt Weedon will be stopping by on Friday for a meeting at 11:30. He's got his own consulting business now, and we're going to see if we can work together on an upcoming proposal," Stan said with a twinkle in his eye. He knew Holly wasn't fond of Matt. Stan and Matt were good friends though, and often rode bikes together.

"I'll put that on your calendar. Thanks for the warning," Holly said with a little laugh. She hadn't seen Matt in 3 years. She began to recall some of the years she worked with him . . .

. . . Matt Weedon was a smart and successful man with a lot of drive. He was a hard worker and demanded plenty from those he

worked with. Holly liked him at first, he had a jovial personality. The trouble was Matt was quite mercurial and would change his mind on something at the last minute, frustrating Holly and the rest of the team. Often his changes would require time-consuming do-overs with little time to get it done. So everyone had to drop everything and rush. Booking travel for that man was a nightmare as well. It was rare for him NOT to make changes after things were booked. She remembered one time that he made so many changes to his flights that it took her a few hours to reconcile the charges. He wanted to know how much he was going to ultimately be billed. She was surprised that he wasn't keeping track of it. Holly had to create a spreadsheet to figure it out, and when she showed it to him he didn't even look at it. He just accepted the final number.

Then there were the client meetings. On more than one occasion, she would have to go to the deli at the last minute to get refreshments when he previously indicated that he wouldn't need any.

"Holly, we have some changes to the meeting today. Our clients will be here through lunch. I need for you to pick up some sandwiches for them," Matt told her shortly before she was getting ready to eat her own lunch. "I have a list of the sandwiches they want and would appreciate it if you could walk to the deli and get them."

It was pouring rain outside, and the deli was two blocks away. She would have to walk since she didn't drive her car to work. She felt she had no choice and should go out in the pouring rain and get the sandwiches. The deli only delivered if the order was for a large party of 20 or more. It seemed like it rained every time he asked her to do something like this. She couldn't recall ever getting sandwiches on a sunny day.

"Sure. I'll go get them," she said, grabbing her purse and umbrella and dreading carrying everything back.

Holly took some money from the petty cash fund and walked down the street in the pouring rain to buy seven sandwiches and a large bag of potato chips. When she returned, she put the sandwiches neatly on a tray, placed the chips in a bowl, and walked into the conference room. She noticed there was an additional guest who arrived late to the meeting.

"Thank you, Holly. Would you mind going back out and getting another sandwich? Tom just arrived," Matt said.

"No, I don't want any lunch. No need to go back out," Tom replied, much to Holly's relief. She was grateful that Tom didn't want her to go back out in the pouring rain to get him a sandwich. She was furious at Matt for even making that suggestion. She despised him for weeks after that. Yes, it would have been a nice thing to do, and if Tom had wanted a sandwich, she would have done it. It was just that this type of incident happened too frequently . . .

Holly was able to laugh at it now. However, at the time it infuriated her to the point of wishing she could hit him over the head with something. She wondered if she worked with this guy in a previous life, and if she was getting karmic payback for something she did.

Holly began to think that maybe she shared some past lives with her coworkers. She got along great with Stan and Neil Peters, even Jack Briggs, who most people tried to avoid. She worked for Jack for a short while after Matt left the company and before she worked for Stan. Jack was a retired military officer who seemed to have more of the military still left in him. He served in the Marine Corps and sometimes seemed overly authoritarian, as if he was still commanding troops. In his late 40s, he still wore his hair in a buzz cut. He was an attractive man, happily married with four sons. She knew he had not been a drill sergeant, although he had the demeanor of one; maybe some of that came from raising four boys. Holly got along well with Jack and liked that he didn't change things at the last minute. He was much more decisive and on top of the things that Matt would let fall through the cracks. She still worked with Jack, as Stan was his boss.

When quitting time came, Holly put on her flat shoes, gathered her tote bag, and left the office to walk to the Metro. It was warm, muggy, and overcast. She saw Charlie walking in the distance ahead of her and was tempted to call out to him so they could walk together. She thought of the tarot card she drew this morning, the Fool, and decided against it. It wasn't the meaning of the card that changed her mind, it was that she felt foolish chasing after him. Her relationship with James was improving, and she still loved him. She had to put an end to her infatuation with Charlie. She would think of him as just a friend . . . which would be a challenge. Maybe that was the real meaning of the card she drew this morning.

Holly arrived at Huntington and walked from the train station to her car, got in, and turned on the radio, and strangely enough, the song "What a Fool Believes" by the Doobie Brothers was playing. She started laughing . . . *I wish the message were more clear* . . . she thought sarcastically as she pulled out of the parking garage and headed home.

James's new work schedule had him working Saturday through Thursday with Friday off. Since this was Wednesday he would be working straight through until next Friday. One of the other chefs suddenly quit, and the restaurant was scrambling to fill the void, which meant just one day off per week until they found a replacement.

Wednesday night was busy at American Steak. James forced himself to focus on his job and not Amber. He was furious with her for not taking her birth control and trapping him with a child. He couldn't bring himself to look at her. Amber picked up on his coldness, and it made her angry . . . *I'm going to have his baby . . . I don't care if he has a significant other . . . He should be with me, and he needs to own up to his responsibilities ASAP* . . . With that thought in her head, she decided to give him an ultimatum.

On one of her trips into the kitchen to check on an order, Amber went up to him and said softly so no one else could hear, "You are lucky I am being generous and patient. Consider this your warning."

"Leave me alone and let me do my job," he said to her hatefully and continued to season chicken breasts while thinking . . . *I've got to talk to Bryce soon. I'll have some time tomorrow morning to pay him a visit. If I can get Amber out of the way, Holly will never know about this.*

Amber quickly turned and left the kitchen . . . *I know I trapped him. He has every right to be angry with me. I don't care, though. I want this baby, and I want James. I WILL make him love me and this baby. He WILL marry me.*

Back at their house, Holly watched TV and thought over the events of the day. She decided to visit the past again tonight. She climbed into bed, turned on her CD player, put on the headphones, and found her way to Atlantis. The past life she experienced came to her in bits and pieces, not a continuous stream . . .

> *. . . Holly finds herself in a strange world, in an area which resembles a college campus. The surrounding landscape is beautiful, with two volcanoes in the distance and the architecture of nearby buildings is slightly Grecian looking. The word "Atlantis" is running through her mind, and her name is Dayani. She is walking toward a large building where people go to learn and realizes she is on her way to school. The people she sees around her look like normal human beings. They are wearing toga-style, or draping clothing. She finds her way into a lecture hall and sits down on a cool marble bench in the front row. The lecture hall is small and similar to a concert hall or theater, with graduated seating up to eight levels and a center stage.*
>
> *A man enters the stage through a side door, and she is incredibly drawn to him. His name is Natom, and he is the instructor. He is tall and handsome, and looks to be in his early 40s with dark hair, a neatly trimmed short beard, brown eyes, and olive skin. She recognizes this man as James. She has been eagerly anticipating this class and*

is excited to hear him speak. There is a large board next to him with diagrams of what looks like chemistry or DNA strands.

More people fill the hall, and Natom begins to talk. He is speaking a strange-sounding language, yet she understands every word, and the lesson is about chemistry and the theory of mixing of different species' DNA to create new beings. She locks eyes with him and instantly knows that he is her lover. She is going to meet him after class for a rendezvous. She senses that they have been together for a little over 1 year.

A short while later she is alone with him, making love in a large bed. He is a good lover and she surrenders herself completely to him. When they are finished, he kisses her and tells her he must be going.

"Please don't leave so soon," Dayani begs him and climbs on top of him to keep him from leaving.

"You know I would love nothing more than to stay here with you for eternity. However, if I don't get home soon, Laneesa will bombard me with questions," he replies.

"Are you ever going to tell her about us?" Dayani asks.

"Yes, my love, when the time is right. We have had this discussion before," he replies.

Dayani is irritated that Natom will not leave his wife, Laneesa, for her. She says coldly to him, "I don't believe that you will ever leave her. You enjoy having two women at your beck and call."

"That isn't true. Dayani, you know you are the one I love. Laneesa will put up a fight if I try to leave her. I have to do this the right way. I don't want to lose everything I have worked for my entire life," he replied.

"I won't wait forever," Dayani replies as she rolls off of him and gets out of bed.

"Honey, you won't have too. I wouldn't do that to you," Natom answers insistently.

She is annoyed with him and says, "Natom, leave and go home to your wife!"

Natom gets dressed and tells Dayani he will see her tomorrow. He kisses her softly on the cheek before he leaves and she returns his affection with a sullen stare and slams the door behind him.

Sometime later she is with Natom again, and they are in a tropical area making love next to a waterfall. Dayani gets the feeling that her relationship with Natom is based more on sex than love, at least for him. She loves him completely, with her whole heart, and yet, she feels like she is nothing more than a sex object. He will never leave his wife, and she can't imagine being with anyone else. She later catches a glimpse of herself in the crystal clear water and notices that she is petite and slender with long, curly, dark hair and brown eyes.

Next they are walking along a dirt path, the surrounding flora and fauna resembles a jungle. They are holding hands and talking. Natom stops and stands in front of her, facing her and says, "Dayani, I have a surprise for you. Close your eyes."

She closes her eyes, and he puts something around her wrist. "Okay, now, you can open them."

Dayani opens her eyes and sees that Natom has given her a lovely gold bracelet. "Natom, it's beautiful. Thank you so much," she says and kisses him.

"You are welcome, sweetheart. I want you to know that I will tell Laneesa soon, and then we can be together forever," he replies.

"I can't wait. I'm so happy!" Dayani exclaims and pulls him close for a kiss.

Time advances, and it feels like it has been several weeks since their rendezvous. Dayani is sitting on the edge of a bed talking to Natom, and she is crying and distraught.

"I'm pregnant. I am going to have your baby, and you still haven't left your wife!" she yells at him, crying uncontrollably.

"Dayani, do not worry. I will take care of you and the baby. I can't leave my wife yet. However, I will ensure that you and the baby are

provided for. You will have everything you need," Natom reassures her.

"Why can't you leave your wife? You keep promising me you will leave her. You buy me expensive presents, and we sneak away to beautiful places while you lie to her. WHAT IS WRONG WITH YOU?" Dayani hurls these words at him. She is furious.

"The truth is that I am afraid of her. Laneesa's parents are important people in the government, and they will ensure my demise if I leave her. I could not leave her if I wanted to, and I want to," he says breathlessly.

"Have you been lying to me this whole time, making up excuses because you don't ever plan to leave her and you are afraid?" Dayani asks him.

Natom is crying now, and he says to her, "Yes. I am so sorry, Dayani. Please forgive me. I love you so much. I don't want to live without you. The only way we can be together is for me to stay with Laneesa. If I leave her, they will make sure I disappear, and I won't be any good to you or our baby if I'm dead. Do you want me to die?"

Dayani believes him and feels bad for making demands. "I love you, Natom. I don't want you to get killed because of me. For the sake of our baby, we can continue on. I will remain your mistress," she says sadly with a heavy heart.

Natom is relieved, and he holds her close and promises her the world. "Dayani, I will take care of you and the baby for the rest of my life. You are the one I love."

A few years later, Dayani sees her little boy, who looks just like Natom, playing happily on the floor with a different man. As the man looks up and smiles at Dayani, she sees that this man is Charlie. In this Atlantis life he has sandy-colored hair and blue eyes. She looks into his eyes and feels complete and total love for him.

"Dayani, will you marry me?" Kam asks her.

"Kam, yes . . . I will marry you," Dayani replies happily and embraces him in a tight hug . . .

Holly wakes up and feels like she has been out for years. It takes her a few seconds to be fully present in the current moment. *Unbelievable . . . I discovered a long buried life with James . . . in Atlantis . . . That was eons ago . . . This is the third lifetime where I have been someone's secret lover . . . Drawing the Fool card was more accurate than I thought. I wasn't a nice person back then, screwing around with a married man and demanding that he leave his wife for me . . . I wonder what happened to Natom. Did he die? Charlie showed up in this life too . . . He and Roger are following me . . . My head hurts, and I'm exhausted . . .*

Holly took off her headphones, turned over, and fell into a deep sleep. James arrived home a little after midnight and watched Holly sleeping soundly as he got into bed. He was tired and sick with worry over his situation with Amber.

The next morning as Holly was eating her oatmeal at the dining-room table, James woke up and came into the kitchen.

"Good morning, honey. You're up early today," Holly said.

"I didn't sleep well last night. You slept like a log," he replied.

"I had another past-life regression, and you were in it this time," she said.

"I want to hear this," he replied.

"You were a teacher in Atlantis, and I was one of your students. You were much older than me, and we were having an affair. You were married, and I got pregnant with your love child. I was angry with you because you kept promising to leave your wife for me, and you never did. You told me if you left her, that her parents would have you killed," Holly said to him.

This particular past life hit James like ton of bricks, and he felt his heart sink down into his stomach. He didn't believe in reincarnation. However, he understood the karmic justice involved and started to wonder if this past life really did happen. *This might be plausible . . .Was Amber my wife back in Atlantis, and I knocked up Holly? . . . Fast-forward to the present and the situation is reversed . . . OH SHIT!*

"James, you look like you just saw a ghost," Holly said laughing.

"No, I'm just shocked by the content of your dream," he said, hoping he sounded normal. "Did anything else happen, other than me not leaving my wife?" he asked, thinking . . . *Did I get killed?*

"In the last part of the regression, or 'dream,' as you call it, I saw our little boy happily playing with another man who said he loved me and asked me to marry him. I accepted his proposal, and then I woke up," she replied.

James felt a pang of jealousy over this and asked Holly, "Who was the guy?"

"I don't know," she lied to him again.

"It seems like you fooled around a lot in your past lives. Is there something I should know about in *this* life?" James asked, hoping to deflect his own guilt.

"NO," Holly replied emphatically . . . *I would never leave him for Charlie . . . Charlie is my fantasy . . . James is my reality.*

"Just thought I should check, with your history," James replied smiling. "Are you going to work?"

Holly looked at the clock and realized she needed to get going. "You're right. I need to speed things up."

While Holly was getting ready, James took his coffee into the living room and sat down in his brown leather easy chair and turned on the TV. He glanced at the coffee table and noticed her deck of tarot cards. He was full of dread and mixed emotions this morning, and his thoughts were scattered . . . *Here she goes with this psychic stuff again . . . I don't know why she has such an interest in these things . . . First, the past-life regressions, now the tarot cards . . . Does she suspect something? Is she keeping something from me? She usually brings out these cards when she's seeking an answer to something . . . I wonder what kind of cards are turning up for her . . .*

That Atlantis dream hit too close to home.

Holly got ready for work and walked into the living room, where she noticed James looked pale and sick again. "Did my past life upset you?" she asked him.

"No, I'm just tired from not sleeping well last night," he replied, thinking . . . *You bet it did!*

"Try to take a nap before you leave for work," she advised him.

"I might do that. You have a great day," he replied.

"You too," Holly said as she kissed him good-bye. "Oh, I forgot to draw my daily tarot card. I'll take the deck with me and do it at work. I should bring the guidebook too," Holly said as she scooped up the deck of cards and the guidebook and put them in her tote bag and left for work.

CHAPTER 5

Conversations with Bryce

James took a shower and got dressed. He couldn't leave the house soon enough to pay Bryce a visit. Bryce owned a chain of martial arts studios, and James knew Bryce would be at his corporate office this morning which was located in Old Town Alexandria. James walked into the lobby of Bryce's office, and the receptionist let Bryce know that James was there to see him. James sat down to wait. He noticed that the walls were covered with pictures of students performing martial arts, and there was a large curio cabinet showcasing trophies from competitions. In addition, there were several plaques on the wall from local civic organizations and charities thanking, "The Decker Martial Arts Company" for their financial contributions and good deeds. *If those organizations knew about Bryce's deals with the devil and the seedy underground world he inhabits, they would never want anything to do with him again . . . The guy is so underhanded and slick, he should run for national office . . .* James thought as he waited for Bryce.

"Mr. Decker will see you now. His office is straight back, at the end of the hall," the receptionist said to James.

"Thank you," James replied as he got up and walked toward Bryce's office.

"James, what brings you here?" Bryce asked as he stood up and greeted him with a handshake.

"Hello, Bryce. I've got a problem, and I'd like to talk to you about getting some help," he answered while returning Bryce's handshake . . . *Damn his office is nice; black leather furniture, large mahogany desk, a great view of the Potomac River, a sofa and wet bar.*

"Have a seat and let's talk," Bryce said, motioning to James to sit down in a nearby chair as he closed the door. "What's the problem?"

"I've been having an affair with a waitress at American Steak for almost a year. She informed me that she's pregnant with my child. She got pregnant to trap me. She admitted that she stopped taking her birth control pills on purpose. She claims that she loves me and that she hasn't fooled around with anyone else. She refuses to have an abortion, and I don't want a kid. She trapped me, deceived me, and I want your help to make her disappear so I can have my life back," James said in a defensive and self-righteous manner.

Bryce was disturbed at this request. He had no problems getting rid of people. He had no problem playing the middleman and arranging hits for a fee. However, to have a woman killed while knowing that she was pregnant was especially distasteful to him, and he didn't want any part of it. The expression on Bryce's face indicated that he was not amenable to this, and James felt his stomach start to churn . . . *I overestimated Bryce . . . I don't think he wants to help with this.*

"You know that I have no qualms taking out anyone who doesn't pay their debts. I give them ample time to comply and get the money. I have no issues with arranging hits for a fee. However, arranging a hit on a pregnant woman or a child under 18 is not something I would ever do; not knowingly anyway. "Who is this woman?" he asked with a look of utter disgust, narrowing his eyes and wanting to take a swing at James for even thinking something like this. Bryce had a soft spot for children, pregnant women, and animals.

"Her name is Amber Conner. She's a waitress at American Steak,"

James replied nervously, suddenly feeling extremely uncomfortable and thinking he made the wrong decision in asking for Bryce's help.

Bryce immediately flinched. He was stunned and speechless for a few seconds. He loved Amber. She was his favorite cousin, and he would take her side no matter what. He glared at James without saying anything, and James suddenly wanted to bolt from the chair and run out of his office as fast as he could. He knew he made a mistake in coming to Bryce with this request. Bryce knew how to keep his cool, and even though he wanted to strangle James and throw his body in the river, he figured it would be better to force James into marrying Amber and supporting the baby.

"Amber Conner is my cousin, a first cousin," Bryce stated coldly.

I'm a dead man . . . "I didn't know that," James replied sheepishly . . . *He's probably going to kill me now . . . Amber and I never talked about our families.*

"You didn't know that because all you want to do is fuck her. You don't care anything about her . . . her interests, her family, none of that matters to you. I didn't know she was fooling around with you. She's like a little sister to me. Let me tell you something, you WILL do right by Amber. You WILL support that baby and MARRY her. If you don't, I will have a special pair of concrete shoes made for you to wear into the Potomac River. I want to kill you with my bare hands right this minute. The only thing that keeps me from doing it is because Amber, for some reason, seems to love you. Family is important to me. I'm old school when it comes to that . . . and I enjoy watching you squirm," Bryce threatened as he glared at James and cracked his knuckles. "WHAT KIND OF MONSTER PUTS A HIT ON A PREGNANT WOMAN?" he yelled as his face turned red, and his eyes shot daggers at James.

"I'm sorry, Bryce. I would have never come to you if I knew she was your cousin. I'll man up and do the right thing. I'll marry her. Please don't kill me," James pleaded, holding his stomach and feeling like he was going to vomit . . . *I half-expect his goons to find me later and beat me up . . . that is, if he doesn't pull a gun out from under his desk and shoot me first.*

"I don't care if Amber trapped you or not. I don't know what she sees in a worthless old guy like you. You'll be 74 when that baby turns 20. You should consider yourself lucky that a woman like Amber would give you the time of day. You have 2 weeks to break up with Holly, or I will tell your woman for you. You don't deserve Holly either, you lying sack of shit. You truly are a useless piece of garbage. If anything bad happens to Amber in the meantime, I'm holding you responsible, and you can consider yourself a dead man. Get out of my office before I change my mind about killing you," Bryce said angrily as he stood up and walked over to open his office door . . . *If he tries to arrange a hit on her through someone else, I will kill him with my bare hands. I shouldn't have given him 2 weeks to tell his lady, but part of me takes joy in knowing that this idiot will be miserable during that time . . . He's one of the most cowardly men I've ever known.*

"I'm leaving right now. I promise I'll make things right with Amber," James said as he stood up and left Bryce's office and quickly walked to his truck. He didn't want to run. He didn't want to do anything more to anger Bryce. *My life is over . . . I have to marry a woman I don't even like anymore, and deal with a damn kid too . . . and Bryce will be family . . . The holidays will be so merry.*

Amber was feeling distressed and frightened and wanted to talk to someone about her pregnancy. She didn't want to tell her sister, Jenny, because as much as she wanted to have James and his baby, she was deeply ashamed that she resorted to trapping him. *I think I'll go see Bryce and tell him what happened . . . He's not going to like it. I never told him I was seeing James . . . He thinks I've just been living my life free and unattached*

. . . she thought . . . *I know he has connections, maybe he can talk to James . . . I'll call him and see if he's doing anything tonight.* Amber dialed Bryce's number and hoped he would pick up and not let it go to voice mail.

"Amber, how are you, sweetheart?" Bryce answered in a concerned voice, hoping to sound pleasant and not let on that he knew about her situation.

"Hi, Bryce. I'm not doing well. I really need to talk to you. Are you going to be home later tonight?" she asked sounding like the weight of the world was on her shoulders.

She wants to tell me about her pregnancy . . . "Yeah, why don't I come over to your place? I'll be done here around 5:30. That way, you won't have to drive out to Vienna," he said.

"That would be wonderful," she replied sounding a little bit relieved. "I'll send out for a pizza."

"That sounds great. I'll be there around 6:00," he replied.

"I'm looking forward to it, see you then," she said.

"Me too, bye," he said and hung up.

Later that evening as he was driving to Amber's place, he wondered why she never introduced him to guys that she was seeing until after she had been with them for some time . . . *I consider Amber to be more than just my cousin . . . we are best friends . . . Although she doesn't know the extent of my dark side, she confides in me, but she never talks much about the men she dates . . . Maybe she's private that way . . . It's true that I never liked the ones she did introduce me to . . . She probably figures I wouldn't like any of them, and she would be right; none of them so far have been good enough for her in my opinion* . . . Bryce arrived at Amber's apartment at exactly 6:00. She buzzed him in and was waiting with her apartment door open at the top of the stairs.

"Bryce, it's so good to see you," Amber said as he walked toward her.

"It's always a pleasure to see my favorite cousin," he replied with a smile.

"Come in, I've got a big meat pizza waiting for you," she said as he entered her apartment.

"Before we eat, I want to know what's troubling you so badly," he said and took a seat on her sofa. She came over and sat down next to him. He could see that she was on the verge of tears.

She turned her body toward him, took a deep breath, and said, "I'm pregnant. The man I've been seeing is in a committed relationship with someone else, and he doesn't want a future with me, although he said he will support the baby financially. I'm scared. I love him more than anything, and I don't want to raise the baby alone. I did a foolish thing and purposely set out to trap James. We've been seeing each other for 8 months, and I thought I could make him mine. I thought once he found out I was having his baby, he would leave his significant other and want to be with me. I guess I thought wrong. I let my heart rule my head, and he's really mad at me. I think he hates me," she said as tears rolled down her face.

Bryce let out a heavy sigh, placed his hand over hers, and asked, "Are you positive that you want to have this baby?"

"Yes, without a doubt. I've wanted a baby really badly for a few years now. I don't want to be an older woman when I have my first child. I love James. I loved him from the moment we met even though he's 20 years older than me. He works as a chef at American Steak. I've dated a lot of different guys over the years, but I haven't really loved or seen a future with anyone until I met him," she replied wistfully.

If she knew that he tried to take out a hit on her earlier this morning she might feel differently about him . . . Maybe I should tell her . . . No, I'd rather see James wallow in misery . . . The guy is a first-class asshole who deserves this and more . . . He is going to pay for thinking about killing a pregnant woman . . . "What can I do to help?" he asked knowing that she didn't have anything to worry about. James was going to marry her . . . or else.

"I know that you have connections and are skilled at the art of coercion. I want James Macklin to marry me. I know that once we're married, I can make him fall in love with me," Amber replied, firm in her conviction.

"Amber, what makes you think that forcing him to marry you will make him fall in love with you? You said that he hates you for trapping him. He's going to hate you even more if he has to marry you," Bryce gently countered.

"I just know he will eventually love me. I feel strongly that once the baby arrives he is going to love it, and he'll forgive me for trapping him and realize that we are meant to be together," she said confidently.

My pretty cousin is delusional . . . She's been headstrong her entire life, and she doesn't back down . . . She gets what she wants one way or the other . . . Like the rest of our family, she will not go quietly into the night . . . Bryce thought as he studied her face and said, "Amber, I would move mountains to help you with anything, even though I don't agree with you or like this choice you have made. I know of this guy, and you can rest assured that he will come around and live up to his responsibilities as a father and husband."

Amber kissed him on the cheek and said, "Thank you, Bryce. I love you."

"I love you too. We can have the wedding ceremony at my house after Thanksgiving. I'll make the arrangements, and you need to start looking for a dress," he said.

"Are you buying me a wedding dress too?" she asked excitedly with wide eyes.

"Yeah. I often feel like your father instead of your cousin, and I know your dad is too frail to participate. I don't think we should tell anyone that this is a shotgun wedding. Let them think that you were dating a man, accidentally got pregnant, and he loves you and wants to marry you," Bryce said.

"I agree," Amber replied, nodding her head.

"I don't understand your attraction to men so much older than you. Whatever happened to that nice boy you grew up with, I think his name was Trey?" Bryce asked thoughtfully. "He was a nice guy."

"Trey Davis. I haven't been in touch with him since a few years after high school. He was one of my best friends. Maybe I'll look him up sometime," Amber replied.

"You should do that. I'm ready to eat pizza now," Bryce said.

"Me too," she agreed, and they sat down at her dining-room table to eat.

CHAPTER 6

The Moon

Holly settled into her office and went through the morning ritual of checking e-mails and looking at her and Stan's calendars to see what was happening today. Stan would be spending most of the day in meetings, and her day was filled with mundane things like uploading documents to a database and working on a spreadsheet for Jack. She remembered that she brought the tarot cards with her and was anxious to see what today's influence would be. She discreetly shuffled the deck thinking about her life in general. The card she drew was the Moon.

The Moon's message can be difficult to interpret. It was one of the more elusive cards in the deck. The card depicts a large moon at night and two dogs barking at it. The dogs are next to a lake, and a lobster is crawling out of the lake toward the moon. The general meaning is that something in your life is not what it seems. Something is hidden, either by you or someone close to you. It indicates caution, confusion, delusion, and relying on your intuition.

She thought . . . *The only thing I'm hiding is an infatuation with Charlie . . . most likely because James took me for granted for so long that I can't turn it off right away . . . I don't think James is hiding anything. We already talked about that . . . Our relationship is on the mend . . . I can't think of anything I need to be cautious about . . . not yet anyway.*

"Holly," Neil Peters said to her. She looked up from her computer and found him standing in her doorway. She quickly hid her tarot cards in her top desk drawer.

"Hi, Neil. What brings you up here today?" she asked.

"I just finished having a discussion with Stan, and I remembered you said that you were going for a psychic reading a few weeks ago. I'm curious, how did that turn out?" he asked.

"It was interesting. She told me that I had a past life in Atlantis and had several lives full of secret love affairs that broke my heart and got one of my lovers killed. I was a Japanese prostitute back in the 1600s and killed my pimp," Holly said and began laughing, thinking . . . *I don't know why it sounds so funny today . . . telling Neil I was once a prostitute.*

"That's probably just the beginning," Neil replied and started laughing with her. "I have weird, recurring dreams now and then about half-human, half-animal creatures in a zoo and I'm walking around taking notes on them."

"That sounds freaky. I remember you mentioned dreams about a tribal ceremony where everyone is naked and writhing around," Holly said and started to giggle. "Your past lives would be fun to watch."

Neil laughed with her, then looked at his watch and said, "I've got to run to another meeting. It's been fun talking with you. I'll see you later."

"Till next time," Holly replied cheerfully as Neil turned to leave.

A few hours later it was time for lunch. Holly brought her lunch today, a salad and an apple. As she began to eat her apple, she remembered the tarot card guidebook in her desk drawer. She took it out and began reading it. She heard a man's voice greeting her and looked up to see Jack standing in her doorway.

"Holly, I'm glad you're here. I wanted to know when you think you'll have the spreadsheet finished?" he asked.

"Hi, Jack. I'll have it ready around 2:00 today. Will that work?"

"That's great. What are you reading?"

"Oh, this is a book on how to read tarot cards. I do my own readings sometimes, and I like to have this guidebook handy," she replied thinking . . . *I'm going to get a reputation as the office nut job.*

"Really? Will you read my tarot cards?" he asked sincerely, seeming interested.

"Sure, I can read your cards. Let me know when a good time is for you and I'll come to your office with my cards and my book. Sometimes I can do a reading without the book, however, I feel better if I bring it for reference," she replied.

"I'll let you know, and we can set up a meeting. I would prefer you not tell anyone about this," he said.

"Of course. I know this is the type of thing you want to keep private," she replied with a smile.

"Thanks, Holly. I'll see you later," he said and walked away.

That's an eye-opener. I never thought Jack would be interested in a tarot card reading. He's such a man's man. The people I work with seem to be open-minded about these things . . . This is good, they won't think I'm crazy . . . she thought. Holly turned and looked out her window. It was October now, and today was a little cooler than usual, although the sun was shining and it was a beautiful day. It was 55 degrees when she left the house this morning. She guessed the temperature was probably 70 at the moment. *I think I'll take a short walk before I work on Jack's spreadsheet.*

Holly slipped on her walking shoes and went outside. She took a leisurely stroll in the direction of The Book Store three blocks away. Her plan was to walk there and back for exercise. She has been stuck behind a desk all morning and a short walk would be refreshing. She saw Charlie up ahead walking with a woman, a tall brunette with long hair and a slim figure. She was dressed in a dark gray suit and matching heels. The two of them stopped in front of a storefront to talk. She was showing him some brochures and had a clipboard. Holly could see that the woman was attractive and she was smiling up at him. She suddenly felt embarrassed and didn't want Charlie to see her, so she turned around and headed back to the office. *If I keep walking, I will go right past them, and I feel awkward and jealous . . . Is this a business meeting? . . . A date? . . . She doesn't look like someone who works for MTAC . . . I have no right to feel jealous. Charlie is free and single . . . I'm not . . . I can't get back to the office fast enough.*

Holly returned to her desk thinking about Charlie and the brunette. *It was probably a business meeting . . . the woman had a clipboard and brochures . . . Or maybe they are planning a vacation together. I never asked Charlie if he had a girlfriend . . . A man that good-looking is bound to have plenty of dating options . . . I wonder what he does on the weekends . . . STOP . . . Listen to yourself and get a grip! . . . Charlie is not your boyfriend . . .You wake up next to your own handsome man every morning . . . Get yourself together and get back to work . . .* Holly took her own advice and channeled her efforts into finishing Jack's spreadsheet.

She was happy when the workday was finally over. As she walked down the street to the Metro station, she heard someone call her name. She recognized the voice. It was Charlie. She stopped and turned around. He was waving to her.

"Holly, wait up," he said and walked faster toward her.

Here comes the great love of my many lives . . . Maybe he will volunteer information about that woman he was with today. Holly waited for him to catch up. "Hi, Charlie. Good to see you," she said cheerfully, happy to see him in spite of his earlier walk down the street with another woman.

"Were you out walking at lunch today?" he asked her.

"Yes. I started to walk to The Book Store and realized that I forgot my purse and went back to the office. Then I got sidelined on a project," she said, hoping he would believe her. They walked together down the street to the Metro station.

"I thought I saw you out of the corner of my eye, and then you disappeared. I was talking to my realtor. I'm thinking of buying an investment property," he replied.

"Do you want to be a landlord?" she asked, relieved that the woman was just his realtor, although she was pretty, and flattered that he would notice her out of the corner of his eye on a busy street.

"Yes. I plan to start with one property and see how it goes. It's something I've wanted to do for a long time," he replied.

"Are you thinking of retirement?" she asked.

"Yeah, eventually. I'd like to have another stream of income other than my military retirement, Social Security, and what I have in my 401K. Just thinking ahead. I'm not ready to retire any time soon, though," he replied. "Do you have any plans for the weekend?" he asked.

"No, James has to work the weekend. I'll find something to occupy my time, though. What about you?"

"I'm going to the Eastern Shore. Me and a few guys drinking beer, camping, and attempting to catch fish," he replied with a laugh as they rode the escalator down to the tracks. "I won't be in the office tomorrow."

"Lucky you. I'll be slaving away over financial stuff," she replied.

They were standing on the platform waiting for their trains. "Holly, if you want to go to happy hour sometime, let me know. I really enjoy your company, and I'll make sure you get home in one piece," Charlie said to her thinking . . . *I really want to know you . . . Even if you want me as just a friend, I can do that.*

They held each other's gaze for a few seconds, and then she said to him, "Thank you, Charlie. I will seriously consider that. I enjoy your company too." She felt a flush creep into her face . . . *I hope he doesn't see me blushing.*

Charlie's train arrived first. He looked at Holly and said, "See you next week."

"Enjoy your weekend," she replied with a smile . . . *One more workday to get through, and then a lonely weekend . . . This never used to bother me before, why now? I find things to do, call or go see friends, catch up on housework, work out until I drop, read books, garden, go shopping . . . I feel like something is missing from my life, and I'm not sure what it is . . . At least I have mornings with James . . .* Finally, her train arrived and she headed home.

While driving to her house, she thought of some items she needed to get at the drugstore. There was a Walgreens close to the house, so she decided to stop there. She needed to get shampoo, conditioner, razor blades, and mascara. As she walked toward the Health and Beauty section, she saw a display for new body sprays with available testers. *I've got to try these . . . I'm a sucker for fragrances. The bottles are large . . . that's a lot of product if I get tired of the scent later . . . Let's see, there are three of them . . . Berry Bliss, Vanilla Wonderful, and Peach Perfection. Vanilla Wonderful . . . I'll try that one first.* Holly sprayed the Vanilla Wonderful fragrance on her wrist . . . *This smells like the vanilla air freshener they use at the restaurant . . . I love it. I'm not going to try the others, I'll get this one. James will like it . . . although, it might make him think about work . . . I don't care, I like it, I'm getting it.* Holly put the new body spray in her shopping basket and went about getting the other items that she came for.

Holly didn't fix much for dinner, she wasn't particularly hungry. She opened a can of vegetable soup, poured it into a large mug, and heated it in the microwave. Then she took her mug of soup and went into the living room to watch TV. She channel surfed until she settled on the History Channel. *American Pickers* was on, and she enjoyed this show. She watched three consecutive episodes and began to get sleepy. Fate was curled up into a ball, asleep on her lap. She relaxed and put her head back for a few moments, thinking about her conversation with Neil that morning. At this point, she had most of the instructions from the past-life regression CD memorized and she went through the meditation in her mind to take her back in time . . .

. . . Holly is back in Atlantis. It feels like many years later. She is working in a lab with a man she recognizes as Neil Peters. In this life, Neil is tall and slim with brown hair and eyes. His name is Hantoro. They are scientists working with animal and human DNA with the goal of eradicating diseases.

"Dayani, I figured it out!" Hantoro says excitedly.

"What did you figure out?" Dayani asks.

"I can make a half-man, half-horse being," he replies.

"Why do you want to do that? What purpose would it serve? What kind of life could it possibly have?" Dayani asks.

"To see if it can be done. We can create new species. I know it will be a success. I'll be famous. This is only the beginning," Hantoro says with a crazy gleam in his eyes.

"That's a wonderful idea, Hantoro. You have my approval, get started." Margan says with enthusiasm. He had been standing in the lab listening to their conversation. She recognizes Margan as Matt Weedon. He was a pain in the ass in Atlantis too.

"NO. Margan, Hantoro, what's the matter with both of you? You're playing God. This experiment will be a disaster, I know it. It's wrong!" Dayani says adamantly to both of them.

"I'm in charge here. What I say is the rule. Hantoro, proceed full speed ahead. Dayani, you can work on other projects. Don't interfere with Hantoro's mission," Margan said sternly and pointed his finger at her.

Dayani is upset with Margan and Hantoro. She knows in her heart that the project will fail and forebodes bad luck. She is more concerned for Hantoro, as he is a good friend, even though he has mad scientist tendencies. She doesn't like Margan and could care less about him. She is in disagreement with many of his work policies.

"Thank you, Margan. I'll mix the cells, prepare the fertilization, and plant the embryo in the chamber," Hantoro replies.

Sometime later, Dayani sees a zoolike compound where many

strange half-human half-animal hybrids live. Animal DNA used to create these hybrids came from horses, goats, bulls, fish, birds, etc. These are the creatures Hantoro helped bring to life, and she feels great sadness as many of them are sick and dying and have horrible lives, forced to live in caged areas and be displayed at science seminars for people to stare at. She takes it upon herself to see to their comfort.

Hantoro is now a sick man, and Dayani visits with him in a hospital. "I should have listened to you, Dayani. I got carried away and acted as God. It serves me right to be so sick," Hantoro confided to her. Hantoro had strange, black growths over a large portion of his body and had trouble breathing. Karma was handing out her painful justice.

"Hantoro, this is karma at work. I know you are truly sorry for creating those half-human creatures. Please forgive yourself. You make yourself feel worse by dwelling on the bad things. You need to focus on getting well and doing what you can to ease their suffering," Dayani said to him . . .

The phone rings causing Holly to come out of her hypnosis as Fate jumps off of her lap. *Who is calling this late? James . . . He must be on a break.*

"Hello," Holly answers the phone.

"Hi, honey. I wanted to call you and tell you that I love you," James said.

"I love you too. What prompted this?" she asked, amused and delighted that he called.

"I was just thinking about you and wanted to hear your voice," he replied.

"This is a nice surprise. How are things at work tonight?"

"A good pace, not too busy, not too boring," he replied. "I don't have a lot to say, I just wanted to connect with you for a few minutes."

"Okay," Holly replied with a yawn. "I think I'm going to go to bed now. I fell asleep on the sofa and your call woke me up. I'm glad it did."

"Sleep well and I'll see you in the morning," he told her.

"Okay, see you soon. Bye."

James was unaware that Amber was listening to his phone call to Holly in the vacant section of the bar. He jumped in surprise when he heard her voice directly behind him, "Why are you trying to make nice with Holly? Are you planning to keep her on the side after we get married?"

"Go away, Amber, this is your fault," he replied sternly.

"That's no way to talk to the mother of your child, and I'm not the sole person at fault here. I'm not going away, and don't you forget it!" she replied angrily and snapped him with a bar towel. The sound of it caused several customers to turn and look. Amber let out a loud laugh. She didn't want them to think the staff was fighting.

"Ouch! Believe me, I wish I could," he snarled at her and walked back into the kitchen.

Wow, that was sweet of James to call... He used to do that in the beginning of our relationship . . . I hope we get back to the way we were . . . He needs to find another job . . . one that won't make him want to go blow off steam with the guys on his days off . . . Holly thought as she changed into her nightgown. *Neil and I worked together in Atlantis . . . Those were some scary and pitiful-looking creatures. Maybe when Atlantis was destroyed something happened to the technology, or human and animal biology changed and the DNA can no longer be mixed like that. It was pretty amazing though. I don't think I'll tell anyone about this, not even Neil. Crappy Matt was there too . . .* Holly put on her headphones this time and listened to the narrator's voice. She found it soothing . . .

. . . Holly finds herself in a store that sells medieval clothes. It is sometime in the fifteenth century. She greets a customer as he walks in

the door and recognizes him as Jack Briggs, who is a frequent customer. His name in this life is Stefano, and they begin to speak in Italian.

"Good morning, Renata," Stefano greets her warmly.

"Good morning, Stefano. It's has been weeks since I've seen you. How can I help you today?" Renata asks him. In this life, Stefano is medium height with dark hair and hazel eyes.

"Today I would like a reading. I want to ask Perla to marry me. My parents think she's a bad woman and want me to find someone else. I love her, and I'm uncertain of what to do," he replies sadly.

"Let's sit down at the table and consult the cards. Mamma, please watch the store while I read for Stefano," Renata addresses her mother, who she does not recognize as anyone that she currently knows in her present life.

Renata walks Stefano into another room where they sit down at a table. She gets her deck of cards and requests he shuffle them while thinking of his intentions with Perla. Once he is done, she selects cards from the top of the deck and arranges them in a cross pattern on the table. She begins to interpret the message. The cards look different from the twenty-first-century version.

"Stefano, your parents are correct. This woman will bring you great sadness. She cares for money more than love. She will not be a faithful wife; she is dishonest. The cards indicate that you will meet another woman soon. She will be a better match for you and will make you happy. My advice is do not ask Perla to marry you. Wait a short while and your feelings for her will change when you meet this new woman," Renata tells him.

Stefano is disheartened, yet he decides to take her advice. "Renata, you have been right about many things in my prior readings. I'll heed your advice. Thank you for this."

"You are welcome, Stefano. Please come to see me anytime you need guidance," she replies. Stefano pays her and leaves the store . . .

Holly awakens gently from her hypnosis session and takes off her headphones and places them on her nightstand. *I was a fortune-teller in medieval Italy . . . that would explain my fascination with anything occult . . . Jack liked to come into my shop for readings. How funny is it that. Centuries later we work together and the subject of tarot cards comes up . . . Everyone I know and have ever known has probably shared some type of past life together . . . I need to get some sleep now.*

She doesn't hear James slip into bed next to her a few hours later. She is sleeping on her back, and he positions himself on his side facing her. He reaches out and puts his arm across her chest and snuggles up next to her thinking . . . *I wish I could take back everything.*

The next morning as Holly is eating her breakfast, James joins her at the dining-room table with a bowl of cereal. "Good morning, beautiful," he says as he walks into the room. He picks up the gallon of milk on the table and takes a drink.

"Good morning. How was work last night?"

"It was moderately busy. What kind of plans do you have tonight?" he asked her.

"I haven't made any, why? Do you suddenly have the night off?" she asked hopefully.

"No such luck," he said. "Did you have any past-life experiences last night?"

"Yes. I was a fortune-teller in medieval Italy and worked in a shop that sold clothing. The tarot cards looked different back then," she replied.

"Well, that sounds better than most of the other ones you've had. No secret lovers, huh?" he inquired.

"No, thank God," she replied, deciding not to tell him about the Atlantis life and the half-human, half-animal creatures. "I need to get ready for work . . . TGIF," she said as she headed toward the bathroom for her shower.

James made coffee, and then walked into the living room and turned on the TV. He noticed Holly's tarot cards on the coffee table and decided to shuffle them and draw a card. As he did, he thought about his problem, what was he going to do? Placing them back on the table, he drew the first card. He didn't know much about them; however, when he drew the Ten of Swords he knew it wasn't good. He decided not to draw another one. He opened up the guidebook and read the card's meaning.

The Ten of Swords depicts a man lying facedown on the ground with 10 swords lodged in his back. There is blood on the swords and blood is oozing from the man's body. He appears to be dead. A red blanket covers the lower half of his body. This card's meaning is failure, ruin, and disaster that cannot be avoided. The failure will not be small, nor will it be easily overcome. The end of something important is about to happen. If you learn from the consequences you will be able to endure and rebuild your life.

Might as well go jump off a cliff . . . he thought as he put the cards away, his heart beating rapidly with anxiety. He pretended to watch the news on TV, but his mind was elsewhere, worrying about Holly and Amber. His stomach hurt. Twenty-five minutes later, Holly walked into the living room looking lovely and smelling like Vanilla Wonderful. *OH SHIT . . . I just drew a card of doom and Holly decides to wear Amber's favorite body spray. I hope she hasn't put two and two together . . . I'd like a little more time with her before my life is over.*

"Smell me," Holly said lightheartedly to James.

"You smell good, a lot like the kitchen spray we use," James lied to her.

"I know. I thought it might remind you of work, so I had to get it," she said while smiling.

"That's okay, whatever makes you happy," he replied forcing a smile

. . . *I deserve whatever I've got coming.*

"I'll see you late tonight or early tomorrow. Don't work too hard," she said as she bent down to kiss him.

"I love you," he said to her.

"I love you too," she replied and headed out the door to go to work. *I enjoy the mornings when James gets up early to spend a few minutes with me. It's been fun telling him about my past lives even though he doesn't believe in that stuff . . . At least he listens and pretends to be interested. I think our life together would be happier if he could get into a different line of work.*

When Holly arrived at work, she realized she forgot to draw her daily tarot card and left them at home. It was quiet today and most of the work she had to finish was routine. She spent an hour checking e-mail and doing miscellaneous administrative tasks, and then went to see Patricia.

Chapter 7

Message from an Old Lover

Holly took the elevator to the seventh floor and knocked on Patricia's office door.

"Hi. What brings you down here?" Patricia asked her.

"I wanted to stop by and see if anything new and interesting was happening with you," Holly replied.

"I signed up to take a Zumba class at the Wakefield Recreation Center," Patricia replied.

"That's great. I'd love to try that. Is there still time to sign up?" Holly asked.

"I think so. Here's the information. I'm sure you can register online. It starts Monday," Patricia replied while writing down the info on a sticky note.

"I want to do this. My regular workout is getting boring, and I need to challenge myself," Holly said. "Got any plans for the weekend?"

"Andy and I are going to see *Evita* at the Kennedy Center tomorrow night," Patricia said.

"I haven't been there in a long time. I know you'll enjoy it. I saw the movie and really liked it," Holly told her.

"How are things with James?" Patricia asked.

"Much better. I feel like we are getting back to a good place. He's been attentive and loving and no plans to go out with the guys," Holly said happily.

"It's about time," Patricia replied. "I've got to finish this report before lunch. Even though Ian's not in the office today he still haunts me through e-mail."

"I'll take that as a hint to stop bugging you and get back to work," Holly said with a smile. "See you later, enjoy *Evita*."

Holly went back to her office and her phone started ringing before she had a chance to sit down. She saw that it was the receptionist calling, which meant Matt was here for his meeting with Stan.

"Hi, is Matt here?" Holly asked as she picked up the receiver.

"Yes, is it okay to send him up?" the receptionist asked.

"Yes, I'll meet him at the door," she replied and hung up the phone . . . *Oh joy, I get to see Matt.* Holly walked to the lobby area to open the door for him.

"Hi, Matt. Good to see you," she said, opening the door. He looked the same, but his hair was grayer and he looked slimmer.

"Hello, Holly. How are you these days?" he asked politely.

"Doing great, no complaints," she replied as they walked down the hallway to Stan's office. "You look like you lost weight," she commented.

"I'm down 25 pounds. Riding bikes is the best thing I ever did," he replied. By this time they reached Stan's office.

"Have a good day," she said to him.

"You too," he replied.

Holly walked back to her desk thinking, *I guess he's not that bad . . . even though he encouraged Neil to create those pitiful creatures back in Atlantis.* She went online and registered for the Zumba class which started the following Monday. The class met twice a week on Monday and Wednesday nights for 8 weeks.

The day went by slowly, and Holly grew more depressed as it got closer to quitting time. She had no plans for this weekend. The weather forecast was cool and rainy the entire weekend. Summer was officially over. She felt sad when summer ended because she enjoyed the long daylight hours and loved the ease of wearing flip-flops and beach dresses. It was the next best thing to living in pajamas. But Holly liked the change of seasons, especially the colorful autumn leaves that usually peaked around the first week of November, and anything edible made from pumpkins.

As she drove home she decided to see how many past lives she could uncover this weekend. *At least it will give me something to do . . . I can't believe I'm actually looking forward to the weekend being over so I can start Zumba on Monday . . . How boring and dull my life has become.*

The rain began to pour shortly after she arrived home. *I'm in for the night. I'm sure not going anywhere in this rain.* Later that evening after she ate her meager dinner, she logged into her e-mail account. She almost fell on the floor when she saw an e-mail from Alex Manning. He sent her a Facebook Friend Request. *Oh my God, I don't believe it . . . I haven't talked to him in 12 years . . . I wonder if he stopped using drugs and got his life together. I wonder if he's still doing guys.* She recalled the years that she spent with her second husband . . .

. . . Holly and Alex met when they both worked for the same company back in the 1990s. He was 6 years older than she. Alex was a handsome man, standing 6 foot 4 with black hair and beautiful blue eyes. He was fun and thoughtful and easy to be with. They lived together for 5 years before getting married in a quickie chapel on a trip to Las Vegas. On the day of their wedding, they hit the casinos early in the morning and they lost on every gamble. She ignored the omen. Their relationship took a sharp nose-dive shortly after their wedding. She wanted to recapture the closeness of their early days and revive their sex life, which, by now, was nonexistent, and he seemed to want more freedom.

She remembers a conversation they had when she was trying to find out if he was still interested in her sexually. He was spending more and more time with his guy friends, and by then, had developed a crack cocaine habit, bringing it home with him after his disappearances and smoking it in front of her. She knew he had battled drug addiction in his past, before they got together. He was back and forth with marijuana, however, she never saw him do any hard stuff. She was developing crushes on other men by now and feeling shut out by Alex, wondering if she would be able to maintain marital fidelity. His new crack habit bothered her the most. She thought he was going to accidentally overdose and die.

"I just can't get it up like I used to. I failed the last few times we've tried. It's a difficult issue for a man to deal with,"Alex had said to her.

"I understand if you are having erectile problems. I'm not going to hold that against you. There are new options for men now. I think you should see a doctor and find out about them. It seems like you don't WANT help for this. I've caught you masturbating several times, so obviously you still have interest in sex . . . just not with me. Is that true? We haven't had sex in almost 2 years,"Holly replied.

She could tell Alex felt uncomfortable, and after a short silence he finally admitted the truth to her. "I'm sorry. I didn't realize it had been that long. I didn't want to hurt your feelings. It's true. I'm not interested in you sexually anymore."

Holly wasn't surprised to hear him say that. She knew deep inside that things weren't right between them, and now she had the answer she needed. It felt like the end was near, but she wasn't ready to leave quite yet.

"Look, if you want to see other men who can fulfill your needs I'm okay with that,"Alex said to her.

"Seriously? You would let me have sex with other men, and then come home to you like nothing happened?" she asked, not expecting him to suggest open marriage.

"I don't want to lose you, I love you. I don't want you to sacrifice your needs because I can't please you," he said.

"Do you think you would be able to hold me and kiss me, knowing I had been with another man?" she said incredulously.

"I think I could, because I don't want you to be unhappy, and I love having you around," he said candidly.

"Okay," she replied softly, thinking about a hot guy at work and thinking maybe she would have a fling with him. She gave serious thought to Alex's offer, except she couldn't bring herself to do this. She was still a good girl at heart. She began to feel like she was Alex's mother instead of his wife.

She was cleaning their apartment a few days later and stumbled upon a collection of porn videos that had gay men on the front covers. She opened up the video case with the intent to watch what was on the film, thinking to herself that maybe Alex had gay fantasies. Her suspicions were confirmed when she saw a photo fall out of the video case of some guy giving Alex a blow job. She was stunned and stared at that picture for about 30 minutes, her hands shaking. Other than their lack of physical intimacy, she never thought that Alex had gay desires. Finding out Alex liked gay sex was the real reason he wasn't interested in her any longer, she knew she couldn't stay in the relationship. It was over. She confronted him about it that evening.

"Alex, can you explain this?" Holly asked, showing him the incriminating blow job photo.

"Oh, Holly . . . I'm sorry . . . and I'm ashamed. I didn't know how to tell you. I love you and don't want to lose you. That was my first gay experience, and I felt enormous guilt. That is why I haven't initiated sex with you. I don't know what to do," he replied, feeling helpless.

"You cheated on me with a man . . . You can go to hell!" she yelled and continued, "We're over! I'll be filing for divorce. I can't live with a junkie, cheating homo husband, and me having affairs with other men isn't going to make me happy. I didn't sign up for this!"

"I'm not homosexual, I'm bisexual. I've struggled with my sexuality for years and kept it a secret. I had trouble admitting it to

myself,"Alex said with great sadness, sitting on the sofa with his head in his hands.

"You should have been up front with me before we got married. Did you think you could hide it forever? I thought getting married would renew our bond. Apparently you had other motives. You wanted to hide behind our relationship and go have fun with boys," she said with exasperation.

"I understand. It was wrong of me to cheat. I'm a coward who couldn't admit I was having problems. I swear on a stack of Bibles that after I started fooling around with men, I didn't have sex with you at the same time. I just couldn't do that to you, so I made up excuses. Holly, you are a lovely woman, and I know you will find someone else. We've been together a long time. You were my best friend. I'd hate for us to be enemies. I won't give you any trouble with the divorce. I'll sign whatever papers you send me," Alex said, and then began crying.

Holly started to feel a little compassion for the man who had been her best friend and who helped her gain confidence in herself. "Alex, you need to figure out what you want in life. You need to get some help. Stop doing drugs! If you prefer guys, find a boyfriend. You need serious counseling, and I'm not qualified to do that. I have to get on with my life," she replied coldly. At this moment the sight of him filled her with revulsion.

Holly moved out 3 days later. They lived in a small condo that Alex owned, and she took just her personal items. She would get a fresh start in her own place. Several months later, Holly and Alex managed to resurrect a friendship and the divorce was smooth and quick. They kept in touch for a short while and gradually went their separate ways. Her years with Alex helped her gain much-needed self-confidence and become a more optimistic and positive person. He was a good teacher and would have made a wonderful life coach, but he couldn't follow his own advice. She never hated him, and she forgave him for what happened. She wanted a man who would treasure her and recoil at the thought of her fooling around with other men . . .

She noticed that Alex sent her a separate e-mail in addition to the Facebook Friend Request. She opened it to see what he wrote.

Holly, I hope this note reaches you. I have thought of you often over the years and wanted to get back in touch. I live in Lynchburg and drive a truck for a living. I joined a 12-step program after we divorced and have been clean for 9 years. After my experimentation with men, I realized that I prefer women and currently have a girlfriend named Rachel. We have been together 4 years and are going strong. I hope this e-mail finds you doing well and happy with James. I would like to reconnect and be friends . . . if that is okay with you. I hope to hear from you soon, Alex

I'm happy he got himself together. His girlfriend is probably a nice person . . . she would have to be. Maybe I'll stop by to visit them on my next trip down to see my folks. She accepted his friend request and replied to his e-mail:

Alex, it was great to hear from you! Yes, I would love to renew our friendship. I am happy to hear that you got your life back, and that you have someone special. James and I are still together and doing great. I have accepted your friend request and might drop by for a visit the next time I head south to see my parents. Talk to you soon, Holly

I'll see if I can uncover a past life with him tonight. Getting this e-mail has cheered me up. I love to hear from old friends.

She spent another hour on Facebook, checking in on her friends. She didn't use it often; she didn't think her life was interesting enough to post about. She tried to check in once a week. When she was done with Facebook, she went into the kitchen and fixed herself a cup of chamomile tea to help her relax. She turned on the TV and watched a few episodes of Pawn Stars on the History Channel.

What an exciting life I have . . . watching reruns of a reality show on a Friday night by myself . . . she thought sarcastically . . . I wonder if Charlie is enjoying his camping trip in the rain . . .I'll ask him on Monday.

Holly put on her headphones and turned on her CD player when she crawled into bed. For some reason, she was unable to concentrate tonight. Her mind kept wandering aimlessly, thinking about Alex, Charlie, Zumba, James, her parents, etc. She turned off the CD player and took off her headphones and went into the bathroom to take a sleep aid. She kept Benadryl around for nights she couldn't fall asleep. There was something in it that caused her to go out like a light. She never took it to relieve cold or allergy symptoms unless there was a bed nearby. Soon she was sound asleep.

When James left the restaurant in the wee hours of the morning, he noticed Bryce's H3 was parked next to his. The engine was running, and the lights were on. He knew Bryce was there to talk to him. As he walked toward his truck, Bryce got out of his car and greeted him.

"Do you have few minutes to talk?" Bryce asked with authority, sounding like the mob boss that he was.

"What's on your mind?" James replied as he started to sweat.

"I just want to remind you of your responsibilities to Amber and your unborn child. Amber called and told me about what happened. I listened to her story, and she is upset at the way you have been avoiding her. She asked for my help. I'm here tonight on Amber's behalf. I want to make it perfectly clear that I expect you to marry her and be a good husband and father. You don't have any other choice. If you try to skip town, I WILL find you," Bryce said menacingly.

"I will do what you ask. I told Amber that I would marry her. I'm working up the courage to tell Holly," James replied with exhaustion.

"Good," Bryce said and got into his Hummer and drove away.

James wished he had the guts to stand up to Bryce. He didn't. He was too much of a coward. *In my next life, if there is such a thing as reincarnation, I want to come back as a Buddhist monk. Stick me in a monastery and let me chant all day. I'll be short and bald and ugly and won't have to worry about women or the local Mafia. I better get home and enjoy my last days with the best woman on the planet . . .* he thought as he got in his truck to head home.

James got home and walked into the bedroom and saw Holly sleeping soundly as usual. He slipped into bed and snuggled close to her again. *I'll make her favorite chocolate chip pancakes tomorrow . . . I don't have to be at work until 2:30 . . . we'll have some quality time together.* He was completely drained of energy and fell asleep quickly.

James woke up before Holly and went into the kitchen to make the pancakes. The smell of fresh coffee woke her up, and she walked into the kitchen yawning, her eyes still blurry from sleep.

"Good morning, Sleeping Beauty. You look like you need some caffeine," James greeted her warmly, appreciating her more than ever.

"Definitely," she replied as she poured her coffee.

"I'm making chocolate chip pancakes this morning. I hope you're hungry," he said.

"Yes, I'm starved. You're the best," she replied.

No, I'm the worst thing that ever happened to you . . . next to that bisexual pansy ex-husband you had and Roger the wife beater . . . "Thanks, honey," he replied and continued, "Did you have any more regressions last night?"

"No, I tried, but I couldn't concentrate enough to make it happen. My mind was racing, and I was unable to focus," she replied.

"What's on your mind?" he asked.

"Well, I got an e-mail from Alex last night. He's been clean for several years, and he's gone back to women. He has a girlfriend named Rachel and lives in Lynchburg. It was good to hear from him and I'm glad he got his life back. We're Facebook Friends now," she said.

The fudge packer returns . . . I wonder if he really has a girlfriend or if he's trying to make a play for Holly . . . I'm sure she wouldn't be interested in him . . . "That's good news. I think it's great when someone gets themselves straightened out," he replied, secretly not caring one bit.

"How was your night?" she asked.

"Busy as hell. I was out as soon as my head hit the pillow," he replied while flipping over a pancake.

"The pancakes smell wonderful. I'm glad you don't go into work until 2:30. I've really missed you," she said.

"I've missed you too. I'm enjoying the sunflowers in their vases," he remarked, hoping to change the subject. Holly picked the sunflowers on Thursday after work and put them in a large vase on the dining-room table and the rest in a smaller vase on the coffee table in the living room. The flower heads were enormous.

"Me too. I gave some to the neighbors since I didn't have enough vases for them. It was time. They won't be alive much longer," she replied.

I probably won't either . . . "They look great," he said as took the last pancake out of the skillet and put it on a plate. "Food's ready." James fixed them each a plateful of pancakes with warm syrup.

"My God, these are awesome!" Holly exclaimed as she took the first bite.

"Glad you like them," James replied happily . . . *I hope that one day you will be able to forgive me.*

After breakfast and showers, Holly was in the mood for romance. They went into the bedroom and started to fool around. James was unable to perform. His guilty conscious had killed his sex drive.

"What's wrong, James?" she asked him. "This keeps happening. Maybe you should see a doctor. You might have low testosterone."

"You're probably right. I guess it was bound to happen sooner or later. My spirit is willing, but my flesh won't cooperate. I'm sorry, Holly," he said thinking . . . *Right now I feel like I never want to have sex again . . . I'm going to have to keep making excuses . . . My guilt is eating away at me . . . My spirit is the biggest problem, my testosterone is fine.*

"No worries . . . I know you will get things working again. Promise me you will make a doctor's appointment soon," she implored.

"I promise," he replied and kissed her thinking . . . *Soon she'll hate my guts.*

They got dressed and went to the living room to watch TV until it was time for James to leave for work. Holly took her tarot cards out of the box and began to shuffle them thinking about Alex and the upcoming Zumba class. The card she drew from the top of the deck was the Six of Cups.

The Six of Cups shows a boy giving a chalice which contains a single white flower to a little girl outdoors in front of two medieval houses. There are four chalices with white flowers in front of them and a fifth chalice with a white flower sitting on a garden stand behind them. The overall feeling is one of happiness and reconciliation. This card portends that family, old friends, and even old lovers are in the process of adding great joy to your life. It indicates reconciliation, leaving the past behind and possibly making a new friend with whom you find many commonalities.

"Wow, this is on target," Holly says happily.

"What does that one mean?" James asked.

"It portends great happiness from friends and family, reconciliation from someone in your past, and possibly making a new friend. I heard from Alex yesterday, and I'm taking a Zumba class on Monday and Wednesday nights starting this Monday. Maybe I'll make some new friends there," she said.

That is uncanny . . . There might be something to these silly cards . . . Lord knows the one I drew yesterday was appropriate . . . "That's good. When did you decide to take a Zumba class?"

"Patricia told me about it yesterday, and I signed up online. It was a spontaneous decision. You know I've thought about doing this," she replied.

"My hot woman is going to look even hotter," he said with a smile.

"That's right," she agreed and asked James, "Why don't you pick one?"

What have I got to lose . . . I already know I'm doomed . . . "Okay," he said and began shuffling the cards. He drew the Death card.

The Death card shows a skeleton wearing a suit of armor and riding on a white horse. The skeleton is carrying a black flag with a strange-looking white design on it. A priest in gold robes stands in front of the white horse with his arms outstretched and his hands cupped, as if to offer a gift. Next to the priest are two children kneeling in reverence toward the skeleton. Underneath the horse is a man lying dead on the ground. Off in the distance the sun is shining brightly and a sailboat floats in the lake. This card indicates a permanent change in your life and severing ties with your past. The loss will be painful; however, accepting the changes and moving forward is the best course of action.

"Looks like big changes are in store for you," Holly said, slightly concerned.

"Does this mean literal death?" James asked thinking . . . *Bryce promised me a new pair of concrete shoes.*

"Most of the time it means a major change in your life and the loss of someone or something important to you. After Death a new life begins. Don't focus on the negative aspect of the card. That's what Martina advised when I drew the Tower, the worst card in the deck," Holly replied.

I might have to tell Holly sooner rather than later . . . I can't take much more of the guilt . . . These stupid cards of impending disaster don't help either . . . "I'm going to put it out of my mind. I don't want to draw anything negative to me," he said and put the card back in the deck.

"Good idea. I hope, for your sake, that whatever happens isn't too bad. Is there something we need to talk about? Are you worried about something?" she asked him.

"No. Maybe I'll get fired from work and be forced into a new job," he said laughing and pretending to not be concerned.

"They would be crazy to fire the man who created 10 different types of baked macaroni and cheese, the most ordered side item on the menu . . . Although I think a new job would be good for you," she replied.

"I know it would," he said, nodding his head in agreement.

They watched TV for another hour, and then James left for work. *What am I going to do today? . . . It's raining and ugly outside . . . past-life regression . . . I'll see if I can find something about Alex and more about James.* With that thought, she went back into the bedroom to listen to the past-life regression CD . . .

. . . Holly is outside drawing water from a well. She is on a farm and sees two little boys running around chasing chickens. The boys are close in age. One of them looks about 5 years old, the other one is taller and looks to be about 7. It is a comfortable spring day. The sun is shining and a light breeze keeps the day from being too warm.

"Calvin, Caleb, stop scaring the chickens. There is work to be done. Gather up the eggs. We have to go into town soon," she yells to them.

"Calvin started it!" Caleb, the younger one, yells back.

"No, I didn't. Caleb lies, he started it!" Calvin yells in disagreement.

"I don't care who started it, gather the eggs now," she yells to her boys. "Your lousy father hasn't been home for 2 days. He's probably lying in a ravine somewhere," Holly says softly to herself.

She is living somewhere out west in the latter part of the 1800s. She is not a happy woman. Her husband likes to drink at the saloon, and lately he spends more time there than working on the farm. They raise sheep and sell the wool in town, along with providing the local general store and restaurant with fresh eggs. She loves her sons. They help as best as they can.

Caleb and Calvin gather the eggs and bring them to Holly. As they get closer, she recognizes Caleb as Alex Manning. He's a cute little boy with curly blond hair, big blue eyes, and freckles. He has a sunny smile and sweet disposition. She doesn't recognize Calvin. He looks much like Caleb except that his hair is darker and his eyes are brown. He has freckles too.

"Mommy, look, Daddy's here." Calvin points to his father riding toward the house on a brown horse.

"It's about damn time," she says under her breath. She watches her husband ride slowly toward her. As he comes closer, she knows that he is James. He has the same curly blond hair as Caleb, with brown eyes like Calvin's.

Caleb is excited to see his father and runs up to greet him. "Daddy, Daddy . . . Come and see the size of the egg I found this morning," Caleb says breathlessly as he tugs at his father's pant leg.

"Not right now, Caleb, I've got to talk to your mother. Get out of the way or I'll step on you," James says hatefully to him as he dismounts from his horse.

Holly notices the hurt look on Caleb's face. This isn't the first time he has dismissed one of his sons like this. He walks over to Holly, and she notices that he reeks of alcohol. She is angry with her husband, and she lets him have it.

"Thaddeus, you are a selfish jackass! Do you know how bad you smell? Booze, booze, booze. That's all you care about. Ignore your wife and sons and go do as you please. How do you expect us to run the farm when you are never around?" she snaps at him and pushes him away from her as he tries to lean in for a kiss.

"I'm sorry, Mary, sweetie. . . I got carried away. I promise I won't do it again. You know I need a break from this place," Thaddeus pleads to her.

"YOU NEED A BREAK?" she screams these words at him and continues, "What about ME? You think I don't need a break? You are never here. I do the chores, cook, take care of the sheep, the chickens, tend to

the garden, raise two boys, and you thinkYOU NEED A BREAK?" Mary begins to cry as Thaddeus rolls his eyes and stands there with his hands on his hips, looking annoyed.

"Mommy, please don't cry," Caleb says and runs up to her for an embrace. He continues, "When I grow up I'm going to marry you and take you away from Daddy . . ."

Holly comes out of her hypnosis feeling sad . . . *Alex was my son in another life. He was such a sweet little boy wanting to take me away from James . . .What a lousy husband and father he was . . . I probably died an angry, old frontier woman . . . Maybe that's why I have a soft spot for Alex.Yeah, he cheated on me . . . However, he seemed like a lost soul, and I had emotionally checked out of our relationship . . . I must have a latent mothering instinct coming through . . . James was named Thaddeus? How awful.* She laughs long and hard about James being named Thaddeus. Holly laughed for several minutes, and then got up out of bed and went into the living room. It was still raining outside, and she started giggling again about the name Thaddeus. *I can't wait to tell James about this tomorrow . . . I'm going to start calling him Thad.*

The remainder of the day was filled with household chores and laundry, anything to avoid going out in the rain.

It was still pouring rain when Holly went to bed that evening. She could hear it beating against the bedroom window. She wanted to see if she could have another past-life experience. She put on her headphones and focused intently on the narrator's voice . . .

. . . Holly is awakened by voices outside of her house. The voices are in German, yet she understands every word. A chorus of people are chanting . . .

"Burn in hell, you witch . . . burn in hell, burn in hell . . .Witches do the devil's bidding . . ."

She smells smoke and realizes her house is on fire. She runs outside just as the vandals are riding away on horses. She is wearing a thin nightgown. It is dark and cold outside. The townsfolk think she's a witch. She knows that she lives alone and is a widow. She notices that her small barn is burning too, which means her horse, her goats, and her chickens are dead; or they were taken by the vandals.

She turns around to look at her house and sees that it has almost burnt to the ground. Rain begins to fall hard, and it helps to extinguish the fires. She falls to her knees and sobs uncontrollably. She doesn't know what to do. She has no friends or family to turn to. She has no means of travel. If she walks into town they will probably hang or burn her. She gets the impression that the year is sometime in the mid-1500s.

"My life is over. What will I do? Everyone hates me. They think I'm a witch. I just want to help people get well. I'm not doing anything wrong," she says out loud to herself and continues to cry.

She looks up and sees someone coming toward her on horseback. As the stranger gets closer, she sees that it is a man. He steps off his horse and walks over to her.

"What happened, miss?" the stranger asks her.

"They burned down my house and barn. They think I'm a witch. Please believe me, sir, I'm not a witch! I am a midwife, and I make herbal elixirs to help heal the sick. I am alone. My husband died 3 years ago. They destroyed EVERYTHING. I have nothing to live for," she says to him through her tears.

"I believe you. My name is Marcus, what is yours?" he asks softly.

"My name is Ursula," she replies as she looks into his face. She realizes that she is looking at James. He is a big man with sharp facial features and blue eyes. His hair is covered by his hat.

"Ursula, do you have any family you can stay with?" he asks.

Ursula is shivering from the cold and replies, "No. I'm alone in the world. I have no family and no friends."

"Come with me. We'll take refuge in the next town, and I'll help you get back on your feet," Marcus tells her.

"I would just be a hindrance to you," she replies.

"No, you would not. I want to help. Let's go," he said.

She follows Marcus to his horse. He helps her up, and then he gets on. She wraps her arms around his waist, lays her head on his back, and they ride away . . .

Holly wakes up and is happy to be back in her comfortable bed. *James saved me . . . We were speaking German . . . This is incredible. I can't wait to tell him that he saved a damsel in distress. Let's see, I have been Japanese, Italian, German, English, Atlantean . . . What else is back there?* She no longer hears the rain beating against the window and hopes that tomorrow will be a nicer day.

CHAPTER 8

A New Friend

James was having a busy night at the restaurant. The rain seemed to bring everyone out to dinner. He was able to take a short, 15-minute break later that evening. He went to his truck and turned on the radio. He sat there for a few minutes with his eyes closed, thinking about how badly he had screwed up his life when he heard a knock on the passenger window. He looked over and saw Amber standing there with an umbrella. *I might as well talk to her; she's going to be my wife . . . I'm going to have a shotgun wedding at the age of 54.* He unlocked the door so she could get in.

"Are you on a break?" he asked her.

"Yes," Amber replied as she collapsed her umbrella, stepped into his truck, and closed the door.

"What's on your mind?" he asked her.

"Are you going to tell Holly soon?"

"Yes, within the next 2 weeks."

"What are your plans after you tell her about us?" she asked, hoping for some reassurance that he would move in with her.

James let out a heavy sigh and said, "I'm certain she'll kick me out. It's her house. She pays the mortgage."

"Where do you plan to stay when she kicks you out?"

"I haven't thought that far," he replied, looking down at his hands and knowing that his answer would make Amber angry, and not caring if it did.

"You should stay with me. We're getting married and having a baby together," Amber said in a hateful tone of voice . . . *I assumed he would move in with me and he hasn't even thought about it.*

James was silent for a few moments. He looked out the truck window into the dark night and had a miserable feeling of ill forebode. "Are you sure this is what you want?" he asked her with resignation, looking her in the eyes and wishing he had never met her.

"Yes, since we are going to be married, the logical thing is to move in with me once she kicks you out," Amber states, her tone more pleading than hateful.

"I can't promise you love. I realize this is not totally your fault. I blame myself too. It was wrong of me to start up with you while I was in a committed relationship with Holly. It was wrong of you to trap me like this. I will support you and the baby financially, and I will be there to help care for it. You can't trap a guy and expect him to love you," James said, thinking . . . *Hell, right now, I don't even like you.*

"I have to get back to work. I'll talk to you later," Amber said with indifference as she got out of his truck, slamming the door with force.

In the rearview mirror, he watched her walk back to the restaurant. The rain had stopped. *She wants a real relationship with me . . . That's going to take time, if ever. I'll marry her to keep Bryce off of my back, although I don't know if I can fall in love with her. I guess I should try. I won't ever fool around again . . . The consequences are too high, and I'm getting too old for this crap.* A few minutes later, James got out of the truck and went back into the restaurant to finish his shift.

Holly didn't hear James come home. He slipped quietly into bed and pulled her close, thinking . . . *I wish I could take it back . . . I'd love you forever. I'm such an idiot.* The next morning Holly woke up first. She was sitting at the dining-room table drinking her second cup of coffee and reading the paper when James walked in.

"Good morning," she said happily.

"Good morning . . . You're in a good mood," he said as he poured his coffee.

"I had some interesting past-life regressions last night, and you were in both of them," she replied with a teasing look.

"What did I do this time?" he asked with an amused look on his face, as he walked to the dining-room table and sat across from her.

"Your name was Thaddeus, and you were a lousy, dirty, alcoholic husband who was mean to our children. We lived out west; it was a frontier life in the late 1800s. We had two boys named Calvin and Caleb. I recognized Caleb as Alex Manning . . . We were his parents!" she said and started to laugh.

"Thaddeus? I was named Thaddeus?" James said and began to laugh hysterically . . . *Enjoy these moments while I still can.*

"Yes, dear . . . and you were hateful to Alex/Caleb. He said he was going to marry me when he grew up and take me away from you," she informed him.

That statement hurts. I know Holly will find another man, although I don't think it will be Alex. "What was the other past life?" he asked.

"You rescued me; I was a damsel in distress. It was Germany in the 1500s. Some townspeople burned down my house and barn and left me with nothing. They were trying to kill me. They thought I was a witch. I was crying in the rain and you were riding by on your horse. I told you what happened and you said you would help me start over. Your name was Marcus and you helped me onto your horse, and we rode off together, and then I woke up," she said.

"I like the name Marcus better than Thaddeus," James stated and continued, "I'm delighted to hear that you had at least one happy past life with me. Do you want me to fix breakfast this morning?"

"I don't want you to go to any trouble. Cereal and milk is fine with me," she replied.

"Me too," James said and went to fix himself a bowl of cereal.

"How was work last night?" Holly asked.

"Busy," he replied and sat back down at the table. "What are your plans for today?"

"Grocery shopping."

The rest of the morning passed without incident. Holly decided not to initiate a romantic encounter with James; she didn't want to deal with another awkward situation. They watched TV together until it was time for him to leave for work.

"I have next Saturday night off. I haven't been free on a Saturday night in a long time. We should plan to go out on the town," James said . . . *That will be our last night out together . . . because then I have to tell you that I knocked up my secret lover.*

"That's great! We'll definitely do something," she replied with enthusiasm.

He kissed her good-bye and left for work. It was overcast and cool outside. The feel of autumn was in the air. Holly went grocery shopping and spent the remainder of the day relaxing and looking forward to her Zumba class tomorrow night. When evening comes, she isn't in the mood to explore any more past lives. She would get back to that later.

Monday arrived and Holly woke up before the alarm went off. James was tired physically and emotionally and didn't get out of bed until Holly was ready to leave.

"You must have had a rough night," she said to him as he walked into the living room.

"It was moderately busy. I'm just tired and burned out," he replied and sat down on the sofa, leaning his head back . . . *I feel like hell!*

"The coffee is ready whenever you are; I've got to get going," Holly said and bent down to kiss him.

"Have a nice day, honey. Enjoy your class tonight," he said with a smile.

"Thanks. See you later," she said and walked out the door to her car.

On her walk from the Metro station to the office, she noticed how beautiful it was this morning. There was a chill in the air; it was cool enough for a sweater or light jacket. The sun was shining and the temperature was forecasted to reach a high of 60 degrees. It currently felt like 45. She suddenly thought about Charlie . . . *I wonder how his camping trip went . . . I didn't think much about him this weekend. I was focused on James and the surprise e-mail from Alex. Hopefully, I'm getting over my crush and won't be plagued by sexy fantasies whenever I talk to him. I'll make a point to talk to him today and see how it makes me feel.*

She settled into her office and took care of the usual tasks, checking e-mail and calendars. She was curious about Charlie's weekend and couldn't resist the urge to go see him. She took the elevator to his office. The floor and offices were quiet this morning. She saw that Charlie's light was on and she knocked on his door.

"Holly, good to see you, come in," he greeted her warmly as he looked up from a report he was reading.

"Hi, Charlie. How was your weekend? Did you get rained out?" she asked as she walked into his office.

"It was okay. We got some heavy rain, but it wasn't constant. We managed to do some fishing and a lot of drinking," he said with a laugh and continued, "Did you do anything fun?"

"No, the heavy rain on Friday night and Saturday kept me from wanting to go anywhere. I just did my usual chores and went grocery shopping yesterday. I live such an exciting life," she said sarcastically. "I'm glad you had a good time. I thought the rain would have ruined it."

She thought about me . . . It's a start . . . She was on my mind most of the weekend . . . She looks beautiful today . . . he thought. Charlie noticed how her expression softened when he talked to her. He held her eyes for a few moments without speaking, and she felt herself melting inside again . . . *I'm not over my crush on this man . . . I feel like I'm floating on a cloud whenever he's around.* Still holding her gaze, he continued the conversation.

"Have you been able to explore any more past lives?" he asked.

"Yes, I uncovered a few of them," she said . . . *Should I tell him about them . . . It might be okay to tell him about the Japanese prostitute one . . . I'm not ready to divulge that we were secret lovers.*

With a slightly embarrassed look she said, "You'll probably laugh at this. I uncovered a past life where I was a Japanese prostitute back in the 1600s. My ex-husband was the house pimp, and we got into a fight over money that he stole from me and I choked him to death. A friend helped me throw his body into the moat while no one was watching."

Charlie laughed and replied with a smile, "He probably deserved it."

"It feels weird to talk about these things. I hope you don't think I'm crazy," she said apprehensively.

"Holly, the subject of reincarnation is fascinating, and I don't think you're crazy. I think it's awesome that you chose to explore it," he replied, hoping that he sounded reassuring.

Mitch Devlin was passing by and stuck his head into Charlie's office. "We have to leave in 15 minutes. I'll meet you at my car in the garage," he said and continued to his own office.

"We have a meeting in Maryland," Charlie said to Holly.

"I'll get back to work. Good talking with you, Charlie," she said as she turned to leave his office.

"Stop by anytime, Holly," he said as she looked back at him and smiled.

I love the way he looks at me . . . I feel things I haven't felt in years . . . she thought as she made her way back to her office. *In my next life, I will request to be with him.* She spent the rest of the day compiling inputs she received for a report that Stan needed to review. She was excited when quitting time came and was looking forward to the Zumba class tonight.

She went home first and changed into her workout clothes. The class started at 7:00. She ate a protein bar for dinner, fed the cat, and then braved rush-hour traffic to get to the Wakefield Recreation Center. She registered at the front desk and went into the gym to wait for class to start. Patricia was already there and talking to a pretty blond woman. She saw Holly and waved to her to come over.

"Holly, I want you to meet Alyssa Thomas. She's a fellow workout freak like us," Patricia said when Holly walked up.

"Hi, Alyssa, it's nice to meet you," Holly smiled and extended her hand to the tall blond woman. Alyssa looked to be about the same age as her and in great shape.

"You both can call me Lisa. It's nice to meet you too. I had some reservations about taking this class. I thought most of the women would be 20- and 30-somethings. I'm relieved to meet some women closer to my own age," Lisa replied and continued, "Do you and Patricia live near each other?"

"We work at the same company, Military Technology Analysis," Patricia replied.

Lisa laughed and said, "You probably know my ex-husband. He works for that company."

"What's his name?" Holly asked.

"Charlie Thomas. I kept his name when we divorced because it sounds better than my maiden name, which is Bumble, like a bee," Lisa replied with a little laugh.

Holly's heart started to beat faster . . . *This must be the pistol that wrecked his truck and pummeled a contractor,* she thought . . . *She doesn't seem like a maniac to me, and she's really pretty.* Patricia was a little stunned too, and she replied back, "Yes, we know Charlie. What a coincidence."

"I'm dating a new man now, and he's great," Lisa quickly replied, starting to feel uncomfortable and thinking maybe she shouldn't have asked if they knew Charlie.

"I've been through a few men myself," Holly said to Lisa, wanting to ease her slight discomfort. "Where do you work?"

"I work for Powell, Brink, and Richards Financial Services. I'm a CPA," she replied.

"I'm a systems engineer, and Holly is an executive assistant. Our asses would be huge if we didn't get regular exercise," Patricia said lightheartedly.

"She's right. My other half is a chef at American Steak and Bistro. He's a fantastic cook. We try to eat healthy, but I'm stuck on his baked macaroni and cheese. We know where that accumulates," Holly replied laughing.

The instructor arrived and everyone quieted down to begin the workout. Holly, Patricia, and Lisa hung together in the back of the class. The class lasted an hour and at the end of the session, the three of them were exhausted.

"That was punishment," Patricia said to them.

"Yeah, however, in a good way," Holly replied.

"I'm thirsty. Would you two like to join me for an iced tea? There's a McDonald's just up the street," Lisa asked them.

"Thank you, Lisa, maybe next time. I just want to go home and hit the sack. I feel my age right now," Patricia replied.

"Actually, she has a terrific husband waiting for her at home. That's the real reason," Holly said and winked at Patricia.

"Seriously, ladies, I'm referring to sleep, not sex," Patricia said with a smirk.

"I'm thirsty too. I'll meet you there," Holly said to Lisa.

"Great. Let's go," Lisa replied.

The three of them walked to their cars, and Patricia headed home. Holly followed Lisa to the McDonald's 1 mile up the street. They got their iced teas and sat down at a nearby table to talk. Holly discovered that Lisa was very chatty and open.

"Did you like the class?" Lisa asked Holly.

"Yes. I thought it was fun, but I hope I can get out of bed tomorrow morning," Holly replied.

"Me too. Are you married?" Lisa asked.

"No, I have a long-term significant other, James. We've been together for 11 years. I'm twice divorced and didn't want to get married a third time. James has never been married. It's worked out well for us," Holly replied.

"I think it's great that you didn't marry a third time. Marriage is a hassle, and I've been married twice too," Lisa said and continued. "One reason I'm taking this class is to help work out some of my aggression. I've had a bad temper my entire life, and it cost me two marriages. My first husband, Bryan, cheated on me with my best friend, and I beat him up and divorced him. My second husband, Charlie, was a good man, but I was a hot mess. I totaled his car chasing down a man who cut me off in traffic, and then I punched a contractor in the nose who messed up a construction project on our house. The neighbors heard me screaming at the contractor and called the police. The cops were coming around the corner as I punched and pummeled the contractor. They arrested me for assault. The contracting company pressed charges and I spent 90 days in jail and was fined $2,500. That was the final straw for Charlie, and he initiated the divorce. I didn't blame him. I took my bad moods out on him. I manage to behave myself when I'm dating a guy but as soon as I make a commitment, my real personality comes out. I've been taking anger management classes for several years, and they have helped me immensely. I feel so much better these days. Spending time in the slammer forced me to change."

"Well, kudos to you for working to get a grip on your anger. My first husband was a wife beater in training, and my second husband was hooked on cocaine and having an affair with a man," Holly replied, and then asked, "Do you have any children?"

"Yes, I have a son from my marriage to Bryan. His name is Glenn, and he lives in Chicago. He's an investment banker. What about you?" Lisa asked.

"No children. I don't think I was meant to have them. I'm 45, and I think my time has passed. I've had a happy life for the most part, and in spite of two ex-husbands," Holly replied.

"I hear you. One kid was enough for me. I don't think I will ever marry again either. I've been dating a guy for 3 months now, and things are going great. I'm open to living with him. It's moving pretty fast," Lisa said. "Hey, would you like to double-date with me and Roger this weekend? Ask Patricia if she wants to come too."

"James is off this Saturday, and we were planning to go out. I'll ask him if he wants to do the double or triple date thing. I think it would be fun!" Holly exclaimed. "I'll let you know on Wednesday at our next session."

"Great. Don't forget to ask Patricia too," Lisa said.

"Okay, I'll see her tomorrow," Holly replied. Lisa and Holly finished their iced teas and walked to their cars. "It was fun talking to you, Lisa. Drive home safely," Holly said to her new friend.

"You too. See you Wednesday," Lisa replied cheerfully.

As Holly drove home she thought about Charlie and Lisa. *I don't believe in coincidence . . . This is too much . . . I really like Lisa. I think we could be great friends. It's good that she's sought help for her anger issues . . . How funny is this. Charlie and Lisa are my two new buddies. He might hate his ex-wife. I don't think I'll tell him I met Lisa*. It was dark when she got home, and she took a shower and went to bed.

When the alarm went off the next morning, Holly felt muscle aches in places she never had before. She walked slowly into the kitchen and felt like an old woman. *I think I'll practice the stretches they showed us last night. I want to be able to move on Wednesday.* She took two granola bars from the pantry and poured herself a glass of milk and sat at the dining-room table. James got up and came into the kitchen as she was eating.

"How was your class last night?" he asked, rubbing the sleep out of his eyes.

"It was great . . . and now I'm really, really sore," she laughed. "I made a new friend, Lisa, and she invited us to triple date on Saturday night with her boyfriend and Patricia and Andy. Are you up for it?"

"Sure, that sounds like fun. Wherever you want to go is fine with me," he said.

"Excellent. We haven't been out with another couple in ages," Holly said. "How was work last night?"

"Slow. Slow nights are worse than busy ones," he said thinking . . . *At least when I'm busy I don't have time to think about my problems.*

Holly finished getting ready and kissed James good-bye. As she got into her car for the drive to the Metro, she was looking forward to talking to Patricia about the class last night and meeting Lisa.

She was beginning to like the chill in the morning air even though it meant the days were getting shorter. She delighted in the crisp breeze and sunny skies on her walk to the office. A tall man in the distance caught her eye. Charlie was walking far ahead of her . . . *I'm going out with your ex-wife this Saturday . . . I really like her, and we have a lot in common . . . If I were dating you it would be weird . . . Sometimes I wish I was dating you . . .You inspire me in ways you'll never know . . .* she thought as she watched him disappear into a crowd of people.

The Zumba workout left Holly feeling tired, yet relaxed enough that she could focus more clearly on her work. She was concentrating intently on a report when Patricia knocked on her door.

"Good morning," Patricia said happily.

"Hey, there. How do you feel today?" Holly asked as she looked up, slightly startled.

"Sore . . . I feel my age this morning, although I enjoyed the class and want to continue with it," Patricia replied quickly.

"Same here. I felt like an old woman when I got out of bed," Holly said.

"What did you think of Charlie's ex-wife?" Patricia asked excitedly.

"I like her. We got better acquainted when we went to McDonald's. She's taking anger management classes and said she has struggled with a bad temper her entire life. She's been married twice, like me. I think there is hope for her; she's dating a new man she really likes . . . I can't remember his name. She invited us out with her and her boyfriend on Saturday night. She wanted me to pass that along to you. James is off Saturday night, and he wants to go out with them. I hope you and Andy can come along," Holly said.

"That should be a fun evening. I'll ask Andy tonight. I'm sure he'll want to go. Are you going to tell Charlie that you are friends with his ex?" Patricia asked.

"No, there isn't a reason to tell him; we're not dating or anything," she replied.

"It's a shame. If you weren't already taken, Charlie is someone I would choose for you," Patricia said with a sigh.

"If I wasn't with James, you know I would be on Charlie like white on paper," Holly replied giggling. "I think we both need to get back to work now."

"I'll talk to you later," Patricia said and turned to leave.

"Have a nice day," Holly replied and went back to working on her report. She thought to herself, *I didn't choose a tarot card this morning . . . I probably don't need to draw one every day. I think the influence of the Six of Cups is still with me; I made a new friend last night. I'm glad I signed up for Zumba. I think I'll have another cup of coffee . . . I'm beginning to feel tired, and it's only 9:30.*

James decides to go running before taking a shower. The cool and sunny morning was calling him and a good run helped to clear his head. He didn't have to be at work until early afternoon. He ran through the subdivision on his way to a nearby shopping center. He wasn't the type to go running while listening to headphones. His shady past had taught him to be keenly aware of his surroundings. As he was running up the sidewalk, he heard a vehicle pull up and follow close behind him. The driver rolled down his window, and James could hear the words to an old AC/DC song, "Dirty Deeds," playing loudly. He stopped and turned around and saw that it was Bryce in his H3.

"Hey, Macklin . . . Enjoying the lovely morning?" Bryce said ominously, his eyes hidden behind sunglasses.

"Bryce, what are you doing here?" James asked, trying to appear calm and cool.

"I was just passing by and saw you running . . . Are you running to or from something?" Bryce asked him.

"I like to go running before work sometimes," James replied.

"I just wanted to say hello. Enjoy your morning," Bryce said with a menacing smile.

"Yeah, you too," James replied and continued his run up the sidewalk as Bryce drove away. *Just my luck that he would be Amber's cousin. He's going to be watching me for the rest of my life.*

James started his shift at 2:30. Amber would be working later that evening. He imagined what life might be like with her. He had uncomfortable thoughts of Bryce checking up on them frequently and Amber reporting to him any perceived infraction. He had an image of them enjoying Thanksgiving dinner and Bryce staring at him with a smug look on his face. *Just one big happy family . . . Maybe I should hit the road and go on the run . . . Nah, I'd never get away with it . . . Bryce has eyes and ears everywhere . . . I'd be going about my life, and when I least expect it, a bullet would hit me between the eyes.*

Later that evening, Amber pulled him aside and showed him the picture of her ultrasound; they were going to have a little girl. "I want to name her Isabella Maria," she said her face aglow with maternal love. "Do you like that name? If not, we can pick another one. My grandmother's name was Isabella Maria Valenti. She was from Sicily. Or we could go with an Irish name from my father's side."

She has Italian roots . . . It makes sense that Bryce is a local Mafia kingpin . . . he thought sarcastically. "I like that name, it's pretty," he said softly, picturing a sweet little blue-eyed girl that looked like Amber and feeling a flicker of excitement which took him by surprise.

"Good, then we will name her Isabella Maria," Amber said with joy.

"I've got to get back to work. Thanks for showing me the picture," James said, having mixed feelings and surprising himself by feeling a small inkling of fatherly pride.

He'll come around as soon as he leaves Holly, and that won't be soon enough . . . Amber thought as she watched him walk back into the kitchen.

Holly was fast asleep when James got home that night. He watched her sleeping and wanted to cry, feelings of remorse and love welling up inside of him . . . *I'm going to make the break soon . . . this Sunday after our night out.* He drank a glass of wine to calm his nerves and then slipped into bed next to her.

Holly had an uneventful day at work and was excited to get to Zumba on Wednesday night. She was almost late due to heavy traffic and rushed into the gym as the instructor began the workout. She looked toward the back of the class and saw Patricia and Lisa and went to join them.

"We thought you bailed on us," Patricia said to Holly.

"No way . . . I love this stuff," she replied happily and joined in.

The women gave it their best effort for the next hour and collapsed on the bleachers when class was over.

"I'm going to sleep good tonight," Lisa said, slightly out of breath. "Patricia said she and Andy will join us on Saturday night, are you in?"

"We'll be there!" Holly said enthusiastically.

"How did James manage to get time off on a Saturday night?" Patricia asked.

"Every now and then the restaurant gives him a Saturday off for good behavior," Holly said jokingly. "So, where are we going this weekend?"

"I was thinking about the Carlyle Grand Café in Shirlington," Lisa said.

"Yes, that place is awesome. I think James knows one of the chefs," Holly replied.

"I agree. Are you going to make reservations?" Patricia asked Lisa.

"I will. This is going to be fun," Lisa said with a smile.

"I'm exhausted. Let's head home and get some rest," Holly said to them.

"Good idea," Lisa and Patricia said in unison and laughed at their perfectly timed response.

The three ladies walked out together and got into their cars for the drive home. *I am really excited about Saturday night . . . The last fun time I had was the evening I got drunk with Charlie . . . That was a crazy night . . .* Holly thought as she pulled onto the highway. Once she arrived home, she took a shower and went to bed. She discovered that she was so tired she couldn't sleep. She got up and took a Benadryl and lay back down. Then she decided to listen to her past-life regression CD. She was thinking about Lisa and wondering if she knew her from a past life. . .

. . . Emily is drinking brandy to numb the pain of losing David and reading a book when she hears a knock on the door. She gets up and opens the door to find Lisa standing there with a sullen look on her face. Emily now recognizes this nineteenth-century Lisa as her new twenty-first-century friend Lisa. Lisa begins to speak angrily to Emily. "I wanted to stop by to let you know that I am leaving, and I hope to never see your face again. I know that David did not rape you, and that Clive killed him in a jealous rage.You and David broke my heart. I will forever hate you for that, and I do not blame Clive for killing him . . . I might have done it myself if I had walked in on the two of you having sex in my bed.You are a horrible, despicable person. I cannot believe you were once my best friend."

Emily feels two inches tall and terribly ashamed. She replies softly, "You have every right to hate me, and I hate myself for everything that happened. I am truly sorry for the affair with David. I was upset with you for ending our friendship and jealous of you being married to him. I have not been happy with Clive for a long time. He is abusive and cruel. I will not lie to you, had we remained friends, the affair still might have happened, although I would have tried harder to resist temptation. I loved David, and wish I had been killed along with him. Lisa, I wish you well and hope that you find someone to love.You certainly deserve that."

Lisa throws her hands up in annoyance and continues to chastise Emily."And I hope that you rot in hell.The neighbors have been talking. They look upon you as a shameful whore, and you will be whispered about and shunned in social circles. I bid you good riddance." Lisa turned and walked away in a hurry. Emily stood there ashamed and wished that Clive had killed her too . . .

Holly came out of her hypnosis with a feeling of astonishment . . . *How can it be? I meet the same Lisa again in this life, and she was married to Charlie . . . and I am friends with both of them . . . She was named Lisa in that life too . . . This is spooky . . . Obviously I didn't rot in hell . . . Not that I remember anyway . . . At least I wasn't responsible for the breakup of their marriage in this life . . . although it is strange that I bought them a greeting card and a gift card back when they first got married, before I ever met Lisa, and Charlie was just some new guy in the company . . . Was there some kind of karmic justice for doing that, even though I was completely unaware of ANY of this at the time? What other little bits of karma are waiting for me?* Holly thought as she sat up in bed and shook her head. She was feeling the effects of the Benadryl and took off her headphones, put them on the dresser, put her head on the pillow, and drifted off to sleep. The rest of the week seemed to fly by, and Saturday night arrived quickly.

CHAPTER 9

Three Swords in the Tower (and a Mallet)

Lisa and Roger arrived at the restaurant early to wait for the rest of the group. They waited outside in front of the building and watched people come and go. The early evening air was crisp and invigorating. The sun was setting, and the sky was clear. It would soon be filled with stars. People were out and about on the street, enjoying the pleasant evening.

"This is a nice place; I think we'll have a great time tonight," Roger said to Lisa, pulling her close and kissing her. "You look fantastic, I'm a lucky man."

"Thank you, honey," Lisa replied with a smile. "Hey, there's Patricia and her husband . . . Patricia! Over here."

Patricia saw Lisa waving and walked over with Andy in tow.

"Hi, Lisa. This is my husband, Andy," Patricia introduced her husband.

"Good to meet you," Andy replied warmly and shook her hand.

"Good to meet you too. This is my boyfriend, Roger," she replied.

"It's a pleasure, sir," Roger said, shaking Andy's hand.

"Are you into working out like these women are?" Andy asked

Roger with a friendly smile.

"I work out when I can. Lisa is a wonderful influence on me. She's helped me drop 20 pounds," Roger replied happily.

"There's Holly . . . Holly, over here," Lisa called out and waved to her friend across the street.

Roger's heart began to pound wildly when he caught sight of Holly. When Holly noticed Roger with Lisa, she almost forgot how to walk . . . She stopped in her tracks.

"What's wrong?" James asked.

Holly knew she had to quickly recover. She took off one of her high heels, shook it, and said, "That's Roger . . . my ex-husband . . . I'm pretending I have something stuck in my shoe."

James laughed heartily and said, "This is incredible" . . . *I'm glad I'm not the only one who has things like this happen to them . . . like seeing my secret lover when I'm in the grocery store with Holly.*

She puts her shoe back on and they walked over to the rest of the group. James was holding her hand, and he noticed it was cold.

"Holly, are you trying to smuggle strange things in your shoe?" Lisa asked her.

Holly laughed and said, "No, it felt like a small rock was stuck in my shoe . . . I think I got it out. This is James, my other half," she said happily as she introduced him to Lisa.

"I've heard nice things about you, Lisa. It's a pleasure," James said, shaking her hand.

"And I've heard you are one hell of a chef," Lisa replied, shaking his hand. "This is my boyfriend, Roger."

James extended his hand to Roger and said, "Roger, nice to meet you." . . .*You don't look like a monster . . . but I'd like to punch you for kicking Holly in the stomach.*

"My pleasure," Roger returned, sizing up James and thinking . . . *He's a big dude. I wouldn't want to fight him.*

Holly and Roger looked at each other and pretended to make

nice for the sake of social company. Holly made the first move. "Roger, it's nice to meet you," she said, extending her hand with a polite smile thinking . . . *He looks better than he did on TV . . . Maybe he's no longer an asshole . . . I knew this was going to happen, that I would cross his path eventually.*

"And you too," Roger said, returning her smile and shaking her hand, noticing that it was cold and clammy. *She must be as nervous as I am* . . . he thought . . . *She looks absolutely beautiful. It was funny that she stopped in her tracks and pretended to shake something out of her shoe when she first saw me.*

"We both know Patricia and Andy. I'm hungry, let's go eat," Holly said happily to the group.

The six of them entered the restaurant and were seated at a large round table. Holly and Roger ended up sitting directly across from each other. The group pondered over the menu, and then placed their orders. It was time for general conversation. Holly decided to strike up conversation with Roger.

"Roger, I saw you on TV recently. I think it's great that your company has done so well. Are you excited to be in the Washington area?" she asked him politely.

"Yes, I am. I'm seriously considering making this area my home base and hiring someone to oversee the California operation . . . I don't like being away from my girl," Roger replied and placed his hand in Lisa's.

"Isn't he the best? See, someone remembers you from TV," Lisa gushed, and kissed him on the cheek.

"You two make a nice couple," Holly replied thinking . . . *I hope he treats you right . . . If he doesn't, I imagine you could really kick his ass.*

"I understand where you're coming from, Roger . . . I've been with Patricia for 32 years, and I still don't like to be away from her for any length of time," Andy said.

Patricia blushed and replied, "We must be soul mates."

"What do you guys like to do for fun?" Roger asked the men.

"Play golf and tennis," Andy replied.

"I practice target shooting and go running. Holly and I both like to work out on our Total Gym. I've never played golf though," James replied.

"Me too. I enjoy target shooting and playing golf. Andy, James and I will have to take you shooting with us, and we can teach James how to play golf," Roger said cheerfully.

"Anytime," Andy replied.

"What do you say, James? Are you interested in learning to play golf?" Roger asked, thinking . . . *I'm curious to get to know this man. There's something about him that doesn't seem right.*

"Sure, why not," James lied, thinking . . . *This is the first and last time I'll ever be together with this group because Holly's going to kick me out on my ass tomorrow.*

The group continued to banter about hobbies and work until the food was served. The conversation flowed for another half hour after they finished eating. The waiter brought the check, and Roger insisted on paying for everyone's dinner.

"This is on me. I hope everyone enjoyed their food," Roger said as he took the bill and pulled out his credit card.

"Are you sure, Roger? Can we at least contribute to the tip?" Andy asked him.

"I guess that's okay. I don't mind picking up the tab. I'm a happy man. I have a beautiful, magical woman, and my company is winning contracts left and right. I feel like paying it forward. I insist," he said eagerly.

"Thanks, Roger, we appreciate it," James said to him.

"Absolutely, we do. Everyone, chip in something for the tip and we'll give the waiter something to be happy about," Andy said to the group. The remaining five of them chipped in almost $80 for the tip.

They walked outside and said their good nights. As Roger and Lisa were walking to their car, he decided to tell her about his past with Holly. "Lisa, I have something I need to tell you."

"Sure, honey, what is it?" she asked.

"Well, I'm going to bluntly say this. Holly is my first ex-wife," Roger said and took a deep breath.

Lisa was surprised by this, and she was speechless for a few seconds, looking at Roger. Then she spoke, "Oh my God, this is the same Holly that you kicked in the stomach? This is amazing. I think you should take her to lunch and apologize for treating her so badly back then."

"You're okay with me doing that?" he asked in disbelief.

"Yes, Roger. If I had the opportunity to apologize to my previous ex-husbands for being a Grade-A bitch, I would jump at the chance, even the one who cheated on me. I guess I'm becoming a nice person in my old age. The years of anger management classes are working, and I really like Holly. I can see us being friends for life. We have a lot in common," she replied and continued, "She works downtown, probably not too far from you. I'll give you her phone number and you call her on Monday."

"Yes, ma'am, your wish is my command. How on earth did I get so lucky to find you?" Roger said and pulled her close for a hug.

"We are meant to be . . . Two mean and angry people who learned how to play nice with others," she said with a laugh and continued, "What did you think of James?"

Roger and Lisa released each other from their embrace. He looked at her and said, "He seems nice enough, except I have a bad feeling about him . . . Something isn't right."

"That's what I think too," Lisa replied fervently and continued, "He seems like a mismatch for Holly, although I don't know why I think that. It's just a feeling I get. It wouldn't stop me from wanting to go out with them again though."

"Me either. I think we would have a good time with them. That is, if Holly doesn't tell me to go hell when I ask her to lunch," Roger said.

"She won't, trust me," Lisa replied.

Holly was quiet on the ride back home. James didn't like the silence and asked her, "What's on your mind?"

"Oh, I was just going over the evening in my head. I'm still a little shocked at everything. Roger doesn't seem like a bad guy anymore, and Lisa is crazy about him. I think they are a good fit. I don't believe in coincidence. I was meant to cross paths with Roger again, for some reason," Holly said thinking . . . *I was meant to meet Lisa. I stole Charlie from her in a previous life, and Roger killed him . . . Can things get any more bizarre?*

James laughed and said, "I don't believe in the spiritual things you do, but I think everything happens for a reason. That's the only spiritual thing I believe."

"Well, I guess there is some hope for you," Holly replied jokingly. "Did you have a good time tonight?"

"Yeah, it was good to see Patricia and Andy again, and I like Lisa. Roger seems to be okay. I still have an issue with him being abusive to you when you were married," James replied.

"So do I. I haven't forgotten how mean he was to me, even though he seemed nice tonight. Lisa struggled with her temper for a long time and it cost her two marriages. I think if Roger tried to physically hurt her, she would do him in," Holly said.

Holly tried to initiate romance with James after they got back home and settled in front of the TV. She curled up close to him on the sofa and started to kiss him. Romance was the last thing he wanted, however.

"Let's go to bed and not go to sleep," Holly suggested to James with the look of love in her eyes.

"Honey, I'm way too tired, and I've got to be at work for the breakfast shift. I need to get some sleep," he replied thinking . . . *I hope she buys that . . . I'm going to have to break the news to her tomorrow.*

"Okay, as you wish," she said dejectedly, and they got up and went into the bedroom for sleep.

James woke up early Sunday morning and made coffee; Holly was still asleep. He noticed her tarot card deck on the dining-room table and decided he would shuffle it and draw a card. He thought about the mess he made of his life and what he had to tell Holly today, and picked a card. The card he turned up was the Tower. *I don't like the looks of this one . . . Holly mentioned she drew this card when she visited the psychic . . . I'm not even going to look up the meaning. I know what's going to happen. I'm going to put these cards back in the box and never look at them again.* With that thought, James put them back in the box and placed them in the same spot on the table. He drank a cup of coffee, and then took a shower.

The smell of coffee woke Holly up, and she stayed in bed for a few minutes thinking about last night. She didn't feel like seeing James this morning and was hurt that he had spurned her affection. *I should be more understanding about this . . . He's not getting any younger . . . I would understand if he truly had an erectile problem, however . . . I can't shake the feeling that something else is going on . . . He's still hiding something . . . I felt it in his kiss last night.* She waited until she heard him get into the shower, and then she made her way to the kitchen. She opened the dining-room curtains so she could look into the backyard. She noticed that the trees were getting their autumn colors, and that made her smile. She sipped her coffee and tried to come to life.

James finished his shower and got dressed. He didn't feel good. He didn't want to tell Holly before he left for work, and he could feel uneasiness from her even though he hadn't seen her yet this morning. He walked into the dining room to tell her good-bye. They locked eyes and he noticed that she looked different somehow; he couldn't explain it, he could only feel it.

"Well, I'm on my way to fix breakfast for the crowds," James said, hoping he sounded normal.

"Have a good day," Holly responded coolly, not moving to kiss him good-bye.

"Don't I get a good-bye kiss?" James asked her.

"Sure, come over here and I'll kiss you," she replied nonchalantly.

James walked over and they kissed good-bye. "I'll see you later tonight," he said.

"Drive safe," she replied, her voice flat and emotionless.

James left the house and got in his truck . . . *I'll tell her when I get home. No use dragging this out any longer . . . She's mad at me this morning anyway . . .* he thought as he pulled out of the driveway.

Holly wasn't hungry. She drank two cups of coffee and decided to get cleaned up and shop for groceries. As she was making herself presentable, she looked at the bottle of Vanilla Wonderful and realized she hadn't worn it much. The bottle was still full. She chose not to wear any fragrance today; she was feeling tired, irritable, and sad. She put on her navy blue sweater coat before she left the house. It was cold and cloudy today, and rain was in the forecast.

She pulled into the Safeway parking lot, parked her vehicle, and began walking toward the store. From a distance, she recognized the petite blond woman looking at the display of pumpkins outside the store entrance. She walked up to her and started a conversation.

"Hi, Amber, funny meeting you here," Holly said warmly.

"Oh, hi, Holly," Amber said, surprised to see her.

"How have you been? Are you keeping everyone straight at American Steak?" Holly asked pleasantly.

"Everyone except James," Amber replied with a nervous laugh.

Holly noticed that Amber smelled like vanilla. "Are you wearing Vanilla Wonderful?" she asked Amber.

"Yes. It's become my go-to fragrance," she replied.

"I like it too. I remember James came home one night smelling like vanilla and he said they were using a new room spray for the kitchen. Then I discovered Vanilla Wonderful at Walgreens and realized it smelled a lot like the kitchen spray," Holly said.

Oh my God, this woman is clueless . . . She has no idea James has been cheating on her. It's time she knew the truth . . . If James can't man up and admit what he did, I'll do it for him . . . "Holly, there is no vanilla-scented spray that we use in the kitchen. We use industrial-strength Lysol," Amber said in a scolding manner. A vertical frown line had formed on her forehead. She looked intensely at Holly.

Holly felt her stomach drop and realized what Amber was saying. She looked into Amber's pretty blue eyes and was rendered speechless for a moment. *James had an affair with Amber . . . I feel like such an idiot . . . No wonder he hasn't wanted to have sex with me . . . I trusted him and believed everything he told me . . . He will rue the day he cheated on me.*

"How long has this been going on?" Holly asked tentatively, feeling like she was suddenly dropped onto another planet, and yet amazed at how calm she sounded.

"We've been having an affair for almost 9 months. I can't believe you never became suspicious. There were many times I had sex with James in your bed. I discovered last month that I'm pregnant with his child. I'm a little over 2 months pregnant," Amber said. Her heart was pounding . . . *I probably shouldn't have mentioned the part about having sex in her bed . . . She looks like she's ready to spit nails at me . . . Maybe this wasn't a good idea.*

"Does he know you're pregnant?" Holly asked. Her voice was calm yet she was smoldering inside.

"Yes. He said he was going to tell you soon," she replied meekly . . . *Please don't hurt me.*

"Thank you, Amber, for telling me what my significant other wouldn't. I hope that you have room for him in your apartment, because he's yours now," Holly barked at her hatefully, turned, and walked back to her vehicle in a hurry.

James is going to be pissed at me . . . But I had to do it. I can't take this anymore. She deserves to know the truth, and he needs to man up to his responsibilities, Amber thought to herself as she watched Holly storm across the parking lot.

Holly couldn't get to her Lincoln fast enough. She loved her vehicle and saw it as a temporary place of refuge. She jumped into the seat, shut the door, put the key in the ignition, and sat there, letting it run and listening to the radio. The heavy intro drumbeat and squealing electric guitars of "Rock You Like a Hurricane" by The Scorpions began to play and she turned it up loud. *I have to get myself together before I drive home . . . I don't want to cause an accident . . . I need to calm down and stifle my anger until I reach the house . . . I'll be home in 10 minutes . . . Save it up for James when he gets home tonight . . . I'm going to rock his world in a bad way . . . keep calm . . . Drive home slowly, put your anger aside for a few moments.* Holly took a deep breath, counted to 10, and drove home slowly.

She made it home safe and sound and sat in her vehicle for a few minutes trying to collect her thoughts. She was furious and her adrenaline was in overdrive. She went back into the house and immediately stripped the bed of the sheets and pillowcases. She threw them in the dirty clothes and put on clean ones . . . *I just changed these sheets 3 days ago, and they probably aren't contaminated with his betrayal . . . humph . . . I DON'T CARE!*

Next, she decided to get rid of James's stuff. She pulled down the stairs to the attic, climbed up, and brought down his two large suitcases. She went into the bedroom and emptied out his drawers and closet. She carelessly threw his clothing into the suitcases, not caring if anything got wrinkled. Dirty shoes were placed on clean white shirts. She sorted through the laundry and placed his smelly clothes on top of clean ones. She was pissed and wanted to do something to hurt him. She got a pair of scissors from the office and opened up his T-shirt drawer. He had a collection of favorite T-shirts he wore on his days off.

She attacked the T-shirts with fury, screaming at the top of her lungs while alternately hacking them up with scissors and ripping them apart with her bare hands. *"YOU LYING MOTHERFUCKER . . . HOW COULD YOU BETRAY ME LIKE THIS? . . . I TRUSTED YOU . . . I BELIEVED EVERYTHING YOU SAID."* Fate was terrified at Holly's rage and ran down to the basement to hide.

Next, she grabbed the bottle of Vanilla Wonderful sitting on her vanity and doused the contents of the first suitcase with it, continuing her rant, *"HERE'S YOUR FUCKING VANILLA WONDERFUL KITCHEN SPRAY . . . I HOPE YOU CHOKE ON THE FUMES!!"* As she threw the shredded T-shirts into the second suitcase, she doused them with it too. *"HELL, I MIGHT AS WELL CUT UP HIS SOCKS . . . I'M ON A FUCKING ROLL!"* After she cut up his socks, she remembered that James kept his jeans in the chest at the foot of the bed and she had a special plan for those too. With a wicked smile, she opened up the chest and took out the five pair of jeans which belonged to him. Then she took the scissors and cut out the crotch in each pair. Just for fun she added some rips in the pant legs. When she was finished, she stuffed the destroyed jeans into the bottom of the suitcase containing the rest of the shredded clothing and said with delight, *"LET'S SEE HOW YOU LIKE THE LOOK OF DISTRESSED DENIM. YOU CAN SHOW YOUR GOODS TO ALL THE LADIES."*

By the time she was done stuffing his suitcases, she had ripped up his favorite T-shirts, each pair of his socks, his jeans, and most of his underwear. She contemplated going back and cutting up the rest of the contents in the first suitcase, however, she realized she didn't feel like expending the energy. The manic beast inside was quieted for the moment. She took the suitcases and set them outside in the front yard. Rain was starting to fall, and she smiled at the thought of his suitcases and ripped clothing getting soaked. She had only partially zipped up the suitcases. James still had plenty of his personal items inside the house . . . *I'll take care of them later . . . He deserves whatever I dish out . . . By this time tomorrow his sorry ass will be parked at Amber's . . . She can have him.*

She had the rest of the day to be miserable. He would be home in 7 hours. She was both furious and exhausted from ripping up his clothes. She decided to watch TV until he got home. She was too upset to do anything constructive and too angry to call and talk to anyone. She couldn't get interested in any of the programs. She could only stare at the TV and think of the past 11 years they shared together. *I'm too mad to cry . . . I just want to beat the crap out of him . . . I think I will hurl this bottle of Vanilla Wonderful at his head when he isn't looking . . . I want to physically hurt him, it's just a plastic bottle . . . however, it's still three-quarters full, and if I throw it hard enough at his head it WILL hurt.*

She looked at the framed picture of the two of them in happier times. It was sitting on top of a small bookshelf next to the TV. *I don't want to look at that picture anymore . . . It's history, and that frame can go too . . . I don't want to make a mess in the house, though . . . I'll drop it on the patio.* She walked over and picked up the picture in its pretty, heart-shaped ceramic frame and walked outside onto the patio in the cold, pouring rain. She stood there and threw the picture and frame on the concrete. It broke into several pieces and she just left it there and walked back inside the house. *That felt good. I wonder what else I can break. I'll sweep up the debris when it stops raining . . . I think I'll get the mallet out of the shed . . . I want to put a big, ugly gash in his pretty new truck.* She walked outside to the garden shed, opened it up, and retrieved the mallet. It weighed 6 pounds and had a steel head. She didn't care that she was getting drenched in the rain, her only thoughts were on ways to hurt James. She went back inside the house with the mallet and changed into some dry clothes. She had a few more hours to sit and stew until he got home.

James had an uneventful day at work and was relieved that Amber wasn't working and he didn't have to see her today. He knew he had delayed the inevitable longer than he should have and would have to give Holly the bad news tonight. It was still raining as he neared the house, and it was dark. He noticed some large objects in the yard. As he got closer, he saw that they were his suitcases and his heart fell into his stomach . . . *She knows . . . I don't want to go inside . . . Amber must have told her . . . Holly set these out in the pouring rain . . . she's probably sitting in the living room ready to let me have it . . . I knew I would have to face the music. This is not going to go well . . .* He pulled into the driveway, turned off his truck, and walked to the house. He suddenly felt chilled and his hands were shaking . . . *I can't believe I'm this nervous.* James turned the door handle and discovered it was unlocked, just like he thought it would be. He slowly opened the door to face Holly sitting on the sofa, waiting for him . . . *If looks could kill I would be dead right now . . . I've never seen her look like that before.*

James turned to close the door behind him and felt a hard object strike his head. "OUCH!" he said loudly and turned to look at Holly. He saw the bottle of Vanilla Wonderful body spray lying on the floor . . . *This confirms that Amber told her.*

"*WHEN WERE YOU GOING TO TELL ME THAT YOU KNOCKED UP YOUR MISTRESS?"* she screamed at him. She was standing up with her hands on her hips; he noticed the mallet lying on the sofa and wondered . . . *Is she going to try to kill me?* Holly glared at him and continued her rant. *"WELL? WEREYOU GOING TO WAIT UNTIL SHE ACTUALLY HAD THE BABY, AND THEN DENY IT? WHY DID YOU WAIT SO LONG TO TELL ME? YOU ARE A FUCKING, LOW-LIFE COWARD!"*

James was frozen in place. He had never seen her like this before.

He was facing a hostile stranger. He took a deep breath and said slowly, "I am so sorry, Holly. I should have been the one to tell you. I was going to, several times . . . and you are right, I was scared."

"Why, James? Why did you feel you needed another woman? What did I do wrong? How many other women have you been cheating with?" she asked in a normal tone of voice this time.

"Holly, you didn't do ANYTHING wrong. Amber is the only woman I ever cheated with . . . *Better not admit to the hookers or Gina right now*. Why did I do it? Because I'm weak. She kept coming onto me, and I tried to ignore her. Eventually she got to me and I didn't want to resist anymore. None of this is your fault. This is all my fault, and I did you wrong, terribly wrong," James said sincerely through his tears. He couldn't hold back anymore and began to cry hard. His body was wracked with sobs. He sank down to his knees in front of Holly. "Please forgive me, honey, I am so sorry. I love you. I never loved Amber. She stopped taking her birth control pills and trapped me. Her cousin has threatened to kill me if I don't marry her. He's got Mafia connections." He looked up at her. His face and eyes were red from crying, and his hands were clasped together begging for her forgiveness. "I love you so much . . ." he pleaded to her.

"YOU DISGUST ME!" she screamed and spit in his face. Holly's ire was rising again, and she snapped these words at him, "You loved me so much that you would go out and fuck another woman repeatedly for almost a year and get her pregnant . . . WOW! I'm supposed to be impressed by the power of your love? HAH! I should kick you in the NUTS. And to think that I felt guilty and conflicted because a coworker kissed me on the lips after happy hour one evening and I liked it. At least I didn't go fuck his brains out. NOW I WISH I HAD. That's the difference between us. I was attracted to another man because you were never around. Now I know that you were too busy having sex in OUR BED with another woman to pay attention to me. I resisted temptation because I valued what we had. YOU DON'T DESERVE

ME. YOU ARE A PIECE OF SHIT. GET OUT OF MY HOUSE!"

James was still on his knees looking up at her, tears spilling down his face. He said softly, "You're right. I'll go. You can keep whatever you want, I just need my clothes. I still love you, Holly. I will never stop loving you."

"GET OUT NOW!" she screamed, stomped her foot, and pointed to the door. She appeared on the verge of hysteria, and James thought that she might become violent.

He got up and took the spare key to her Lincoln off of his key ring and laid it on the coffee table along with his house key, and then he walked out the door. It was still raining hard outside. Holly went over to the sofa and picked up the mallet. While James was loading the wet suitcases into the passenger-side door and getting soaked, Holly went around to the back of his truck, took hold of the mallet with both hands, and smacked the tailgate hard. She laughed with glee and struck the tailgate two more times in different spots. James heard the loud thumps and crazy laughter and realized what Holly had done. He went around to the back of the truck and saw her standing there, holding up the mallet in strike position, and the dents she made in the tailgate.

"I wanted to give you a little something to remember me by," she said with a wicked smile. James couldn't believe the radical change in her. He felt like he was living a real-life horror movie . . . *She's gone bat-shit crazy . . . She beat up my new truck . . . I'll be lucky to get out of here in one piece.*

"Holly, I beg you, please, please stop," he cried, and continued, "I promise I will never set foot on your property ever again. You can keep the Total Gym in the basement. Anything you don't want you can throw away. Please, just let me go. You will never have to see me again."

Holly stood there glaring at him with the mallet raised in attack position. James was frozen in place. It was like a bad dream. *I don't want to try to disarm her with force . . . She's got a mallet in her hands . . . I wouldn't put ANYTHING past her.* After what seemed like an eternity of her evil stare and the cold rain, she lowered the mallet and said softly to him, "You aren't worth the trouble."

The maniac inside of her retreated, and her eyes were vacant and unfeeling. She walked past him, back into the house, and closed the door. James stood there for another minute or two looking at his beat-up tailgate and feeling afraid to move. *She might come back . . . I better get going before she changes her mind.* Still in a state of shock, he got into his truck and drove away. *I guess I will go knock on Amber's door. I have never seen that side of Holly. In her state of mind, I think she could fight the devil himself . . . I swear on my mother's grave that I will never, ever, cheat on a woman again.*

Holly stood inside the door and heard James's truck drive away. She had her back to the front door and didn't look out the window to watch him leave. She was soaking wet and dripping a puddle onto the floor. She was still holding the mallet. She stood there for several minutes trying to regain her composure . . . *I feel better now . . . I'm glad I didn't hit him . . . He truly isn't worth it. I would have had to call the ambulance and probably would get arrested for domestic violence . . .* She let out a big yawn . . . *I'm feeling kind of tired . . . I think I will get out of these wet clothes and go to bed.* She stripped, towel dried her hair, wiped up the floor, put on some warm pajamas, and collapsed on the bed. About an hour later, Fate slowly crept into the bedroom, softly jumped on the bed, and snuggled close to Holly.

James arrived at Amber's apartment building and called her on the intercom so she could unlock the main door and let him in. She was waiting for him and promptly opened the door. "You look like a drowned rat," she said with concern.

"Can I stay here tonight?" he asked feeling humbled and ashamed, yet relieved to see a friendly face and suddenly feeling a new appreciation for Amber . . . *I have to be nice to Amber. I have nowhere else to go.*

"Yes, I told you that you can stay with me. Come in; let's get you out of those clothes and into something warm," she replied, feeling a mixture of happiness and guilt . . . *I'm happy that he's finally here with me.* "Where are your suitcases?"

"I left them in the truck. They're soaking wet and I imagine the contents are too. Holly left them sitting in the front yard for me when I got home and they were only partially zipped up. Do you have a big blanket I can wrap around myself?" he asked.

"I can do better than that. I bought a robe and slippers for you. I was planning to give them to you for your birthday. I'll go get them. Would you like some hot tea?" she asked, wanting to please her man and make him feel at home.

"Yes, that would be wonderful. Thank you, Amber," James said, relieved that the worst of the storm had passed. *I feel a little better now; everything is out in the open. I hate myself for hurting Holly so badly . . . I'll just have to live with that.*

Amber went to her bedroom to get the new, soft and fleecy robe and shearling-lined slippers that she bought for James. The robe was thick and plush in a dark wine color. The shearling slippers were tan-colored suede. She knew that he would eventually be staying with her and she wanted him to feel so welcome that he would never want to leave. She helped him out of his clothes and the new robe and slippers felt warm and welcoming against his cold body.

"I'm going downstairs and putting your wet clothes in the dryer. We can deal with your suitcases tomorrow. You know that there is a laundry room on the lobby level, and you can use the dryers for your clothes. I doubt if anybody will be using them early on a Monday morning. The laundry room key is hanging up on the side of the refrigerator," she said to James.

"I really like the robe and slippers, Amber. I can't thank you enough," he said with sincerity.

"You're welcome. You know that I love you," she said sweetly.

James sat down on her living-room sofa feeling numb from this emotional roller coaster. His thoughts drifted back to Holly's fit of anger and how she beat up his tailgate. A few minutes later, Amber came back to the apartment and began to fix him a cup of hot tea. She microwaved a mug full of water, inserted a bag of chamomile tea, and brought it to him.

"Here you go, let it steep for 5 minutes," she said, placing the mug on a coaster on the end table next to where James was sitting.

"Thanks," he replied somberly, having had a few minutes to think about what happened with Holly.

"I assume that you had a tough time with Holly," Amber remarked, sitting down next to James and wanting to have a conversation about the breakup.

"Yes, it was terrible. I've never seen her lose her temper like she did tonight. She took a mallet and put three big dents in my tailgate. I wouldn't be surprised if the clothes in my suitcases are ripped to shreds. I know that you told her. Did you call her?" he asked, looking her straight in the eyes. She could feel his irritation.

"I ran into her outside of Safeway this morning. That's when I told her. I felt she should know, and I honestly didn't think you were ever going to tell her," Amber replied defensively.

"She had the whole day to stew about it. I'm sure most of my clothes are ruined. I was planning to tell her today when I got home from work, so it really doesn't matter," he said with exasperation. "I don't feel like talking about it."

"I understand. I won't mention it anymore," she said. Amber felt a deep sadness emanating from James and she decided to be supportive and not ask further questions . . . *I have to make him fall in love with me.*

The next morning Amber had to be at her day care job early and James didn't have to be at the restaurant until shortly after lunchtime.

He had the morning to take care of getting his clothes unpacked and washed. He retrieved the two suitcases from his truck. They were still damp. He brought them upstairs to Amber's apartment. He noticed that they smelled faintly like vanilla . . . *She did this on purpose. Amber must have been wearing the Vanilla Wonderful spray when she told her.* He placed the suitcases in the middle of the living-room floor and filled with dread, he sat down to open one of them. . . . *This is going to be a disaster . . . I know she did something to my clothes.* James unzipped the first suitcase . . . and his heart sank. There wasn't a complete piece of clothing in the entire suitcase. His favorite T-shirts were ripped to shreds, along with his socks and underwear. Every item was damp and shredded. He discovered his jeans were thrown in with the rest of the tattered clothes and each pair had the crotch cut out. *She cut out the crotches . . . If I didn't feel so miserable this would be funny. I know Amber is going to laugh herself silly when she sees this.* There was nothing salvageable in this suitcase. He sat there staring at Holly's handiwork and thinking of everything that transpired last night. *I'm thankful that she didn't kick me in the groin. Better to have the crotches cut out of my jeans. I should check the other suitcase and see what kind of damage she did in there.*

James opened up the second suitcase and was relieved to find that the clothes in this one were whole, even if they were a little bit dirty. She had placed his dirty laundry in this suitcase. *I can't believe she went through the laundry and picked out and packed my dirty clothes. Actually I can believe it. She was home the entire day and got angrier by the minute. She must have packed this suitcase first, and then sliced up the stuff in the other one. Hey, at least I found some spare underwear and socks I can wash!* Most of his shoes were in this suitcase along with his dress clothes. Holly had placed his shoes, sole-side down on top of some crisp, white dress shirts that were now dirty. *At least I have a few shirts . . .* he thought with relief. His dress pants were on the bottom and he was delighted that they had been spared her wrath, crotches still intact . . . *I'll have to go shopping for some new clothes. At least I have a pair of pants to wear to work today.* James gathered up his dirty clothes and put them in a large plastic garbage bag. *Time to do laundry . . .* he said to himself as he took the key to the laundry room off of its hook. *I said I would never cheat on a woman again, and I mean it. No hookers either . . . I vow today that I will be faithful to Amber, even though I don't love her . . . Amber has a mean streak. She would be worse than Holly . . . She would have Bryce torture me . . . so much to look forward to when you marry the mob.*

CHAPTER 10

After the Storm

Holly woke up several times during the night racked with grief and was finally able to cry. When the alarm went off, she was in a deep sleep and waking up was physically painful. *Should I go into work today? I feel like I've been hit with that mallet . . . I have to wash and dry my hair too . . . or maybe I'll just put it up in a bun. . . . . . I think that's what I'll do . . . I don't have the energy to blow-dry it . . . I'm still not hungry . . . and I didn't eat anything yesterday.* She got out of bed, put her hair in a shower cap, and took a long, hot shower.

She looked at herself in the mirror and saw that her eyes were red and puffy. *I need a double dose of eye drops and some heavy concealer today . . . I'm going to have to dress nice to make up for feeling so wretched* . . . Holly continued to make herself look presentable; the process of bringing herself back to life was therapeutic. She replayed the events of yesterday over and over again in her mind and felt a sense of relief combined with deep sadness . . . *I can't cry at work today . . . I'm going to have to repress my feelings . . . That psychic reading last month was completely accurate . . . I didn't want to admit to myself that James and I were headed for Splitsville . . . I emotionally checked out of my previous relationships when they ended . . . Not so with this one, and that's why it hurts more . . . I really beat up James's tailgate . . . God, what in the world possessed me? I'm not sorry for cutting up his clothes, I want him to pay! Calm down, girl, calm down . . . finish making yourself pretty and get on with your life.*

Holly was finally ready to go to work, and she looked at herself in the full-length mirror before leaving the house . . . *I actually look pretty good today. I'm thankful for the transformative power of heavy makeup. I'll be okay as long as I don't succumb to a meltdown.* She was wearing a black suit with black hose and patent leather pumps. She had a beautiful face, and wearing her hair up in a soft bun suited her well . . . *Eat your heart out, James.* When she walked out of the house, the sun was trying to peek out of the clouds and the air was crisp and cold. She buttoned up her sleek, black leather coat, got in her car, and began her drive to the Metro.

The clarity of the morning light helped her to feel better. She was now free to start her life over again. While riding the Metro, she thought about Charlie and realized that she wasn't interested in him romantically at this moment. She was too hurt to think about being with another man . . . *Maybe I'll get the chance to date him in the future... . . . Right now, I feel nothing except emptiness toward everything . . . I am totally numb.* As she stepped off of the train, lost in her thoughts, she didn't realize that Charlie was walking a few feet behind her.

"Holly, wait up," he called out to her . . . *I like her hair that way . . . the sexy librarian look.*

She turned around and saw him and was pleasantly surprised. She greeted him with a smile. "Hi, Charlie." They continued to walk toward the escalators.

"Are you okay? You look like you don't feel well," he said with a slight frown as he gently placed his hand on the small of her back and walked close beside her.

Gee . . . That feels good . . . I wasn't expecting this . . . "You sure know how to make a girl feel pretty," she laughingly responded and continued, "I kicked James out last night. He was having an affair with a waitress at work and got her pregnant."

Charlie was stunned by this news and said, "You're joking, right?" *I hope it's true . . . then I might have a chance with her.*

"It's true," she replied, "His secret lover was the one who told me. I saw her on my way into the grocery store and stopped to chat with her. I know her from the restaurant."

"Do you want to talk about it?" he asked as they stepped onto the escalator. "I'm not in a rush to get to work, and I don't have any pressing appointments until later this morning. I'm flying out to Albuquerque tonight and will be there the rest of the week and, unfortunately, the following week as well."

"I guess so . . . I feel like a zombie, and I'm still numb from the shock of it. I was a raging monster last night, and it wasn't a pretty sight. I'm so ashamed of myself," she said uneasily.

"You can tell me when we get to street level. This will give you a minute or two to get your courage up while we ride the escalator . . . I'm curious. Now I *have* to know," he said good-humoredly.

A few minutes later they were on level ground and he gently pulled her aside so they could talk without interrupting the flow of people. They stood facing each other, and she felt comforted by his presence and the concerned way he was looking at her.

"Tell me, what did you do to that asshole?" Charlie asked point-blank.

Holly replied slightly embarrassed, "You might not want to be my friend after I tell you . . . You are the first person I have talked to since last night."

"If you told me that you kicked him in the nuts, I'd be proud of you," Charlie said with sincerity.

"I thought about doing that . . . except he was at work and I had 8 hours of time on my hands. Instead, I had fun with scissors and sliced up his favorite clothes, his socks, and his underwear, and then doused them with the body spray his mistress wears. I stuffed his tattered belongings into his suitcases, including whatever was in the dirty clothes hamper, and put them out in the front yard. The suitcases were only partially zipped and it was pouring rain . . . They got rained on for at least 6 hours . . . I'm sure everything was soaked. When he got home and walked in the door, I threw the bottle of Vanilla Wonderful at his head, and it whacked him pretty hard . . . It was almost a full bottle. I yelled and screamed at him, and he begged me for forgiveness. I told him to leave, and while he was putting the wet suitcases in his nice, shiny new truck, I took a steel mallet and put three dents in the tailgate . . . That's the part I'm ashamed of. I've never been that angry before or purposely destroyed anyone's stuff," she said with a sad look in her eyes.

Charlie looked at her for a few seconds wanting to take her in his arms and comfort her, then he replied with a serious demeanor, "You have nothing to be ashamed of. I completely understand your reaction. James deserved your wrath, he had it coming. The tailgate can be fixed; if it costs him money, even better. I still think you should have kicked him in the nuts, along with everything else, though. And I still want to be your friend." *I think I'm in love . . . I'm going to marry this woman.*

"Thank you for saying that, Charlie, it feels good to get it off of my chest," she replied with a deep sigh of relief.

"I mean it . . . The man is a fool for hurting such a wonderful person. You can do better than him, and I think you look pretty with your hair up like that. I think you look pretty every day," Charlie said to her, his eyes sparkling like the way they did the evening they spent at Jake's.

"Thank you, Charlie," she replied sweetly.

"Are you ready to go to work now?" he asked. "If not, we can talk more."

"Yes, I think I can face the day now. Patricia will be surprised when I tell her this," Holly replied.

They joined the throngs of commuters walking along the sidewalk on the way to the office. This October morning was cool and invigorating and the sun was shining brightly. Holly noticed that there were no more clouds in the sky. Charlie put his arm around her shoulders in a side hug and she responded by putting her arm around his waist. He pulled her close for a moment, and then let go.

I'm not ready to jump in with him yet . . . My heart is too heavy . . . But I want to enjoy his company and get to know him better.

"I know what it feels like to be cheated on. My first wife did a number on me too. It's a long story, and I'll tell you about it sometime," Charlie said as they crossed the street.

"I look forward to hearing about it," Holly said . . . *Maybe he's a man I could trust . . . although I thought the same about Alex and James too.*

Patricia happened to be in the lobby of the building dropping off a letter and saw them crossing the street together. *Those two are perfect for each other . . . She needs to get rid of James . . . I have a feeling he is bad news, and it's only gotten stronger from the things she's told me about him. She should be with Charlie, or someone like him. Holly probably didn't notice that James acted really strange Saturday night. Something's not right with that man.*

"Happy Monday," Patricia said cheerfully to them when they entered the building.

"Good morning, I need to talk to you for a few minutes," Holly said to her.

"Have a nice day, ladies. I'll talk to you later," Charlie said and winked at Holly as he walked toward the elevators. Holly remained in the lobby to talk to Patricia.

"You too, Charlie, have a safe trip," Holly replied with a smile.

"And what was that wink about?" Patricia said eagerly.

"I kicked James out last night. He was having an affair with a waitress at work and got her pregnant. He was too chicken to tell me. His tramp spilled the beans when I ran into her at the Safeway yesterday," Holly said calmly.

"Oh my God! I knew something wasn't right. He seemed so strange at dinner Saturday night." Patricia exclaimed.

"I feel like such an idiot. I overlooked the obvious. I'm too trusting. I feel like hell this morning," Holly replied somberly, beginning to feel the physical effects of too little sleep and major emotional upset.

"Did you tell Charlie?" Patricia asked.

"Yes, he made me tell him the whole, sordid story. He's so sweet. Maybe I'll go out with him sometime when I feel better. I was beginning to think everything was improving between me and James, then I got blindsided by this. I exploded on James. I think I scared him," Holly replied, starting to get agitated and angry.

"Please tell me you are going to Zumba tonight. You need to keep doing physical things to get rid of your aggression," Patricia replied, pleading with her.

"I'll be there," Holly said with a slight laugh. "I must get to work. I need something to focus on today, and it will help take my mind off of things temporarily."

Holly and Patricia walked toward the elevators to begin the workday. Patricia got off on her floor, waved good-bye to Holly, and then took another elevator to go see Charlie. *It's none of my business . . . however, I want to let Charlie know I'm in his corner if he wants to start dating her.* Charlie looked up from his work as Patricia walked into his office.

"Hi, Patricia. I assume Holly told you what happened?" he asked.

"Yes, she did. I think she can do better than James. Actually, I think that you and Holly would make a great couple," Patricia said sincerely to him.

Charlie laughed and said, "Nothing gets past you. Yes, I like Holly. I know how hurt she is right now. My first wife cheated on me too. She needs some time to get over the pain. I don't want her to feel pressured into going out with me. I know her feelings are raw right now. With that said, I think she's interested in me, but I want the timing to be right. I have some ideas to win her over."

"I want you to know that I am in your corner. Let me know if I can do anything to help out," Patricia replied.

"Well, there is something I need to know about Holly. What are her favorite flowers?" he asked, smiling.

"She doesn't have one favorite. I know that she loves sunflowers and roses. Sunflowers will be out of season soon, and she grows them in her yard. Roses are a safe bet," Patricia said happily.

"Good to know. I can take it from here," he said.

"Win her over, Charlie. I think you two should be together!" Patricia said emphatically. "I've got to go, have a good day."

"Oh, one more thing. What time does she leave for the day?" he asked.

"She normally leaves the office between 5:00 and 5:15," Patricia replied.

"Thanks, Patricia. I'll talk to you later," Charlie said as she left his office. *I need to plan out my strategy to land the next Mrs. Thomas . . . Holly is the one . . . Holly Thomas.*

Holly settled into her office and opened up the blinds. *I want as much sun as I can get. It makes me feel better.* She drank a cup of coffee as she read through her morning e-mails and saw that she had multiple inputs for a report she was compiling for Stan. *This is good. I have something meaty to work on today.* She put her troubles aside and was able to focus closely on the report. Three hours later, her phone rang. She saw on the caller ID that it was "Chase TechNet." *Roger's calling me? What the hell?*

"Hello," Holly said as she picked up the phone, anticipating Roger's voice.

"Good morning, Holly!" Roger said enthusiastically, "How are you today?"

He sounds like a used car salesman. "Okay, how are you?" she responded, sounding apprehensive.

"I'm doing great. Look, I don't want to bother you and if you tell me to go to hell, I'll understand. I called to see if you would like to meet for lunch one day soon. Don't worry about Lisa, she suggested it. She knows we used to be married. I know it's been a long time, and I was a total dumbass of a husband. I'm truly sorry for the way I treated you," Roger said genuinely.

"Sure, we can meet for lunch. What day is good for you?" she asked, intrigued and surprised by his offer.

"Thursday is good for me. We could meet at Jake's Joint at 11:30. Will that work for you?"

"Yes, that's good. I'll meet you in front of the restaurant," she replied.

"Wonderful. Have a good day. Thanks, Holly," he replied happily.

"Thank you, bye," she replied and hung up. *I'll verify with Lisa tonight that it's okay to have lunch with him. I don't want her to think I'm making any moves on her man . . . not after the past life where I stole Charlie. It was really nice of Roger to ask me to lunch . . . WOW . . . still not sure what to feel or think about him.*

Holly put her heart and soul into work and was still engrossed in compiling the report when quitting time came. A knock on her door made her jump. "Hey, it's past your quitting time, Holly . . . There's no rush on that report. I need to deliver it the middle of next week; you should go home and enjoy your evening," Stan said to her.

Holly looked at her watch and saw that she had worked over an hour past her quitting time. "I totally lost track of time," she said in amazement.

"Is everything okay? You look like you don't feel well," Stan said with a concerned look.

"Thanks for asking, Stan. I lost track of time because I needed something to take my mind off of my problems. I kicked James out last night. I found out that he was cheating on me," Holly replied.

"Oh dear, I'm sorry to hear that. Would you like to take some time off? I can finish up the report," Stan asked.

"That's a nice offer. However, work is therapy for me. If I'm busy, I don't have time to think about it," she replied.

"Okay, whatever you want. I'll understand if you decide to take a sick day or two this week," he said with a smile.

"You're the best," Holly replied thankfully. She gathered up her coat and purse, logged off her computer, and left the building.

Holly arrived home and went about her usual routine of checking the mail, feeding the cat, and trying to unwind for a few minutes before heading out to Zumba class. As luck would have it, most of the mail was for James. *I will just throw it away . . . too bad, so sad . . .* she thought as she threw his mail in the trash. She noticed the bottle of Vanilla Wonderful on the living-room floor from last night; she picked it up and threw it in the trash too . . . *I never want to smell vanilla anything EVER again.* She recalled the broken picture frame she smashed last night and went outside to sweep it up. As she was sweeping up the broken porcelain and glass, she noticed that the wind had blown the picture of her and James into the grass. It was lying facedown several feet away. She went to retrieve it and when she turned it over, she ripped it up. *I never want to see him again . . . Any pictures I find of us are going in the garbage.* She finished taking out the trash, ate an energy bar, and got ready to go dance her aggressions away at Zumba class.

She was running late again due to traffic and slipped into the back of the class with Patricia and Lisa. They both smiled and greeted her as they moved to the music and followed the instructor. This was exactly what Holly needed; she let herself go and got into the rhythm of the class. When it was over, Lisa gave her a hug.

"Patricia told me what happened. I'm so sorry," Lisa said as she hugged Holly. "How are you holding up?"

"I'm doing okay. Taking this class is the best thing I ever did," Holly replied, trying to catch her breath.

"You were really getting into it tonight," Patricia remarked.

"It felt good . . . Whew, I'm glad I came," Holly said with a sigh of relief. "It sure beats sitting at home crying."

"I told Patricia about Roger being your ex-husband," Lisa said laughing.

"Yes, she did. I've had two shockers today: first you and James break up, and now I find out that Lisa's Roger is your ex-husband," Patricia said in amazement.

"Did Roger call you today?" Lisa asked.

"Yes, we're meeting for lunch this Thursday. Why did you encourage this? I'm curious," Holly asked.

"Because I think it's the right thing to do. He's truly sorry for being a bad husband, and I can relate to that since I was an awful wife to my exes. We are trying to be better people. Roger has helped me with new techniques to keep my anger under control, and he continues to work on his. I think I will look up my exes and apologize, even the one who cheated on me," Lisa replied.

It will be interesting to find out Charlie's reaction when she apologizes . . . "That's wonderful, Lisa. It sounds to me like you and Roger are soul mates," Holly said.

"I'm starting to think that might be true. Patricia and Andy should give classes on how to stay happy with one person for the rest of your life," Lisa said teasingly to Patricia.

"I wouldn't know where to begin. Andy and I just got lucky," Patricia replied.

"Holly, if you need someone to talk to you can call me anytime, even in the middle of the night, it doesn't matter. I know what it feels like to go through a bad breakup, especially a betrayal," Lisa said earnestly to Holly.

"Thank you, Lisa. I'll try not to call you in the middle of the night, though. I believe people should get their sleep, and I think I'll sleep deep and sound tonight," Holly replied thoughtfully.

The three of them gathered their belongings and walked to their cars together. The night air was chilly and the wind had picked up. As Holly drove home she reflected on the recent events of her life. *How did it happen that I befriended both Lisa and Charlie within several weeks of each other? To top that off, my abusive ex-husband has turned into a nice person and invited me out to lunch with the blessing of his girlfriend who is Charlie's ex-wife . . . and I find out my cheating significant other got his secret lover pregnant . . . This is soap opera material . . . and then there is the past-life connection.* She laughed so hard that tears were rolling down her face . . . *I feel pretty good now.*

Holly was tired when she got home. She took a shower and went to bed, and no sleep aids were needed tonight.

When the alarm went off before dawn, she realized how exhausted she was both mentally and physically. *I think I'll call in sick today. I need to sleep.* She picked up her phone and left messages for Stan and Patricia to let them know she wouldn't be in today. She put her head back on the pillow to sleep and didn't wake up until noon. She might have slept even later if Fate hadn't jumped on the bed to pester her for something to eat.

I haven't slept this late since my 20s . . . I guess I needed it . . . I still feel exhausted . . . I think I'll fix some coffee and feed my fur baby . . . she thought as she walked into the kitchen. She opened the curtains so she could look at the backyard and sat down at the dining-room table. It was overcast today, and the weather seemed well suited to her mood. She thought about James and his betrayal and discovered she had no appetite. She felt sad and hurt beyond tears. She was too sad to cry. She thought back to the past life she shared with James in Atlantis where he was married to someone else and got her pregnant . . . *oh my God . .*

. little bits of karma have come home to me . . . I wouldn't be surprised if Amber was his wife back in Atlantis . . . they had sex in my bed . . . in Victorian England I had sex with David/Charlie in the bed I shared with Clive/Roger . . . and it got him killed . . . Then why is Lisa my friend in this life? . . . Things make sense, and then they don't.

She remembered Kavi's words, *"I want to add that you are not required to clear bad karma. As an eternal being of love and light your soul desires to clear it, and so you make the choice to do so in agreement with the other souls involved . . . in agreement with the other souls involved . . ."*

Now it makes more sense. I'm going to be extremely careful how I treat people from this day forward . . . I don't want to incur any more bad karma . . . I don't know what else is out there that I have elected to clear that I don't know about. Knowing this doesn't lessen the pain . . . It does help me understand, though. I think I'll box up James's stuff and let him know he can come and get it . . . I won't trash it like I originally planned. Even if we planned this scenario before reincarnating, it still hurts.

Holly got herself together and went about boxing up her ex's personal items. She realized she would have to get some new tools of her own and start mowing the grass again. The rest of her day was spent cleaning house and clearing it of James. Early in the evening, she thought it was time to see if she could uncover more about the Atlantis past life, to see if Amber was James's wife back then. She relaxed and listened to the CD without the headphones. She was able to experience another piece of the story . . .

> *. . . Dayani is at a fancy social event, she is back in Atlantis. She is walking around with a tray of food and serving well-dressed guests. The room is circular and has high ceilings and the walls appear to be made of glass. Everything is accented beautifully with touches of gold. She notices that her fellow servers are young. This must be during her college years. She sees Natom talking with several other people standing in a circle. She notices the beautiful woman on his arm and is*

stricken with pangs of jealousy.

She recognizes that the beautiful woman is Amber. In this life she is known as Laneesa. Laneesa is tall and elegant. She has long, golden brown hair and hazel brown eyes. Her facial features are soft and delicate, and Dayani feels like a short, ugly duckling in comparison. She walks over to Natom's group of friends and offers them delights from her tray. Laneesa casts a cold, hard stare at her. She knows.

"Hello, would you like a delicious treat to start the evening?" Dayani asks the group and holds out her tray filled with delectable offerings, ignoring Laneesa's cold stare.

"Thank you," Natom says without looking at her. He takes one of the treats from her tray and turns to Laneesa and says, "Open up, darling, these are delicious." She opens her mouth and Natom feeds her the small morsel.

Laneesa's eyes light up, and she looks at Natom and says, "Sweetheart, that was wonderful." She kisses him on the lips, and he pulls her close, kissing her head.

Dayani turns and walks away; she feels like she is going to be sick.

Sometime later she is standing outside at night, taking a break, and Natom comes and stands next to her.

"Go away, I don't want to talk to you right now," Dayani says tersely to him.

"Dayani, please, you know I can't tell her yet. I have to pretend everything is fine. You know that I love you," Natom pleads to her.

"She knows about us. I could tell in the way that she glared at me. She will never give you up, Natom. Even if she decided she didn't love you, she would do everything to keep you, just to spite me!" Dayani shouts at him.

"It won't be long, I promise," he says softly.

"That's what you always say. I know that you will never leave her. Just go away and leave me alone," Dayani replies and begins to cry . . .

Holly comes out of her hypnosis with a lump in her throat and notices that she has tears running down her face. She lets loose and cries hard . . . *It's true . . . I was right . . . Karma came back to bite me in this life . . . That was a long time ago, eons ago. I can only guess what kind of karma I have yet to redeem . . . I was such a mean little brat.* Holly got up and decided to fix herself something to eat as she feels weak from not eating, even though she isn't hungry. She put a small frozen dinner in the oven and glanced at the tarot cards lying on the dining-room table. *I think it's time for a reading.*

Holly shuffled the cards thinking about the recent turn of events her life has taken and drew the first card, the Hermit. The Hermit shows a solitary man with a long white beard, wearing a long hooded cape and holding a glowing lantern in one hand and a walking stick in the other. He is looking down at the ground in contemplation. This card is symbolic of seeking spiritual enlightenment and means that you need to take a step back and carefully examine your decisions and the situation. A period of inner reflection and soul searching is needed, for by understanding yourself you will better understand others.

Unbelievable . . . This one is right on the money . . . I think I will see if I can uncover a past life with Lisa tonight. Holly watched TV until it was time to go to bed. She listened to her regression CD thinking about her new friend and caught a short glimpse of a time when she generated good karma . . .

> *. . . She is swimming in the ocean. It's a warm and sunny day at the beach. She looks to the shore and sees men and women in funny-looking swimsuits and surmises that she is in the 1920s. She sees thick dark hair on her arms and realizes that she is a man and is named Joseph. He hears someone yelling and gasping for air and looks further out to sea and realizes that another man is drowning. The man is struggling against the current. Joseph swims fast with all the energy he can muster and manages to save the drowning man. He rescues him*

and helps him back to the shore.

"Thank you, sir, thank you from the bottom of my heart.You are an incredible swimmer," the stranger says as Joseph collapses on the beach from exhaustion. Joseph recognizes the stranger as Lisa. Lisa is a man in this life too.

"You're welcome . . . I'm glad I was . . . able to get to you in time . . .What is your name?" Joseph asks trying to catch his breath.

"My name is Paul. I owe you my life. I have a wife and two children in New York. I'm here on business and wanted to take a nice swim in the ocean. I shouldn't have gone out so far. I became caught up in the current, it was pulling me down. What is your name?" he asked. Paul was a man of medium height and build with brown eyes and hair. He looked to be around 30 years old.

"Joseph. I'm pleased to meet you, though I wish it had been under different circumstances," Joseph replies heartily and extends his hand.

"I'd like to buy you dinner. It's the least I can do," Paul offers, returning the handshake.

"Sure, I'll take you up on that," Joseph replies . . .

Holly opens her eyes . . . *I saved his/her life . . . Maybe that's how I made it up to her . . . I wonder how long I lived if I was alive in the 1920s . . . I was born into this current life in 1969 . . . I feel better knowing that I have some good karma to help mitigate the bad. I'd love to know what I looked like as a man. I sure was hairy. It's time to get some sleep now . . . I think I'll go into work tomorrow.*

Holly woke up the next morning and felt better. She was rested and anxious to get back to work. Today was Wednesday, and her lunch with Roger was tomorrow.

Holly got to work early. She wanted to make up for being out yesterday. She felt sad this morning. She kept thinking about the Atlantis past life and what a selfish bitch she had been. *I know I need to move past this . . . I can't keep dwelling on this stuff.* She spent an hour answering e-mails and had plenty of work to keep her occupied. Then she began to work on the unfinished report and saw an e-mail notification from her computer. She looked at her inbox and saw that it was from Charlie.

Hello, Sunshine. I hope you are feeling better. I just wanted to let you know that I'm thinking about you and looking forward to seeing you when I get back. If you need to talk, feel free to call me anytime, day or night. Have a great day. Charlie

Her heart filled with joy and she felt suddenly happy and giddy. *Oh my God, what a sweetheart . . . I'm looking forward to seeing him too. I will definitely reply to his e-mail.*

> *Hi, Charlie. Yes, I'm feeling better. I stayed home yesterday to get some rest, didn't get out of bed until noon. I'm taking Zumba classes, and they kick my butt; going to another one tonight. Thanks for checking on me. You have a great day too. Holly*

She heard a knock on her door, and saw that it was Patricia. "Hey, girl. Are you feeling better today?" Patricia asked cheerfully.

"Yeah, although my feelings alternate between sad, angry, happy, and relieved. Oh, and I got an e-mail from Charlie!" Holly said excitedly.

"I take it you are in happy mode right now, correct?" Patricia said grinning.

Holly smiled and replied, "Charlie has that effect on me. It might be easier to get over James than I thought. He really hurt me, but I honestly don't feel that I love him anymore. It's almost like the love I had for him just vanished. His cheating was the final nail in the coffin. I've been down this road before. When I left Roger and Alex, I was checked out emotionally, and it still hurt. Breaking up a longtime relationship seems to have a fair amount of pain, even if you no longer love the person. The memories will be painful for some time. However, if Charlie asks me out, I won't turn him down."

You should be with him. He's crazy about you . . . Patricia thought, and then she replied, "I think you should expect that. You know he has eyes for you."

"I know, and it's mutual. We'll have to wait and see what happens," Holly said.

"I'll let you get back to work. Are you going to Zumba tonight?" Patricia asked as she turned to leave.

"Yes. I need to increase my hotness factor since I'm single again," Holly said laughing.

"That's what I want to hear. See ya," Patricia replied joyfully and left her office.

Thank God for friends like Patricia . . . Holly thought as she went back to working on the report. A few hours later, she began to get hungry and couldn't stop thinking about Chinese food. Stan walked into her office and read her mind.

"Are you doing anything for lunch today?" he asked.

"I've been thinking about Chinese food for the past hour. I might walk to The Dragon Dynasty for some Kung Pao Chicken," she replied.

"Great minds think alike. I was going to call in an order. If we call in two orders the delivery is free," Stan replied and asked, "Are you in?"

"Yes, I want a small order of Kung Pao Chicken," Holly answered; her stomach was growling.

"I'm going to get the Beef Chow Mein. Lunch is on me, and I'll call it in," Stan said smiling.

"Thank you, Stan, you're the best boss ever," she replied, and she felt a little more settled now. She looked out her window and saw that it was raining, not a hard rain, just enough to discourage walking to the restaurant.

Holly ate the Kung Pao Chicken and had enough room left for a fortune cookie. She noticed that there were two of them. The Dragon Dynasty usually included multiple fortune cookies, even with small orders. She opened up the first fortune cookie and it said,

You will soon receive a beautiful gift.
Hmmm, that's interesting . . . Let's see what the next one has to say.
Your soul mate will find you.

Holly laughed out loud at this and immediately thought of Charlie. The image of a teddy bear flashed in her mind. *I'm going to tape these to my computer monitor . . . I want them to come true. Who wouldn't want to receive a beautiful gift and find their soul mate?* She felt uplifted and happy for the rest of the day.

CHAPTER 11

Theo Barry

It was Thursday and she was feeling anxious about her upcoming lunch date with Roger. The rain stopped earlier that morning, and it was a perfect, sunny, and cool October day. She put on her walking shoes and leather coat and headed out to meet him at Jake's. Her stomach was turning and her heart was beating a little faster as she neared the restaurant. *What in the world are we going to talk about . . . How uncomfortable is this going to be . . . I hope he doesn't try to come on to me . . . This whole thing is just WEIRD. At least he's on time . . .* she thought as she saw him waiting for her in front of the restaurant. He was dressed in a navy blue suit with a red tie. He looked nice. He saw her approaching and smiled. He greeted her amiably as she walked toward him.

"Good afternoon, Holly," he said warmly to her.

"Hi, Roger," she replied cordially, noticing the lines around his eyes as he smiled.

He sensed immediately that she was nervous, as he was feeling the same way and wanted to put her at ease. He looked into her eyes and said, "I feel nervous about this, and I'm sure you do too. I want you to know that I'm not going to put any moves on you."

Holly replied with a slight laugh, "Yes, thank you. With that said, I think we can get through lunch."

"Good, let's go get something to eat," he added with relief.

They were seated at a cozy table for two, perused the menu for a few minutes, and were ready to order when the waiter appeared.

"Ladies first," Roger said to her.

"I'll have the Chicken Cordon Bleu with a side of rice pilaf," Holly said to the waiter.

"I'll have the 10-ounce rib eye with a baked potato," Roger said.

"And what would you like to drink?" the waiter asked.

"Just water for me," Holly said.

"Same here, just water," Roger agreed. The waiter gathered their menus and left to get their drinks.

Roger broke the silence with an apology. "So, Lisa told me about what happened with James. I'm sorry to hear that. For what it's worth, I apologize for being a total asshole of a husband. I went to counseling for a long time after you left me. I've made anger management a priority since then. I got married for the second time five years after you left. She was a complete witch and fooled around with lots of guys behind my back. I should have seen it coming. That's what I get for marrying a stripper and being blinded by lust. When I found out she was having affairs, I smacked her across the face, and then she knocked me unconscious with a frying pan. That was the only time I ever hit her, and I shouldn't have. I found out the next day that she was pregnant. DNA tests eventually confirmed it was mine. I've never hit a woman since then. Like I said, I've made anger management a priority. I'm calm and happy most of the time. I've learned self-control and patience the hard way," Roger said.

Holly laughed out loud at the mental image of Roger's ex-wife knocking him unconscious with a frying pan, and she replied, "Did you have to go to the hospital when she knocked you out?"

"Yes, I had a concussion. Her name was Olivia. Our daughter's name is Denise. She turned out to be a wonderful young lady. She's attending college and wants to be a teacher," Roger said.

Holly felt more comfortable with Roger and felt that she could finally forgive him. "I forgive you, Roger. I didn't think I would ever say that. You have grown up and seem to be a good-hearted man. I know we got married too young, and we weren't right for each other. I am happy that you've become so successful and made a good life for yourself."

"Thank you, Holly. You've done well too. You are a sweet and beautiful woman. I know you won't have any trouble finding another man. I hope the next one, if you want a next one, will be good to you and won't break your heart," he said emphatically.

"Well, James was a good man for 9 years, and then he changed. I want the next one to last the rest of my life. I do think there will be a next one," Holly replied candidly while thinking, *If the next one is Charlie we probably won't be able to double date with Lisa and Roger.*

"I'm sure Lisa won't mind helping you screen them. If you want, you can bring them on double dates with us. Sometimes men can sense things about other men that women can't. When I met James, I told Lisa that something seemed 'off' about him, like he was hiding something, and she said she sensed the same thing," Roger offered to Holly.

Holly was touched by this, even though she knew she would never bring Charlie on a double date with them. "Thank you, Roger, that is really sweet," she replied cheerfully. The waiter brought their lunch, and they began to eat.

"I'm glad you asked me to lunch and we had this conversation," Holly said.

"Me too," Roger replied.

"I think you and Lisa make a nice couple. You both have the issue of conquering your anger in common and can help each other. I sometimes think our generation is meant to have more than one or even two marriages. It just seems that way to me," Holly said.

"I've often thought the same. I think we learn how to love better and be a better person with each experience, most of the time. There are many people who give up and decide to live alone. I understand that too. I felt that way before I met Lisa," Roger replied philosophically.

"I'll give it one more try before I call it quits. I like having a partner to go through life with and I don't have any children, just some nieces and nephews that I see once or twice a year," Holly said.

Roger had a playful look in his eyes and he said, "Is there someone you have your eye on?"

Holly couldn't hide her surprise at his question and she blushed and looked guilty. Roger knew right away that she was interested in someone.

He laughed and said merrily, "You do. Your face just gave you away. Tell me about him."

Holly did her best to be dismissive, "There's a guy at work who's been sweet to me, and I know he likes me. I would go out with him if he asked me."

"What's his name?" Roger asked.

Holly didn't want to spill the beans because she knew he would tell Lisa. The teddy bear image flashed through her mind and she answered, "His name is Theo."

"Well, I hope that Theo asks you out," Roger said with gusto. "Maybe we'll get to meet him in the near future."

I should have said his name was Ted, however, if pressed for a last name I can't say "Bear" because that sounds fishy . . . Theo Barry will be Charlie's secret name . . . Holly thought . . . *He's kind of like a sweet teddy bear anyway.*

"We'll see," Holly replied with a smile. They finished eating lunch, Roger paid the bill, and they left the restaurant.

"Can I walk you back to your office?" he asked.

"Sure," Holly replied smiling.

"I don't believe in coincidence. I think we were meant to meet again, for some reason," Roger said thoughtfully as they walked down the sidewalk.

"Do you believe in reincarnation?" Holly asked him.

"Yes. I believe we've lived many previous lives and we learn new things every time we come back. I believe everyone that we've ever met, we have known in another life," he added.

"I agree with you. I believe the same thing," Holly said.

"Lisa is open to the possibility of reincarnation. However, I don't think she gives much thought to those types of things," Roger replied.

"I've been listening to a past-lives regression CD and have experienced a few of my past lives," Holly said, and then immediately thought . . . *Why in the world did I say this?*

"Did you have any which involved me?" he asked with uneasiness.

"Yes. I don't know if we should talk about them right now. We just became friendly again. I'm surprised at myself for blurting out that I've been practicing past-life regression. You've managed to put me at ease," Holly replied with concern.

"That's okay. I hope that us being friends gets rid of whatever bad karma we've carried through the centuries," he said with sincerity.

"I hope for the same thing. If I get to heaven before you do, I'll tell them that we've resolved our negative karma," she said with enthusiasm.

Roger laughed and put his arm around her shoulder for a brief moment and said, "Good. Everything in my life now is good."

Holly came to a stop and said, "This is the building where I work."

Roger held out his hand, and she placed her hand in his for a firm and friendly handshake. She looked him in the eyes and said with a delighted smile, "Thank you, Roger. It was great talking with you."

"Same here. I'll talk to you again soon," he replied returning her smile, and then turned to walk in the other direction.

Holly was in a good mood. She felt happy and was grateful for the chance to reconcile on friendly terms with Roger. She went back to her office and noticed that there was a large box sitting on her desk. *What is this? . . . It's addressed to me and it's from . . . The Vermont Teddy Bear Company. Someone sent me a teddy bear?* Holly laughed out loud . .

. My life is one big coincidence. Here I am calling Charlie "Theo Barry" and someone sends me an actual teddy bear. Now . . . Who is it from? I hope it's not from James . . . Holly thought as she carefully opened up the box. She lifted the teddy bear out of the box and marveled at how beautifully it was crafted. It was 15 inches tall with movable arms, legs, and head. It had soft, suede paw pads. The bear was light brown and wearing a red bow tie.

"This is the sweetest thing!" Holly exclaimed in delight and hugged the bear close.

"Who is it from?" Stan asked, startling her. He had been standing quietly in her doorway for a minute or two and watched her open up the box.

"I didn't know you were there," she said laughing, feeling embarrassed that her boss watched her hug a teddy bear and feeling a flush creep into her face.

"Busted. Look and see if there's a card," Stan said excitedly.

Holly put the bear down in her chair and saw a card in the box. She opened it up and read, *"Hug the teddy bear whenever you feel blue, I want you to know that I am thinking about you. Love, Charlie."*

"Well, who's it from?" Stan insisted.

Holly was speechless. She just stared at the card and said softly to Stan, "It's from Charlie."

"Charlie Thomas?" Stan said loudly with surprise.

"Yes," Holly replied. She was glowing with happiness and felt like she had just won the lottery.

"Well, that's interesting. I didn't know you two were friends," he remarked.

"We run into each other frequently on the Metro and have developed a friendship. He was the first person I talked to after my breakup with James," Holly replied.

Stan had a mischievous look on his face and said, "I think he's in love with you. Men don't usually send gifts like that to just friends."

Holly thought Stan was right, and that Charlie's intentions might be serious. She replied, "It's so soon to get into another relationship. I like Charlie. I just want to get to know him better before I jump in."

"He's a good guy. I think you should see where it goes," Stan replied as he turned to leave.

"I think I will," Holly said while gazing lovingly at the precious teddy bear.

Holly couldn't concentrate on her work. She kept looking at her lovable teddy bear and feeling completely giddy. She had it sitting in her guest chair. *Charlie is amazing. Charlie is going to get a big kiss from me when he gets back . . . What a sweet, sweet man . . . Maybe I can let myself get lost in him, it would be so easy to do . . . I don't think I will be pining for James much longer. I have to tell Patricia.*

Holly dialed Patricia's office. "Hey, guess what Charlie sent me."

"Flowers?" Patricia asked, recalling the earlier conversation she had with him.

"No. He sent me a teddy bear, a really nice one. Come up and see it," Holly said eagerly, resisting the urge to jump up and down in excitement.

"I'm on my way," Patricia said happily and hung up the phone.

Patricia arrived at Holly's office about 3 minutes later. "Wow, this is great!" she said with excitement as she picked up the teddy bear. "It's so well made and adorable," Patricia said with a happy sigh and continued, "Are you going to start dating Charlie?"

"I'm going to give him a big thank-you kiss when he gets back in town, and we'll see where it goes from there. I'm afraid to get my hopes up. However, when I look at this sweet bear, I feel like a kid at Christmas," Holly replied.

"Are you going to take him home with you?" Patricia asked.

"Yes, I plan to sleep with him," Holly replied and started to giggle.

"The teddy bear or Charlie?" Patricia asked with teasing eyes.

"Both!" Holly replied and both women succumbed to a fit of

giggles like 16-year-old girls.

"How was your lunch with Roger today?" Patricia asked once she stopped laughing.

"It went really well. He was a gentleman and apologized for being such a rotten husband. He seems to be a good man now. We had a great conversation, and I think he and Lisa will be happy together for a long time," Holly replied.

"Good. He seemed like a charming man at dinner last Saturday. It's hard to imagine us throwing his dead body off of a balcony back in Japan," Patricia said and began to laugh again. The two of them were cracking up with laughter at the mental image.

"You are too funny. I hope Stan didn't hear that comment. I don't want to have to explain it," Holly said while gently wiping away the tears of laughter and hoping her eye makeup wasn't too messed up.

"I need to get back to work. I'm happy about the teddy bear," Patricia said kindly.

"Me too. See you later," Holly replied, smiling and happy . . . *I should call Charlie and thank him . . . let me dig out his number* . . . she said to herself as she pulled out his business card. She dialed his number . . .

"Well, hello there," Charlie said, sounding jubilant.

"Charlie! Thank you so much for the teddy bear. I love it," Holly said, overjoyed with happiness.

"You're welcome, Holly. I thought you might need someone to help you get over James. Teddy bears are good for that, so my daughter tells me."

"I'm going to call him Theo Barry," Holly said cheerfully.

"I like it. That's a good name," Charlie replied.

"I have a kiss for you when you get back," Holly said, her heart pounding with excitement.

"Then I can't wait to get back. I'd like to take you out to dinner or something," Charlie said, suddenly feeling nervous.

"That would be great. I'd like that. You'll be back on Halloween, according to the calendar," Holly said.

"Yeah, what a day to be flying. I won't get back until almost midnight, when the deviants are making trouble," he said jokingly.

"Do you want to go out on Saturday night, November 1?" Holly asked.

"Yes, that's perfect. I was going to suggest that," Charlie replied.

"I'm really looking forward to it, Charlie," Holly said sweetly.

"So am I. I hope Theo will keep you smiling until I get back," he said.

"He will, no doubt," Holly smiled.

"Well, I'll let you get back to work. If you need someone to talk to in the middle of the night and Theo isn't enough, just call me," Charlie said lovingly.

"Thank you, Charlie, I'll talk to you soon," Holly said.

"I hope so. Have a good evening," he replied.

"You too. Bye," Holly said and hung up the phone.

The next week is going to go by so slow . . . I have a date next Saturday . . . my first date with someone new in 11 years . . . at least I have time to figure out what to wear. Holly glanced at her two fortune cookie predictions taped on the side of her computer monitor and realized that one of them had just come true: "*You will soon receive a beautiful gift.*" *Theo Barry is my beautiful gift . . . Is Charlie my soul mate? Time will tell for the second prediction.*

A few hours later it was quitting time and Holly gathered her things together and left the office. She took her teddy bear with her. She placed him in her tote bag on top of her high heels. The evening air was chilly, and it was beginning to get dark. A light breeze was picking up and she could smell the damp leaves from the morning rain. She was so happy that she felt like skipping down the sidewalk or doing a happy dance . . . *Like Roger said, "Good. Everything in my life now is good." This has been a fantastic day . . . The best day I've had since, well, Charlie rode the Metro home with me from happy hour last month. I've been broken up with James for less than a week and a new man is waiting in the wings . . . Does it get any better than this?*

When she got home, she sat Theo on the sofa for the time being. He would later end up next to her in bed. She fell asleep that night holding him close. Sometimes a grown woman needs to sleep with a teddy bear.

Friday and the rest of the weekend passed slowly. She used the long stretch of time to clean house and get herself back on track. She updated her Facebook status on Saturday afternoon to Single, and she posted a short summary of what transpired to cause her and James's breakup, leaving out the parts where she lost her temper, bashed his tailgate, and ripped most of his clothes to shreds. Saturday night Charlie called her to see how she was doing. It was quite late in the evening.

"Hi, Sunshine. How is your weekend going?" he asked pleasantly.

"Hi, Charlie. It's going good, I'm done boxing up James's stuff, and I gave the house a thorough cleaning. It's not the most exciting weekend, but I've gotten a lot done," she replied sweetly, suddenly feeling on top of the world again.

"Has Theo been doing his job?" Charlie asked, like he was checking up on one of his minions.

"Yeah. Theo has been wonderful, I'm glad you hired him for the job," Holly said with enthusiasm. "He's sitting on the sofa with me, watching TV."

"What are you watching?" Charlie asked.

"I'm watching *Pawn Stars* reruns on the History Channel," she replied.

"So am I," Charlie said laughing. "I know there are more interesting things to do in Albuquerque on a Saturday night, except I don't feel like going out. I'm anxious for the weekend to be over and the workweek to go by fast so I can come home. I shouldn't have to travel again for several months after this trip is done."

"What kind of things do you like to do for fun?" she asked, wanting to get a glimpse of what a potential future with Charlie might be like.

"I'm kind of a homebody. I traveled so much when I was in the air force, and this past year I've been traveling a lot for business. I enjoy quiet evenings, watching TV, doing things around the house. I'm a handyman type, woodworking in my garage. I go running and lift weights to keep up my strength. I like long walks in the park or the woods, outdoor concerts, good restaurants, oh, and I love to cook. I would love to cook for you some time," he said, hoping that the part about being a homebody didn't turn her off. "What about you, what kind of things do you like to do?"

"I go to Zumba class on Monday and Wednesday nights with Patricia, I like to work in my garden, sleep in late on the weekends, work out on my Total Gym several nights a week, and I like outdoor concerts, and I love taking long walks anywhere," she replied and continued, "I'm an okay cook, but since it's just me, I live on frozen dinners and nutrition drinks. I got spoiled living with a chef for 11 years, so you can cook for me anytime. I'm curious, what kind of things do you make in your woodworking shop?"

"I build custom cabinets, bookshelves, baby cribs, almost anything that can be created out of wood. I have a side business called 'Charlie's Custom Carpentry.' It's a nice break from working in an office," Charlie replied . . . *I hope she's turned on by a handyman who can cook and build things.*

"Charlie, that's fantastic. I'd love to see your work. Do you plan to make a second career out of carpentry one day?" Holly asked, imagining herself bringing Charlie a cold beer while he works on a project. She was definitely turned on.

"No, it's a side thing that I enjoy and provides some extra money. Have you thought about where you want to go on Saturday night?" he asked expectantly.

"Anywhere is fine with me. There's an Outback Steakhouse up the street from my home; we can go there if you like," Holly replied, not caring where they went as long as she could spend time with him.

"Sure, that's good. What time do you want me to pick you up?" he asked, anticipating how nice it will be to see her lovely face again.

"Is 5:30 good for you? I'm hoping we won't have a long wait if we get there early," she suggested.

"Yes, that's perfect. Did you want to do anything afterward?" he asked, hoping that she would invite him to spend the remainder of the evening at her house.

"Would you like to come back to my house and just watch TV?" she asked . . . *I want to do more than watch TV.*

"Yes, I'd like to do that," he replied . . . *I hope she wants to do more than watch TV, but I don't want her to feel pressured.*

"Do you have any plans for tomorrow? It's not much fun to hang out in a hotel room," Holly asked.

"I'm going to visit the Old Town area of Albuquerque. I think it will be a fun place to walk around and explore. I went there a long, long time ago and enjoyed it. It's a good way to bide my time," Charlie replied . . . *I wish she was here with me . . . Maybe I can bring her back something.*

"I would love that. Old Town historic areas usually have shopping and museums and other fun stuff. I've been to Colorado several times and enjoyed the little shops that sell natural stones. I'm a bit of a rock hound," Holly said.

Now I know what I can bring back for her . . . "What about Old Town Alexandria, do you ever go there?" Charlie asked, knowing that she lived near the area.

"I've been there a few times. I'd like to go more often, except that I hate trying to find a parking space," she replied.

"I understand that," Charlie said and asked, "What are you planning to do tomorrow?"

"I don't know. I'll decide when I get up. Most likely grocery shopping and a good workout," Holly replied . . . *and daydreaming about you.*

"Are you doing anything on Halloween?" he asked.

"No, just handing out candy to the kids and hoping no one vandalizes my property. I'm a little concerned about karmic retribution since I bashed up James's tailgate last weekend," she said.

Charlie laughed at this and said, "You never intended to beat up his tailgate. I think there's a difference. You were acting out of anger and hurt, not premeditated, malicious intent. Besides, he deserved everything he got." *I'd like to tell her about my cheating first wife, although I think I'll save that for our date next Saturday.*

"Thank you for saying that, Charlie. If I do get vandalized, at least I have insurance," she quipped.

"That's true," Charlie replied and couldn't stifle an oncoming yawn . . . *I hope she doesn't get the wrong impression; she's not boring . . . I'm feeling sleepy.*

"Did you just yawn?" she asked.

"Yes, I'm sorry, Holly. I think jet lag has caught up with me. I've loved talking with you tonight, and I can't wait to see you again," he said fondly.

"No problem, I think we should hang up so you can go to sleep. I've loved talking with you too. Enjoy tomorrow in Old Town and I'll talk to you again soon," Holly said thoughtfully.

"Okay. I'll talk to you soon, Sunshine. Have a good night," Charlie said.

"You too. Bye," Holly replied and hung up. Two hours later Holly was asleep on the sofa in front of the TV until Fate woke her up and she finally went to bed.

Sunday was spent grocery shopping and remembering what transpired last weekend. James had been gone for 1 week, and it felt much longer. In 1 week's time so much had changed. Charlie was in her life and things looked promising with him. She still felt a little love for James, as they had been together for a long time. However, she knew she would eventually get past these feelings. She sent James an e-mail that evening to let him know he could stop by and pick up his things at his convenience. She wondered how he was doing and what his reaction was when he discovered that she destroyed most of his clothes . . . *I would love to have been a fly on the wall when he opened his suitcases . . .* The thought of that made her laugh.

She checked her e-mail on Sunday night before she went to bed and noticed that she had a message from Alex.

> *Hi, Holly. I saw that you changed your Facebook status to single and I want you to know that I am here for you if you need to talk. I assume that you and James broke up. If he did something stupid, you are better off without him. Take care of yourself and don't hesitate to contact me. Alex*

What a sweetheart. That was nice of him. I'll send a quick reply.

> *Hi, Alex. It's good to hear from you. Yes, James and I broke up last weekend. He had a secret lover and got her pregnant, so I kicked him out. I'm doing fine and getting over him is easier than I thought it would be. Thank you for caring. I hope everything is well with you and Rachel. Holly*

Monday was a busy day at work and she was looking forward to Zumba class that evening. Holly got to class with 5 minutes to spare this time.

"Hey, there," Lisa greeted her kindly. "You don't look so sad anymore. I take it you are getting along fine without James?"

"Yeah, I'm doing great. I think getting over him will be easier than I thought," Holly replied.

"Roger said you two had a good lunch and have buried the hatchet. I'm happy to hear that," Lisa said. "He told me that a guy at work likes you and you kind of like him. Tell me, who is he? I might know him."

Oh, you definitely know him . . . He's your ex-husband . . . I'm not ready to tell you yet . . . But I can tell you about Theo . . . "His name is Theo Barry. We'll see if things progress now that I'm single again," Holly replied.

"I don't remember anyone named Theo," Lisa said thoughtfully.

"I don't think Holly's in a hurry for someone new," Patricia threw in, hoping to come to her friend's rescue. "I think she might want to play the field a little bit."

"That's a good idea, don't jump in too quickly," Lisa said with a serious demeanor. "You have friends who can help weed out the bad ones once you're ready. Roger is amazingly perceptive and intuitive. He's worked hard on developing his intuition. He could probably spot a bad man fairly quick."

"You girls are terrific. I appreciate your support," Holly said happily and put her arms around both of them. The music began to play, and they followed along with the instructor. An hour later they were sweaty and exhausted.

"Are you ladies doing anything for Halloween?" Lisa asked them as she stretched out her hamstrings.

"No, just handing out candy," Holly replied trying to catch her breath.

"Same here although Andy likes to turn off the lights and scare the trick-or-treaters with a ghoulish costume," Patricia laughed. "Are you and Roger doing anything?"

"No, he's coming over to hand out candy with me. I keep thinking it might be fun to go to a Halloween party, except no one I know is having one, and I'm not one for throwing parties," Lisa said with a laugh.

"Me either," Holly agreed. "James was usually at work most Halloweens and I got used to handing out candy alone. I think that's one reason why it doesn't seem so lonely with him gone. I got used to being alone because he worked varied shifts. I do think that a Halloween party would be fun, though."

"Maybe I'll have one next year. Halloween will be on a Saturday night," Patricia said.

"You have the room for it. I'd love to have a house the size of yours!" Holly said with enthusiasm.

"Me and Holly will stay and help you clean up. The men can go outside and smoke cigars or something," Lisa said. "Does Andy smoke cigars?"

"He does if one is offered to him. He likes smoking a pipe on occasion," Patricia said.

"So does Roger. Maybe Holly will be hooked up with Theo by then," Lisa said good-naturedly.

Holly smiled at this remark and said slyly, "We'll see." *If I'm with Charlie we probably won't be there.*

"I'm ready to roll, ladies. Let's go home and get some rest," Lisa said.

The three of them walked to their cars and headed home.

Tuesday morning as Holly was checking her e-mail, she saw there was a message from Charlie. *He must have sent this last night; the time stamp says 11:30 p.m.*

> *Sunshine, I enjoyed talking with you Saturday night. This week can't go by fast enough. I hope you have a great day. Charlie.*

That was thoughtful. He didn't say much in his e-mail, and yet he said plenty. He's thinking about me, he likes to call me Sunshine. This makes me feel so good. James never had a pet name for me. I want to send a reply, but what should I say?

> *Hi, Charlie. I enjoyed talking with you too. I wish I could have been walking the streets of Old Town Albuquerque with you and buying pretty rocks that I don't need. Holly*

She hit the send button and her reply was on its way . . . *I hope he doesn't take it the wrong way and think that I only wanted to be with him to buy pretty rocks.*

Tuesday and Wednesday went by slowly and Holly couldn't stop thinking about Charlie. Visions of her and Charlie with two children in a big roomy house flashed through her mind more than once. *Where are these thoughts coming from? I skipped over my childbearing years, and I can't imagine having them at this point in my life, and Charlie is 8 years older than I am . . . He's already a grandfather . . . albeit a sexy and handsome one.*

She realized by Thursday afternoon that she hadn't thought about James much at all. The few times that he did cross her mind, she felt a pang of sadness, however, it didn't last long. She felt happy and serene most of the time, and curled up with Theo Barry when she went to sleep at night. She checked her e-mail before she left work for the day and saw that Charlie sent her another message.

> *Hey, Sunshine. Happy days are here again. I'm leaving here tomorrow. Have a safe Halloween and make sure you lock your doors and windows. See you Saturday. Charlie*

He's protective, thinking about my safety on Halloween . . . That is so hot. Each time I hear from him my heart soars. I need to reply to his e-mail.

> *Hi, Charlie. I hope you have a safe flight home, and I look forward to seeing you on Saturday . . . I'll be sure to lock my doors and windows*

to keep the goblins out. Holly

On the way home from work she stopped at Safeway to pick up a few items. She had a feeling that Charlie would be staying over on Saturday night and she wanted to have extra food in case he wanted to stay for breakfast. *I know I shouldn't get my hopes up, yet the feeling that he is going to stay the night is strong . . . Even if it doesn't happen, I want to be prepared.*

The last time she stopped for groceries at this Safeway she ran into Amber and found out about the affair. She told herself she wouldn't shop here anymore, except that it was convenient and as she pulled into the parking lot she felt no emotion other than anticipation for Saturday night. She walked into the store, picked up a shopping basket, and headed to the dairy section to get eggs. Her head was in the clouds thinking about Charlie and she didn't notice the couple several feet across from her putting milk into their cart. They saw Holly, and James wanted to tell her that he would come by Sunday morning to collect the rest of his belongings. With his heart pounding in his chest and an apprehensive Amber standing next to their shopping cart, he walked over to Holly as she was checking the eggs for cracks.

"Hi, Holly," James said tentatively as he walked up to her.

She recognized his voice immediately and turned around to face him. "Hello, James," she replied dismissively.

"I got your e-mail about picking up my things, and I'd like to come by Sunday morning around 10:00 to get them, if that's okay with you," he said nervously . . . *Please don't smash an egg in my face.*

"Sure. I'll be home," she replied coolly and noticed that he looked haggard and tired . . . *He doesn't seem too happy.*

"Good, I'll stop by then. Have a nice evening," he said politely.

"You too," she replied calmly and went back to checking the eggs for cracks. She didn't even look to see if Amber was nearby. The crate of eggs that she was planning to buy was perfect. She set them in her basket, left the dairy section, and headed toward the meats.

James walked back to the cart and Amber. She looked at him questioningly and said, "How did it go?"

"Fine, she's okay with me coming over Sunday morning to get my stuff," he replied, feeling heavy remorse and thinking that Holly looked as pretty as ever.

Amber sensed his feelings and she felt like a fat hag. Her pregnancy hormones were wreaking havoc on her emotions. She was jealous of Holly and did her best not to say anything mean. She wanted James to love her. "That's good, sweetie, then you can finally close that chapter of your life," she said, trying to be nice.

They continued their shopping, and Holly picked up packages of ham and bacon and went to the checkout counter. They didn't cross paths again in the store. Holly paid for her groceries and walked to her car. It was getting cold, and the wind had picked up. It was almost dark, and she felt a fit of laughter coming on. As she put her groceries in the back of her vehicle, she began to laugh hysterically . . . *Just my luck that I would run into them at the same place where I discovered they were having an affair. I don't even feel sad . . . I feel nothing at all . . . Seeing James caught me off guard, except that I truly don't care anymore . . . Is it possible for love to die that quickly? I guess I'm so happy over Charlie's attention that it doesn't matter.* She started her car and drove home, realizing that she hadn't told Patricia that she and Charlie had exchanged several e-mails and a phone call and that she was seeing him on Saturday. Patricia had been stuck in meetings this week and she didn't want to tell her at Zumba class within earshot of Lisa . . . *I need to tell her the good news.*

Friday morning Holly went to Patricia's office to see if she was there. Her Outlook calendar indicated that she had no meetings today. Patricia was sorting through items on her desk when Holly knocked on her door.

"Happy Halloween," Holly said cheerfully.

"Hi, there. I'm so glad those meetings are done and I can catch up on the latest with you. I've been dying to ask about Charlie," Patricia said with optimism.

"We're getting married next weekend," Holly said jokingly.

Patricia laughed and said, "What's up with the two of you?"

"He called me Saturday, and we had a nice conversation. He asked me out to dinner for tomorrow night. We've been exchanging e-mails this week. The anticipation is intense," Holly replied dreamily.

"Wonderful! I'm happy to hear it. He's the one for you, I know it. If I were a gambling woman I would place a large bet on it," Patricia said with conviction.

"Do you think he would still want to be with me if he knew I was friends with Lisa?" Holly asked.

"Somehow I don't think that's going to matter. He might be surprised by it, but I don't think it will stop him from wanting to be with you," she replied with certainty.

"I hope you're right," Holly replied, looking serious. "Oh, I saw James at the Safeway last night. Isn't that crazy?"

"The same place where Amber broke the bad news to you? Yes, that is interesting synchronicity at work," Patricia said with surprise. "How did you feel?"

"I was caught off guard, but I didn't feel anything. James looked haggard and tired, and I don't know if Amber was with him. I was checking out the eggs, and then I went to get some meat. He wants to come over Sunday and pick up the rest of his belongings," Holly replied.

"What if Charlie stays over?"

"If Charlie is there when James shows up, so be it. I'll open the shed for James to get his things and lock it up when I hear his truck leave the driveway," Holly replied with a naughty smile.

"You go, girl," Patricia replied laughing and wishing she could be a squirrel in Holly's front yard this coming Sunday.

"I better get back. Stan's having a new client meeting at 10:00 and I want to set up the conference room with refreshments. I'll talk to you soon," Holly said and turned to leave.

"Bye," Patricia replied.

The rest of the workday went by quickly, and Holly enjoyed handing out candy to the children that evening.

CHAPTER 12

Falling in Love Again

Saturday afternoon finally arrived and Holly was excited for her date with Charlie. She wanted to look her best for him. She had spent the day with her long hair up in hot rollers so it would be bouncy and full this evening. She decided to wear her dark denim boot-cut jeans with her low-heeled black leather boots and a soft, cashmere, V-neck pullover sweater in a lovely shade of royal blue. The sweater enhanced her bust, and the jeans fit her well without appearing too tight. She accented her outfit with large, gold-toned hoop earrings. She wore light makeup and pondered on whether or not to wear perfume. She sprayed some Curve Crush fragrance on her hair and was ready for Charlie. She sat down to watch TV until he arrived.

Holly heard a vehicle pull into the driveway and knew it was Charlie. She glanced at the clock and it was exactly 5:30. The butterflies in her stomach were aflutter as she waited for him to knock on the door. She heard a car door shut and seconds later he knocked on the door.

"Hi, Charlie," Holly greeted him joyfully as she opened the door and let him inside. He was wearing dark Levi's jeans, a white, button-down shirt, and a black leather aviator-style jacket. His shoes were casual, dark brown oxfords with a thick sole. She thought he looked handsome.

"Hello, beautiful. It is so good to see you," he replied with an admiring look. "You look great, Holly."

"Thank you, Charlie," Holly replied sweetly as she smiled and reached up to embrace him. He met her halfway with a kiss. This time it was a long, passionate kiss and he pulled her close to him. They stood kissing in the doorway for several minutes. When they came up for air he looked at her and said, "I hope that kiss doesn't scare you off."

He makes me forget how to speak . . . She looked at him and smiled and said, "I'm not going anywhere, unless it's with you, and you can kiss me like that anytime." And then she kissed him again.

"If we keep doing this, we won't end up at the Outback," Charlie said laughing and hugging her.

"I guess we should go eat then," she said happily . . . *Although I could skip dinner and hit the sheets with him right now.*

"We can come back here, right?" he asked teasingly.

"You can count on it," she answered cheerfully.

"I see that Theo is comfortable on your sofa," Charlie said, noticing the teddy bear sitting on the middle sofa cushion.

"He is. He's been an excellent companion," Holly replied, her eyes dancing with delight.

Holly was surprised when they stepped outside and she saw that Charlie drove a truck. It was an F150 4x4 just like James's, except that it was black instead of gray. There was a lot of shiny chrome on it. She enjoyed the sound of the autumn leaves crunching beneath their feet as they walked to his truck, and the early-evening air was chilly . . . *Autumn is a nice time of year to fall in love.*

"Charlie, I want to promise you that no matter what happens between us in the future, I will not hurt your pretty truck," she said as he opened the door for her.

Charlie thought this was funny and he laughed and said, "I'll never give you a reason to even think about it."

"Good. I like the sound of that," she replied smiling as he shut the door and went around to the driver's side.

I'm in way too deep with this one already . . . Charlie thought as he got into his truck and they rode up the street. "I saw the Outback on my way to your house, so I know where I'm going," he said.

"You're a man who has his act together, I like that," Holly replied flirtatiously.

"I picked up something for you in Albuquerque," Charlie said to her as they were waiting at a stoplight. "Open up the glove box."

Holly did so and saw a little white box. "Is this it?" she asked reaching for the little box.

"Yes."

She took the lid off of the box and saw that it contained a beautiful, tumbled turquoise stone that fit perfectly in the palm of her hand; it would make a terrific paperweight.

"I love it, it's perfect," she said with appreciation. "You were listening when I said that I liked rocks. Thank you, Charlie, it will make a great paperweight. I can use it on my desk at work."

"I'm glad you like it," he said . . . *There's more where that came from . . . She inspires me to do these things for her . . . I never thought I'd want to get married again, but I see a diamond ring in her future.*

"Do you think you can get me the moon and stars too?" she said playfully.

"That's a tall order, but I'll see what I can do," he replied.

They arrived at the Outback and he parked the truck. They went into the restaurant and didn't have to wait for a seat. They were seated in a small booth and looked at the menu for a few moments while the waiter went to get their drinks. They were ready to order when he brought them to the table.

"I'll have the 10-ounce rib eye, cooked medium well with a baked potato and a house salad," Charlie said to the waiter.

That's interesting . . . Roger ordered a 10-ounce steak at Jake's . . . "I'll have the salmon with a loaded sweet potato and a house salad," Holly said.

"Great. I'll put that order in for you and bring you some bread," the waiter said and left to place the order.

"Holly, I remember you saying that you were exploring your past lives with a hypnosis CD. How has that been progressing?" Charlie asked, curious to know if he shared a past life with her.

"That's a loaded question, brace yourself for what I'm about to tell you," she replied apprehensively.

"You can tell me anything. I hope you know that," he said reassuringly.

"We were secret lovers in a past life. You were a married soldier stationed in Sweden and I was working as a type of nurse, caring for the sick and wounded. You weren't just a regular soldier. You were in a higher position, although not a commanding officer. We fell in love and carried on a secret affair for a year, until we were discovered and you were threatened with losing your position and being sent home. We tried to be more discreet and were caught again. You lost your position and were ordered home. You came to tell me good-bye and said that you had a wife, who you didn't love and married for convenience, and a son. I was extremely hurt and upset that you kept that hidden from me. You promised that you would return for me and we were both heartbroken and crying before you got into a carriage to take you away. One of your soldiers turned you in, and the last thing I remember was slapping him in the face, and then I woke up," Holly said, concerned what Charlie's reaction might be.

Charlie sat there silently for a moment taking in Holly's beautiful face, and then he said, "That's an incredible story. I believe it's true. I've had a recurring dream throughout my adult life of saying good-bye to a pretty blond girl and we were both terribly sad and crying. Now I know that you are that girl."

"I am. I looked into a mirror when I was under hypnosis and saw that I was a pale blond girl, and quite young, most likely a teenager," she replied.

"Do you know who it was that told on us?" he asked.

Holly hesitated for a moment, and then said, "You will find this incredible. The person who told on us was my first ex-husband, Roger."

"That is wild," Charlie said with astonishment. "I wonder if I crossed paths with him at some point in this life. Was he ever in the air force?"

"No, he was in the navy, an enlisted man. His name is Roger Chasen. We lived in Rota, Spain, for a little while. We weren't together long. He was an abusive husband," Holly replied.

"Roger Chasen? I saw him on the morning news. His company is doing great. How did he abuse you?" Charlie asked.

"He hit me numerous times and was extremely possessive and controlling. My parents sent me the money to come home. I worked on base as a typist and two of my Spanish friends encouraged me to leave and helped me do it," she replied.

"You've had the same good luck with choosing partners as I have," Charlie said shaking his head. Their food arrived, and they started to eat. They resumed their conversation about past lives and loves when they were done eating.

"So, Charlie, tell me about your past relationships," Holly said. "I take it you've been married twice?" she asked.

"Yes, my first wife was Kelly Morris. That woman sent me to the poorhouse. We met in my senior year of college and got married shortly after I graduated from Officer Training School. We moved around a lot, being in the military, and she would usually find some kind of job to keep her busy wherever we were stationed. She had a history degree and little work experience. She got pregnant with our son, Tyler, 2 years after we married and decided to be a stay-at-home mom. That was okay with me, and it worked out well for a while. But she became a spendthrift as Tyler got older. She was friendly with many of the higher-ranking officers' wives, and she wanted to keep up with them or outdo them as far as material things were concerned. She had to have the best and latest and greatest of everything. She got pregnant with Brianna when Tyler was 3 years old. Things were strained between us when Brianna came along, and they got progressively worse after that. I was often away on tours of duty, and I think she resented my not being at home. There was nothing I could do about that, it was part of being in the military. Many times when I would come home, I would find that our credit cards were charged up over the limit and most of the regular bills were overdue. She just left them for me to take care of, and it was difficult trying to pay them down. The late fees would drive up the balance. At one point, we had over $150,000 of credit card debt. The icing on the cake was when I found out she was having an affair with a medical doctor that she met through one of her friends. The decision to divorce was mutual. And that is the saga of my first failed marriage," he said.

"Would you like dessert?" the waiter appeared and asked them.

"I could go for a piece of cheesecake. Holly, would you like anything?" Charlie asked.

"Nothing for me, I'm stuffed."

"One slice of cheesecake coming up," the waiter said and left to get it.

"I'm happy to share my cheesecake if you change your mind. So, you told me about Roger. Was there anyone after him?" Charlie asked, curious to know if there was someone before James.

"Several years later there was Alex Manning. We met at work and lived together for a few years before getting married on a trip to Las Vegas. It was a spontaneous and stupid thing to do. He had drug problems before we met and he seemed to be fine for a long time . . . until years later when he started disappearing for days at a time and smoking crack cocaine with his friends. I later found out that he was struggling with his sexuality. Our sex life was nonexistent for nearly 2 years and during that time he was doing cocaine and having sex with other men. I found an incriminating picture of some guy giving him a blow job when I was cleaning our apartment. I confronted him about it and told him I was leaving. I had emotionally checked out before this happened. The drugs and lack of physical intimacy were big issues for me. Somehow we managed to remain on good terms throughout the divorce, and to this day we remain friends. He's done exploring his sexuality and is living with a woman named Rachel down in Lynchburg," Holly said.

The waiter arrived with the cheesecake and the check. "Thank you, have a great night," he said and walked away.

"At least that was a friendly divorce; neither of mine were," Charlie said shaking his head. "I don't understand how any man could lose sexual interest in you. If I was your partner, you would never have a moment's peace," he said with a loving look in his eyes.

"Hurry up and eat your cheesecake so we can get back to the house," Holly said playfully.

Charlie stuck a fork in his cheesecake and said to her, "Here, help me out." Holly took a bite, and they polished off the cheesecake together.

When they arrived back at Holly's house she felt a little nervous. Charlie pulled his truck into the driveway, turned off the engine, and took hold of her hand. He turned to look at her and said, "Do you still want me to come in? I don't want you to feel any pressure. I'm happy just to watch TV and talk."

"Yes, I want you to come in. I'm having such a great time with you. I don't want it to end," she replied . . . *I hope you stay the night.*

"Good, because I don't want to leave," he said with relief.

They went into Holly's house and sat on the sofa close together to watch TV. They channel surfed for a while and couldn't find anything interesting to watch. Then they started kissing and became lost in each other.

"Charlie, I don't want to stop. At the risk of sounding aggressive, I want you to stay the night and do me all night long—I can't believe I just said that," Holly said to him, feeling the heat rise into her face . . . *That was a brazen thing to say.*

Charlie was pleasantly surprised and laughed out loud and replied, "I can stay as long as you want me to. I can even make you breakfast, rake the leaves, check the air in your tires, you name it."

Holly looked him in the eyes and said, "Right now, I want you follow me into the bedroom."

"Lead the way, Sunshine. I'm yours," he replied passionately.

Holly and Charlie retreated to her bedroom and made crazy passionate love several times during the night. Their chemistry was off the charts, and they both knew there was no turning back. They fell asleep from exhaustion somewhere around 4:30 in the morning. The sun came streaming through the windows and woke them up hours later. Holly discovered that they had slept in a spoon position, and she was wrapped up in his arms. *I can't believe this is happening to me. Exactly 2 weeks ago I kicked James out and had a meltdown . . . I never thought I would have Charlie in my bed this soon. I know relationships can start out hot and heavy and fizzle into nothing, and he might be a rebound romance, but I want to see where this goes, even if it means I get my heart broken in pieces again.*

Charlie woke up and seemed to read her mind. "Good morning, Sunshine," he said while still wrapped around her. "Are you having any regrets? It's okay if you are, I understand."

She turned to face him and said, "I have no regrets, Charlie, I'm happy you stayed the night."

He gently touched her face and looked at her with those adoring brown eyes and replied, "If you start to have them later please tell me. I know this has happened fast. I can slow down if you want me to. I'm crazy about you, Holly. I don't want to see anyone else, and I'd like to be exclusive, although I want it to be at your pace. I'll let you lead. You let me know what you want, and I am yours for as long as you want."

Holly was touched by this and closed her eyes for a moment to fight back the tears, and then she replied, "I feel wonderful when I'm with you. I want to see where this goes, and I want to be exclusive. If you value your truck, you better be true," she said with a little laugh.

Charlie laughed and kissed her forehead, and he replied teasingly, "You said no matter what you wouldn't beat up my truck."

Holly smiled and said, "You know I was joking. Even if you did cheat, I wouldn't touch your truck. The aftermath of what I did to James made me feel awful. I didn't realize how much I hurt myself when I did it. I don't have a bad temper, even though it might seem that way. I've never gone off like that before. I was blindsided and furious, I felt like our entire relationship had been a lie."

"You never, ever have to worry about that. I've been alone for several years. I've dated a few women here and there and never really hit it off with anyone. I've had my eyes on you for a long time and wished that you were single so I could ask you out," Charlie said lovingly.

"I've been attracted to you since that day I ran into you at the deli. I tried to do the right thing and salvage my relationship with James, so I fought my feelings for you, especially after we got drunk at Jake's. Then, when I found out he cheated on me and got Amber pregnant, it infuriated me. If I had known then what I know now, we might have gotten together sooner. Oh, and Stan knows that you sent me the teddy bear. He walked in on me hugging it and was insistent to find out who sent it. I don't think we'll be able to hide our relationship, and I don't want to hide it," Holly said.

"I don't either. As long as we don't show physical affection at work, I think it will be fine. However, if I see you alone in the elevator, you know I will steal a kiss," he replied.

"I hope so. Are you hungry?"

"Yes, and I'd love a cup of coffee," he replied.

"I'll get the coffee started, and then we can figure out what to fix," she said.

"Do you like omelets? I make excellent omelets," he said.

"Yes, I love them. I have plenty of eggs, and cheese and ham and bacon too," she replied.

"I'm going to fix us an omelet while you make the coffee," he said.

"After breakfast we can take a shower, I have some new toothbrushes and can designate one for you," she replied smiling.

"That's nice of you, and you will probably think I'm nuts, but I keep an extra set of essentials in my truck. I have a toothbrush, toothpaste, a change of clothes, and deodorant, along with flashlight batteries and a first aid kit," Charlie said slightly embarrassed that his new lady love might think him weird.

"I don't think you're nuts. You're a man who likes to be prepared. I think keeping those items handy is a good thing," she replied nodding her head in agreement.

"If you still want to designate a toothbrush for me, I'd like that," he said with a smile . . . *I hope to stay with you each weekend until you move in with me.*

They got out of bed, and Holly put on a silky, dark green robe and slippers, and Charlie put on his jeans and remained shirtless. She admired his toned torso and stomach. He wasn't overly muscular, yet his arms and chest had definition, and she didn't see an ounce of fat on him. He was physically similar to James as far as his build and height. *I'm attracted to a certain physical type . . . I can't help what I like . . . and I LIKE Charlie . . .* she thought.

"You look so hot right now," she said, thinking that she wanted a repeat performance after breakfast.

"Not as hot as you do!" he replied with enthusiasm.

"I would like a repeat performance after breakfast," she said teasingly.

"Your wish is my command. I aim to please," he replied and pulled her close in a tight embrace.

They went into the kitchen to make breakfast. She looked at the kitchen clock and saw that it was 9:15, and she remembered that James said he would be over at 10:00 to get his things.

"Charlie, I just remembered something, and I hope you won't be embarrassed," she said with a hint of apprehension.

"What is it?"

"I remember that James said he was going to stop by this morning at 10:00 to pick up the rest of his items. I have them stored out in the shed. I had so much fun with you that I completely forgot about it," she said.

A sly smile crossed Charlie's face, and he had a devilish look in his eyes as he replied, "This is going to be fun. Let's enjoy our breakfast, and I'll come to the door with you when he knocks."

Holly let out a sigh of relief and said laughingly, "Keep your shirt off."

"Yes, ma'am," he replied cheerfully.

Charlie prepared a hearty omelet, and they sat down at the dining-room table to eat. Holly took a bite of the omelet and said, "Charlie, this is delicious. Thank you for fixing breakfast." She was glowing with happiness.

"I'm glad you like it. I like to cook. I'm not in a hurry to get home . . . *Being with you feels like home*. However, I don't want to overstay my welcome, and if you have things you need to do today, feel free to kick me out," he said thoughtfully.

"You can stay as long as you want," she smiled.

Charlie noticed the box of tarot cards on the dining-room table and was intrigued. "Do you read tarot cards?" he asked.

"Sometimes. I don't read them well enough to do a reading without my reference book. However, I have brought them to parties before and done readings for fun. I consult them every now and then when I have a pressing issue," she replied.

"How often do they provide the answer that you seek?" *I'd like to consult them to find out where we're headed.*

"You need to focus on your issue or question while you shuffle the deck. The more specific the question, the more accurate the answer. General readings are usually less clear, although sometimes interesting things will show up. If you are not focused, then the readings won't offer much guidance. The tarot cards are just a tool to access your intuition," she replied.

"You'll have to read them for me soon," he stated.

"I look forward to it," she replied and touched his arm. Just as they were finished eating, they heard a knock on the door. "There's James," Holly said with a giggle and picked up the key to the shed.

"Let's go greet him. I'll ask him if he needs some help," Charlie replied.

Holly and Charlie answered the door together, and James felt his heart sink . . . *I knew there was another man here when I saw that truck parked in the driveway. She didn't waste any time. It's only been 2 weeks, and he's no slouch. He obviously spent the night. They're only partially dressed . . . I know she did this on purpose.*

"Good morning. I'm here to get my things," James said feeling uncomfortable and humbled.

"Your stuff is in the shed. I put your name on the boxes. Here's the key," Holly said coolly.

"Do you need some help?" Charlie asked.

"No, I've got it," James replied looking down at the ground with a scowl on his face.

James unlatched the fence gate and walked to the backyard shed to retrieve his belongings. Holly and Charlie stood in the doorway and watched him load up his truck, which was parked on the street. It was a lovely autumn day, sunny and cool and the leaves were brilliant with color.

"He's a big guy. We're almost the same size," Charlie remarked.

"You're a little bit taller and whole lot nicer," Holly replied and snuggled close to him, reveling in his sexy, shirtless chest . . . *Charlie is a beautiful man inside and out.*

He squeezed her tight and asked, "How are you feeling right now?"

"Happy," she said smiling and looked up at him . . . *I hope you are my future.*

He touched her disheveled hair and said, "Me too." Charlie noticed the dented tailgate on James's truck and began to laugh as he remarked, "He still hasn't fixed the tailgate. You really did a number on it," he said as he kissed her on the head.

"Remember that," Holly replied playfully.

James finished loading the boxes into his truck and returned the key to Holly. "Here's your key back. Thank you," he said coldly, handed her the key, and turned to walk away. He couldn't get to his truck fast enough. He practically ran to it thinking . . . *She didn't waste any time finding another man . . . That pisses me off. She destroys my clothes, bashes my truck, and hops into bed with another guy 2 weeks later . . . DAMN that bitch.* His tires squealed as he sped up the street. As he exited onto the highway he remembered the large stash of cash he had in the basement closet. "DAMN, DAMN, DAMN!" he yelled out loud and banged his fist on the dashboard . . . *Holly didn't know about those hidden boxes. I hate to have to ask her to dig them out. She might start asking questions, or worse, she might open up those boxes and see the cash . . . SHIT . . . I have to think about how to get it back without arousing suspicion . . . Better think more about this.* He drove on down the highway, angry with himself for doing stupid things and wrecking his life. He was driving a good 20 miles over the speed limit, flying down the highway engrossed in his anger and had to slam on the brakes to avoid hitting the driver in front of him, who had come to a sudden stop due to a traffic jam. "LIFE SUCKS!" he bellowed, and sat there stewing for the next 30 minutes until the traffic started moving again.

"Let's take a shower," Holly said and closed the front door, feeling elated at having made James angry. It was a small and satisfying revenge.

"Lead the way," Charlie replied.

Holly and Charlie took a shower together which led to hours of passion in the bedroom. *I can't get enough of him . . . I feel like I took some kind of drug. I haven't felt this way in years.*

"Do you have any plans for next weekend?" Charlie asked as they relaxed in the afterglow, bodies still entwined.

"No. Would you like to get together again?" she asked smiling.

"You know the answer to that," he replied passionately and kissed her.

"What would you like to do, other than sex?" she asked.

"Anything or nothing. Think about it and let me know," he replied and kissed her again.

"How did I get so lucky?" she asked.

"No, how did *I* get so lucky?" he replied.

They spent the rest of the day curled up in front of the TV and sent out for pizza for dinner. Fate was usually shy around strangers, yet she warmed up to Charlie and did her best to nestle in between the two of them. She vocalized her annoyance whenever they would kiss. He thought Fate was adorable. Charlie didn't want to go home and Holly was having fantasies of what their life could be like living together, but it was getting late and tomorrow was a workday.

"Holly, I've had a great weekend with you, and I need to get going, even though I don't want to," Charlie said.

"I've enjoyed being with you too. You make me feel happy and carefree. You are welcome to stay over anytime, even during the week if you want," she said . . . *I don't know if I should have said that so soon.*

"And you can stay at my place anytime too," Charlie said.

"We could stay at your place next weekend," Holly said.

"Sure, I think you will like it. I can show you my woodshop and some of the things I've made. Can you come over on Friday and stay the weekend?"

"I'd love to Charlie," she replied happily.

"You make me a happy man," he said and put his arms around her in a tender embrace.

They walked outside to his truck. The night air was cold, and millions of stars made the night sky resemble the Milky Way, like the first time he kissed her back in September. A crescent moon was on display tonight.

"Good night, Charlie, I'll see you tomorrow," Holly said looking up at him.

"Good night, honey, I had a great time," he said and took her in his arms for a long kiss.

He got into his truck and pulled out of the driveway. She watched him drive away and went back into the house . . . *I have a new boyfriend . . . It's been a long time since I've said that. I can't believe my good luck. I hope this isn't just a rebound romance. I have never rebounded this quickly.* She was too happy and excited to go to bed so she took a sleep aid and read a book until she was able to fall asleep.

As she was getting ready for work the next morning and happily replaying the events of the weekend over and over again in her mind, she remembered that tonight was Zumba class and she would see Lisa. *I'm going to have to come clean with her and Charlie soon. I don't want to lose either of them or have them be mad at me. I don't want a repeat of the Victorian life in any way. We never talked about his past relationship with Lisa, we were too eager to jump in the sack, or rather I was . . . and Charlie didn't seem to have any complaints.*

While riding on the Metro, she wondered what work would be like now that they were a couple. *Should I make the first move this morning and go see him? I don't know what to expect.* Her apprehensions vanished into thin air when she stepped off the train and walked toward the escalator. Charlie was standing next to the escalator waiting for her. She started walking faster and when he saw her coming toward him, his face lit up with a big smile. *I want to throw myself in his arms. This is such a crazy feeling. If I was any happier I could fly.* When she got to him, he took her in his arms and gave her a big hug.

"Good morning, Sunshine," he said as he squeezed her in close to him.

"Good morning, Charlie, it's nice to see you again," she replied sweetly. This man took her breath away. She was in deep; there was no turning back. He was wearing a black trench coat. She liked it much better than the tan ones she saw everywhere.

"You look beautiful today," Charlie said and kissed her on the lips.

"Thank you, Charlie," Holly replied smiling.

"I guess we should get to work. Now I have something to look forward to every day . . . seeing you," Charlie said, thinking . . . *I love you.*

"You know where to find me," Holly said laughing.

They rode the escalator up to the street and walked to work together. This November morning was frosty, one of those days where you see your breath when you talk. The sun was shining, and it was going to be a beautiful and chilly day. Since they were going to the office, they decided to remain professional and not hold hands. They walked close to each other resisting the urge to touch.

"I didn't realize how difficult it would be not to touch you," Charlie said as they walked toward the office. "I need to practice restraint, which makes it even harder."

"Is it unladylike to say that I'm getting turned on hearing you say that?" Holly asked.

Charlie laughed at her comment and replied, "No. I'm constantly turned on when you're around. Now you know what we guys have to deal with."

"It's too bad the hotels around here are so expensive. I'm open for a rendezvous at lunchtime," Holly said flirtatiously, having a flashback to the Swedish life where they took secret getaways to a nearby inn to satisfy their lust.

"Please behave, dear lady, you are driving me crazy," Charlie said smiling. "We are nearing the office now and need to be respectful."

"I can't wait until this weekend when we *don't* have to be respectful!" she replied enthusiastically.

They walked into the building and waited for the elevator. The lobby area was quiet and void of people at this early hour. When the elevator arrived there was no one on it, and they kissed passionately before it opened at Charlie's floor.

"I'll call you around lunchtime and we can go for a walk or something," Charlie said as he exited the elevator.

"See you then," Holly replied cheerfully, thinking . . . *I've got to tell Patricia about our weekend. This will make her happy.*

Holly settled into her office and started the daily ritual of checking e-mails. Shortly thereafter, Patricia appeared at her door.

"Good morning," Holly said cheerfully.

"How was your date with Charlie this weekend?" Patricia asked excitedly.

"Awesome. He didn't leave until Sunday night!" Holly exclaimed, her face glowing.

"That *is* good news. I knew you two were perfect for each other. He probably waited for you at the Metro and walked with you to the office this morning," she said.

"How did you know?" Holly asked.

"Lucky guess. I can see Charlie doing that. He will probably walk you to and from the Metro every day. I'm extremely happy for you," Patricia said with a sincere smile. "Now, when are you going to tell Lisa and Charlie?"

"I don't know. I need to do it soon. Charlie mentioned going for a walk at lunch today. I should probably tell him then. I feel nervous about this," Holly said with a serious expression.

"Honestly, I don't feel that you have anything to worry about. I think both of them are mature enough to understand. Besides, Lisa is dating your ex-husband. She is the last person on earth who should be upset with you, and Charlie is in love with you. He's not going to let you go over something like this," Patricia assured her.

"Charlie hasn't said that he loves me; we're just beginning. It's too soon for I love you," Holly replied.

"I still don't think it will matter," Patricia said with conviction.

"I hope you're right. I'll tell him at lunch and get it over with," Holly declared.

"Good. Don't worry about it and I'll talk to you later. Bye," Patricia said as she turned to leave.

"Thanks," Holly said as she walked away.

Holly forced herself to focus on the many tasks she had to accomplish this morning and several hours later Charlie knocked on her door, startling her as she was concentrating on her work.

"What are you doing for lunch today, pretty lady?" he asked.

"Hopefully, taking a walk with you," she replied smiling and noticed that he had his black suit jacket on. He was wearing a dark red shirt and a colorful tie in shades of black and gray. He looked handsome.

"Do you want to get something to eat at the deli?" he asked.

"Yes, that sounds good," she agreed, starting to feel worried about what she had to tell him.

Holly slipped on her leather coat and walked with Charlie to the lobby. Stan was getting off the elevator and saw them standing there. He smiled at both of them and said, "Have a good lunch."

"You too," Holly replied and stepped into the elevator with Charlie.

He reached for her hand and noticed a look of concern on her face.

"Holly, is something wrong?"

"Yes, Charlie. I have something I need to tell you, and I'm not sure how you are going to take it."

"Are you planning to ditch me?" he asked in a joking manner, yet inwardly he was feeling very alarmed.

"Oh God, NO!" she replied emphatically and squeezed his hand. "That's the last thing I want to do."

Charlie breathed a sigh of relief. "Good. I was a little worried for a moment there."

"I'll tell you when we get outside," she said and they both stopped holding hands when the elevator stopped on the fourth floor and more people entered.

They reached the main lobby and walked outside together. "Okay, please tell me before I go nuts," he said to her.

"Okay, here goes. I am worried because tonight I have Zumba class and one of my new friends in that class just happens to be your ex-wife, Lisa," Holly said with trepidation.

Charlie stopped in his tracks and turned to face Holly. He looked in her eyes, and then began to laugh. "*That's* what you were worried about?" he asked incredulously and continued laughing and resumed walking with her. "I haven't seen or talked to Lisa in years. I have no feelings about her anymore, either good or bad. She's just a distant memory and a difficult lesson learned. I don't know what, if anything, she told you about us, however it must not be too bad since we are here together now." Charlie placed his arm around her shoulders for a moment and said, "I will never tell you who you can be friends with, as long as it's a female, and a male would require some questioning first," he replied lovingly to her.

Holly was relieved and wished she could hug Charlie, but she refrained as there were many people from MTAC milling about on the sidewalk. She replied, "You don't have to worry about male friends. The only ones I have are currently married or related to me. For the record, Lisa said that she was a terrible wife and that you were a good man. When Patricia and I got acquainted with her on the first night of class, we mentioned where we worked and she asked if we knew you.

The next thing I have to tell you is even crazier."

"I guess that you haven't told her about us yet," Charlie stated as they continued walking down the city sidewalk, leaves crunched beneath their feet and the wind was picking up.

"I haven't. I was waiting until the right time. I wanted to tell you first. She thinks I like a guy at work named Theo Barry," Holly said with a laugh.

Charlie laughed at this remark and said, "Thank you for doing that. I appreciate it," and briefly touched the small of her back. "What is the other crazy thing you wanted to tell me?" he asked as they approached the deli, one block away.

"This one is a real showstopper. Lisa is dating my first ex-husband, Roger Chasen. It's serious, and they're talking about moving in together. Before James and I broke up, we went to dinner with Roger and Lisa and Patricia and Andy one weekend. It was a shock to see Roger again. We felt uncomfortable yet managed to get through the evening and were civil to each other. Come to find out, Roger has been going to anger management classes for years, and Lisa has been going to them for the past few years. They have that in common and seem to be fun and nice people now. Roger took me to lunch last week to apologize for being a bad husband. Lisa gave him the idea and said she would jump at the chance to apologize to her ex-husbands for being such a bitch," Holly said.

They reached the deli, and he held the door for her. "You're right, that is an amazing story. Lisa was never one to apologize to anybody for anything," he replied, feeling surprised by this news. "I hope you won't be upset if I'm not anxious to go on a double date with them."

"No worries, Charlie. I understand completely, and I wouldn't expect you to double date with them. The whole thing is just weird. I can't find a better word for it," she replied with a loving look.

"I'm not saying I would NEVER go out with them, I just need to get used to the idea first. Let me buy you lunch. What would you like?" he asked.

"A ham and cheese on whole wheat," she replied . . . *What an angel of a man. He would actually consider going out with them someday.*

Charlie bought lunch for them, and they sat down at one of the nearby tables. As Holly was getting ready to bite into her sandwich, she saw someone she knew come through the door. "Oh my God, there's Roger," she said to Charlie.

"Are you serious?" he asked with raised eyebrows.

"Yes, and he sees me and is coming this way," Holly replied and put down her sandwich so she could greet him. Roger saw Holly sitting with a good-looking man and surmised that it must be Theo.

"Hi, Roger," Holly said cheerfully. "What brings you here today?" she asked.

"Hi, Holly. I was in the neighborhood and stopped in to get a sandwich to take with me. Are you going to introduce me to your friend? Is this Theo?" Roger asked heartily and curious to find out if this was the guy she mentioned to him last week.

"Yeah, I'm Theo, pleased to meet you," Charlie quipped, and held out his hand.

Holly wanted to laugh hysterically at Charlie introducing himself as Theo, yet she held it in, not wanting to embarrass Roger. The two men shook hands.

"Nice to meet you," Roger said with a friendly smile. "I'm just passing through and realized I had a few minutes to grab a sandwich. I'll leave you two alone and go get something to eat" . . . *I don't want to impinge on their date.*

"Have a good day, Roger," Holly replied.

"Same to you both," Roger said and waved as he went up to the counter to place his lunch order.

Charlie had an amused look on his face and so did Holly. They ate their sandwiches and didn't speak much until Roger left the deli. "I'll be Theo until you are ready to tell Lisa about us. Roger might give Lisa a call and tell her you are having lunch with a man and she will ask you questions tonight," Charlie said thoughtfully to Holly.

"You are an angel, Charlie, my angel, and thank you," she replied gratefully.

"Anytime, Sunshine," he said and winked at her.

"I feel so much better since I told you," Holly said with relief.

"I can't think of anything you could do that would turn me away," he said to her, his dark eyes seeming to look deep into her soul.

I think I just fell in love with this man . . . "Same here, Charlie," she replied.

They finished eating their lunch and left the deli to walk back to the office. "Do you have any more surprise stories for me?" he asked lightheartedly as they left the deli.

Holly remembered that she hadn't told him about the past life in Victorian England. Her momentary silence increased his curiosity.

"There must be something because you hesitated," he said playfully.

"There is something else. It's about a past life you and I shared with Lisa and Roger, and it's another showstopper," Holly said with a half-serious demeanor.

"This is from one of your regressions, correct?" he asked.

"Yes, brace yourself," she warned.

"Were we in a kinky foursome or something?" he asked jokingly.

Holly laughed at this and said, "No. Roger shot and killed you because he was my husband and he walked in on the two of us having sex."

"Seriously?" Charlie said and questioned in disbelief.

"Yes, I saw the whole thing, and it was terrible. It was back in Victorian England. You were married to Lisa and I was married to Roger. The four of us were friends, especially me and Lisa. We used to meet for tea and have long talks. Roger was an abusive husband who treated me badly and worked long hours away from home; he was a policeman. I was unhappy with him and harbored a secret crush on you. I envied Lisa even though we were best friends. You liked me too, and told Lisa on many occasions how beautiful and kind I was and what a lucky man Roger was. She grew jealous of me because of your comments and ended our friendship. I was terribly upset over this and you found me crying and tried to console me. We ended up in my bed later that day while Roger was away. We had an affair for about 6 months until we got careless, and Roger walked in on us having sex in his bed. He shot you twice, and you died immediately. He threatened to kill me if I told anyone, and proceeded to vandalize the house to make it look like you broke in to rape me. His fellow police officers believed him. Sometime later, Lisa came by to tell me she was moving away from the area and wished me to burn in hell. And that is another sad story in our past," Holly said. They were now standing in front of their office building.

"Holly, that's an incredible story, and a sad one. I'm not the cheating type, and neither are you, at least not in this life. I apologize for getting us in trouble. I don't blame Roger for killing me. Maybe Lisa was so hateful to me when we were married because there was some karmic payback going on. I will have to think some more on this, but I'm glad you told me. It seems we have chased each other through the centuries. Let's be careful in this life to stay together and not let anything come between us. I'd love to know if we had any happy past lives together," Charlie said, looking at her adoringly.

"Absolutely, I agree," Holly replied. "I think we should get back to work before our bosses find out we've been gone longer than an hour."

They turned to walk into the building. "I hope no one is on the elevator because I really want to kiss you," Charlie said as they waited in the lobby.

"I feel even closer to you now that I've spilled my guts," she replied.

"I listen with an open mind, and I don't want you to be afraid to tell me anything," he said reassuringly.

The elevator arrived, and it was full of people. Charlie rode up with Holly and walked her to her office. He stole a kiss when no one was looking and said that he would be back later to walk with her to the Metro at the end of the day.

About 15 minutes later, Stan walked into her office and said, "I approve of your new boyfriend."

Holly was tickled at his remark and she said, "Thanks, Dad."

Stan laughed at her comment and replied, "I'm leaving early for a dentist appointment. I'll see you tomorrow."

"I hope it turns out well and you have no cavities," Holly said and saw that she had recently received a number of e-mails that required her attention. It was time to get her head out of the clouds and get back to work.

Later that afternoon across town, Roger was back in his office and had just finished eating his sandwich. He called Lisa every day to check in. He was happy for Holly and thought Lisa might like the new tidbit of information he had to tell her about seeing Holly with Theo. He closed his office door and used the speakerphone to call her.

"Hi, Honey," Lisa answered.

"Hey, Beautiful, you know I just called to hear your voice," Roger flirted with her.

"How's your day going?" she asked him.

"It's going great. I stopped by a deli near MTAC to grab a sandwich and saw Holly having lunch with a man. She introduced us, and his name is Theo," Roger reported.

"That's wonderful, good for her. She mentioned a guy named Theo at Zumba. What did he look like?" Lisa asked.

"He was taller than normal, at least 6 foot 4 and slim. He had dark hair with streaks of gray and a bald spot on the back of his head. I think his eyes were brown," Roger replied.

"That's interesting; his physical description sounds a lot like Charlie," Lisa said.

"Your ex-husband?" Roger asked.

"Yes. Not many men are 6 foot 4 and work at MTAC. I remember Charlie used to color his gray when we were married. He was vain about his looks. It must be a coincidence. There are other really tall men in this world," Lisa replied.

"I think it is, because he shook my hand and said his name was Theo," Roger said with certainty.

"Then it must be a new guy. I'll tease her tonight about hooking up with Charlie," Lisa said with glee.

Roger had a fleeting thought as he looked out his office window that maybe Holly really was seeing Charlie and using the name ofTheo as a ruse because she was afraid to tell Lisa about it. "Roger, are you still there?" Lisa asked thinking maybe the line had gone dead.

"Yes, I'm still here. I had a strange thought just a second ago," Roger said slowly as he was pondering the possibilities of Holly dating Lisa's ex and what a funny turn of events that would be.

"Tell me your strange thought. When you have those thoughts it usually means something. Your intuition is generally on target," she insisted.

"Okay, what if Holly really *is* seeing Charlie and they are using the name of Theo as a ruse because she's hesitant to tell you the truth? Maybe he stopped covering his gray. I used to do that too, and I had a hard time keeping it up. It's just a thought, but if it were true, would that bother you?" he asked, hoping that she loved him enough that she wouldn't be troubled by lingering feelings for her ex-husband.

Lisa laughed and replied, "Don't you worry, I have no lingering feelings for Charlie. We were quite the mismatch. If she is seeing Charlie, then it's fine with me. I would welcome the chance to apologize to him. I was a first-class bitch and made his life miserable. I'm still going to tease her tonight and watch her reaction, though."

Roger was relieved that she didn't have any residual feelings for her ex and he said, "I'm happy to hear that. You know I love you and would jump off a cliff if you left me. Have fun at class tonight."

"I love you too, Roger, bye," Lisa said and hung up the phone.

Later that day when it was quitting time, Charlie went to Holly's office to see if she was ready to go home. "Are you ready?" he asked her.

"Yes. Where's your coat?" she asked, noticing that he wasn't carrying his trench coat or his briefcase.

"I need to stay another hour to finish up a presentation for the client tomorrow. I just wanted to walk you to the station," he replied.

"What a sweetheart and a gentleman you are, wanting to walk your lady to the train," Holly said with adoration.

"I have meetings most of the day tomorrow. One of them starts at 7:00 and another one ends at 5:00, which means I won't get out of there until at least 5:30 or 6:00. I won't get the chance to see you tomorrow," he said with some dismay.

"I'll be here working and thinking about you," she replied sweetly as she slipped into her walking shoes and put on her coat while he watched her intently, thanking his lucky stars that he found her.

They left the building and walked to the Metro station. He rode the escalator with her down to the turnstile area, and then pulled her aside to a corner where they could be alone for a few minutes.

Charlie took her in his arms and kissed her good-bye. "Have a good evening and I'll see you on Wednesday. Have fun at Zumba. I imagine that Roger probably already called Lisa and told her that he met Theo," he said.

"He probably did, and it will be interesting to see if she says anything tonight. I'll see you sometime Wednesday," she replied, feeling warm and happy inside. She kissed him again, and he watched her walk through the turnstiles. She turned and waved to him. *He sure is keeping an eye on me . . . He's afraid we'll lose each other like we did in our past lives. I hope things continue going well and we stay together. I think breaking up with James was a blessing in disguise . . .* she thought as she waited for her train.

Holly makes me crazy in the best way . . . Charlie thought as he walked back to the office to finish his presentation. *I think I'll give her a key to my house this weekend. I'll hold off on buying a rental property. I can't find anything that I want to fork over big bucks for, and then have to worry about finding and keeping renters. Maybe we can rent Holly's place when she moves in with me. I shouldn't assume that she will, however, I feel that it will happen down the road. The past lives she told me about are amazing . . . Being married to Lisa was hell in this life . . . Maybe I deserved her wrath for cheating on her in the past. Roger seemed like a nice guy, although I get angry when I think about him hitting Holly . . . best to not think about that right now.*

Holly made a point to leave for Zumba a little earlier than usual. She knew traffic made it a hassle to get there, and she didn't like being late to anything. She felt nervous when she pulled into the community center parking lot and saw Lisa's car. She walked into the gym and saw Lisa and Patricia sitting and talking on the bleachers with a few other women.

"You're on time," Lisa called out jovially to Holly as she walked toward the bleachers.

Maybe I should come clean with her tonight . . . "Yeah, I'm trying to get my butt here on time now," Holly replied as she walked up to the ladies.

"Roger said he met your new boyfriend today," Lisa stated with a playful look on her face. "He told me what Theo looked like and I swear, he sounds just like Charlie. Are you dating my ex-husband?" she said in mock seriousness.

Holly wasn't sure how to respond to Lisa's teasing and Patricia had a knowing and uncomfortable look on her face. Lisa knew from

Holly's expression and delayed response that she *was* dating Charlie. Holly decided to fess up, "Guilty as charged," she replied tentatively.

"I had a feeling you were. Actually, Roger is the one who put the idea in my head. I'm constantly amazed at that man's intuition. With more practice he could be a psychic. Now we have even more in common, each other's men," Lisa said laughingly and opened her arms for a hug. "I don't have a problem with that."

Holly smiled and hugged Lisa. "Thank you, I am so relieved!" she said emphatically.

"I have no reason to be mad at you. This is the strangest thing that ever happened to me," Lisa replied. "I'm guessing double-dates are off the table, although I would like to apologize to Charlie sometime. I'm pretty sure he still hates me."

"We talked about that, and he might be open to going out with you and Roger eventually," Holly said. "He needs time to get used to the idea."

"Oh, that's good. By the way, where did you get the name ofTheo?" Lisa asked.

"Charlie bought me a teddy bear to cheer me up a few days after James broke my heart, and I named him Theo Barry. Using the name Ted Bear sounded too made up," Holly smiled.

Lisa laughed and said, "That is really cute. Although I think Ted Bear or even Teddy Barry probably would have worked. Hey, I just thought of something. The name Teddy Brown would have worked. You could have used that one. I'm happy for you, Holly, and I hope that things go well for you and Charlie. Patricia, how long have you known about this?" Lisa asked.

"Charlie's had a thing for Holly for a while now. He was hoping that she would break up with James so he could ask her out," Patricia replied.

"I can see why he's attracted to Holly. She's pleasant and easygoing and not a drama queen like I was—and still am at times," Lisa said to them.

"Thank you, Lisa, although James might say otherwise. He stopped by to pick up the rest of his things on Sunday morning and saw me with Charlie," Holly said with a mischievous smile.

"Yes! I love it, revenge is sweet," Lisa replied with enthusiasm. The class started and the ladies worked it for the next hour.

Holly was exhausted when she got home that night and took a long, hot shower before going to bed. *I'm so happy that Lisa is okay with me seeing Charlie; she's turning out to be a great friend.*

For the rest of the week, Charlie waited for Holly every morning next to the Metro escalator so they could walk to work and leave together. They were growing incredibly close and found an enormous amount of joy and happiness with each other. Holly savored each moment, as she thought the beginning of a new relationship and learning about each other was the most exciting time. Charlie was ready to marry her. He thought that she was perfect, and he would do anything to make her happy. They were both excited when Friday rolled around. She was coming to his place for the weekend.

"I'm so happy it's Friday," Charlie said excitedly as he walked close to Holly on the way to the train station. It was still early November, although it felt more like a cold January evening.

"Me too. What do you want to do for dinner tonight?" she asked.

"I was thinking that we would order a pizza. I want to time it so it arrives around the same time you do," he replied.

"I should be at your place by 6:30. I already have my bag packed. I just want to make sure Fate has enough food for the weekend," she said.

"You don't need to bring a lot of clothes," Charlie winked.

"Good, because I haven't packed much to wear," she replied teasingly.

"Will you bring your tarot cards?" he asked.

"Sure. It'll be fun to see what the cards have to say about us," she replied and reached for his hand as they crossed the street.

"It feels so easy to be with you. It must be from our past-life connection. I think we are meant to be together," he said.

"I think so too. Timing is everything. I had quite the crush on you after our drunken night at Jake's. Things weren't going well between me and James, and I had fantasies about you whenever I saw you," she said, still holding his hand and not caring if anyone from MTAC saw them like this.

"You've been my fantasy girl for a long time. I want to make you happy so that you never develop a crush on any other man," Charlie said with a serious look on his face.

"Things were going downhill between me and James for a long time before I developed a crush on you. As long as you don't take me for granted and run off with the guys every chance you get and keep secret lovers on the side, I won't develop crushes on other men," she replied and squeezed his hand for emphasis.

"You are going to get so tired of me constantly being around that you will rejoice on the rare occasion that I do spend a weekend with the guys," he said half-jokingly and continued, "You will bug me to give you some space. You should know that you NEVER have to worry about other women."

"I know that, and it makes me love you even more," Holly replied dreamily . . . and then realized that she had blurted out that she loved him . . . *Oh no, I said the L word!*

Charlie felt her flinch as soon as she realized what she had said, and he wanted to do a happy dance. They reached the down escalator and Charlie led her over to a corner out of the line of foot traffic and turned to look at her, and he said, "Holly, I love you too."

Holly's world stopped turning, her posture softened, and she was speechless for a few seconds, looking into Charlie's eyes . . . *He loves me, I knew it, and yet it feels incredible to hear him say it . . .* "I can't believe I just blurted out that I love you in such an unromantic place," she said and her heart felt like it was going to jump out of her chest.

Charlie laughed and pulled her close in an embrace and said, "That makes it even more special. You make everywhere romantic. I'm glad we got that out of the way. Now I can freely tell you how much I love you and not worry that I'm going to scare you off."

Holly gently pulled away from the embrace so she could look up at him and she said, "I love you, Charlie Thomas, you are my gentle giant."

Charlie kissed her and said, "Let's get going. I can't wait for you to get to my house." They stepped on the escalator, went through the turnstiles, and kissed good-bye when their respective trains arrived.

"I'll see you shortly," Holly said with a smile.

"Drive safe," Charlie replied.

Holly arrived home and changed her clothes, set out plenty of food and water so Fate wouldn't starve, placed the tarot cards in her overnight bag, and left the house. Charlie lived about 8 miles from her in a large town house in Springfield. She was excited as she drove down the road, and reminded herself to maintain the speed limit. *I think I'll give him a house key . . . This is a whirlwind romance. I've never had one progress at this speed with this much intensity . . . I need to stop analyzing it and just go with the flow. Something tells me that this isn't a passing thing and I don't need to worry about getting my heart broken . . . It just FEELS right.*

Holly turned into Charlie's neighborhood and even though it was dark, she could see that the townhomes were large and beautiful. They were at least 2,500 square feet with a driveway and a garage and a little bit of a yard. Charlie lived in an end unit on a cul-de-sac. She pulled into his driveway and got out of her car. She walked up the steps to his front door and found him standing there waiting for her. He opened the door and let her in.

"Did you have any trouble finding the place?" he asked and took her overnight bag and set it on the sofa.

"No. I had an idea of where you lived, and it was easy to find," she replied looking around his open and airy living room . . . *I can see myself living here. What a beautiful house.* "Charlie, you have a lovely home. I love how spacious and open it is."

"Thank you. I purposely made it as masculine as possible after I separated from Lisa," he said with a laugh.

"It's masculine, however, your furnishings and their placement are well done," she said with sincerity. She loved his wine-colored leather furniture and rustic, honey-colored end tables. The floors were hardwood and continued throughout the house.

"Brianna helped me with that. She seemed to know the perfect balance between masculine and suitable for bringing home a date. I have a maid service that keeps it clean. I've already told my kids about you, and they are anxious to meet you," Charlie said as he took her in his arms and kissed her.

"I look forward to meeting them," she replied and rested her head on his chest. She looked at several family portraits that were hanging on the wall and she could easily pick out Brianna and Tyler. "Your children take after you. They have your coloring and your smile." . . . *I wonder what our kids will look like . . . Wait a minute! Where the hell did that come from? I'm past my prime for childbearing and Charlie's a grandfather.*

"You never had any children. Was that by choice?" he asked wondering why such a sweet woman like her was childless. She seemed like the nurturing type.

"Yes and no," she replied. "I was open to having children, it just never happened. Roger wanted kids, but he was abusive and cruel, and I wanted to get out of that situation before I got pregnant. I think he wanted them as a way to keep me from leaving. Alex didn't want any kids and got a vasectomy before we met. James and I were open to it and didn't try to prevent it from happening, yet I never got pregnant. I think I'm infertile. I've never had the strong desire to have a child like a lot of other women, and that's probably why I never got depressed about not having one, although I think I would have been a good mother."

"I know you would," Charlie replied and squeezed her tight. They heard a knock on the door. "That must be the pizza. I hope you're hungry," he said. Charlie paid the pizza delivery guy and Holly followed him into the large, gourmet eat-in kitchen for dinner. Charlie's kitchen was bigger than her living room, kitchen, and dining room combined. The appliances were stainless steel, and the countertops were a lovely, smoky gray granite. The kitchen was painted a pale gray and the cabinets were black. There was a large island in the middle with the same granite countertop and a small table with four chairs off to the side looking out the French doors into the small backyard. They sat down at the table.

"You've got it all, Charlie. A fabulous home with an awesome kitchen. I could be inspired to cook here," Holly said as she picked up a slice of pizza and took a bite.

Charlie had an amused look on his face, and he stood up and reached into the front pocket of his jeans. "I have something for you. Last week you asked if I could give you the moon and stars. This isn't exactly what you were referring to, however, I hope it will suffice for now," he said as he took out a cute little keychain which depicted a colorful rendering of the sun, moon, and stars beneath an acrylic circle that spun around, and handed it to Holly. "Here are the keys to my house, Sunshine. You can come over anytime, day or night," he said with that adoring look in his eyes that made her melt.

Holly swallowed her pizza, took a drink of water, and replied, "Thank you, Charlie. The key chain is lovely. We must be on the same wavelength. As I was driving here tonight, I was thinking that I wanted to give you a key to my house. We can go to the store tomorrow and have one made" . . . *I adore this man, he's incredibly thoughtful.*

Charlie was delighted that she was thinking the same thing and he replied, "That's a good plan." . . . *Hopefully, she will want to move in with me 6 months from now and we can put her place up for rent. She has a cute little house in a prime location. We could easily charge $1,800 a month or more for it.*

Holly and Charlie ate their pizza, and then she expressed a desire to see his woodshop. "Charlie, I would love to see your woodshop. I noticed your truck wasn't anywhere in sight when I pulled up. Do you have enough room in your garage for a woodshop and a truck?" she asked.

"My woodshop is in the basement. It's more of a lower level. It's a walk-out basement so it's not underground. That was another thing I did after Lisa left. I expanded my woodshop to encompass the entire lower level. I made a lot of the furniture that you see in this house. I made the living room end tables, the coffee table, and the table and chairs we are currently sitting on. Woodworking is therapy for me. I can get lost in a project and before I know it, 10 or 12 hours have passed. I haven't done much woodworking these past several months since I've had to travel. Now that I have a pretty lady in my life, I would rather spend time with you than make furniture," he said and stood up "Come on, I'll show you."

They walked downstairs to the expansive, finished basement devoted to woodworking and Holly was impressed. "Charlie, this is amazing," she said in awe, as she looked at the equipment and tools. "I'm impressed that you made such lovely pieces." . . .*When I move in, I want him to keep this workshop . . . I don't care what I have to get rid of. I'm proud of him and he can do woodworking whenever he wants.*

"Thank you, Holly. If the day comes when you want to move in, I can look into renting a space for this," he said.

"When that day comes, I wouldn't ask you to give up this

woodshop. I think it's wonderful, and I think there's enough room in your house for me and my stuff. I'm proud of you and the beautiful things that you've made. You have a wonderful talent," she said lovingly and reached for his hand.

She said "when I move in" . . . YES! "You said 'when,' so that means you have thought about us living together," he said teasingly. "You and Fate can move in whenever you're ready. It doesn't matter if it's next month, 6 months from now, or a year or 2 from now," he said and kissed her.

"We've happened so quickly, and yet I'm not worried about anything with you. I see a future together, and thank you for remembering my cat," she replied.

"Fate is sweet. It's been a long time since I've had a pet, and I'm partial to cats. Speaking of fate, did you bring your tarot cards?" he asked in jest.

"Yes. Do you want to consult them now?"

"Sure. Since we are on the topic of the future, let's find out what they have to say," he suggested.

They went upstairs and Holly retrieved the tarot cards and guidebook from her bag. They sat down across from each other at the kitchen table and Holly explained the options. "Okay, there are several types of readings. We can do a one-card reading, where you think of a question and draw a single card for the answer, or we can do a three-card reading telling the past, present, and future. We could do a Celtic Cross reading where we go more in-depth as to the circumstances and influences surrounding you and how they might impact the final outcome. So, which one would you like?"

"I'd like a one-card reading," he replied. "If the one card isn't clear, can I draw another one?"

Holly handed him the cards and said, "Yes, I do that sometimes. Think of your question and shuffle the cards until you feel you are ready for the answer. When you are done, place the cards back on the table and draw the first card off of the top."

Charlie shuffled the deck for a few moments thinking . . .*What's in store for me in my future with Holly? . . . Is this the real thing, or am I just a rebound romance?* He placed the cards on the table and drew the first one from the top of the deck. The card Charlie drew was the Sun. The Sun shows a naked child smiling and riding on a white horse. Behind them is a row of sunflowers and a large yellow sun. This card is positive and portends joy and energy and overall good fortune. It can indicate a new friendship or relationship that will bring much happiness, or that you are approaching a moment that will change your life for the better.

"This looks like a good card," he said with a smile. "You are my Sunshine, the card indicates that plain and simple. Your sunflowers are pictured too."

Holly smiled and said, "This card portends much happiness and overall good fortune. It can indicate a new relationship that will bring great joy and a change in your life for the better. I think this is a good omen for us."

"You are the change in my life for the better," he replied. "Are you going to consult the cards?"

"No. I feel good about us," she replied with certainty.

"I have an idea, would you like to see the bedroom?" Charlie asked with a devilish smile.

"Yes," Holly replied eagerly, "show me the way."

Holly and Charlie went up the staircase to his bedroom. His room was large with vaulted ceilings and a gas fireplace. The room was painted a cream color. Charlie had a king-sized bed with a tan leather quilted headboard. The floors were the same honey-colored hardwood as the living room. The bedspread was made from a dark brown velour-type fabric. The nightstands on each side of the bed matched the hardwood floors exactly.

"Charlie, did you make these nightstands too?" she asked, marveling at how perfectly they matched the floors.

"Yes. I made the chest at the foot of the bed as well," he replied.

"They are beautiful, and I love the earth tones of this room," she said approvingly as she looked at the dark brown window treatments and coordinating area rug with its soft shades of cream, brown, and tan. Charlie ignited the gas fireplace, and then came over to Holly and they started kissing. They spent most of the weekend in his bedroom, consumed with passion.

CHAPTER 13

A Shotgun Wedding

James and Amber got married the weekend after Thanksgiving at Bryce's home in a quiet neighborhood in Vienna. He lived in a spacious, five-bedroom, 4.5 bathroom home, with 5,000 square feet of living space on a half-acre lot. His home was valued somewhere around 2.5 million and looked like it should be in the pages of a magazine, with its soaring ceilings and light-filled rooms. Bryce hated clutter, and his home was immaculate. He had plenty of community connections and was able to arrange a small wedding ceremony for his cousin. A few of Amber's nearby relatives, including her older sister Jenny, and some mutual friends from American Steak were invited. Her father was in an assisted living facility several hours away and wasn't able to travel. Her mother died of cancer 10 years ago. Amber and Jenny were close to Bryce and his older brother Luke, who was even more corrupt than Bryce. Most of the relatives in attendance were her cousins. Her mother came from a family of five kids, and her father from a family of six.

The ceremony was held in the enormous sunroom adjacent to the kitchen, with long French doors leading to an outside patio and porcelain-tiled floors in a sandy beige color. The sun was shining bright today even though it was cold outside. Bryce temporarily relocated the furniture and set up folding chairs auditorium style, 15 on each side, for the expected guests. James stood in the sunroom with Bryce, Luke, and Father Derek Davidson, and chatted with the arriving guests while Amber got dressed in one of the upstairs bedrooms.

Father Davidson, affectionately known as "Father Derek," was a catholic priest who lived in two worlds. He played the role of pious priest better than any actor ever could. Beloved by his parishioners, his masses were consistently filled to capacity as he was a charismatic speaker. He enjoyed the adulation and attention that life as a priest provided. He was at the forefront of many civic good deeds, such as feeding and providing shelter for the homeless, helping disadvantaged youths find their way, overseeing a local food bank, and sponsoring community fundraisers for worthy causes. It helped that he was physically attractive and in his late 30s. Standing 6 foot 2 with light brown hair, hazel eyes, a handsome face, dazzling smile, and slim build, he relished attention from women. He had no homosexual or pedophile tendencies. He never had sex with women from his church. Bryce happily provided expensive call girls for him. Bryce enjoyed his friendship with Derek, it helped to have a popular priest in your corner when it came to crafting a good guy image in the public eye. Bryce and Derek had each other's back. Bryce knew that Derek loved drinking, gambling, sex with hookers, especially threesomes, and the occasional drug binge. Derek agreed to conduct a secular ceremony for Bryce's cousin in exchange for a week's worth of call girls. Father Derek was easily bought and never refused doing favors in return for cash or hot women.

"James, how are you feeling on your big day?" Luke Decker asked sarcastically with an evil smile and smug look on his face. Luke resembled Bryce so much that people often asked if they were twins. He was a few inches shorter and 1 year older with the same hard, muscled body, shaved head, perfect white teeth, and his eyes were brown. Luke was mean. Where Bryce arranged hits, occasionally beat someone up, and sometimes felt compassion, Luke was a hired gun.

James was dressed in his well-tailored and expensive navy blue suit, which survived Holly's wrath, and he could feel himself start to sweat. "I'm feeling fine, doing what I have to do," he replied with a stone-cold face . . . *How would you feel if you had a shotgun wedding on your birthday at the age of 54? I hope you and Bryce end up as someone's bitches in prison and get butt fucked unmercifully.*

"You know the alternative if you decide to back out at the last minute," Bryce whispered in his ear.

"Yes, I'm well aware of that. I want my birthday to be a happy one," James replied without smiling.

"James, smile, be happy. This is a big day for you and Amber," Mike Collins, a shift manager at American Steak, said to him and slapped him on the back. Mike never met Holly. He was one of the newer managers and good friends with Amber's Mafia cousins. They helped him get the job. "You're a lucky man. Amber's a beauty." Mike had a big crush on Amber; alas, he wasn't her type. He was 37 and on the small side, standing about 5 foot 8 and skinny, with curly brown hair and glasses. He was too nerdy looking to suit her taste.

"Oh, I'm happy, Mike. I'm feeling a little nervous, getting married and having a baby at my age," James lied with a fake smile. James liked Mike, thought he was a good guy and a decent shift manager.

"I would trade places with you in a heartbeat," Mike replied with enthusiasm.

Oh, how I wish you could . . . Do you know any genies? "I'm sure you'll find someone, Mike, you're a great guy," James replied sincerely . . . *I'd like to help him bulk up, dress better, and get the ladies.*

"James! You look so handsome," Gina Porter squealed as she gave James a hug, her large breasts pressed firmly against his chest. He had a fling with Gina for a few weeks before he moved in with Holly. They liked to do it in the restaurant booths after closing. He broke it off with her once he was settled at Holly's. Gina was okay with that. She just liked having sex with James and wasn't in the market for a committed relationship. Gina was a bartender at American Steak, and she stood 6 feet tall, with a voluptuous and curvy body, long dark hair, and brown eyes. He didn't usually go for tall women, however, she was fun, and he never tired of staring at her chest when he could get away with it.

"Thank you, Gina. It's nice that you could make it," James replied.

"I haven't forgotten the fun we used to have. I know with Amber being pregnant that you might have 'needs.' I'm still available to help, just let me know," Gina said softly, out of earshot from Bryce and Luke, and kissed his cheek.

I haven't wanted sex or been able to perform since before I broke up with Holly . . . Gina just did the trick . . . Damn, I could do her over and over again right now . . . I guess I'll have to fantasize about her tonight. I know Amber will want to do it, and I need something to get me excited . . . No more cheating . . .
"I'm trying to be a good boy now," James replied jokingly, with a laugh.

"Good luck," she said with a sexy smile, gently flipped her hair, and turned her eyes toward Father Derek.

Amber's baby bump was showing, and she had gained 15 pounds. Her petite frame showed the extra weight and made her appear heavier than she really was, and as Jenny zipped her into her wedding dress, Amber looked at herself in the mirror and wanted to scream. "I'm so fucking fat and ugly. I hate this dress. My boobs are gigantic, and my face looks like a puffer fish!" She wailed and dissolved into a teary mess, crying and ruining her makeup. Her wedding dress was white satin and featured an empire waist, long and sheer lace sleeves, a sweetheart neckline and an A-line skirt, not overly full, which draped nicely and concealed her little baby bump. It had a small, chapel-length detachable train. The dress was stunning and looked lovely on Amber, even though she didn't feel pretty.

"Amber, honey, please stop. You look beautiful. It's natural to gain weight when you get pregnant. You have a wonderful, sweet new life growing inside, and you should be happy about that. And you are getting married to a good-looking man who loves you. Just focus on eating better, more nutritious food, fruits, and vegetables, stay away from the sweets and breads. That will minimize your weight gain. It's not too late to do that," Jenny said, taking her in her arms and hoping to calm her sister's nerves.

He doesn't love me; he doesn't even like me anymore . . . I wish I had told Jenny the truth . . . "That's easy for you to say. You're taller, and can easily carry extra weight without looking like a balloon. When you were pregnant you looked gorgeous, both times, not like a fat blimp," Amber replied and continued to sob heavily. She was envious of Jenny. Jenny had the same pretty, long blond hair and blue eyes. She was 3 years older than Amber and 5 inches taller. Jenny was happily married with two children and a husband who adored her.

Bryce knocked on the door to find out if they were close to being ready. "Hey, how's it going in there?" he said as Jenny walked over and opened the bedroom door.

"Not good. Amber's having a meltdown. She's got a bad case of nerves and hates the way she looks," Jenny replied with exasperation.

Bryce entered the room and saw a distraught Amber. By now, she looked like a raccoon. Her eye makeup was smeared from crying. His heart sank, and he took her in his arms. This made her cry again. She was deeply touched by his concern, and saw him as a father figure even though he was just a few years older than she. She clung tightly to him.

"Hey, sweetheart, you're going to be okay. I guarantee it. Shhh, stop crying. There's a room full of people waiting to see you get married. Let Jenny fix your makeup. Think happy thoughts of your baby and the new family you're creating," he said soothingly and stroked her hair as he held her for a few minutes. This seemed to do the trick. Bryce felt especially protective of Amber. Even growing up he watched out for her, and she knew she could come to him for help with any problems.

Thank God for Bryce . . . He's like a father and big brother combined . . .

He planned this entire wedding for me, bought me this dress, and took care of the details . . . I need to straighten up and get on with it . . . "Thank you for everything, Bryce, you're the best. I'm so happy you're here," Amber replied as she released him from the embrace and smiled up at him.

"That's my girl, and there is nothing wrong with that dress. It looks beautiful on you," he said. "We'll see you in a few minutes, right?"

"Yes," Amber replied, and Bryce left the room so she could finish getting ready.

"Feeling better?" Jenny asked, relieved that Bryce was able to calm her down.

"Yeah, and I'm sorry for the meltdown. I appreciate you being here and helping me get ready," Amber replied humbly, and Jenny helped her fix her makeup and look pretty for the ceremony.

The guests were seated although a few were standing. A string quartet played classical music until they received the cue from Bryce to play the bridal march. Jenny was the first to walk down the aisle. She was wearing a strapless burgundy satin gown and carrying a bouquet of white roses; she wore her hair in a soft and stylish updo. The "Wedding March" played and Bryce and Amber walked down the aisle to the front of the sunroom where Father Derek and James were standing. Amber decided against wearing a veil. Instead, she wore a small, crystal-studded crown and her long, blond locks were full and softly curled. She carried a bouquet of red and white roses. She looked like a princess.

Amber does look beautiful . . . I wish I could feel happy . . . This is the worst day of my life . . . James thought as he watched her walk toward him, his stomach twisting into knots . . . *Bryce looks so damn smug . . . He's getting his kicks out of this . . . I wonder what he offered Derek to perform this ceremony . . . I've seen him at the gambling tables . . . He's just as bad as the rest of us . . . He's the high priest of pussy hounds.*

James is so handsome . . . Why do I love him so much? . . . He doesn't return my feelings . . . I thought of backing out at the last minute when Bryce was consoling me . . . except that I can't disappoint him . . . He went to all of this trouble for me . . . If I backed out, I would hate myself . . . because then I would lose James completely . . . I can't let that happen . . . My baby deserves to know its father . . . Amber thought as she saw James at the end of the aisle . . . *I'll make him love me . . . I refuse to give up.*

Bryce and Amber reached the front of the room and he kissed her on the cheek, then she took her place next to James and Father Derek began to speak. "Dearly beloved, we are gathered here today to join this man and woman in the loving bond of marriage. You are adding to your life not only the love and affection for each other, but the sacredness of a deep and enduring trust. You are agreeing to share strength, responsibilities, hardships, disappointments, happy times, and most importantly, love. Love is nurturing tolerance, understanding, and a sense of humor. Love is having the capacity to forgive and forget, and giving each other an atmosphere in which each can grow to their full potential. James and Amber, please join hands and recite your vows."

James and Amber faced each other and joined hands. Amber searched his face for a trace of love, however, his face and eyes were void of expression . . . *I'm looking at a robot . . . I feel so bad . . . I've dreamed of this day since I was a little girl . . . I never thought it would happen like this . . . What have I done?* . . . she thought.

Numb, I feel completely numb . . . Forced to marry a woman I don't love because she trapped me, or end up at the bottom of the Potomac . . . I'm such an idiot . . . James thought, and then stiffened his spine and said the following words, "I, James, take you, Amber, to be my lawfully wedded wife, to have and to hold from this day forward, for better or for worse, for richer, for poorer, in sickness, and in health, to love and to cherish until death parts us." . . . *Thank God that's over with.*

"I, Amber, take you, James, to be my lawfully wedded husband, to have and to hold from this day forward, for better or for worse, for richer, for poorer, in sickness, and in health, to love and to cherish until death parts us," Amber said, and meant every word.

"Wedding rings are made from precious metals and symbolize the sacred circle of your love and devotion. Wear them with pride every day as a constant reminder of your promise to each other," Father Derek said. "You may now exchange rings."

"Amber, with this ring, I take you to be my wife," James said and slipped the gold band on her finger. At this point in the ceremony, James felt his heart soften as gave her the ring . . . *Where is this feeling coming from?*

Amber sensed the change of energy, and her heart became a little lighter as she said, "James, with this ring, I take you to be my husband. I love you." She slipped a ring of tungsten steel onto his finger and smiled at him, and to her surprise, he smiled back.

"With the power vested in me by the Commonwealth of Virginia, I pronounce you husband and wife. You may kiss the bride!" Father Derek said joyfully.

Amber and James shared a passionate kiss as the wedding guests clapped loudly, and he pulled her close into a warm hug and whispered, "Don't worry, honey. We'll make it work."

"Thank you, James, and happy birthday," Amber replied and felt the weight of the world lift from her shoulders.

CHAPTER 14

Into the Future

As the weeks and months went by, Holly and Charlie fell deeper in love. They were like two peas in a pod. They wanted the same things from a relationship. They were older and experienced in long-term commitments and deep, heartbreaking disappointments. They knew what did and didn't work for them in their past relationships. They met each other's family, and everyone was happy for them. There were no family issues of not liking each other's relatives. Holly continued her Zumba classes with Lisa and Patricia and enjoyed a girls' day out once a month, usually meeting them for lunch on a Saturday or Sunday and shopping or seeing a movie.

Holly moved in with Charlie in May. She opted to keep her house and rent it instead of selling. Charlie was happy with that as he would get experience managing a rental property. She was delighted to let him oversee it, and she would keep the $800 monthly profit. The house would be paid off in 3 more years. As they were cleaning out her house, Holly had a feeling she should double-check the closet underneath the stairs. The closet was empty, but she had the nagging feeling that she was missing something. She bent down and put her arm underneath the bottom shelf above the floor and felt some boxes. She pulled out four boxes and noticed they were sealed with packing tape. She was curious as to what could be inside, yet she was exhausted and didn't feel like opening them to investigate. She brought them upstairs and put them into a larger box.

"What's in those?" Charlie asked, watching her place the smaller boxes into a larger one.

"I don't know. I'm too tired to check them out right now. They must belong to James. I'll send him an e-mail to come and get them," she said.

"It might be something valuable. It's strange they are sealed up like that," he said.

"I'll open them later," she replied. "I'm exhausted and want to get home, to my new home with you, and go to sleep."

"No problem, Sunshine, I'll let you sleep tonight," he said and winked at her. "Why don't we label it buried treasure?" Charlie asked sarcastically.

"That's a good one," Holly replied and wrote the words "Buried Treasure" on the sides of the boxes. Holly sold most of her furniture. She was happy to start over with Charlie. She loved his town house and everything about him. He was her home now.

James and Amber became parents on April 28 and named their little girl Isabella Maria. As James held his baby daughter in his arms for the first time, he started to cry and realized that he loved her dearly . . . *She's so tiny . . . and precious . . . and I'm actually happy to meet her.* He thought of how he initially wanted to have Amber killed, and then broke down into tears and felt deeply ashamed. Amber thought he was crying tears of joy, and she was touched by his display of emotion.

"I'm going to call her Belle," he said to Amber as she was lying in the hospital bed.

She noticed the expression on his face as he looked at their baby girl, and she breathed a heavy sigh of relief . . . *I knew he would love our baby. He's really come a long way.* "I like that. We'll both call her Belle," she replied.

"I know I've given you a lot of grief and I want to apologize. I hated that you trapped me into becoming a father and marrying you, however, I love this little angel, and I promise I will do whatever it takes to make our family work. You've put up with a lot from me," James said to her with deep sincerity . . . *and I'm ashamed for wanting to put a hit on you.*

"That's because I love you, James. I know you don't feel the same, and that's okay. I hope that one day you will," she said.

James looked at her and said, "I have deep feelings for you, Amber, and I stopped hating you on the day we got married. I'm committed to you and Belle." . . . *It's true, I don't love Amber like I loved Holly . . . even so, we can make it work.*

"That's enough for me," Amber replied . . . *We can build on those feelings,* thankful that James was planning to stick around. When he first moved in he reminded her almost daily of how she trapped him. After their wedding, and as her pregnancy progressed he became more caring and thoughtful. She hoped that one day he would love her in return.

"Thank you for this beautiful baby," James said and kissed her. He hadn't forgotten about the stash of money he left at Holly's. Amber's pregnancy was difficult, and he was preoccupied with helping her and just getting through each day. He felt the money was safely hidden and that he would get it from Holly at some point in the future. He thought about it as he gazed at his new daughter . . . *That money will come in handy. It will pay for her college . . . I've got to get in touch with Holly and try to get it back, even if I have to confess how I acquired it . . . I WILL man up this time . . . I will do whatever it takes.*

Charlie and Holly made plans to go to the beach at the beginning of June, before the summer rush started. They drove to Virginia Beach for 3 days of sun, riding bikes, and strolling on the boardwalk. Holly hadn't been to the beach in several years and was excited to go. Charlie made reservations at the Courtyard Marriott, an upscale hotel on the boardwalk overlooking the ocean. As they walked into the bright and airy hotel room, the first thing Holly did was open the curtains to the balcony. The sun was high in the sky, and it filled the room with its warmth. She unlocked the sliding glass doors and stepped onto the balcony to look at the ocean. The sun was blinding. She closed her eyes and let it encompass her for a few moments while she stood there relishing its warmth, listening to the ocean and the sound of seabirds . . . *I love the sun . . . I wonder if the light people see when they die and go through the tunnel is like this, drawing you in . . .* Her thoughts were pleasantly interrupted when Charlie joined her on the balcony. He wrapped his arms around her and kissed her neck.

"Are you ready to hit the beach?" he asked.

"Yes, let's go," she replied happily.

Charlie was blind to the other pretty women walking around. He couldn't take his eyes off of Holly's taut and toned body. She felt completely and totally loved, and she trusted Charlie. The sun was beaming down upon them as they sunned themselves on the sand, listening to the sounds of seagulls and the waves washing ashore. Charlie had a present for her. He slipped it into their beach bag when she wasn't looking. He reached into the bag and pulled out a small jewelry box and placed it into Holly's hand while she had her eyes closed.

"What's this?" she asked and sat up.

"Open it and find out," he said with a smile.

Holly opened the little box to find a diamond ring inside. It was a lovely and round, two-carat diamond surrounded by a halo of small blue topaz stones and set in yellow gold. It was unusual to find colored stones in an engagement ring. He wanted something unique and different. He had it specially designed for her. She stared at it for a few seconds, and then looked at him . . . *Is he going to propose?*

"Charlie, it's absolutely beautiful," she said, and moved the box around a little to watch the diamond sparkle in the bright sun. "It has a lot of fire, and I love it!" she exclaimed happily.

"I love you. I want to spend the rest of my life with you. Will you marry me?" he asked with the most serious look on his face that she had ever seen.

She handed the ring box to him and said happily, "Yes, now you have to slip it on my finger."

Charlie smiled and slipped the ring onto her left ring finger, kissed her, and said, "You make me the happiest man on earth."

Holly looked at him lovingly and said, "I never thought I would want to get married again. I lived with James for 11 years and never wanted to marry him. I thought it would ruin our relationship. Now I know why. It's because I'm supposed to be with you. We feel right. I love you, Charlie."

"I knew I wanted to marry you the day you told me that you kicked James to the curb. I never thought I would want to get married again either. Do you want to have a formal wedding? I'll do whatever you want. If you want to keep your last name, I'm okay with that too. As long as you become my wife, anything goes," Charlie said sweetly.

Holly smiled and said, "I want to take your name, and I don't want a formal wedding. We can go to the courthouse, and then have a dinner later and invite our friends to celebrate."

"That sounds perfect. I don't want a formal wedding either, although I would happily do that if you change your mind. You know I'm not fond of Lisa, and I don't know Roger. However, if you want to invite them to our celebratory dinner, I'm okay with it," he replied with a laugh. "When do you want to get married?"

"I'd like to get married in September. That's the month I started falling for you and we had our first kiss," she replied, remembering the lighter-than-air feeling as she walked down the city sidewalk with Charlie on the evening they shared at Jake's.

"I agree, September it is. We can figure out the exact date later," he replied.

"This ring is so pretty, I don't want to take a chance on losing it, though. Let's go back to the hotel and lock it in my suitcase," Holly suggested.

"Sure, and while we are there we can do something else," Charlie said playfully.

"Or, we could wait until we get married," she teased.

"No way, I'd be a crazy man by then," he said laughing.

"I wouldn't be able to wait either," she replied, and they started walking back to the hotel room. "Holly Eileen Thomas, I think that sounds nice," she said as she slipped her hand into his.

He squeezed her hand and said, "It sounds beautiful, just like you."

The rest of the beach trip was picture-perfect and filled with passionate nights and fun days. Neither of them wanted to leave. "What do you think of living down here one day?" Charlie asked as they loaded up her Lincoln for the drive home.

"I would love to. You know I love basking in the sun almost as much as I love you. Are you thinking we could move here after you retire one day?" she asked.

"Yes. I don't know when that day will be, however, I'm glad you agree. We can visit here more often until then," he replied.

James called Holly's home phone and discovered it was disconnected. He then called her work number and got her voice mail. He decided to leave a message. "Hi, Holly. I'm sorry to bother you, but I remembered that I left some boxes in the basement closet and was wondering if you might have found them. I don't know if you are still living there. I hope that if you've moved that you found the boxes and still have them. I'd like to get them back. I hope things are going well for you and that you get this message. Please call me back at 555-552-6185. Thanks." *She probably moved in with that guy who was at her house. If she did, I hope that she's happy with him and that he treats her well. She deserves the best and that certainly isn't me . . . I hope she returns my call . . . I need that money.*

Holly returned to work on Wednesday. Her mind was still at the beach and she didn't feel like working. She checked her voice mail and heard James's message . . . *I wonder what is in those boxes . . . I'll call him back and see if he wants to come and get them.* Holly was curious, however, she was so happy that she was going to marry Charlie that she didn't give any more thought to the contents of the boxes. She called James, and he picked up on the third ring.

"James, this is Holly," she said politely. "How have you been?"

"Holly, it's nice to hear from you. I'm doing well. Did you happen to find those boxes?" he asked tentatively.

Holly sensed his anxiety, and she wanted to put him at ease. She forgave him for everything. It was water under the bridge. If they had never broken up she wouldn't be with Charlie now. "Yes, I found four boxes. Is that how many there were?"

"Yeah, I'd like to get them back. I can come and get them," he replied, relieved that the money wasn't lost or spent and now Belle would get a good college education and have money to be on her own one day.

"Sure. I'm living with Charlie. He's the guy you met when you came to collect your stuff. We're renting out my house and I found the boxes when we were cleaning it. We live in Springfield," she said cheerfully.

She sounds happy . . . This is good, "I can come to Springfield. Let me know when it's a good time for you," he replied.

"Sunday is good. Can you come by before you go to work?"

"I'm off this Sunday so I can be there at 10:00," he said.

"That's fine. Oh, did Amber have the baby?" Holly asked excitedly.

"Yeah, we named her Isabella Maria. She's beautiful," James replied and Holly picked up from his tone of voice that he adored his new baby.

"Congratulations. Are you and Amber married now?"

"Yes," he replied.

"Good. Charlie and I are getting married in September," Holly said happily.

"I'm happy for you, Holly, truly I am. I hope he's good to you," James said thoughtfully.

"Charlie is wonderful to me. I'll e-mail you the directions to our house, and I'll see you on Sunday morning," she said.

"Great, see you then," James said and hung up the phone . . . *That went better than I thought . . . She probably hasn't opened the boxes, and that's a good thing.*

Amber overheard his conversation. She was putting away laundry in the bedroom. "James, what's in those boxes?" she asked and walked into the living room, suddenly curious.

James looked at her and said, "It's time you know about my less-than-stellar past. Those boxes contain a combined amount of $200,000. I made that money illegally. I used to deal drugs and gamble. That's where the money came from. Holly never knew about my past. Thankfully, she discovered the boxes when she was cleaning, and as far as I know, she hasn't opened them. She's living in Springfield with a guy named Charlie, and they're renting out her house. I'm going to pick them up on Sunday. I was thinking that we could use the money for Belle's college education. We can gradually put it in the bank, little by little, in the coming years so we don't arouse any suspicion."

Amber was surprised at James's admission of guilt. However, she was elated at the financial windfall. She wanted the best for their child. "That's wonderful. I'm so glad she found it!" Amber said and began jumping up and down with delight. "I know you have left your past behind and you are making a new start with us. I'm okay with that. The money will help our daughter, so it's not entirely bad."

"I knew you would understand," he replied and took Amber in his arms and held her close. Things were going well for them, and James loved Belle. He gladly got up in the middle of the night to tend to her so Amber could sleep. Belle was his new reason for living, and he looked forward to coming home to his ladies after work. His appreciation for Amber was growing. He thought she had the patience of a saint to put up with him and realized that he was in love with her . . . *I'll stop by a jewelry store on the way home from Holly's and buy her something beautiful . . . and then tell her how much I love and appreciate her.*

The rest of the week passed uneventfully for James, Amber, Holly, and Charlie, until Saturday evening. James was thinking of Belle's sweet little face and the way her tiny hands gripped his finger as he placed a bunch of steaks on the grill for a large dinner party. He was looking forward to his day off tomorrow, collecting the missing money, and planning Belle's future . . . *Things have turned out better than I could ever imagine . . . and I'm actually happy.* Suddenly his heart began to race and he became so dizzy that he lost consciousness and fell to the floor.

"James! Someone call 911! James is down!" Tony Hudson, one of the lower-ranking cooks in the kitchen, called out. The kitchen staff dropped what they were doing and ran over to James. Mike Collins, the manager on duty, was in the kitchen and he immediately whipped out his phone and called 911. Tony noticed that James wasn't breathing. He felt for a pulse and couldn't find one. "He's not breathing, I can't find a pulse," Tony cried out helplessly.

American Steak was located directly across the street from the local fire and rescue and minutes later the ambulance arrived and the paramedics raced into the kitchen through the back door. They did their best to revive James with CPR and a portable defibrillator, but it was too late. James Macklin was dead at the age of 54. Less than 15 minutes earlier, he was putting steaks on the grill and whistling happily to himself. A somber mood fell over the kitchen as the paramedics zipped James into a body bag, placed him on a stretcher, and carried him out the back door.

Tony Hudson started crying as they put James in the ambulance and closed the doors. He didn't want to work the rest of his shift. The other kitchen workers were crying too and hugging each other for comfort. James was one of the more difficult head chefs to work for because he was demanding and a perfectionist. In spite of that, he was well liked and respected by most everyone. Mike Collins had the unpleasant task of calling Amber to let her know that her new husband just dropped dead from an apparent heart attack. In addition, he needed to motivate the kitchen staff to get back to work after this tragic incident and let the customers know what was happening.

"I hate to do this, they just had a baby. Amber is going to be devastated," Mike said to himself as he dialed Amber's number, thinking in the back of his mind . . . *When she's ready to date again, I'm going to make a play for her.*

"Hello," Amber answered cheerfully.

She sounds so happy. Damn, I hate this . . . Mike took a deep breath and said, "Amber, this is Mike from American Steak. I really hate to tell you this. James is dead. He was cooking steaks on the grill and suddenly collapsed. We called the ambulance, and they did their best to try to revive him, but unfortunately, it was too late. I am so, so sorry. If there is anything you need, please don't hesitate to call me. We are here if you need us."

Amber's perfect new world of family bliss came crashing down. She was in shock as soon as Mike uttered the words, "James is dead." She could hear her own heart pounding in her chest and Belle started crying. Somehow she managed to pull herself together for a few seconds and replied, "Thank you, Mike. I don't know what I'm going to do. I'll let the rest of the family know, and I'll be in touch."

"Please do, Amber. You and James are part of our family, and we're here for you," Mike said as he thought . . . *Especially me. I'm here for you anytime day or night . . . I could be a good stepfather.*

"Thanks again," Amber said and ended the call. Belle was crying hard. She was screaming. Amber went to her and tried to calm her down . . . *I wonder if she knows that her daddy isn't coming home . . . I think she must know on some level.* Amber sat down in the rocking chair holding her crying daughter and began to cry along with her . . . *If James were here he would be able to stop Belle from crying. She always perks up when he's around and she's not even 2 months old. I have to be strong for her. James would want it that way. I've got to get that money from Holly too. I'll call her when this settles down . . . I have so much to do . . . retrieve his belongings, arrange a funeral, notify the life insurance company . . . sit here and cry.*

On Sunday morning Holly and Charlie were waiting for James to arrive and pick up the boxes. Holly placed them on the living room coffee table. An hour later when he failed to show, they thought maybe he was lost, although their house was easy to find and she figured James would call if he was lost or going to be late. Charlie was reading the newspaper and Holly was channel surfing when she started to get a bad feeling about James.

"Holly, I know why James hasn't shown up yet," Charlie said with a serious look on his face.

"How do you know that?" she asked.

"He died last night. He literally dropped dead while he was working at American Steak. There's a small article about it right here," he said, and she leaned over him to read the article.

Top Chef at Local Restaurant Dies on the Job

American Steak Bistro and Pub lost their top chef last evening around 6:30 p.m. as he was preparing steaks for a large dinner party. James Macklin, age 54, collapsed and died quickly from what emergency personnel believed to be sudden cardiac arrest. Paramedics rushed into the restaurant's kitchen and worked to revive him using CPR and a defibrillator, but sadly, it was too late. Restaurant manager Mike Collins was left with a vexing problem. The dining room was full of customers and most of the staff were distraught with grief and had difficulty returning to work; and he had to notify Mr. Macklin's wife of her husband's untimely death. James Macklin is responsible for creating 10 different varieties of baked macaroni and cheese entrées, prompting the restaurant to have a separate menu for the beloved comfort food. James is survived by his wife Amber and their baby daughter Isabella.

Holly's eyes welled up with tears as she read the last line of the article. She thought it was so sad that his little girl would grow up never knowing her father. She snuggled close to Charlie and started crying.

"I'm not crying because I still have loving feelings for James. I think it's sad that he won't live to see his daughter grow up. They will never get to know each other. James wasn't exactly a good guy. However, when I talked to him on the phone he sounded happy and proud about Isabella," Holly said as she tried to stop the tears. "I was so mean to him. I truly regret cutting up his clothes and bashing his tailgate."

Charlie was also saddened by this situation and wanted to say something to make Holly feel better. "I feel sad about it too. At least you had a pleasant conversation with him before he died. I'm sure he knew how badly he hurt you, and that you were in a fit of rage when you vandalized his belongings. I think you should forgive yourself for being human," he said and kissed her softly.

"In a strange way I should have thanked him for his betrayal. If he had never knocked up Amber I probably wouldn't be here with you," she replied.

"I think fate would have put us together eventually. He dropped dead, you would be single again and I believe we would have ended up together," Charlie said lovingly.

"I harbored a secret crush on you, so that's probably true," she agreed. "I think I'll open these boxes and see what's inside. It might be something Amber would like."

"I'll go get the box cutter," Charlie replied and went to retrieve it from the kitchen. He returned to the living room and opened the first box. "Holy crap! There's a boatload of money in here," he exclaimed as he saw the stacks of bills in denominations of mostly 100s and 50s, although there were quite a few stacks of 20s.

Holly gasped in disbelief and said emphatically, "Open the others!"

Charlie opened the remaining three boxes and saw that they were filled with cash too. "Unbelievable. I wouldn't be surprised if this was drug money," Charlie said in astonishment as he looked at Holly.

Holly thought of James's disappearances and unusual behavior the last two 2 years of their relationship and she replied, "I think there was more to his disappearances than having an affair with Amber. If he was truthful when he said they had been seeing each other for about 8 months, then he was doing something else behind my back before he hooked up with her. Let's count the money and see how much is here." She said the last sentence excitedly. She was anxious to know how much money James had been hiding from her.

"Good idea, let's start counting. I'll go get something to write on. We can divide this up and write down our counts," Charlie replied eagerly and walked to the den to retrieve pens and paper . . . *This guy was a piece of work . . . That money might be from a combination of illegal activities. Obviously he didn't want to put it in the bank, and he didn't want to share it with Holly . . . After we count it, I wonder what she will want to do with it . . . More importantly, does Amber know about it and will she come knocking on our door?*

Holly sat on the sofa staring at the stacks of money, her thoughts racing . . . *Why did he hide this from me? What else do I not know about? . . . Does Amber know about the money? . . . What should we do with it? . . . Will Charlie want to keep it? . . . That's a lot of money.*

Charlie returned with pen and paper, and they began to count it. Sometime later they added up their counts and discovered that it totaled exactly $200,000.

Holly and Charlie looked at each other, and he spoke first, "So, what do you want to do about this?"

"You're going to think I'm crazy. I have an overwhelming feeling that we should give it to Amber. This money belonged to James, regardless of how he acquired it. It's not mine. Yeah, I found it, and most people would say take the money and run. However, we don't know if Amber knows about it. I was going to give it to James anyway. I had no idea of the contents and didn't really care. If he hadn't called and asked me about it, these boxes would have stayed buried for who knows how long. Had he lived, he would have stopped by and I would have handed him the boxes, and he would have lied about what was in them had I asked. If Amber doesn't know about it, I will admit that I would be tempted to keep it, although my guilty conscious would eventually get the better of me and I would give it to her. I feel that he wanted this money for his daughter's future. I have a strong feeling that Amber does know about it and we will hear from her soon," Holly replied . . . *And I don't want to incur any bad karma to pay back in a future life or this current one.*

This woman is amazing . . . I can't believe I found her . . . "I was thinking the same thing, Sunshine. You amaze me more and more each day. A lot of women would feel justified in keeping some or all of that money for the pain and heartache he caused you. Honestly, we are in good shape financially, and I have a comfortable nest egg for our retirement. I agree that we should give the money to Amber. It will help ensure a good future for his little girl. I love how thoughtful you are. A lesser person would keep this money," he said and kissed her passionately.

Later that evening as Holly and Charlie were sharing a bottle of wine and watching TV, Holly's phone rang. The caller ID said "James Macklin," she knew that it was Amber calling about the money.

"Hi, Amber," Holly said.

"How did you know it was me?" Amber asked.

"We read about James's death in the *Washington Post* this morning. There was a small article in the Metro Section. I am so sorry, Amber," Holly said, feeling like she was going to cry and managing to hold back the tears.

"I didn't know it made the newspaper. I'm still in shock. I'm functioning on autopilot, trying to get things squared away for his funeral. It just doesn't seem real. I called because James said he was planning to stop by and pick up some boxes that he left behind. Is it okay if I come over tonight and pick them up?" she asked with trepidation, wondering if Holly had found the treasure inside.

"Yes, of course. I want to let you know that we opened them to see what was inside. It should make your life a little easier and it will be great for Isabella. You can come over now if you want," Holly said kindly.

Amber was touched by Holly's kindness, so much that she was moved to tears. "Amber, are you still there?" Holly asked.

"Yes . . . I'm a bit . . . of a mess . . . right now," Amber replied through her tears. "I have the directions to your house. I'll be there in about an hour. Thank you, Holly."

"You're welcome. We'll be waiting for you," Holly replied.

"See you soon," Amber said and ended the call . . . *Holly really is a nice person . . . I can see why James loved her.*

Charlie leaned over and kissed Holly, "I love you," he said.

"I love you too, Charlie," she replied. "You better not drop dead on me. You have to live to be a really old man."

Charlie laughed and said, "I plan on it, and the same goes for you."

"If you go before me, I'll come chasing after you," she replied, resting her head on his shoulder.

"I'm not going to let you get away. I'll follow you too," he said and kissed her head.

Amber arrived an hour later. She brought Isabella with her. When Holly opened the door to let them inside, she noticed how pale and sad Amber looked. She wasn't wearing a speck of makeup and her pretty blond hair was pulled back in a messy ponytail. She had Isabella in her carrier.

"Hi, Amber, come in," Holly said with a smile.

"Hi, Holly. Thank you for letting me come over at this hour," Amber said gratefully as she stepped inside with Isabella.

"No problem," Holly replied as they walked into the living room.

Charlie stood up to greet her, "Hi, Amber. It's nice to meet you."

"Hi, Charlie. Nice to meet you too," Amber replied and took a seat on the sofa with Isabella next to her.

Holly looked at Isabella and thought that she resembled Amber. "Isabella is a lovely baby. I think she's going to look just like you. Those big blue eyes are mesmerizing," Holly said as she took a seat in one of the nearby leather chairs, and Charlie did the same. Amber noticed the four boxes of cash were sitting on the coffee table.

"Amber, we counted the cash, and it totals exactly $200,000," Charlie said, sensing her uneasiness and feeling sorry for her loss. He wanted her to feel comfortable.

"That's what James said, thank you," she replied, her facial expression softening with a little smile.

"Would you like something to drink?" Holly offered. "Iced tea, coffee, soda, water?"

"A glass of iced tea would be nice. It's hot outside," Amber said.

"Do you want it with sugar?"

"Yes, thanks," Amber replied.

Holly went to the kitchen to prepare a glass of tea, leaving Amber and Charlie alone to talk for a minute.

My God, he is a handsome man . . . He seems nice too, and rich . . . "Charlie, you have a beautiful home. It looks like something that should be in a magazine," Amber said as she admired the surroundings.

"Thank you, Amber," he replied pleasantly and walked over to the sofa to get a closer look at Isabella. "Your little girl is adorable." At that moment Isabella started crying. "Do you mind if I hold her?" Charlie asked.

"Please, go right ahead," she replied.

Charlie picked up Isabella, and she stopped crying a few seconds later. He carried her back to the leather chair, cradling her in his arms.

"She would stop crying whenever James picked her up. I think she loves men," Amber said with tears in her eyes, remembering how much James adored his baby.

"She's precious," he replied, gazing tenderly at the child . . . *If I had gotten together with Holly sooner, maybe we could have made a beautiful baby.*

Holly came back into the living room with the iced tea and smiled when she saw Charlie sitting in the chair with Isabella. "Here you go, Amber," Holly said, handing her the tea.

"Thank you. You've got a good man there," Amber said looking at Charlie holding Isabella.

"I know," she said happily and sat down in leather chair across from Charlie . . . *James can't hold a candle to him*. "Amber, I know this is none of my business, and you don't have to answer if you don't want to. Do you know how James acquired this large amount of money?" she asked.

"Yes. James told me that he used to deal drugs and gamble. This is how he saved it. He was afraid to put it in the bank. He thought it would draw suspicion to him," Amber replied and took a sip of tea.

"That would explain some of his behavior the last 2 years of our relationship. I wouldn't be surprised if it was going on before we ever got together. He was good at keeping secrets," Holly said, remembering the times when he was "out with the guys."

"He told me just a few days ago. It really surprised me. I know James wasn't a good guy, however, once Belle was born, he became a new person. He instantly became a doting father. He got up with her at night every time she cried, he changed her diapers, and he was there for her. He loved to buy her things. She has an unbelievable toy chest and clothes for when she gets older. She became his world," Amber said, and then began crying. She was overcome with emotion, remembering the wonderful changes in James, and now, Holly and Charlie's kindness, and the tears wouldn't stop.

Holly felt Amber's deep sadness and came over to sit beside her on the sofa. She put her arms around her, and Amber cried on her shoulder for a few minutes . . .*Who would have thought that I'd be comforting the woman who stole my man . . . That's okay, though, everything is forgiven now.*

When Amber regained her composure she said, "I'm sorry we hurt you. I fell in love with James and wanted him for myself."

"It's water under the bridge; things happen. Sometimes we can't help who we fall madly in love with," Holly replied thinking of the crush she had on Charlie when she was trying to patch things up with James. "Isabella is what's most important right now. You have to be strong for her."

"When James showed me his butchered clothes and bashed in tailgate, I knew I would have done something similar. I laughed hysterically about the clothes. Cutting the crotches out of his pants . . . That was brilliant," Amber said and started laughing.

Holly smiled and said, "In hindsight, it is pretty funny. Although I still feel bad about bashing his tailgate."

"He got it fixed 3 weeks later. Don't feel guilty about that. I would have done more than bashed his tailgate," Amber replied.

"Well, that makes me feel a little better," Holly said.

"I think I should be going now. I have so much to do," Amber said and stood up.

"Let me get you a tote bag for the boxes," Holly said and went to the kitchen. She returned with a large canvas bag. "Here you go. The boxes should fit in here," she said, and Amber placed the four boxes into the tote. "You can keep the bag. I've got plenty of them," Holly told her.

"Thank you," she replied with a smile and looked over at Belle sleeping peacefully in Charlie's arms. "Belle looks so sweet with you, Charlie. I hate to disturb her. Maybe I'll get lucky, and she'll sleep until we get home."

Charlie got up and gently secured Belle in her carrier. She was sleeping soundly. "Here, let me carry the tote bag and you carry Belle," Charlie said, picking it up. Charlie and Holly walked Amber out to her car and placed the tote bag in the backseat.

"Thanks again for everything. If I can ever be of help to either of you, please don't hesitate to call me," Amber said thoughtfully to them.

"Have a nice evening," Holly replied.

Amber started her car and waved to Holly and Charlie as she drove away.

"That went well," Charlie said.

"I feel good about giving her the money," Holly replied.

"I hope she's responsible with it and doesn't try to live off it until it's gone," Charlie said with concern.

"Let's hope so," Holly replied as they went back inside the house.

They sat down on the sofa and Charlie looked at her and said, "We need to set a wedding date, and the more I think about it, I'd like our wedding to be something more special than just a civil ceremony."

"Do you want to have a formal wedding?" Holly asked, hoping he would say no. She didn't want to plan a big shindig.

"No. I was thinking of hiring a wedding celebrant and having a small ceremony on the beach. I'm thinking of the second weekend in September, the 12th or 13th," he replied.

"I like that idea, Charlie. Do you want it to be just the two of us?" she asked . . . *What a romantic he is. Usually women think about these kinds of things.*

"Yes, if that's okay with you," he replied and kissed her.

"I love the beach ceremony idea. Just the two of us and a wedding celebrant. What do you want to do about wedding vows?" she asked.

"We could write our own or search for some on the Internet, or we could go with the traditional vows," he replied.

"I like the idea of writing our own vows and letting them be a surprise to each other," she said excitedly. "I'm sure we can find some on the Internet to give us ideas. It might be easier to do that than create them from scratch."

"Perfect," Charlie replied happily. "What type of wedding ring would you like?"

"I would like just a simple gold band. What about you?"

"The same," he replied and pulled her in close. "I love that you aren't fussy about things. My previous wives were divas," he said with a laugh.

"We need to decide if we want to get married during the day or wait until evening. Oh, and what should we wear?" Holly asked.

Charlie looked at her lovingly and said, "I'm picturing you in a flowing white sundress with your hair long and loose and bare feet, although if we get married during the day the sand will probably be too hot for your feet. I'm picturing a sexy, bohemian goddess look."

Holly started laughing and said, "Do you want me to wear flowers in my hair too?"

Charlie smiled and said, "I'd marry you no matter what you were wearing."

"I want to look like the picture in your mind. I'll start looking for the white sundress. I think I'll skip the flowers in my hair, and I think we should get married in the early evening," she said happily.

"Early evening it is. I'll start looking for a wedding celebrant and book a hotel," he said.

"I love you, and now, let's go to bed," she replied, and they went upstairs.

Chapter 15

Light at the End of the Tunnel

At Zumba class on Monday night, Holly was anxious to tell Patricia and Lisa about her upcoming wedding plans. She was going to tell Patricia at work when she realized that Patricia was out of the office for a few days at a symposium on the other side of town. She walked into the gym and saw her friends waiting for her.

"Hey, ladies, we finally set a wedding date. We're getting married September 13," Holly said joyfully.

"That's on a Saturday. I thought you were going to get married on a weekday and celebrate on the weekend," Patricia replied.

"We were, and then Charlie suggested we get married on the beach, at Virginia Beach," Holly informed them.

"I love that idea," Lisa said cheerfully, seeming happier than usual. Holly thought that something about her face looked softer. She was glowing.

"Are you going to have a celebration dinner back here?" Patricia asked, hoping she could be a part of it.

"You know, we didn't even talk about that part. I'll talk to Charlie and find out what he wants to do. I'm just really happy right now. I feel like I could Zumba for 2 hours tonight!" Holly replied with enthusiasm.

"Marriage must be contagious because Roger asked me to marry him last night," Lisa said with a happy smile.

"Congratulations," Patricia and Holly said in unison.

"Did he give you a ring?" Patricia asked.

"Yes. I left it at home because I don't like to wear jewelry while I'm exercising," she replied.

"This is fantastic. Hopefully, our third time around, we both will be as happy as Patricia and Andy," Holly said sweetly.

"I sure as hell hope so!" Lisa replied emphatically. "Now that I've learned to manage my anger and some other personal issues, I think I can be a good wife. Roger's been a dream come true, helping to keep me straight. I don't want a third divorce, and neither does he. We are committed to do whatever it takes to make it work."

"Have you set a date?" Holly asked.

"We're thinking of getting married on New Year's Eve," Lisa replied.

"I married Andy on New Year's Day back in 1982," Patricia chimed in lightheartedly.

"You can be our marriage guru. We'll come to you for advice," Holly said playfully.

The instructor's name was Shawna, and she announced that it was time to start Zumba, and the theme for tonight was '70s Funk. Holly, Patricia, and Lisa liked it and enjoyed the beat. They worked it hard for an hour. At the end of class, Lisa teased Holly about her comment that she could do 2 hours of Zumba.

"Hey, Shawna, Holly said she wants to go for another hour," Lisa called out to the instructor.

"I can do another hour for you if you want," Shawna said playfully.

"I think I've had enough," Holly replied laughing and trying to catch her breath.

The three of them sat on the bleachers for a few minutes talking and saw Roger walk into the gym.

"Hey, sweetie, over here," Lisa called out to her man.

"Did he drive you here tonight?" Patricia asked.

"Yeah, I went out to get in my car and noticed that the tire was flat so he drove me," she replied.

Roger walked over to the exhausted women and said, "The three of you still look great, even when you're drenched in sweat."

"You're just trying to score points," Holly said teasingly.

"Did it work?" he asked with a smile.

"Yeah," Patricia kidded. "I'm going to go home and tell Andy that another man thinks I'm hot."

"You are hot. I hope my body looks as good as yours at 57," Holly replied observing that although Patricia was older, she had good muscle tone and a smooth complexion and wasn't gasping for breath as much as she and Lisa.

"I agree, you don't look 57," Lisa chimed in. "I'm 7 years younger than you and struggle to get through the class. You make it seem easy."

"Thank you," Patricia replied feeling extremely flattered.

"I'm here to escort you three beautiful ladies to your vehicles," Roger said, anxious to get going because he had an early-morning meeting.

"I think that's our cue that we need to get out of here," Holly smiled.

"Yeah, it's quitting time," Lisa replied.

The four of them walked out of the building to their cars. This summer night was hot and muggy and without a breeze.

"My car's over there," Holly said to them and turned to walk in the opposite direction. "Have a good night everyone," she said and walked a few feet toward her Lincoln. Holly didn't see that less than 2 minutes ago, someone dumped out a cup of ice onto the parking lot and she slipped and fell backward, hitting her head on the pavement. Patricia saw her fall.

"HOLLY!" Patricia screamed, and the three of them came running over to her. Holly was lying on the pavement unconscious.

Lisa gently touched her and tried to bring her around, "Oh my God, she's not responding. Call an ambulance!" she said in a panic. Roger was already dialing his phone.

"911. How can we help?" the 911 dispatcher said.

"Yes, we are in the parking lot of the Wakefield Rec Center. Our friend just slipped and fell and hit the pavement. She's unconscious and still breathing okay. Please send an ambulance right away," Roger pleaded . . . *Please let her be okay. Holly, please come around.*

"We are dispatching a team right now. They will be there in just a few minutes," the dispatcher said.

"Thank you!" Roger said emphatically and hung up the phone. "We've got to tell Charlie. Patricia, do you have his number?"

"Yes, I'm on it," she said as she called Charlie's phone with shaking hands.

"Hi, Patricia, what's going on?" Charlie asked as he answered the phone slightly alarmed and wondering why Patricia would be calling him instead of Holly.

"Charlie, you are not going to believe this. Holly slipped and fell on some ice in the parking lot and hit her head. She's unconscious," Patricia said as she heard the distant sound of an ambulance making its way to the community center in the background.

"Is she breathing?" Charlie asked, his voice sounding like a croak.

"Yes, the ambulance is on its way. I can hear it getting closer. I'm going to follow it to the hospital," Patricia said, her heart pounding in her chest and thinking of everything that could possibly go wrong and how sometimes people never recover from a head injury.

"I'm on my way. I'll see you there," Charlie said and hung up the phone. He grabbed his keys and rushed outside to his truck . . . *Stay calm, you can't have an accident on the way to the hospital . . . Holly, my sunshine, please be okay, please come around . . .What if she has brain damage? . . .*

What if she never comes around? . . . Can't think like that . . . not yet.

Patricia, Lisa, and Roger watched as the paramedics carefully loaded Holly into the ambulance. "We're going to follow them to the hospital too," Roger told Patricia.

"Good, I'll see you there," Patricia said as she turned to walk to her car.

. . . Holly is flying through a tunnel. In the distance she sees a warm, glowing light and thinks . . . I'm going into the sun. What an incredible dream . . . I feel so happy, and I'm going right into the sun . . . As she gets closer to the welcoming light, she is abruptly pulled in another direction and sees a beautiful, crystal structure that reaches up into a blue, cloudless sky as far as the eye can see. This structure resembles a large cluster of polished quartz crystals, with the one in the middle reaching into the sky . . .

The ambulance arrives at the hospital, and the paramedics bring Holly into the Emergency Trauma Center. Patricia, Lisa, and Roger arrive a few minutes later and confirm what happened and provide what personal information they can to the emergency room doctor and the admissions center. The three of them take a seat in the waiting area and see Charlie coming through the door 20 minutes later, looking just as shocked and upset as they do. He sees Patricia waving to him and walks toward her, noticing Lisa and Roger . . . *They came too, that was nice . . . What's Roger doing here? . . . Maybe he was picking up Lisa.* Charlie suddenly felt grateful and does his best to choke back the tears as he greets everyone.

"I'm glad you are here," he said to them.

"They're running tests on her, both an MRI and a CT scan. We don't know how long until we find out something. She's still unconscious. They are closely monitoring her blood pressure. If it goes up that means there could be some swelling on the brain," Patricia said, her face pale and sad with worry. "Her blood pressure was normal when she arrived."

"I called the ambulance as soon as she fell. Some idiot dumped out a cup of ice in the parking lot," Roger said with irritation, wanting to show Charlie that he was a good guy . . . *I don't know what Holly told him about me . . . I want him to know that I'm not a monster anymore.*

"I'm grateful to the three of you and thankful that you acted quickly. I'm sure that Holly was walking and talking and not watching her step," Charlie replied and sat down, running his fingers through his hair, tears falling down his face. "I don't know what I'm going to do if she doesn't come around. Head injuries can be the end of normal," he said, fighting to regain his emotional composure.

"We can stay as long as you need us too," Lisa said to him, feeling awkward around her ex-husband, yet wanting to say something comforting . . . *I still want to apologize to him for being such an awful wife . . . but this isn't the right time or place.*

"Thank you, Lisa," Charlie replied sincerely and looked her in the eye. "I appreciate that you can stay, although I can take it from here. I'll let you know her condition if you want to go."

"We're going to be worried sick about her, and I won't get any sleep tonight," Lisa replied.

"Me either!" Patricia said emphatically.

"If you want to stay that's great. I appreciate the support. I don't want you to feel that you have to on my account," Charlie replied humbly.

"I want to know the results of the MRI and CT scan," Patricia said.

"So do we," Lisa said, and Roger nodded his head in agreement.

"I guess we sit and wait then," Charlie replied with a heavy sigh.

. . . Holly is in awe of this crystalline structure, and as she continues to look at this strange new world she notices there is a long and winding, slate gray stone path leading up to the entrance of the building with simple wooden benches every few feet on either side of

the pathway. She starts to walk along the path and toward the crystal building . . . "I'm having a lucid dream, this is fun," she says. She observes people milling about. Some of them are walking dogs and everyone is wearing long robes which touch the ground so that you can't see their feet. The robes are colorful, and she sees colors she's never seen before. The people seem to be floating instead of walking. The surrounding scenery is spectacular, with lush green rolling hills and full-leaved trees. As she walks/floats toward the building, she thinks that she recognizes a man standing in front of it. He is tall and handsome with blond hair and wearing a green robe. He looks at her and smiles. Holly realizes that she is looking at James, and he is waiting for her. He appears 20 years younger.

"James, it's good to see you. What are you doing here?" she asks him.

"I should be the one asking you that," James replies laughing.

"Where am I?" she asks, feeling confused and thinking she should be getting home soon.

"You fell down and hit your head," he replies without answering her question.

"Is this payback for hitting you upside your head with the body spray bottle?" she asks, trying to remember how she fell and hit her head. Something was blocking her memory.

"No, your fall was an accident, and this place is real. I heard you coming, and I wanted to thank you for getting the money to Amber and Belle. It means a lot to us. I want to apologize for betraying you and breaking your heart," he said thoughtfully.

"I forgive you, James, it doesn't matter now. I think we planned our situation before we were born. We had to learn certain lessons and clear karmic debts. I want to apologize for bashing in your tailgate and cutting up your clothes. I felt really bad about that the next day," she says while remembering the Atlantis lifetime . . . "Strange that I can remember Atlantis and not how I wound up here," she says to herself.

James let out a hearty laugh and says, "I deserved it. I want you to know that I NEVER held any of that against you and totally understood. And you are right about the prebirth planning. We did that before we came back, however, it was merely a blueprint," he replies. "To answer your first question, I am on my way to school, and then to consult with my guides about my next incarnation."

"When will you be reincarnating?" she asks excitedly.

"I don't know. There is no time in this place. I have plenty to do here, and I'm keeping a watchful eye on my sweet Belle," he replies, smiling. "I know that I will eventually be reincarnating as a Buddhist monk. No wine, women, or song for me next time," he says jokingly.

"Good luck, James, and thank you for meeting me here," Holly says happily . . . This place feels so good to her.

James reaches out and touches her pretty face with both hands. They felt warm and comforting. He looks into her eyes and says, "I'll see you later, Holly." And then he was gone . . .

Forty-five minutes later a doctor came toward them. "Are you the folks with Holly O'Rourke?" Dr. Chris Tanner asked.

"Yeah. How is she?" Charlie asked.

"She is still unconscious. The good news is that the MRI and CT scans are not showing any signs of brain damage and her breathing and blood pressure are steady, which indicates no brain swelling. It's my opinion that she has a concussion. With a concussion, brain cells are temporarily damaged or dysfunctional. I expect her to regain consciousness, although I can't say exactly when. We are going to keep monitoring her until she regains consciousness, and then we want her to stay a day or 2 to make sure she is out of the woods," Dr. Tanner explained to them.

"I'm her fiancé. Is it okay if I stay overnight with her?" Charlie asked feeling hopeful that he wasn't going to lose his wife-to-be.

"Yes, of course," he replied.

Patricia, Lisa, and Roger each breathed a sigh of relief. "I feel better now. I think I might be able to sleep tonight," Lisa said.

"Me too, although she isn't out of the woods yet," Patricia replied cautiously.

"Are you ready to go?" Roger asked Lisa.

"Yeah, we can go. Charlie, please let us know how she is tomorrow," Lisa said with concern.

"I will, definitely, and thanks again to the three of you for being here and for calling the ambulance," Charlie replied shaking hands with Roger and smiling at Lisa.

"I'll tell Stan what happened so you don't have to call him. I'll let Mitch know too," Patricia said to Charlie.

"Thank you, I really appreciate that," Charlie replied and hugged her, and then the three of them left to go home. It was almost 11:00 p.m. now.

Charlie followed the doctor into Holly's room. He knew this was going to be a long night. He sat beside her and held her hand and said, "I'm here for you, Sunshine. You concentrate on getting well, and I'll be here when you wake up." . . . *Please wake up . . .You have to wake up.*

. . .After James vanished, someone Holly wanted to meet appeared. Standing in front of her was a Middle-Eastern-looking man standing 5 foot 9 with shoulder-length, curly black hair, dark eyes, and the beginnings of a beard. He was wearing a white robe and he exuded kindness and joy.

"Are you Kavi?" she asked, knowing that he was.

"Yes, my dear. It is good to see you," he replied.

"Am I in heaven?" she asked.

"You are in a heavenly realm, so yes," he replied.

"Am I dead?" she asked.

"Not yet. Come with me and I will show you a comfortable place to rest and recover," he said and took her hand.

They floated right into the crystal building as there was no entry door. The inside of the building was filled with sunlight and a fabulous atrium containing a plethora of different plants and flowers in those strange new colors she had never seen before, as well as colors she knew. She was astonished at the beauty surrounding them. They were standing in the tallest part of the crystal structure. It was shaped like a hexagon. She looked up and saw that a golden balcony encircled each floor as far as the eye could see.

"Is this a halfway house for people with head injuries?" she asked. "James said that I fell and hit my head, but I don't remember anything other than I was doing Zumba and now I'm here."

Kavi laughed and said, "No, sweetheart, this isn't a halfway house. This is a place for rest and learning. Many activities go on here."

"Kavi, where are the elevators?" she asked, looking around and wondering how they could reach the upper levels.

"We don't need elevators. See that point of light three floors up?" he asked and pointed to a small, glowing light.

"Yes, I see it," she replied.

"Focus on that light and imagine you are inside of it," he said.

Holly focused on the light and then noticed they were standing inside a beautiful room with long, almost floor-to-ceiling windows on two walls overlooking the garden outside. She studied her surroundings more closely and saw that her room was decorated with striped wallpaper in alternating colors of pale pink, pale orange, and white. There were pink, white, and orange roses sitting in a clear vase on a little white table next to the bed, which was draped with a quilted white bedspread and a brass headboard. The room was large, with a pale pink sofa and pale orange easy chair sitting on top of a white area rug, looking out one of the large windows. The floors were pale gray marble.

"You need to lie down and rest; try not to think too much. I hope you will be comfortable here," Kavi said.

"Thank you. This place is beautiful," Holly replied as she continued to look around the room.

"I'll check back with you in a little while," Kavi said, and then he disappeared.

Holly walked over to the bed and lay down . . . It feels divine, she thought. As she relaxed into the comfy pillow she heard his voice . . . "I'm here for you, Sunshine. You concentrate on getting well, and I'll be here when you wake up . . . Please wake up . . . You have to wake up" . . . . CHARLIE! . . . I have to get back to Charlie . . . It feels so good here, though, she thought as she surrendered to the dizziness, and then found herself in a completely different place . . .

. . . Holly is standing in a grassy area looking at the backside of a large house when she hears a child's voice call out to her, "Mommy, come look at the treehouse I built with Daddy!" She turns to look behind her and sees an excited little boy around 4 years old with red hair and hazel green eyes jumping up and down with glee. "Look what Daddy built," he says and points to a fancy treehouse. She sees that the little boy looks a lot like her.

"What do you think, Sunshine?" Charlie asks her, beaming with pride at the treehouse he built.

"Charlie, it's wonderful," Holly replies as she looks at this fantastic creation. Charlie looks a bit older, and he has more gray in his hair. She hears another little voice and feels someone tugging at her skirt. This time it belongs to a girl. "Daddy said he is going to build me a dollhouse," the little girl said and Holly sees that this child is the same age as the boy, and she has dark brown hair and eyes. This one looks like Charlie . . . Where am I, and when did we have kids? . . .

Holly opens her eyes and she is back in the tower room . . . Did I just have a dream . . . a dream when I'm already unconscious? . . . Here comes that dizziness again . . .

"She's awake! She's awake! Nurse, she's awake!" Charlie yelled loudly and a nurse hurried into the room. Holly looked at Charlie as he entwined his fingers with hers and smiled.

"How do you feel?" the nurse asked Holly.

Holly surveyed the room and said, "What am I doing here?" . . . *This doesn't look like the room in the crystal building.*

"You fell and hit your head. We're happy that you have regained consciousness. You have a concussion. You've been out for a little over 2 hours," the nurse replied. "What is the last thing that you remember?"

"I was doing Zumba, and then I was floating toward the light, and then I walked toward the crystal palace. I stayed there for a while, and now I'm here. I don't remember falling," she replied trying to process what happened and feeling extremely groggy and disoriented.

"Do you remember me?" Charlie asked with concern and wondering what kind of strange, alternate reality she just experienced.

"Yes, Charlie. You are my husband and we have two kids. You built a treehouse for our son," she replied and her head was aching. "My head hurts."

"I'm sure it does," the nurse replied. "I'm going to get you something for the pain and tell Dr. Tanner that you have regained consciousness." The nurse left to get some pain meds and find the doctor.

We have two kids . . . I built a treehouse for our son . . . Where the hell was she . . . I don't think she's back 100 percent yet . . . "Holly, we don't have any kids. I think you were dreaming. We aren't married yet. We are engaged, though, and we are planning to get married on the beach in September," Charlie said gently.

"That's right, we are. I must have dreamed it, Charlie. I swear I was in the most amazing place. I met my spirit guide, and I saw James. Can you believe it? He apologized for hurting me, and he thanked me for getting the money to Amber and Belle," Holly said wide-eyed with amazement.

Sometimes people in comatose states experience other dimensions . . . That must have happened to Holly . . . "I think you might have glimpsed the afterlife. I'd like to think that what you experienced was real, and that James can rest easy knowing his daughter is taken care of," Charlie replied and bent down to kiss her. "I'm so glad that you are back. I thought I was going to lose you."

"James seemed happy, and he said he was planning to be a Buddhist monk in his next life. It was an incredible dream, and I was in a great place. I can remember it so vividly, yet I can't remember falling," she replied feeling irritated. "What happened exactly?"

"You, Patricia, Lisa, and Roger were done with Zumba and were walking out to your vehicles when you slipped and fell on some ice. Someone dumped out a cup full of ice, and you were walking and talking and slipped and hit your head on the asphalt. Roger called the ambulance, and they followed you to the hospital. Patricia called me as the ambulance was arriving. We've been worried sick about you. At the risk of sounding like a scolding parent, I beg of you, PLEASE watch where you are going in the future. You got lucky. That fall could have killed you . . . or worse," Charlie said, agitated.

"I promise I'll be more careful. I don't remember any of that. Maybe it will come back to me in a few days. What was Roger doing at Zumba?" she asked.

"He was picking up Lisa. He gave her a ride because her car had a flat tire," Charlie replied. "He seems like a nice guy. It'll be interesting to see how long he stays with Lisa."

"They're planning to get married. She told me before Zumba that he proposed and wanted to get married on New Year's Eve," Holly said happily . . . *Thank God I can remember a few things.*

Dr. Tanner walked into the room happy that Holly was conscious. "Welcome back. I'm Dr. Chris Tanner. It's a pleasure to meet you," he said. "How are you feeling?"

"I have a headache, and I still don't remember much before the accident. I think I'm okay. I had strange dreams, and when I woke up I thought that Charlie and I had kids, which we don't," she replied.

"Confusion is normal with a concussion. I've got some pain meds for you. It's prescription Tylenol. I want to talk to you about treatment," he said as he gave her the pain meds in a little plastic cup and she swallowed them with a drink of water. "I want to keep you here 2 days for observation. You were unconscious for a long time for just a concussion. I'm amazed that you don't have a large cut on the back of your head. I'm sure there will be a bruise, and you will need to be careful when styling or brushing your hair.

"There are some things we need to watch for postconcussion. In the next few days you may experience headaches, the sensation of spinning, light-headedness, fatigue, poor memory, inability to concentrate, sensitivity to light or noise, irritability, depression, and anxiety. You might develop impaired thinking. These symptoms are common during the week after a concussion and usually resolve during the second week. However, sometimes, symptoms persist for months or, on rare occasions, years. People who have suffered a concussion seem to be predisposed to another one if a new injury occurs before symptoms from the previous concussion have completely gone away. I recommend no vigorous physical activity until your symptoms clear and you have a thorough medical exam. You need to watch your step more carefully. People who experience more than one concussion are at risk for dementia and Parkinson's disease. Do you have any questions?"

"I guess no Zumba for me for a while. Is it okay to go for walks and work out on my Total Gym? I'm used to a lot of physical activity," she replied.

"Yes, walks are fine as long as you watch your step. You can use the Total Gym, however take it easy and don't overexert yourself. Wait at least 2 weeks," Dr. Tanner said.

"I will. Thank you, Doctor," Holly replied.

"Get some rest now," Dr. Tanner said and left the room.

"If you need anything during the night, just press the buzzer to your left and it will notify the nurses' station," the nurse said and followed after Dr. Tanner.

"Charlie, you should go home and get some sleep. It's late, and I'm okay," she said lovingly to him.

"I don't want to go; however, I know that you need your rest. I'll be back in the morning. Patricia is notifying Stan and Mitch on why we won't be at work," he said.

"That's sweet of her. She's such an angel. Let her know I'm okay, and Lisa and Roger too," she replied and yawned.

"I'll see you in the morning, Sunshine," Charlie said and kissed her. "I love you."

"I love you too," she replied.

Charlie left to go home and Holly quickly fell asleep. She was exhausted from the Zumba class and her head injury. She had weird dreams through the night as her brain cells tried to recover. She experienced two brief segments of past lives and some other interesting phenomena . . .

. . . "Friedrich, get down on your knees and lick my shoes clean, you good-for-nothing boy!" The large blond woman with a mean and scowling face and hair piled on top of her head in a bun said to her. "If you don't, I'll beat you black and blue with this rope!" Roger is a woman this time. . .

"Mommy, please don't. I'll clean your shoes. I'm sorry I left the barn door open," Friedrich pleads as he bends down and starts to lick her shoes clean. The disgusting taste of mud and soot make him want to vomit.

"You better not throw up this time," the big woman warns, and then laughs menacingly . . .

. . . Holly is speaking a strange language and having sex with a native-looking man around a large fire. Other people around them are copulating and changing partners. She recognizes the native man as Neil Peters . . .

. . . Holly is back in her room at the crystal palace. She is sitting on the pink sofa and Kavi is sitting across from her in the orange easy

chair. Sunlight is pouring through the windows . . . I'm back here again, she thinks. "Kavi, was that a segment from one of the past lives you told me about when I visited Martina?"

"Yes. Roger is working diligently to be a better person in his current life, and he has learned much from his experiences. You are both evolving beautifully and are on the right path. It often takes several lifetimes to learn your desired lessons," Kavi replied with a smile.

"I don't remember you saying I lived as a native in a primitive life, but I experienced a sex dream about that with one of my coworkers, who I feel no attraction to. I feel embarrassed," Holly said, dismayed that she ever participated in something like that.

"You have lived many past lives. I told you just a few of them. There is no need to feel embarrassed," Kavi replied laughing.

"What am I supposed to learn from this life as Holly?" she asked.

"Would you like to see a segment of your prebirth planning session?" he asked.

"Yes. Show me please!" she replied with enthusiasm.

"Let's go to the movies," Kavi replied, and they were suddenly sitting in a theater looking at a movie screen . . .

. . . Holly sees herself in a room with Kavi and two other spiritual advisors discussing the blueprint of her upcoming life which has been laid out on a grid, resembling a chessboard you would find on earth. She sees herself trying on the body of Holly O'Rourke. The image of Holly is transparent, as she isn't ready to reincarnate at this moment. She sees James, Alex, Roger, Amber, and Charlie in their equally transparent body images.

"You should focus on gaining self-confidence. You need to learn that your opinions and desires are important and have merit. This is overdue. You need to learn to stand up for yourself and not let others walk all over you. You should learn not to sacrifice your own happiness and be miserable to please another," the female spiritual advisor with short brown hair and blue eyes said to Holly.

"I agree. I see that in many of your past lives you stayed in abusive situations and were afraid to speak up for fear of retribution. I would like to see you become strong and confident in your next earthly life and go after what you want," the male spiritual advisor with a completely bald head and kind blue eyes said to her. "How would you like to go about this?"

"I agree with your assessment. I think that I should have another abusive relationship with him, except that I leave before it turns into something worse. Having the courage to leave early will make me stronger and more self-confident. I want to clear more of my negative karma too," Holly replied.

"Roger, are you up for this again?" the brown-haired advisor asked.

"Yes, although it saddens me to hurt her again. I hope that she will want to leave me, and this time she will be strong enough to do so. I know that this fits into my plan to learn to control my anger and help others overcome similar problems. I hope we both get it right this time," Roger replied.

"I would like to clear my negative karma with Amber," Holly said.

"You don't have to do this, my friend," Amber replied.

"I know, except that it will make me feel better when I return here," Holly said.

"How would you like to do it?" Amber asked.

"You can steal him away from me, and I will experience the devastation you felt in Atlantis when he got me pregnant," Holly explained.

"Holly, you know that clearing karma doesn't require an even exchange. There are other ways. Wouldn't you rather save her life or do something else? Are you sure you want this?" the male adviser asked.

"Yes," Holly replied.

Amber laughed and said, "I volunteer to trap and steal him and even the score for you. I think I should get pregnant with his child too. I want to have the single-mother experience again for a little while. My romantic relationship with James shouldn't be for life. I want to learn to be strong without him."

"Yes, that's a good idea. James, are you onboard with this?" Holly asked.

"Again? Ugggh, the drama!" James replied in jest. "I love you both so much that I will do this again. This will prepare me for the Buddhist monk lifetime that is slated for the life after this one. I have other karma I want to clear before I experience a spiritual life free from romantic entanglements. I'd prefer a later midlife death, maybe around 54."

"Thank you, James and Amber," Holly replied. "Back to things that would make me strong, I think there should be another relationship that causes me to stand up for myself and leave an unwanted situation, although I do not want additional physical or mental abuse."

"Holly, let me play that part," Alex said. "I want to experience overcoming drug addiction, reaching rock bottom and pulling myself out, and bisexuality and the conflict of being true to myself. I can be your partner for a period of time."

"Here's a thought. Alex, your bisexuality and drug problems will be the undoing of your relationship with Holly. Holly, are you sure you want to experience three difficult relationships?" Kavi chimed in.

"Yes, I think that will be enough. I would like to eventually find a partner to love and grow old with, save the best for last, and truly appreciate him. I would like for him to be Charlie," Holly replied.

"I would love to be with you, Holly. We haven't been together in an honest relationship since Atlantis, and we both died in our late 30s when the continent was destroyed. I'm happy to be your husband. I have two unhappy marriages planned that will help clear my karma with Lisa and Kelly. I would love to experience happiness in my later midlife years with you," Charlie replied.

"I'm looking forward to it, Charlie," Holly said.

"Holly, it seems we have the adult romantic relationships set for your next life. We will now talk about the timing of these relationships

and your other areas of work as well as alternative futures in the event of freewill overrides," the male advisor said and the female nodded her head in agreement . . .

. . . "Kavi, that was amazing. I remember it now, I remember being there and planning this. It seems like things have unfolded according to the plan," Holly said with wonder.

"Yes, although there have been many lives where you did not follow the blueprint, the same goes for all of us. Free will overrides everything, which is why alternate plans are made. No matter what you experience in your many lives, you learn and grow in some way. I have shown you just a small piece of your plan.You are here to work on more than gaining self-confidence and standing your ground," Kavi replied.

"Why do we change genders?" Holly asked.

"For the experience," he replied.

"I prefer being a woman," she said.

"Most souls eventually develop a preference," he replied.

"Why can't you show me the rest of my life plan?" she asked teasingly.

"Because, it could hinder your progress. It's best to live your life and see it unfold according to the choices that you make."

"Once my brain recovers, will I see you again?" she asked.

"I am here to guide you for the rest of your earthly life. This accident will leave you with some psychic abilities, and I think we'll have these talks more often," he said . . .

Holly woke up. It was still dark outside. Her head felt better, and she lay in her hospital bed pondering her otherworldly experience . . . *That was amazing . . . I remember every bit of that dream. I wonder how long I'll be able to remember it . . . Roger was a mean and ugly woman. I should probably tell him about our shared past lives sometime . . . EWWW, I can't believe I had native sex with Neil in another life. I have zero physical attraction to him . . .This will remain a deep, dark secret that I tell no one. I want to forget it . . . I can't wait to take a shower . . . I think I'll keep the prebirth planning to myself, although I might tell Charlie . . . Something like that is hard for most people to believe and accept . . . to think that you actually plan negative experiences for yourself and ask others to do mean or bad things to you . . .What a concept, and I think I believe it . . . It makes me think twice about judging others. I'm going to try not do that anymore, although it won't be easy . . . I feel incredibly tired . . . going back to sleep now.*

Holly woke up again when the morning light brightened her room. A nurse walked in to check on her and Holly noticed that the woman had a pink aura surrounding her . . . *That's weird; I've never seen colors around people before . . . I'm seeing auras without even trying.*

"How are you feeling this morning?" the nurse asked as she took Holly's blood pressure.

"Much better, thank you," Holly replied . . . *Should I tell her about her aura?*

"Your blood pressure is normal, how's your head? Do you still have a headache?" she asked.

"Not right now. My head's okay except that I'm seeing auras," Holly replied with a laugh.

"Do you see one around me?" the nurse asked with surprise.

"Yes, you have a pink aura!" Holly said excitedly. "This has never happened to me before."

"I'll let the doctor know. Head traumas affect people differently. The auras will probably go away as you continue to recover," she told her.

"I think it's neat," Holly said with a smile. "I'm hungry. Will you please bring me some breakfast?"

"Yes. I'll put the order in now," the nurse replied and left the room.

Holly was eating breakfast when Charlie came to see her. She noticed that his aura was green.

"Did you get any sleep last night?" she asked, happy to see him.

"Some. I had a feeling you would be okay, and I'm relieved to see you awake and alert," he said and kissed her forehead. "How do you feel?"

"I feel better. I don't have a headache at the moment. I still don't remember leaving the rec center and walking to the car, though. The other strange thing is . . . get this . . . I'm seeing auras, and yours is green!" she said with enthusiasm. "I'm not even trying to see them, they are plainly visible."

Charlie didn't know if this was good or bad. He said, "Maybe it's only temporary, let's hope so."

"Right now it's fun, although I can see where it might be a major distraction if it doesn't stop," she replied. "The nurse's aura was pink. I want to know what color mine is. I'm going to look in the mirror," she said as she started to get out of bed.

"Careful getting up," Charlie said and reached out for her.

"I got up a time or two last night on my own, with a nurse's supervision," she said as she slowly got out of bed and stood up straight. "I'm a little dizzy when I first stand up . . . There, it's gone," she said as she took hold of Charlie's arm and walked to the bathroom. She looked in the mirror and gasped in surprise, "I look like death warmed over . . . Oh my God . . . My aura is pink too . . . I also see some orange. The room I stayed in at the crystal palace was decorated in pink, orange, and white wallpaper, with a pink sofa and an orange chair. This is amazing."

She seems really happy and upbeat . . . I think she's going to be fine . . . "It makes me happy to see you recovering so quickly, Sunshine. I'm concerned though. If you continue to see these auras they may become a nuisance," he said, his eyes showing concern as he embraced her from behind and nuzzled into her neck.

"I'm not worried about it. Kavi said that I would have some psychic abilities as a result of the concussion," she said.

"Who is Kavi?" Charlie asked.

"He's my spirit guide. Each of us has a spirit guide to help us through our earthly incarnations. They guide us via our intuition, and some people have the ability to communicate with them psychically," she replied.

"I don't know what to think about that. As long as you are safe and happy I'll try not to worry about your sanity," Charlie said half-jokingly. "What does Kavi look like?"

"He's about 5 foot 9. He's a Hindu man with long, curly black hair, a beard, and dark skin. Don't worry; I'm not attracted to him in *that* way," she teased.

Charlie laughed and said, "I trust you. Besides, you have to be unconscious to see him."

"That's true, at least for now," she replied. "I want to take a shower."

"I'm going to help. I don't want to take a chance on you falling again," he replied as he looked in the shower and saw there was a chair.

"You're an angel. I'm going to get the shower started, and you can stand by to catch me if I fall," she said sweetly.

"I'll be right here. Tell me when you're done and I'll help you stand up," he replied.

Charlie helped her into the shower and the warm water felt heavenly. *Finally . . . I feel human again . . . I can feel the bruise on the back of my head . . . I'll be extremely careful.* Holly felt rejuvenated from the shower, and Charlie happily helped her stand up and dry off.

"I hope they don't keep me here past tomorrow. I'll go crazy from the boredom, and I just *love* these gowns," she said sarcastically as Charlie helped her into her hospital gown.

"I brought you some lounge pants if you want to put them on. And I think you should stay as long as the doctor recommends. I'm here for you, and you don't have to be alone," he replied.

"I guess so. The headache has returned, although it's not as strong," Holly said. "I still see your aura."

"Is it still green?" he asked.

"Yes," she replied. "We'll have to find out what the colors mean."

Holly and Charlie watched TV for a few hours, and then received a visit from Lisa and Roger. Lisa was carrying a bouquet of pink, white, and orange roses in a clear vase.

"Hey, there," Lisa greeted them cheerfully as she walked into Holly's room with Roger.

"It's good to see you awake," Roger said with a smile.

"Those roses are so pretty. Thank you! I'm glad you guys were with me when I fell. I still don't remember it," Holly said . . . *Those are the exact same flowers that were in the crystal palace . . . This is amazing.*

"Charlie called us after you gained consciousness, and then I was able to get to sleep. I expect Patricia will show up soon," Lisa said as she placed the flowers on a nearby table.

"Thank you so much for stopping by. I'm not sure how long they'll keep me," Holly replied feeling touched and grateful that they cared enough to take time out of a busy day to visit.

"How do you feel?" Lisa asked.

"I feel a little dizzy when I stand up, and then it goes away. I don't remember anything except doing Zumba and waking up here, and I'm seeing auras without even trying," Holly replied.

Roger laughed and said, "I can see auras. I have to relax and focus a little bit first, and then I see them."

"Do you know what the colors mean?" Holly asked. "Your aura is yellow."

"What color is mine?" Lisa asked.

"Yours is red," Holly replied.

"That seems appropriate, and I don't know what the colors mean," Lisa said with a laugh.

"That's correct. Lisa's aura is usually a clear red, although I've seen it turn orange-red and orange-yellow quite frequently. Holly, I see that yours is mostly a soft pink with some orange," Roger said. "And I see that Charlie's is an emerald green."

"I guess that proves what Holly is seeing is correct," Charlie said. "She told me I had a green aura and that hers was pink and orange.

Lisa, red and green are the happy colors of Christmas, yet when we were together, it was anything but," Charlie said jokingly to her.

Lisa laughed, feeling hopeful that Charlie didn't hate her anymore and replied, "Amen to that. This might not be the best time and place, however, I want to apologize for being such a witchy wife and taking out my anger on you when we were married. I don't blame you for kicking me out."

"Thank you for saying that," Charlie replied. "I think we've both found our true soul mates. Roger, what do these colors mean?"

"Generally, they correspond to what people automatically think of certain colors. From what I know about them, your aura will change colors depending on your emotional state. I think we each have a main or basic color and strong emotions can cause it to change. I'm going to search the Internet for a better explanation," he replied as he searched the Internet on his smart phone. A few minutes later he said, "Here we go. This site provides a good description of what aura colors mean. Lisa's currently clear red aura indicates a powerful, energetic, competitive, sexual, and passionate nature. I can vouch for that."

"That is true. I'm working on the competitive part and trying to be more cooperative," Lisa replied.

"Charlie's emerald green aura indicates someone who is a natural healer and is love-centered. This sociable person loves nature and animals and people and would make a good teacher. Is this true, Charlie?" Roger asked.

"For the most part. I don't know about being a natural healer, though," he replied.

"Holly, your mostly light pink aura indicates that you are a romantic, loving, sensitive, and affectionate person with much compassion. The orange indicates courage, energy, and stamina, and an outgoing social nature."

"That sounds right," she replied.

"My yellow aura indicates that I am developing psychic and spiritual awareness, I'm optimistic, easygoing, and positive, and a natural-born leader. I sure didn't used to be," Roger said. "Once upon a time my aura was probably cloudy and gray."

"Mine was probably black," Lisa said playfully and turned to look out into the hallway. "Here comes Patricia."

Patricia walked into the room and Holly noticed that her aura was yellow too.

"I'm glad to see you awake and laughing," Patricia said to her.

"It's great to see you too. I think I gave everyone a pretty bad scare," Holly remarked.

"You sure did. From now on, watch where you're going," Patricia teasingly reprimanded her. "How are you feeling? Do you remember falling?"

"No. I remember doing Zumba, and then waking up here. My head aches off and on, and I'm currently seeing auras. Yours is yellow. Roger can see auras too. Roger, am I right about Patricia?" Holly asked.

"Yes," he replied. "My aura is yellow too. Do you want to know what that means?" he asked Patricia.

"Sure," she said.

"A yellow aura indicates that you are developing psychic and spiritual awareness, are optimistic, easygoing, positive, and a natural-born leader. I'd say that sounds right," he said.

"I agree, that is cool," Patricia said with an air of surprise and looked at Holly. "I wonder what other abilities you might have from this accident."

"I'll have to wait and see. The doctor said I should avoid vigorous physical activity until I've had a complete medical exam. You and Lisa will have to enjoy Zumba without me. That is such a bummer. I love Zumba," Holly lamented.

"There are six more Zumba sessions, and then they take a break until September. Maybe the three of us can sign up for Pilates. That way, we can still get a good workout, just not as vigorous. Then when

September rolls around, Holly should be ready to Zumba again," Patricia said.

"I think that's an excellent idea, I'm in!" Lisa said with enthusiasm.

"Me too. Let's plan to do that," Holly agreed, optimistic that she would be fully recovered by then . . . *I just love looking at people and their auras, this is incredible. It's so nice that they stopped by to check on me . . . I'm a lucky lady.*

"So, how long are they keeping you?" Patricia asked.

"The doctor said 2 days for observation, I think that means today and tomorrow, and then I can leave on Thursday morning. I should give Stan a call," Holly replied.

"You don't need to. He wanted me to tell you not to worry about work, just concentrate on getting better," Patricia told her. "Everyone in your group is pulling for you, and I have to give them a full report when I get back."

"That's nice to know. Stan's such a good guy, and I want to go in Friday if I'm feeling up to it," Holly said and noticed that Dr. Tanner was standing in the doorway.

"Hello. I need to check on Holly."

"Let's step outside," Lisa said, and the three of them stepped out of the room for a few minutes.

"How are you feeling today?" Dr. Tanner inquired.

"Much better. I still don't remember the events leading up to my fall. My head aches off and on," Holly replied.

"The nurse said that you are seeing auras. Are you seeing them now?" he asked.

"Yes, yours is green like my fiancé's," Holly replied.

"I don't recall ever getting a report of seeing auras from someone who had a concussion. However, I'm not too worried about it. I think it will gradually diminish as you get better. Head injuries and the healing process are different for each person. We want to keep you here through tomorrow and discharge you on Thursday, providing you continue to improve," Dr. Tanner said.

"Doctor, she seems to be doing great. She's been talking and laughing with our friends and doesn't appear to have any problems following a conversation or train of thought," Charlie said.

"Good. I'll stop by tomorrow. The nurses will continue to monitor your progress. You two have a good day," Dr. Tanner said with a smile.

"You too, thank you, Doctor," Holly said, and Dr. Tanner left the room.

Lisa, Patricia, and Roger came back into the room. "We're going to get back to work and are happy that you will make a full recovery. I'm seeing more orange in your aura now," Roger said.

"Thanks again for coming to check on me. I have the best friends!" Holly said emphatically with a big smile.

"Yes, I'm grateful to you too," Charlie said to them.

"Give me a call when you get out of this joint," Lisa said.

"Yeah, and stop by my office if you come in on Friday," Patricia chimed in.

"I will, and you guys have a great day," Holly said happily as they left her room.

"I have another idea for our beach wedding," Charlie said.

"Let me guess, you want to include them?" Holly asked with a knowing look.

"If you're okay with it, I thought it might be nice to invite them to share our ceremony, and then I'll treat everyone to dinner at Catch 31. It will be a nice little weekend at the beach for them, and we can stay a few extra days," Charlie said.

"I think that's lovely. I know our families won't be able to make it. Our parents aren't in good health, and our siblings and your children are scattered across the country. I'm impressed that you would want to invite Lisa and Roger to the ceremony. You are so evolved," Holly replied, never expecting Charlie to come up with something like this.

"I like Roger. He seems like a good guy, and Lisa has changed. Her entire demeanor is now pleasant. I can see that she's a good friend to you. It was kind of her to bring you flowers. The three of you seem like sisters. With the two of them and Patricia and Andy, I think it will be a good time. They can take pictures that we can send to our families," Charlie said.

"I'm thrilled to be marrying you, and I love you even more now," Holly replied and squeezed his hand.

"If you're happy, I'm happy," he said and kissed her.

Holly stayed in the hospital through Wednesday and Charlie drove her home on Thursday morning. She still had amnesia about the events leading up to her fall. In the days and weeks that followed, she experienced some mild episodes of vertigo and lingering headaches. However, she made a full recovery and stopped seeing auras around people. She was disappointed when this happened and purchased a book to learn how to see them at will. With a little practice, she discovered what Roger said was true. She could see auras around people anytime, if she focused her gaze in a certain way.

CHAPTER 16

Better Than a Fairy Tale

Holly recalled what Kavi said about her potential for psychic ability as a result of the accident, *"This accident will leave you with some psychic abilities, and I think we will have these talks more frequently."* It was now late August and other than learning to see auras, she didn't notice any additional psychic abilities, nor had she dreamt of Kavi since she left the hospital. She was blissfully preoccupied with her upcoming beach wedding and wasn't too concerned with her lack of psychic ability. Patricia, Andy, Lisa, and Roger were going to be there with her and Charlie when they took their vows. As she looked out her office window, thinking about her wedding day coming up in less than 3 weeks and getting ready to go home in the next 20 minutes, she heard someone knock on her door.

"Hi, Jack. What brings you up here?" she asked when she saw Jack Briggs standing in her doorway.

"Hi, Holly. I know it was sometime last year, and I apologize for getting back to you so late on this. I was wondering if you had time this week to come down to my office and do a tarot card reading," Jack asked tentatively. Holly sensed that he was worried about something. He looked tired and upset.

"Yes, I'd be glad to. I can bring my cards in tomorrow. What's better for you, the morning or the afternoon?" she asked.

"Tomorrow morning at 9:30 would be perfect. The rest of my day from 10:30 on is booked solid. Hopefully 30–45 minutes will be enough time," he replied.

"That's perfect. I'll come down to your office tomorrow morning at 9:30," she replied with a smile.

"Thank you. I'm looking forward to it," he said and turned to leave.

He's stressing over something . . . It will be interesting to find out what it is . . . she thought as she returned to reading her e-mails. A mental picture flashed through her mind of a sick woman resting in bed and a harried man trying to keep up with his kids . . . *That's it, Jack's wife is ill . . . That poor guy, he's so worried about her . . . Now I feel bad . . . Try to focus on something else, we'll see what the cards say tomorrow.*

"Hey, Sunshine, are you ready to go home?" Charlie said as he walked into her office and sat down in her guest chair.

"Yeah, it's been a long day," Holly replied with a sigh.

"What's wrong? You seem a little down," Charlie asked.

"Jack Briggs asked me for a tarot card reading tomorrow, and he seemed upset and stressed. As I was reading my e-mails, I had a mental picture of a sick woman and an upset man flash through my mind. I take that as a sign that Jack's wife is very ill and he's struggling with it," Holly said. "An image of a teddy bear flashed in my mind shortly before you sent me Theo Barry, so I take that as an intuition. The mental image of a sick woman was followed by a sad feeling, and you picked up on it."

"Jack keeps to himself and rarely ever talks about his family life. He is strictly business 24/7. I don't have any information from the grapevine on what it could be, so you might be right," Charlie replied. "If he is worried about his wife, I know how he feels."

"I know I tell you crazy things and you still love me. When I was having my experience in another dimension, Kavi mentioned that I would have some new psychic abilities as the result of the accident and this might be it, enhanced intuition," Holly said as she logged off her computer and slipped on her flats for walking.

"I believe everything that you tell me, even if it sounds strange at first. I hope that if something is wrong with his wife that she recovers from it. Having enhanced intuition could come in handy. We should play the lottery the next time you feel lucky," Charlie said as he took her hand and they walked to the elevators.

"I've been so happy since we've been together, I feel like I've already won the lottery," Holly replied sweetly.

"Me too. And I'm especially grateful that your head injury wasn't life-threatening," Charlie replied with a smile and squeezed her hand. "Still, winning the lottery would be awesome. We could do whatever we wanted and not have to wait for retirement."

"When you put it that way, I think we should buy tickets real soon. Let's buy a ticket on our wedding day!" she said excitedly.

Charlie laughed and said, "Okay, we can do that."

Later that evening while Charlie was in the basement putting the finishing touches on an end table that Andy asked him to make, Holly was in the living room reading her tarot card guidebook and determining which spread would be the best to use for Jack's reading tomorrow . . . *The five-card spread looks like a good one . . . I don't know Jack on a personal level, I don't think anyone does, and the five card provides a little more information than the three card . . . It indicates what influences are affecting his thoughts and feelings . . . I'll use that one . . . It's strange, I'm not getting a feeling that anything terribly bad is going to happen to Jack . . . I feel that worry is consuming him and things are going to be okay somehow . . . whatever his current situation is.*

Holly showed up in Jack's office the next morning at 9:30 sharp. "Good morning, Jack. Are you ready?" she asked.

"Yes, let's get started," he replied and closed his office door so they could have some privacy.

Holly noticed that he didn't look as stressed today as he did yesterday. However, it was still early. Jack had a small, round table in his office with four chairs. They both sat down and Holly put her deck of cards on the table.

"So, how does this work?" Jack asked.

"It's easy. You shuffle these cards and think about your question. When you are done, place the deck facedown and choose the first five cards. The first card will indicate your question, the second card will provide some background information, the third card represents you and your feelings, the fourth card indicates your environment or outside influences, and the fifth card will be your answer," Holly said as she handed him the deck.

"I hope that I can count on you not to tell anyone about this. It's okay if you tell Charlie, I know he's your fiancé and he's not a gossip. I'd appreciate it if no one else knew," he said.

"I respect that, Jack, I won't tell anyone that we've had this interaction, and I'll ask Charlie to do the same," Holly replied reassuringly.

Jack shuffled the cards while thinking of his question . . . *Will my wife carry our fifth child to term and recover her health? . . . She's been bedridden for 4 months, she's got 3 more to go . . . We never thought she could get pregnant again . . . I don't know what to do . . . I would be devastated to lose our new baby . . . or her or both of them . . . With this little one we will be a family of seven.* Jack finished shuffling the cards and Holly watched him draw five cards from the top of the deck and line them up next to each other. He took a few moments and looked carefully at each card, as if he was trying to discern its meaning.

The first card Jack drew was the Four of Swords which shows a man lying at rest upon a bed with three swords on the wall and one sword decorating the outside of the bed frame. The sleeping man looked peaceful. A stained glass window decorated the wall of his room.

The second card he drew was the Empress which shows a pretty woman with long flowing hair sitting in a fancy, plush red chair holding a scepter. She is wearing a crown on her head and a long gown with what appears to be strawberries printed on it. Behind her are trees and a river running through the trees which empties into a lake.

The third card he drew was the Nine of Swords which shows a man sitting up in bed with his head in his hands, the background of the card is black with nine swords on the wall beside him. This card's overall feeling is one of despair.

The fourth card he drew was the Hanged Man which shows a man hanging upside down from a tree. His head has a yellow aura around it. One of his feet appears to be bound and the leg is straight, his other leg is bent at an angle, his hands are behind his back.

The fifth card he drew was the Ace of Wands which shows an illuminated hand coming out from a cloud holding a tree branch with leaves on it. The sky is blue and there are rolling hills in the background, and a castle sits atop one of the hills. The card has a positive feel.

Holly looked at the cards and images began to form in her mind . . . *His wife is pregnant, and he is worried about the future; she might be sick and having a hard pregnancy which is what is keeping him up at night and causing him stress.*

"So, what does this mean?" he asked.

"At first glance, I'm going to guess that your wife is pregnant and you are extremely worried about her health and your unborn child," Holly said.

Jack was speechless for a moment; his face indicated surprise. "You just hit the nail on the head," he replied. "Please tell me what each of these cards mean and what kind of outcome we can expect."

"The Four of Swords in the first position indicates withdrawal, rest, and healing from an affliction. This pregnancy has been rough on your wife, and she is confined to bed for the rest of her pregnancy. Is this correct?" Holly asked.

"Yes, exactly," Jack replied.

"This card usually points toward recovery and is not negative," Holly said. "The Empress card in the second position points to a motherly, nurturing, and fertile woman and can indicate much creativity. This is a good card overall, and I feel that this represents your wife. The Nine of Swords in the third position indicates depression, grief, and mental anguish. I'm going to surmise that you have experienced many sleepless nights of worry about the future of your family."

"That is true," he replied.

"The Hanged Man in the fourth position indicates transition and sacrifice. Those are the forces surrounding you now. Adding a new baby to your family is both a transition and a sacrifice. Many things are unknown to you at this moment, and you must make new goals and plan accordingly as the situation unfolds. This card is neither positive nor negative.

The Ace of Wands in the last position indicates a new beginning. Aces are positive cards and I take it to mean that your wife and new baby girl will be just fine. My intuition keeps telling me that you and your family will be okay," Holly said.

"How did you know we are having a girl?" he asked.

"I don't know, the words just rolled off of my tongue," Holly replied . . . *Damn, maybe I am becoming psychic . . . I didn't use my guidebook once . . . I just realized that.*

Jack laughed and Holly noticed that he looked relieved. "I hope that what you say is true. I'm not a spiritual person, yet I'm inclined to believe you. I don't know what prompted me to ask you for a reading. I can't explain any of it. When I first asked you about a reading last year, I was focused on a troubling business concern that eventually turned out in my favor," he said. "My wife has been bedridden through most of her pregnancy and it's been difficult getting through each day, more so for her than me. She was so active until this surprise pregnancy. We thought we were through having kids. Thankfully, her mother is able to stay with us to help around the house. We are so looking forward to having a girl. Thank you, Holly, I appreciate the reading."

"You're welcome, Jack, anytime," Holly replied. They both stood up and Holly gathered her tarot cards and placed them back in the box. "You have a good day."

"You too, Holly," Jack replied with a smile as he opened the door and she left his office.

Amazing, I can't believe I did that without the book . . . Everything just came to me. When Charlie retires, I think I'll look into giving tarot card readings at fairs and parties . . . That would be fun . . . Holly thought as she took the elevator back to her office on the tenth floor. As she walked into her office, her phone rang and she saw that it was Charlie.

"Hey there. I just got done," she said.

"How did it go?" he asked.

"It went great. I didn't need to use the guidebook, and I didn't open it once. Stuff just came into my head, and I found myself interpreting the cards like a pro. It felt right. Oh, and Jack doesn't want you to tell anyone about this," Holly said.

"No worries, I haven't told anyone. Is he going to be okay, do the cards portend good things?" Charlie asked, curious and hopeful that nothing was seriously wrong with Jack's wife.

"Yes. His wife is pregnant with their fifth child and unfortunately she's bedridden for the next several months. He's so worried about her, but I believe they're going to be okay and happy. That's what was in the cards," she said happily.

"Five kids . . . holy smoke . . . That's a lot to take . . . I sure wish the guy well," Charlie replied.

"Me too. I've got to go. Stan just sent me an urgent e-mail. I'll talk to you later," Holly said.

"Okay, bye," Charlie replied and hung up.

In the weeks that followed, Holly and Charlie anxiously awaited their beach wedding. Holly found her wedding sundress on a shopping trip with Patricia and Lisa. It was a floor-length, white sundress made from a gauzy-type of cotton material with an attached slip to prevent it from being see-through. It had a halter-style neckline with a fitted waist and flared fuller skirt. It was the perfect, beachy bridal dress. She planned to wear white flip-flops because the sand would most likely be too hot to go barefoot. They were getting married at 4:00 p.m., on a Saturday afternoon, with drinks and dinner afterward at Catch 31 on the boardwalk. She decided against carrying flowers. She just wanted her and Charlie, their wedding rings, and friends present.

On Friday morning, September 12, they left for the beach and arrived about 4 hours later. The weather was hot and sunny and the feel of summer was still in the air. Saturday's forecast indicated another warm and sunny day and would be perfect for their beach nuptials. They decided to stay at the Courtyard Marriott again, and their friends opted to stay there too. The morning of their wedding day, they met Roger, Lisa, Patricia, and Andy for breakfast at a nearby pancake house and spent time lazing around the hotel swimming pool before getting ready for their ceremony.

"You ladies look so fine. We are the luckiest guys here!" Andy exclaimed as he appreciated how fit and toned Patricia, Holly, and Lisa looked in their swimsuits. "All that hard work is paying off."

"We are pretty hot," Lisa said as Patricia and Holly laughed in slight embarrassment and made their way into the swimming pool. The guys were content to sit and veg in the lounge chairs.

"Yes, we have the finest ladies anywhere," Roger agreed. "Speaking of luck, I think we should buy Powerball and Mega Millions tickets. This is a big day for Charlie and Holly, and the jackpots are huge."

"Funny you should say that. Holly mentioned a few weeks ago that we should buy lottery tickets on our wedding day. She's probably forgotten about it," Charlie replied, having forgotten about it too.

"You do realize that this is the 13th. I've never thought of 13 as a lucky number," Andy said. "But it is a happy day for Charlie and his bride, so maybe I'll put my superstitions aside and buy a ticket or two."

"I have no qualms with getting married on the 13th; it's not like it's a Friday," Charlie said with a laugh . . . *Although I would marry her on Friday the 13th if she wanted me to . . . I'd do anything for her.*

"We should probably get tickets before the ceremony. I can go get them. I saw a sign in a storefront a few blocks down. I can walk there and back in 20 minutes," Roger offered.

"I'm in," Charlie said and reached into their beach tote for some cash. "I want to bet specific numbers on Powerball this time." He knew that Holly liked to keep a pen and small notepad handy, so he wrote down the following numbers, 9, 20, 14, 54, and 46 with a Powerball of 13. "Here you go, please get me these numbers and two other random number tickets," he said as he handed the note and cash to Roger.

Roger looked at Charlie's numbers and said, "Let me guess, the 9 is for September, 20 and 14 are the current year, you are 54 and Holly is 46 and today is the 13th."

"Why do you have to be so smart?" Charlie asked sarcastically.

"I'm not overly smart, just perceptive," Roger replied with a laugh.

"I'm in. I'll take whatever numbers are generated, three Powerball tickets please," Andy replied and handed his money to Roger.

Roger started walking toward the sidewalk. "Where are you going?" Lisa called out to him.

"Lottery tickets," he yelled back with a big smile.

"Good idea," Holly called out in agreement.

"I hardly ever play the lottery. When I do I'm lucky if I get one number to match," Patricia said.

"I'd rather get lottery tickets on a gorgeous day, especially a happy occasion like this," Lisa replied. "I usually don't get any matching numbers either."

"I never remember to buy a ticket. I think about it after the fact and tell myself that I will buy a ticket next time," Holly said. "When I married Alex, we were in Las Vegas and that morning we did some gambling and didn't win a thing. It was like an omen of foreboding because the day before we won $100. I mentioned to Charlie a few weeks ago that we should buy lottery tickets on our wedding day. I forgot about it until just a few seconds ago."

"Even if you don't win any money, you've won the best thing . . . a wonderful man who loves you to the moon and back," Patricia said sweetly.

"Yes, I agree. If we win something, great, if not, no big deal," Holly replied.

"The three of us are already lucky. We have good men, good figures, good jobs, the list just goes on and on. Roger's helped me to become a more grateful person. I try to think of something I'm thankful for every morning," Lisa said.

"I've been so happy with Charlie this past year. I'm glad we switched partners," Holly said to Lisa teasingly . . . *When I think about the past life where the four of us had our terrible falling out, it fills my heart with joy that things turned out so well in this current life.*

Lisa laughed heartily and replied, "Ain't it the truth."

As Roger walked down the street, he had a good feeling about buying these lottery tickets . . . *One of us is going to win something big . . . maybe not the jackpot but a nice little sum of money . . . It just feels strong . . . Today is a good day. I'm happy to be here with Holly and Charlie and share in their happiness* . . . he thought as he took notice of the clear blue sky and the bright sun beating down on him. He bought the lottery tickets and walked back to the hotel.

"I got your winning tickets," Roger said to Charlie and Andy who had joined the girls in the swimming pool.

"Put them somewhere safe and come in," Lisa said to her man. Roger took off his shirt and joined the rest of them in the pool. Holly noticed that Roger was in pretty good shape. Lisa put him on a diet and got him into lifting weights, and he looked much better than when she first saw him on TV last year. His potbelly was gone.

An hour later they retreated to their rooms to get ready for the ceremony. While Charlie was taking a shower, Holly finished blow-drying her hair and went to retrieve her jewelry pouch from her suitcase. She opened up the pouch and noticed two tarot cards were placed inside . . . *Where did these come from? . . . Charlie must have placed them in here . . . Did he draw these? . . . These are good ones, the Ace of Cups and the Ace of Pentacles . . . the Ace of Cups . . . I drew this one at my psychic reading with Martina last year. The Ace of Pentacles indicates prosperity, successful endeavors, and good luck . . . pentacles usually represent financial matters . . . lottery tickets* . . . Holly's heart began to beat fast and she suddenly felt excited and giddy. She retrieved her jewelry and the two tarot cards from the pouch and continued to get dressed as she waited for Charlie to step out of the shower. She heard the water stop and decided to wait until he stepped back into the room before she asked him how these cards found their way into the jewelry pouch.

The Ace of Pentacles is similar to the Ace of Wands in that an illuminated hand comes out of a cloud holding a large coin, or pentacle, set against the backdrop of a light blue sky and pretty scenery. This card portends financial success along with emotional stability and happiness. Aces portend new beginnings and good luck.

As Charlie stepped into the room to get dressed he paused to look at the beautiful lady standing in front of the open door to the balcony. The afternoon sunlight filtering into the room brought out the lovely copper highlights in her long red hair. Holly looked like a goddess in her white dress.

"You are the most beautiful woman I have ever seen. At the risk of sounding cliché, you are a vision of loveliness," Charlie said to her with that adoring look in his eyes that she knew and loved so well. "I could stand here and stare at you for hours."

"Thank you, Charlie," she said with a smile and asked, "Did you draw those aces?"

"Yeah. I woke up Thursday morning around 3:30 and couldn't get back to sleep. I went into the living room to watch TV and saw the cards on the coffee table and decided to shuffle them to see what they had to say. The first card I drew was the Ace of Cups and the second was the Ace of Pentacles. I couldn't locate the guidebook, and then I figured it didn't matter because I drew two aces. I know that aces are good omens, and I had the idea to place them somewhere in your suitcase," he replied. "I've never had any doubts about us, and the cards just solidify what I know to be true."

"When I went to see Martina for my psychic reading last year, the Ace of Cups was the last card I drew to get an overview of the future. The Ace of Cups indicates a loving and balanced relationship and the Ace of Pentacles indicates financial and emotional prosperity; that's the short version. Aces signify new beginnings," she replied and walked over to kiss him.

"You better let me finish getting ready. We don't want to be late for our wedding," he said and squeezed her tight.

Even though it was still quite warm outside, Charlie wore a white dress shirt and black trousers. He didn't wear a tie, he just unbuttoned his shirt a little to keep cool. As he put on his socks and dress shoes, he said, "I know I'm going to get sand in my shoes, but you're worth it."

"You look handsome. Let's go meet the others," Holly said happily, and they left the room and headed for the hotel lobby.

Roger, Lisa, Patricia, and Andy were waiting for them. The ladies were dressed in colorful and pretty floor-length sundresses, and the men were dressed similar to Charlie . . . nice shirts and slacks, no ties. As Charlie and Holly walked toward them, they saw that their friends were having a lively conversation with the wedding officiant, Cynthia Hobart. Cynthia was a wedding officiant for hire; they found her through an Internet search. She was a former minister in the Unitarian Church who retired and made a good living performing wedding ceremonies for those who didn't have any particular religious affiliation or belong to a church. Charlie and Holly exchanged e-mails and telephone conversations with her and felt comfortable hiring her to perform their ceremony. An older lady, Cynthia was in her late 60s with short blond hair, blue eyes, wore glasses, and had an engaging smile and energetic personality. She stood 5 foot 6 and was slightly plump, wearing a dark blue pantsuit.

"Here comes the happy couple now," Patricia said when she noticed Holly and Charlie coming toward them.

Cynthia smiled and greeted them warmly. "Hello. It's wonderful to finally meet you two in person," she said and shook hands with each of them. "What a beautiful couple you make. Are you ready for wedded bliss?" she said sweetly.

"I feel like we're already there," Charlie replied, looking lovingly at Holly.

"Yes, we've been ready for months," Holly said and leaned into Charlie.

"Great. Let's head to the beach," Cynthia suggested.

The seven of them walked along the boardwalk toward the north end where there were fewer people. A soft breeze kept the late-afternoon sun from being uncomfortable. Since it was September, the beach was blissfully uncrowded and it was easy to find a roomy area of sand unpopulated.

"I like that area," Holly said and pointed to a deserted stretch of sand with just a lone couple nearby, building a sandcastle with plastic molds and wet sand.

"Me too," Charlie replied and their group turned and walked onto the beach. As Holly surveyed their surroundings and they walked closer to the water, the couple looked up and Holly instantly recognized the man. His hair was salt-and-pepper like his Facebook photo, and he appeared slimmer than she remembered. He was wearing dark blue swim trunks and a white T-shirt. His face was lightly sunburned.

The woman with him was a petite brunette with shoulder-length hair, nicely tanned skin, and a slim figure. She was wearing a bright pink beach cover-up.

"Oh my God, that's Alex!" Holly exclaimed.

"Your ex-husband?" Charlie asked with surprise.

"Yes. I think he recognizes me too," she said with a laugh and waved to him. Alex recognized Holly and waved back.

"It looks like we're going to see a wedding. I know that woman," Alex said to Rachel. "She's my ex-wife."

"That's Holly?" Rachel said with surprise. "This is unbelievable."

"They make a good-looking couple," Alex replied. "I'm going to congratulate them and offer to buy a round of drinks tonight." He took Rachel's hand and walked toward them.

"I've performed a lot of weddings, and this has never happened before," Cynthia said with a hearty laugh. "I assume you are on friendly terms?"

"Yes, it was a friendly divorce, and we are Facebook friends. That must be his girlfriend Rachel," Holly replied.

"Holly, this is hilarious running into you here!" Alex said excitedly. "Are you getting married today?"

Holly laughed with delight and said, "Yes. We are having our ceremony on the beach, right here. This is my fiancé, Charlie."

Charlie thought this situation was funny, and he extended his hand to Alex and said, "Great to meet you, now I've met all of Holly's former husbands. Roger, here, was Holly's first husband, and that's his fiancée, Lisa, who is my ex-wife." Everyone erupted in laughter at Charlie's statement.

"Pleased to meet you, Alex," Roger said and shook Alex's hand.

"Holly has generated some interesting karma to have her two ex-husbands show up at her wedding," Lisa said.

"This could only happen to you, Holly," Patricia teased.

"Don't I know it! Alex, is this Rachel?" Holly asked, hoping that it was . . . *It would be so embarrassing if she was a different woman.*

"Yes, I'm Rachel. I think it's so special that you are getting married on the beach," Rachel said pleasantly with a sweet smile.

"I hope that you two will stay to watch and join us for drinks and dinner," Charlie said, feeling generous and hoping Holly would be okay with that. He didn't need to worry because Holly was in total agreement.

"We'd love to. Thank you, Charlie," Alex replied.

"Charlie's already reading my mind. I was thinking the same thing. Let's get this party started," Holly replied feeling joyous and supremely happy and blessed.

"Okay, gather 'round," Cynthia said and their friends stood in a semicircle formation to give them space. Charlie had Holly's wedding ring in his pocket and Holly gave Charlie's ring to Cynthia since she didn't have an available place to keep it.

"Let's begin. Holly and Charlie, please join your hands together," Cynthia said as they faced each other, with joined hands, and continued, "We are gathered here on this glorious day to witness and celebrate the formal union of this loving couple who want to share their lives with each other in the bonds of marriage. A good marriage must be created. One is never too old to hold hands. It's remembering to say I love you every day, and it is not just marrying the right person, it's being the right partner. In marriage, the little things are the big things. It requires having the ability to forgive and forget. It is giving each other a supportive atmosphere in which each can grow. It is speaking words of appreciation and demonstrating gratitude in thoughtful ways. It is remembering to not take each other for granted and truly listen to what each other has to say. With that said, let's commence with the wedding vows. Holly, you can go first."

"Charlie, I am honored to take you to be my husband, my partner in life, and my one true love. I will cherish our union and love you more each day than I did the day before. Your thoughtful and loving way warms my heart. I will trust and respect you, laugh and cry with you, love you faithfully through good times and bad, regardless of the obstacles we may face together. I give you my hand, my heart, and my love, from this day forward until the end of my days. With this ring, I take you as my husband," Holly said and placed the ring on his finger. "I love you," she said with a smile.

"Holly, I invite you to share my life. You are the most beautiful and generous person I have ever known, and I promise always to love and respect you. Your lovely smile and caring heart lights up my life. With kindness, unselfishness, and trust, I will work by your side to create a wonderful life together and encourage your dreams. I promise to be a faithful and honest husband. I am proud to make you my wife, to cherish you, for better or for worse, for richer or for poorer, in sickness and in health for as long as we both shall live. With this ring, I take you to be my wife," Charlie said and placed the ring on her finger. "I'm so happy that we found each other. I love you, Sunshine."

"I would ask that you always treat yourself and each other with respect and remind yourselves often of what brought you together today. Give the highest priority to the tenderness and kindness that your marriage deserves. When frustration and difficulty assail your marriage, as they do to every relationship at one time or another, focus on what still seems right between you, not just the part that seems wrong. If each of you will take responsibility for the quality of your life together, it will be marked by abundance and happiness. By the power invested in me by the Commonwealth of Virginia, I pronounce you husband and wife," Cynthia announced, "And now you may seal your union with a kiss."

Charlie and Holly shared a passionate first kiss as husband and wife and everyone clapped their hands. After their kiss, he embraced her in a bear hug, lifted her off the sand and twirled her around.

"About this time last year I ran into you in the deli," Charlie said softly to her.

"And I was thinking how handsome you were and picturing us on the beach," she whispered in return . . . *According to the calendar, this would be the weekend of our meet-up at Jake's . . . and my visit with Martina . . . I NEVER imagined it would lead to this . . . the Ace of Cups indeed.*

"Congratulations," Cynthia said to them.

"Will you do our wedding on New Year's Eve?" Roger asked her.

"Let me check my schedule. I think I'm available," Cynthia replied. "Here's my card. Please call me and I'll see if we can work something out."

"That was a lovely ceremony," Lisa smiled and slipped her hand into Roger's, their fingers entwined, and he gave it an affectionate squeeze.

"I think Patricia and I should renew our vows on our anniversary next year," Andy said as he put his arm around her waist.

"Yes, and we'll have a party too," Patricia said in agreement.

"Cynthia, would you like to join us for drinks and dinner?" Charlie asked.

"Thank you, Charlie. I'd be delighted to, but I have another appointment this evening. It was a pleasure performing your ceremony, and I wish you the best of luck. Thank you for choosing me," she replied sincerely.

"Thank you, it has been our pleasure," Holly replied.

"Alex, are you and Rachel going to join us?" Charlie asked.

"Yes, and I'll buy the first round of drinks, except that we aren't exactly dressed for the occasion. Where are you planning to go?" Alex asked.

"Catch 31," Holly said.

"We can meet you there in 20 minutes. We just need to gather up our beach toys and change our clothes," he said.

"We'll wait for you at the boardwalk entrance," Charlie told him.

"Great, see you shortly," Alex said as he and Rachel left to gather their belongings.

Catch 31 was an upscale seafood restaurant on the boardwalk and the food was scrumptious. It featured an indoor/outdoor lounge with fire pits on the terrace, perfect for sipping drinks and watching the waves. The inside dining area featured soaring ceilings and cool, blue-tiled walls. It was Holly's favorite restaurant.

Holly and Charlie and the three other couples enjoyed a fun-filled evening of drinks, dinner, and spirited conversation. Holly felt like she had completed an important chapter in her life and had come full circle. Her two ex-husbands were celebrating her happiness and marriage to Charlie, along with his ex-wife Lisa. She talked with James while unconscious and in another dimension and forgave him and Amber for their affair and the ensuing heartbreak it caused. In her wildest dreams she never imagined how wonderful their future would unfold.

The next morning Charlie woke up before Holly and fixed a small pot of hotel coffee. He knew she would want it when she finally awakened. He sat on the nearby sofa and watched his beautiful new wife while she slept. She drank a lot last night and he fully expected her to be hung over. *I'm such a lucky man . . . I married a woman like Holly, incredibly good-looking and not a diva . . . not even a little . . . the lottery . . . I need to check the Powerball numbers . . .* With that thought he turned on his smart phone to see the winning numbers . . . 9, 20, 14, 54, 46, 13 *. . . No . . . It can't be . . . These things don't happen to me . . . I can't believe this . . . The exact same order as my ticket . . . Holy shit! I just won the jackpot . . . $186 million! . . .* Charlie's heart felt like it was going to beat out of his chest, and he was temporarily in a state of shock *. . . We won the lottery! . . . We won the lottery! . . .* He could no longer hold it in and he shook Holly awake and said to her with breathless excitement and a slightly high-pitched and funny-sounding voice, "Holly, wake up, wake up! We won the lottery!"

Holly was extremely groggy and most certainly hung over. She opened her eyes, looked at him, and said with a yawn, "I just had a dream that you won the lottery."

"It's not a dream. We won the lottery. The numbers came out in the exact order that I played them. Look!" He showed her the ticket and the winning numbers from the Web site and she rubbed her eyes to make sure she was seeing things correctly.

"This is unbelievable, Charlie," Holly exclaimed. "And what makes it even better is that 13 is the Powerball number. We're rich!" Suddenly she felt awake and alive. She threw her arms around Charlie and pulled him close and said, "Thank you."

"No, I should be the one thanking you. If it wasn't for you this would never have happened," he replied and pulled away so he could look in her eyes.

"Correction, if it wasn't for *us*, this would never have happened," she said with a big smile.

"So, what do you want to do now?" he asked.

"I guess we have to decide if we want to continue working at MTAC or retire early and enjoy the rest of our lives," she replied with a huge smile.

"I think we should retire and have fun," he declared.

"Me too," she agreed. At that point, someone knocked on their hotel room door.

"Hey, it's Roger and Lisa," Roger called out through the door.

Holly slipped on her robe while Charlie opened the door.

"Have you checked your lottery numbers?" Roger asked excitedly.

"YEAH, I can't believe it. We were just talking about it. We just found out 5 minutes ago," Charlie said elated.

"Congratulations!" Roger said enthusiastically and shook Charlie's hand.

"Thank you, Roger," Charlie smiled.

"It couldn't happen to a nicer couple," Lisa said kindly and shook

Charlie's hand too.

"Come on in," Charlie invited, and Roger and Lisa walked into the room and greeted Holly with a hug.

"I'm still in shock; it doesn't seem real," Holly said happily.

"Roger, you were the one who purchased the tickets, so I'm going to give you a large chunk of cash once we collect our winnings," Charlie said, feeling generous and grateful to the man who suggested they each buy lottery tickets before the ceremony.

"You don't have to do that. I'm already a multimillionaire. I just play the lottery for the hell of it. However, if you want to make a sizeable donation to some of my favorite charities, I would be forever grateful. I'm biased toward animal rescue and children's charities," Roger said. "I'll be able to sell my business in another 3 years and retire with Lisa and enjoy the good life."

"Aren't we the luckiest women alive?" Lisa exclaimed with elation, happy for her friend's good fortune as well as her own.

"Without a doubt," Holly said cheerfully.

Holly and Charlie retired from MTAC a few weeks later, and by mid-December Holly discovered that she was pregnant with twins. Charlie was ecstatic with this news. They sold her rental house and his townhome in Springfield and moved closer to the Virginia Beach area where they purchased a beautiful mansion on 2 acres of land and thanked the universe every day for their good fortune. Neither Holly nor Charlie was the type to sit around and let the world go by. Charlie enjoyed woodworking and reinvigorated his small business making furniture. He didn't need the money, he did it for pure enjoyment. They both delighted in being full-time parents to their twins, and Holly liked giving tarot card readings at local fairs and helping Charlie with the administrative part of his carpentry business. They stayed in contact with Lisa and Roger who married on New Year's Eve as planned, and Patricia and Andy. The six of them remained lifelong friends, and they lived happily ever after.

CPSIA information can be obtained
at www.ICGtesting.com
Printed in the USA
FSOW01n0931280416
19803FS